What People Are Saying About

Wreath

Captivating, moving, haunting at times—yet hopeful;
Judy Christie's *Wreath* is a dynamic and adventurous read.
Highly recommended for all audiences.
—Alice J. Wisler, Christy Award finalist and author of *Rain Song*
and *How Sweet It Is*

Wreath Willis will win her way into your heart with her tenacity
and tenderness. Judy Christie has crafted a wonderful, gripping
story of overcoming hardship against all odds. Teens of all ages
will love Wreath's story.
—May Vanderbilt, coauthor of *Emily Ever After* and The Miracle
Girls series

Compelling, gripping, and relevant to what today's teens are
facing, *Wreath* grabbed hold of my heart and would not let go. I
found myself rooting for Wreath and caring for her as I would a
long-lost child. A must-read for every teenage girl.
—Janice Hanna Thompson, author of the Backstage Pass series

From the first scene of *Wreath*, when Wreath has to say good-bye
to her beloved mother, this girl—this Wreath—drew me into her
story and her struggle. I found myself rooting for her. Wreath's
story is one I will share with my own teenage daughter.
—Marybeth Whalen, director of She Reads (www.shereads.org)
and author of *She Makes It Look Easy* and *The Mailbox*.

Wreath

❋ A NOVEL ❋

JUDY CHRISTIE

BARBOUR
PUBLISHING

For more information about Judy Christie, please access the author's website at the following Internet address: www. judychristie.com

Published by Barbour Publishing, Inc., P.O. Box 719, Uhrichsville, OH 44683, www.barbourbooks.com

Our mission is to publish and distribute inspirational products offering exceptional value and biblical encouragement to the masses.

 Member of the
Evangelical Christian
Publishers Association

Printed in the United States of America.

To Mel

With Gratitude:
Thank you to all those who brought *Wreath* to life, including
Etta Wilson, Janet Grant, Becky Germany, Jamie Chavez,
grandaughter Gracie, and my husband, Paul.

❋ Chapter 1 ❋

As much as Wreath wanted to stay, Frankie pushed her to go.
"You need to leave," her mama said. "Today."

"Not yet. Please, Frankie, not yet." Wreath hated the way her voice trembled. "You're better this morning. Let me stay a little longer."

Her mother lifted her hand and pulled Wreath weakly down to the bed. The skinny teenager snuggled as she had done hundreds of times, Frankie running her fingers through Wreath's long, reddish-brown hair.

"Be strong for me, sweet girl. Show the world what Willis women are made of." The words were little more than a whisper. "When you get scared, remember that I'm in your heart."

Wreath was already terrified.

She wished Frankie's words were not more and more difficult to hear. Her mother's breathing sounded ugly and strained, like the time the window fan motor went out and the blades kept trying to turn.

"You want me to get your oxygen?"

Frankie shook her head, and for the first time Wreath noticed tears in her eyes. She moved even closer to Frankie and kissed her forehead.

"Wreath Wisteria Willis!" Frankie's voice startled Wreath with its sudden fierceness. "What's our motto? Tell Mama our motto!"

Wreath propped herself up on her elbow and looked into her mother's eyes. "Where there's a Willis, there's a way," she said with a trembling smile.

Her mother nodded, her chin bumping into Wreath's shoulder. "Don't ever forget that. It'll see you through the hard days."

"I won't forget."

"You need to get out of here before it's too late. I don't want Big Fun to know where you're headed. Are you ready?"

"Everything's set." Wreath turned away from Frankie and sat up on the side of the bed. Her stomach churned. She didn't mention that she'd never called the number on the piece of paper and that she had no intention of signing up to be a foster child.

"Be sweet. Make good grades. Help around the house. You're good at that," Frankie whispered. "Your new family'll treat you right."

"Yes, ma'am." The fact that Wreath had fooled her mother into believing she would live in a house with strangers showed how out of it Frankie was.

"Promise me you'll go to college."

Wreath said nothing. She wondered how she would get through her senior year of high school, much less pay for college.

"Promise Mama. Promise." The words seemed to take all of Frankie's energy and frightened Wreath with their intensity.

"I promise."

"Good, Wreath. . ." Her mother's voice trailed off as she squeezed the teenager's hand.

"Shhh, Frankie. Rest. Everything's going to work out okay."

A slight smile came to the dry, cracked lips. "You've been telling me that since you were a little bitty girl. 'It okay, Frankie, it okay,' you'd say. I was supposed to be the one telling you that."

"You've told me lots of stuff." With her hands shaking, Wreath poured a cup of water from the pink plastic pitcher on the bedside table, a remnant of one of her mother's hospital stays, and held it for Frankie to sip.

"I should've given you another daddy after yours got killed. I never could find one who would take good care of you."

"Don't worry." Wreath tensed at the rare mention of her father, who had died before she was born, not even married to her mother, his name never spoken.

Frankie rubbed Wreath's arm gently, the glass of water sloshing onto the sheet. "Your daddy was a nice guy, but we were both just kids." She looked past her daughter as though she could see someone standing on the other side of the room.

Uneasy, Wreath pulled the worn bedspread up around her mother's shoulders.

"I'm sorry I wasn't a better mama to you," Frankie said.

"No one ever had a better mama. You're the best."

"I love you, Wreath Willis."

"I love you, Frankie Willis."

"Remember our plan, sweetie. Do better than I did." Frankie's voice stopped. She didn't gasp or wheeze. She just slipped away.

"Not yet, Mama." Tears rolled down Wreath's face.

She held her mother's hand until it grew cold, folded the bedspread back neatly, stroked her fine brown hair, and reached under the matress until she found what she needed.

Fighting sobs, she made the call to 911, mimicking the grown-up voice of a neighbor, and headed to the back door.

"Good-bye, Frankie." She walked out as though leaving for school or an errand.

If her mama heard her at all, Wreath knew it had to be from a better place.

❀

Slipping behind a neighbor's house, Wreath watched.

She couldn't leave her mother's body until someone came to the run-down house.

A lonely pain shot through her. No amount of planning or the many lists she had made could have prepared her for how much this hurt.

When a sheriff's car pulled up, siren blaring and lights whirling, neighbors spilled out of run-down houses and loudly told each other what they saw, thought they saw, or wished they had seen. Some shook their heads with regret, while others grew animated, as though part of an exciting event.

The entire scene reminded Wreath of one of the police shows on television where bad things happened and the wrong people got hurt.

A deputy marched up the rickety steps, knocked, called out, and gave the door a shove with his shoulder. He disappeared inside, and Wreath could picture the path he took, finding the thin body of her mother.

Within minutes, the officer was back and spoke tersely into the radio in his car, the squawk of a reply impossible to understand. As he talked, an ambulance whirled around the corner, the flashing lights making the street more garish than usual.

"She's kind of uppity, keeps to herself most of the time," a woman with bleached-blond hair said, smoking a cigarette and flirting with the deputy. Wreath had seen that woman sit close to Frankie's boyfriend on the porch the past couple of weeks and knew he'd left the house with her a handful of times, at least.

"They haven't lived here very long," a man who worked on cars in his yard said. "She and that girl of hers won't take no help from the neighbors. Ain't like they got two nickels to rub together. They're just too proud to ask."

"They told me they didn't have any kinfolk around," the nice old lady who lived next door said. "It's a real shame. She and her daughter were real close. Somebody needs to find that child and tell her. She's the sweetest little thing. It's going to break her heart."

For an instant, Wreath thought about throwing herself in the woman's arms, begging to stay. She had gone with her to the library four or five times and even visited church with her once.

As she considered asking the woman for assistance, Big Fun, her mother's boyfriend, pulled up in his shiny old Chevrolet, painted the color of tropical punch. The silver wheels spun, and the radio blared. Wreath's heart pounded, and the nausea she had been feeling for the past few minutes threatened to spill over.

That man should have been named Big Mean. He *was* big but lacking in the fun department. He'd had little patience with Wreath from the beginning and even less as her mama's end drew near.

"Nice car," the blonde said, moving from the deputy over to Big Fun, who took the cigarette out of her mouth and used it to light one of his own. "Isn't it about time you take me for another ride?"

In the background, paramedics rolled Frankie out, a sheet over her, the body strapped to a gurney.

The sight of her mother drew Wreath out of her hiding spot with the pull of a strong magnet. She took three steps toward the still figure and glanced toward Big Fun, leaned up against his car, his arm draped around the blonde.

He caught sight of Wreath, and she knew she'd made a mistake. Pointing at her with pure evil in his eyes, he sneered at her, always the bully. She turned to run, then wheeled around to look at Frankie one last time. Big Fun turned to see what she was looking at and moved toward the ambulance, cursing loudly.

The commotion that followed made it easy for Wreath to slip away, propelled by fear.

Once out of sight, she walked deliberately, staying behind garages that listed to the side, stinky chicken coops, and huge trees that must have been planted when the neighborhood was new. She wove through backyards, over broken-down fences, and around piles of trash. A dog or two barked, and she jumped and looked around to make sure no one noticed.

Stepping inside a rusty tin shed two streets over, Wreath caught her breath and adjusted to the gloom. She wrapped her arms tightly around her middle but could not keep her body from shaking. A repressed sob, something like a hiccup, escaped.

She took a deep breath and rubbed tears from her eyes, mad at herself for crying and trying not to be mad at Frankie for dying.

Moving a bag of dog food, a collection of yard tools, and a burlap sack, Wreath pulled a backpack and black garbage bag from their hiding places, double-checked for the seventy-four dollars, notebook, and pencil in the sandwich bag, and considered stealing the owner's flashlight. She couldn't bring herself to do it.

Wreath's plan was under way, a variation on the one she and her mother had worked up carefully when the cancer hit. "Forgive me, Frankie, for misleading you," she whispered into the dank darkness. "I'll make a better life. I promise."

She exited the building and set off through the nearby woods, pausing to pet a neighbor's dog. His tail wagged.

The first few miles were easy, fueled by grief and determination. Wreath moved briskly but casually, as though out for pleasure, hanging close to whatever she could hide behind. An elderly couple sitting in lawn chairs smiled and waved as she walked past the back of their house. Wreath, dismayed that she had been seen, mumbled a greeting in return.

The last thing she needed was to be noticed, a girl wandering down the road with all she owned.

She did not want to be hunted by one of her mother's supposed friends, the same people who had taken off with their TV or stolen the grocery money. Most of all she did not want to be found by Big Fun, who liked to punch Frankie and had made ugly suggestions about how much he liked Wreath, who had done terrible things and liked to tell her about them. She gagged as she remembered his hand on her arm, and now with her mother gone. . . She couldn't bear the thought.

Nor could she stomach the possibility of being swept into some welfare system, peppered with official titles and severe faces. She had gotten her fill of those with Frankie as they'd drifted from place to place and in trying to get help when her mother got so sick.

After her grandmother died, Wreath had clung even tighter to Frankie, knowing only her mama stood between her and strangers, hearing kids at her many schools talk about being moved from family to family or sent to group homes.

Now she had one year to graduate.

She would make a better life.

The awful day she realized her mother would soon die, Wreath decided. She would no longer be at the mercy of other people.

She intended to run away. She would disappear right under their noses.

❀ Chapter 2 ❀

Fatigue swept into Wreath's body as she realized she had underestimated how long it would take her to walk to the junkyard in Landry.

Worn out and wrung out, her mother a day dead, she stashed her black garbage bag in the thicket where she'd slept, hiding it in the midst of a patch of poison ivy. She pressed her pack against her chest.

With the Central Louisiana woods as camouflage, she swatted mosquitoes and waited nearly an hour for the Tourist Welcome Center to open. When she walked in, the air was deliciously cool, but the hostesses not welcoming.

Groggy, hungry, bug-bitten, and grimy, she imagined she looked like a runaway or druggie, ratty after a night spent on the ground in the woods. Longing to tell them about Frankie, she almost asked for help. "You have to sign here for a free map." A stern lady's voice interrupted her thoughts. "Give your address." Suspicion rolled off the woman like rain running off the roof into the yard.

Wreath took a deep breath and tried to look calm and collected. Carefully writing the fake address she had come up with weeks before, she scrawled her name in unrecognizable script and picked up brochures about the area.

"Only take the ones you need," the worker said. "We don't like to waste those." Wreath managed a small smile, pretended to read one, and put it back, taking another instead.

Hearing the worker give an exaggerated sigh, Wreath looked desperately for the bathroom and charged in, leaning against the cool, blue tile wall to catch her breath.

Rattled by the hostility and fatigue, she stumbled to the sink and splashed water on her face. When she looked into the mirror, she scarcely recognized herself, her thick hair pulled back in a messy ponytail, her cheeks flushed, and her hazel eyes sunken.

She shook her head, as though the action might shake off her despair, and cleaned up, grimacing at the employee sent in to check on her. Without a doubt, she stood out like a shiny toy on a run-down porch.

"My mother's waiting in the car, but you know how we girls are," Wreath said, speaking in a snobbish voice one of the rich girls at school had used. "She'll appreciate the tourist material. We've never visited Louisiana before."

With her heart nearly pounding out of her chest, she wandered outside to a soda machine, bought an expensive bottled soft drink she couldn't afford, and acted as though she were walking to one of the cars in the parking lot. Looking over her shoulder to make sure she wasn't being followed, she turned around to find herself not a car's length from Big Fun.

"Did you think you could get away that easy?" he snarled and jerked her arm, his long, greasy hair lifting with the movement. "You and I have unfinished business. I'll hunt you down wherever you run and wring that scrawny little neck of yours if you don't do what I say."

"You don't scare me," Wreath hissed, wondering what in the world to do.

"Girl, you don't know what scared is," he said. "You've crossed Big Fun one time too many. Did you call the cops on me, too?"

"No," Wreath whispered, trying to hide the backpack from his line of sight. "I didn't do anything."

"Shut up! I've had about enough of your snotty attitude. If you think I intend to let you get away from me, you're crazier than a bedbug."

"All you ever cared about was Frankie's paycheck," Wreath cried out. "I will never let you treat me the way you treated my mama. Let me go, or I'll scream."

"Don't even think about it." He grabbed her wrist so hard she thought it might snap. "Get in my car. Now. Or you'll regret it."

When Wreath was about ten, she'd seen a pit bull attack a chicken, and she thought she knew now how the chicken had felt. Judging the distance to the edge of the woods, she knew she couldn't outrun Big Fun. She considered rolling under the car, but didn't think she had room. Maybe she could jump out of the car once they got started, or push him out and take the wheel.

Who was she kidding? She'd seen him hit Frankie repeatedly over a few dollars in tips from her mother's day at the café, and he had backhanded Wreath more than once for defending her. If only her mother hadn't gotten sick, they could have moved away from Big Fun, the way Frankie had planned. Maybe they could have gotten away from him and his fists and his horrible secret.

Hope evaporating, Wreath heard a quiet whirring sound. A security guard in a golf cart with a flashing yellow light rolled to a stop and stepped out. "Take your hands off that girl immediately," he demanded. "What's all the shouting about?" Although he was ancient and overweight, he spoke with authority and looked oddly threatening with his hand on the spray he wore snapped to his belt.

Cursing under his breath, Big Fun let go of Wreath but stepped so close to her that his arm touched her shoulder.

"You in trouble, young lady?" the guard asked.

Big Fun spoke first. "Teenage daughters!" he said with a weird laugh. "They certainly have a mind of their own." When he spoke, she could smell the tobacco and beer on his breath, his threats ringing in her ears.

The guard relaxed his stance slightly, and Wreath knew only her wits would get her away now. "My *dad's* upset because I need to go to the bathroom again," she said, rubbing her wrist. "He gets mad when I throw him off his schedule."

"Well, now, missy, why don't you run on into the bathroom there," Big Fun said, pinching her back where the guard couldn't see.

Her frightened look must have caught the guard's attention because he nodded, pulled the cart over to the curb, and walked next to Big Fun and her, talking in a grandfatherly way. "Fathers don't always understand their little girls, and they sometimes handle them wrong. Go on inside and freshen up." He almost blushed as he said the last words.

Wreath paused outside the bathroom and looked around for a place to hide, clutched her backpack, and considered dashing behind the counter with the two women. Compared to her mother's boyfriend, they seemed downright loving.

"Don't even think about it," Big Fun whispered behind her. "You walk in that bathroom and turn around and walk out, or I'll break every bone in your body."

Stepping through the bathroom door, Wreath felt like she was in a completely different place than minutes before. She looked for a way to lock the door or block it, but could see nothing to stop the bull of a man. There were no windows, and she contemplated getting into a trash cart but knew she'd be caught.

If she screamed, Big Fun would somehow convince the guard she was a hormone-ridden teenager with an attitude, or the police would come and she'd be shipped off to a foster home.

For months Wreath had observed Big Fun's every move, anticipating what he would do next. Now she hoped the element of surprise would be on her side. She went into the middle stall, locked the door, secured the pack around her front shoulders, in case he had a knife or punched her, and stood on the toilet, hunching down just enough that her head didn't show.

As she suspected, after only a couple of minutes, she heard the creak of the bathroom door, and Big Fun called out in a voice that sounded like something from a family movie. "Wreath, honey, hurry it on up now. We need to hit the road."

His slight emphasis on the word *hit* did not elude her.

Holding her breath, Wreath heard his steady steps and the sound of the industrial-strength hand dryer. "They won't be able to hear you yell over that thing," he said in a normal voice. "I intend to have what's mine. Give it to me."

Still Wreath waited. If her unstable life had taught her anything, it was patience.

The dryer shut off, and the doors to the first few stalls crashed open as Big Fun made his way down the line. Then she heard the creak of the main door again and the shrill voice of one of the desk clerks.

"Sir, you shouldn't be in here. This is the ladies' room," the woman said. Wreath's heart nearly exploded with relief.

"My daughter's not feeling well," he said. "I had to check on her."

"Well, make it quick. We don't want to upset other customers."

The bathroom door clicked shut, and Big Fun grabbed the door to the stall where Wreath hid, giving a maniacal laugh when it wouldn't open. "You're trapped," he said. "You have gotten away from me for the last time."

Wreath said nothing.

"There's no way out." His voice was more ominous now, and he jerked the door three times, so hard the stall rattled.

Waiting for the precise moment when he yanked on the door again, Wreath shoved as hard as she could, causing him to stumble back into the row of sinks.

He regained his balance in only seconds, but by then she was closing in on the bathroom door, which swept open just as she reached it, the security guard entering. Wreath brushed past him and glanced back to see the flustered man spray something into Big Fun's face.

Wreath never slowed down, ignoring the calls of the guard and the other employees and diving out of sight into the woods.

Crouching like a hunted animal, she grabbed the trash bag from its hiding place and disappeared into the thorny vines and thick trees. Wreath plowed through the woods, pausing frequently to loosen her pack from a briar or wayward limb. The trash bag had several large rips, and she rearranged the blanket inside to keep other items from falling out.

Trying not to cry and desperately missing Frankie, she ran until her side hurt and she thought she would throw up. She stopped behind a large tree and drew deep breaths, her eyes moving from side to side, every sound a terror. After a few moments, she pulled out her new map, the one that was supposed to be free. Instead it had cost her an overpriced soft drink, a bout of second-guessing that tore her apart, and an encounter with Big Fun.

"Don't ever let people scare you," Frankie had often told her. "You're strong and brave."

"Easy for you to say," Wreath muttered out loud and then felt guilty for the ugly words. A big chunk of faith in her plan had been ripped away, but at least she hadn't been caught.

Frankie had once said that Big Fun could talk himself out of any situation, and Wreath figured he was painting her as a juvenile delinquent to whatever authorities had shown up at the tourism center.

She could almost imagine the conversation. "She doesn't look like a troubled girl," he would say, "but her mother and I get painted in this bad light all the time. I'd appreciate it if you wouldn't intrude on our family business. She'll run home to Mommy, and this is something for us parents to work out." The two women at the desk would swoon over him and tell tales about their bad children before it was over.

Maybe his ego and argumentative nature would stall the process and throw off the search. The police and Big Fun would then probably focus on the four or five towns in Louisiana and Arkansas where she and her mother had lived over the past eleven years. The little town of Landry with its faraway junkyard seemed promising after all.

Wreath had chosen Landry because it was where Frankie had been born, close enough—and far enough—from Lucky, where they had most recently lived. She could think of no reason anyone would look for her down in Rapides Parish. Wreath, her mother, and Big Fun had driven through Landry on a fishing trip, and from the backseat, she fretted about Frankie's illness and considered the town. It had looked big enough to go undetected but small enough to get around by foot, the perfect place to finish high school.

When a snake slithered over her shoe, Wreath screamed and clutched her belongings, running until she had another stitch in her side. Panting, she collapsed in a clearing, put her face down, and wept. She longed for shelter and one more day to hold the glass to her mother's lips, to count out her pills, to brush her hair.

Wreath's pace was not nearly as good as she got weaker; she was tired and hungry. Red bug bites plagued her, itching at her waist, the back of her knees, and her armpits. She spent three more miserable nights in the woods, a can of Vienna sausages and a bottle of water her only meal. She looked longingly at a bruised banana and a package of peanut butter crackers, but knew she had to save what little food she had.

The urgent hurt in her heart and need for distance subsided to a tired ache that made her slow and unsteady. She had sometimes felt alone before, with Frankie at work or sick, but that had been nothing like this.

Wreath constantly swept her eyes about to make sure no one followed. She asked herself questions to make sure she had not gone crazy—and then wondered if that was a sign of losing her mind.

When she spoke aloud, her voice sounded rusty and scared.

"What did you love most about your mother?"

She laughed unsteadily and answered. "She believed I could do anything."

"What is your favorite food?"

The last question made her stomach growl, and she wondered again if she should turn back and confront the known ugliness, rather than hoping for something better.

If life were a race, she was definitely starting from the back of the pack.

Wreath walked on.

❀ Chapter 3 ❀

A woman in a shiny new car pulled to the shoulder of the highway as Wreath tripped over a root, tried to catch herself, and fell backward, cushioning the blow with her pack.

"Need a ride, young lady?"

"No thanks." Wreath put her head down, not knowing if she could go on and afraid of being noticed.

"Looks to me like you need help." She was African American, wearing a fancy shirt. "I'm happy to give you a lift. I'm going toward Landry. Can I drop you somewhere along the way?"

Wreath needed to get to Landry, and the lady seemed nice enough. Wreath nodded her head and turned toward the car.

"I'd appreciate a ride," she said. "I can give you gas money."

"Headed that way anyway, no pay necessary," the woman said. "Hop in."

As the car pulled slowly onto the road, Wreath breathed the cool air and tried not to relax into the comfortable seat. Still, she gave a deep sigh, thankful the ride was free. Wreath had read warning after warning about hitchhiking and had memorized Frankie's lecture about accepting rides with strangers. She'd decided two weeks ago that it would be too dangerous and intended to walk the entire way. But surely accepting this offer did not mean she couldn't make it on her own, and the woman was probably harmless. It was smart and would save her time and energy.

Wreath cut her eyes over to the driver and thought she could outrun her or beat her up if necessary and then almost laughed out loud at the thought. This was not the kind of woman who got into fights.

"You look like you could use something to drink," the lady said. "This time of year I don't leave home without an extra bottle of water." She motioned to the console between the seats. "It's probably not very cold, but it's wet."

Wreath gulped the water, wiping her mouth and thinking nothing had ever tasted so good.

"My name's Clarice, by the way," the driver said. "Clarice Johnson. I live north of the Wooddale community, close to Landry. How about you?"

"I'm Wreath." She winced when she gave her real name instead of the made-up name she had practiced for days. At least she hadn't given her last name.

Being on the run was harder than the movies made it look.

"What a lovely name," Clarice said. "Were you a Christmas baby?"

Wreath shook her head and lied to make up for blurting out her name. "That's what most people guess, but it was my mama's aunt's name. My mama always said if she had a little girl that's what she would name her."

"You live down this way?" the woman asked.

"Visiting relatives near Landry. I'm meeting my mama."

"I see."

Wreath turned to look out the side window, inching away on the leather seat, and was relieved when Clarice didn't ask her anything else.

A silence fell between them and, despite her best intentions, Wreath dozed, her neck crooked against the door, the shoulder strap pulling, her hair tangled.

"Wreath," she heard Clarice murmur, barely above a whisper. "I wonder what in the world your story is."

Sleep pulled at her, but Wreath roused herself and sat up straighter. The sound of gravel forced her wide awake.

Clarice had pulled off the main highway onto a side road and stopped the car. "Sleepyhead, I'm getting close to my house and don't know where to drop you. Would you like to come home with me for a bite of supper?"

Wreath sat up straight and tried to shake off her grogginess. She could think of nothing she would like more than a home-cooked meal and a place to wash up, but she had already risked more than she should have by accepting the ride. For her plan to work, she had to survive alone and make quick and good decisions.

"My family's expecting me, so I'd better move along," Wreath said. "I'll get out here. This'll be great."

Clarice gave the kind of laugh a friend makes when another friend says something stupid. "Here? In the middle of nowhere?"

"My cousins don't live far." Wreath began to sweat, despite the air-conditioning blowing on her face. "This is good."

"I can't leave you here," the woman protested. "You must be turned around. There's nothing around here but a junkyard and the state park."

Wreath practically leapt from the car, jerking on the back door and panicking when she realized it was locked. She couldn't leave her backpack! "Just a second, honey," Clarice said, hitting a button. "Now try it."

Wreath yanked the back door open, dragging her pack out and catching the trash bag on the door, tearing it down the side. Her clothes and stash of food spilled into a ditch next to the road.

Humiliated, she scooped the items up, wrapped everything in the blanket, tied it into a knot, and stuck the trash sack, which was her tarp, rain cover, and suitcase, into her pack. At this point, she could afford to get rid of nothing.

She lifted her hand for a quick wave and felt a familiar lump in her throat. Her fear, along with Clarice's kindness, air-conditioning, and the thought of a real meal, made the departure harder.

"Thank you for the ride," she said through the open window. Something about the woman made her want to use her best manners.

"Are you sure you won't let me take you to your kinfolks' house?" Clarice asked.

"I'm good." Wreath backed away from the car, tripping over her own feet.

"At least let me give you this." Clarice held out a twenty-dollar bill.

"I've got plenty," Wreath said. "Thanks anyway."

She started walking purposefully, as though she had been here a thousand times and knew just where she was going. She fought the urge to look back.

"Godspeed, Wreath," Clarice called out and slowly drove off.

Wreath waited until the car disappeared and leaned against a tree, scooting away from a hill of ants.

She pulled out her map and tried to figure out where she was.

Clarice had mentioned a junkyard, and the teenager hoped that didn't mean locals paid attention to the overgrown spot. She wished the woman didn't know it existed, didn't know *she* existed. She wished she'd taken the twenty dollars. *No, I don't.*

Her thoughts whirled.

Stepping into dense woods, she squirmed to arrange the trash bag as a cushion and plopped down. She fished around for her notebook and a pen, her hand brushing against the crackers. She wanted to eat them, but they needed to last. She had so little of everything.

After making eye contact with Big Fun at the house and catching the eye of the old couple in their backyard—and, oh my, now hitching a ride—she wanted to add "avoid notice" to her list of goals. Her words were printed carefully in a small brown binder, bought for a quarter, including extra paper, at a garage sale. The journal was her treasure and felt like her only friend. In elementary school, she had named it Brownie—and at the moment it comforted her.

"It's just you and me now, Brownie," she wrote in the book, patting it as though it were a pet. "The journey has begun."

She tried to remember the date. June 3, she decided it was, wishing she had brought a calendar. "A fresh start," she scrawled, her hand shaking so hard the writing was almost illegible.

She flipped through the lined pages for the thousandth time. On the first page, she had written the word *CONFIDENTIAL* in matter-of-fact capital letters. On the second page, she had used big, loopy, bubble-shaped words: *Wreath Wisteria Willis! Plans, Goals, and Dreams! Get Ready, World!*

She had felt full of hope when she started writing in the notebook, but now the words seemed silly. She looked back at the pages labeled *WHAT TO DO*. She had made note after note, most entries updated and expanded. She had written about the town of Landry and the abandoned junkyard where she would live. She had even sketched the way she wanted her future room to look, copying ideas from design magazines.

Her main list was basic:

Choose a place to live. (Done!)
Do research. (See notes.)
Travel to destination. (Walk? How far? How long?)
Set up home. (Supplies?)
Buy CHEAP food. (Don't spend much money!!!!!)
Scope out high school. (How to enroll?)
Get a job????? Where??? (Make list of skills.)
Go to college.
Make lots of money!!!!!$$$$$

And, today, her latest entry:

Avoid notice!

She glanced at the list of supplies she would require, studied her list of mean and interfering people who might decide they knew what was best for her, read over a short list of job skills.

Exhausted, she daydreamed about the books she wanted to read and the places she planned to travel, starting with New Orleans and ending with Nova Scotia, a place she had read about in Louisiana history in eighth grade, and Prince Edward Island, where one of her favorite books was set.

As Wreath started to close the little notebook, an unfamiliar entry near the back jumped off the page at her, and her heart leapt into her throat.

Lo, I Am With You Always, it said.

Lo, I am with you always?

The words were printed precisely, in small block letters. The phrase sounded vaguely familiar, but the sight of it unsettled Wreath. Frankie must have made the entry, although it didn't look like her handwriting, and Wreath couldn't figure out how or when her mother had gotten her hands on the journal.

The wind blew.

"Mama?" she whispered.

❧ Chapter 4 ❧

Wreath's first glimpse of a rusted van thrilled her as she clawed her way through a wall of green vines.

An ancient school bus and a half-dozen cars sat near the van, along with a storage shed, similar to where she had hidden her belongings in Lucky, and three or four abandoned mobile homes, their doors standing open and insulation hanging from the ceilings.

But the place was creepier—much creepier—than she had imagined, not nearly like the quaint fairy home she had fantasized about. She picked up a tree branch for protection. "Hello," she called out in a low voice. "Anyone home?"

Relieved and terrified when no one answered, the combination of emotions burned most of her spurt of energy. The light faded quickly in the dense undergrowth, and she squinted to check the time on her cheap plastic watch. It was close to seven, and night noises were cranking up.

She hadn't realized it got dark so fast. She slapped at an invisible mosquito that buzzed in her ear.

Wreath tried to talk herself into feeling safe here in the abandoned junkyard she had chosen for her home. This jumbled mess offered excellent protection from prying eyes. Only birds, insects, and frogs punctuated the quiet.

She could fix up a spot here to stay until she graduated in a year. This was her plan.

The idea evaporated as an owl hooted in the distance.

"What was I thinking?" she groaned out loud and wondered what the easiest way to get in touch with welfare people would be. She pulled out the piece of paper with the words *Foster Care* on it, written in her mother's handwriting.

She walked up the broken stairs of one of the trailers, and a cat shot out from inside and brushed against her leg, causing her to scream.

No one appeared at the shrill sound. She was alone in this place, with the exception of who knew what kind of varmints.

She was alone in the world.

The collection of beat-up cars went on and on, scattered here and there, right up to a swampy area. The size of the junkyard swallowed Wreath up.

From the road, it looked like a few cars and then trees, but it was huge. A mass of metal, everything was rusted, dented, crumpled, or moldy. The discards spread across what she guessed were quite a few acres, but she couldn't remember how big an acre actually was. She loved books and drawing, but didn't particularly care for math. Was an acre something you studied in math? She couldn't remember.

Wreath had finished her junior year only a week and a half ago, but the details disappeared in her tiredness, and she didn't try to snatch them back. Her thoughts resembled the cars, piled up and rusty.

Only days ago she had been in charge at home, caring for Frankie, making sure food got cooked and clothes washed. She had taken care of her mother in one way or another most of her life, but she wasn't as grown up as she had thought.

She was only sixteen. She wouldn't even be seventeen for six months. This new life was already an on-the-run fiasco.

No, Wreath had vowed to her mother she'd get an education. She'd earn money. She didn't want to live in a run-down rent house with skuzzy people the rest of her life. She'd make her senior year work out somehow.

Big Fun hadn't been *that* bad. Their old neighbor liked Wreath. Some of the cousins hadn't been so bad when she was little. If not, someone else would take her in.

Take her in.

Wreath hated the way that sounded, like she was a stray dog waiting to be adopted at the pound, but she wouldn't be a burden.

She was smart and strong and knew how to do all sorts of things around the house. Her mama used to say Wreath had always been a little adult, even though she was younger than most in her class.

Only one year stood between her and freedom.

She would rely on others until she graduated, and then she wouldn't need anybody—not foster parents who'd feel sorry for her, not nice people like that woman Clarice or the old lady next door in Lucky.

NEW PLAN, she wrote in big letters in the notebook and made another list:

> *Scrap old plan.*
> *Make safe place to sleep tonight.*
> *Call foster care office.*

Her stomach growled.

> *Buy a hamburger, no matter how much it costs.*

Tomorrow she could go into Landry and figure out how to get in touch with someone who could tell her what to do. She'd live like a normal girl—find someone to stay with, get a part-time job, go to school, graduate from high school, and grow up. She'd find a way to pay for college and make lots of money. She'd wear pretty clothes and have a handsome husband and sweet children who had lots of toys and books and were never left alone.

Never.

They would stay in one place, and she'd always be there for them.

But tonight?

She could try to find Clarice's house and admit she needed help. But the path back to where she had been dropped off had been a long walk in daylight. It'd be safer to stay put. Start fresh tomorrow.

She'd been on her own for only five days, and she already felt stuck. That's what she was. Stuck.

She was stuck in this weird place that had seemed so perfect. Or she was stuck with living with someone she didn't like.

What kind of dream world had she been living in? She missed Frankie so much. She wanted to lie down and sleep.

Wreath tried to find the best place to make her room for the evening and looked for escape routes in case danger appeared. She picked up the stick again and gripped it like a club.

The memory of Big Fun made her rub her arm. She stuck the diary into the waistband of her jeans and took a few practice swings with the wood. Her arms felt weak and trembly.

As she searched for a place to rest, she held the stick out in front of her, grasping it with both hands, like she had seen swashbuckling heroes do in movies. She pretended it was a saber and she could cut someone in half or evaporate them on the spot.

The marshy area behind the place, with a stream that would have to do for water, housed frogs croaking in an array of tones. She pulled out her notebook and squinted at her entries in the gloom, reading her research notes.

Don't be afraid.
Frogs will not hurt you.
You will get used to them.

She had not expected them to be so loud.

Unnerved, Wreath chose a crazy van, a maroon color like the cover of an old record album one of her mother's cousins had. The van, with tiger-striped shag carpet on the floor and walls, looked as though someone had left it in midsentence. Magazines and a faded photo album sat on a fake wood end table, a suitcase of rotten clothes and a stack of paperback books rested in the corner. The windows had been covered with old sheets so no one could see in, nice for privacy but no good for lighting.

Wreath chastised herself for heading out without a flashlight, mad that she had let the detail slip past her.

That meant she had likely overlooked other essential details.

Closing the doors, in the eerie night, she fidgeted with the locks until she made them work. For one frightening moment, she thought she had permanently locked herself in and panicked, imaging her decaying skeleton discovered years later. She frantically dug a pair of rusty pliers from the glove box and forced the side lock open, drawing a deep breath of fetid air when it worked.

Trembling, Wreath spread her blanket on the rough carpeted floor and laid out her clothes, ate a banana, and put her stick nearby. She lay awake for a long time, afraid to sleep.

A loud tapping noise caused Wreath to roll over and rub her eyes.

She needed to get to the door before the knocking woke Frankie up.

Frankie.

A sick feeling roiled in her stomach. Frankie was gone.

Wreath froze and tried to figure out where she was.

The rough carpet rubbed against her aching arm, her familiar blanket bunched up. A trail of ants inspected the banana she had left nearby.

The tapping continued, and Wreath reached for her stick.

"Who is it?" she asked, her voice sounding like one of the frogs the night before. The knocking noise went right on, as though she had not spoken.

"I'm armed," she said louder, clearing her throat and trying to clear her mind. "What do you want?"

She heard the shrill call of a bird, and the noise stopped.

Crawling to the front seat of the van, she tried to roll the window down to peek outside, but corrosion had jammed it. Tentatively, she pushed against the door and looked, blinded by bright sunshine.

She jumped back, slammed the door, and waited.

Nothing happened.

Then the knocking started again.

Agitated, Wreath opened the van door, the branch in her hand. A large woodpecker sat at the top of a rotten tree, ignoring her as he tapped at the wood.

The bird sounded exactly the way the neighbor had in Lucky when she knocked on the front door, soup in hand or with a piece of misdelivered mail. Wreath's anxiety vanished at the sight of the bird. She looked up at the clear sky and back at her watch. Twelve o'clock!

She had slept until noon.

In desperate need of a bathroom, Wreath wondered if any of the rotten trailer houses had commodes. She settled instead on a spot in the woods, embarrassed, and wandered back to her campsite, thankful no one was around.

As she strolled back to the van, a warm breeze lifted her hair. She yawned and stretched and savored the sunshine. Sadness lurked, but she felt rested.

Almost refreshed.

The junkyard looked slightly more inviting by day, and its vastness felt almost safe, like a giant metal cocoon where no one could find her. The panic of the night before seemed excessive.

Her original plan had not been off base after all. If no one knew she was here, no one could hurt her.

She rocked back and forth for a moment, the daytime thoughts more agreeable than the dark doubts of the night before. She felt almost giddy, although part of that could be weakness brought on by hunger. She knew she couldn't eat nearly as much as she wanted, so she brushed the ants off the banana peel and wondered if it was edible.

Wrapping up half a package of peanut butter crackers instead, she decided to go on an expedition. *This is an adventure, Brownie*, she wrote in her diary. *I will not give up. Frankie taught me to be strong and brave. I will not let her down.*

Scouting nearby vehicles, Wreath found similar setups to the van, places that looked as though the owners had walked away with nothing. The Tiger Van already seemed more familiar and less foreboding than the other cars, trucks, and trailers, and her inspection revealed details of lives that reminded her of the home she had left behind.

To cheer herself, she pretended to be honest-to-goodness house shopping, like she loved on those home channels on TV and in magazines that Frankie brought home from the café. Within a few minutes, Wreath assumed the role of both buyer and real estate agent. She spoke aloud to calm her nerves, finding the lack of human noise unnerving.

"This van is small enough to be safe, has several exits in case of emergency, and is carpeted from top to bottom, floor to ceiling," Wreath said, using her stick as a pointer. "The previous owners might have gone a little overboard with the furry, tiger-striped carpet, and I am not thrilled that the wall and ceiling will require vacuuming. Perhaps it comes with air freshener?"

Realtor Wreath was gregarious. "Are you sure you wouldn't prefer one of our larger models, maybe the school bus that can accommodate a crowd, or one of these tiny sports cars that are cozy and easy to heat in the winter? You might find a camper trailer to your liking. They're musty, but they have breathing room. You'll have to commit soon because the property is flying off the market."

Wreath laughed out loud, the game of charades a relief. "I'm quick to know what I want," she spoke aloud again. "I'll stick with my original choice. Have your people get in touch with my people, and perhaps we can discuss a Tiger Van reality show."

She took a small bow and then felt ridiculous rather than playful, the woodpecker still knocking in the distance. She heard another bird call, and it sounded as though the woodpecker paused and answered.

Even the birds had more friends than she did.

She inhaled deeply, the air a mix of fresh summer and moldy ruin. A breeze moved through the trees, and she felt a moment of calm.

During her explorations in various trailers, Wreath pilfered a half-dozen tiny painted flowerpots, made in Mexico, a cracked mixing bowl, and a mildewed Bible that reminded her of her grandma. She took a tire iron to replace the tree branch as a weapon, removing it from an Opal GT, a car she'd never seen before.

She was disappointed but not surprised to find no lights and no running water in the area and began to consider her first trip into town.

Too soon, she told herself. *Wait.*

As evening fell, the mosquitoes were big and aggressive, and she added insect spray to her shopping list. As she wrote, she knew that no matter how good she was with money, hers would not go very far. She would have to find a job.

She hoped Frankie'd had a nice funeral and wondered who had paid for it.

❧ Chapter 5 ❧

After three sweltering, unnerving nights in the junkyard, Wreath thought there must be truth to Frankie's motto.

Where there is a Willis, there's a way, she wrote time and again in her notebook. She considered putting it at the top of every page.

Without a strong will, she never could have survived. Her brain was shaken up, like the snow globe Frankie had brought her from a weekend trip to Hot Springs.

By night four, filthy and hungry, her meager food gone, she yearned for a break from what she now called Wreath's Rusted Estates. Worried that it was too early to show her face in town, she longed for a shower and a real meal and was willing to trade precious cash for cleaning supplies.

She had spent most of the first stifling forty-eight hours huddled in the van, exploring only briefly before scurrying back like one of the mice she saw every time she turned around. At least she preferred to think of them as mice. Some looked big enough to be rats, and they grew when she sketched them in her notebook.

On the fifth morning, Wreath emerged from the van, forcing herself to look around, happy to hear the familiar *tap-tap-tap* of the woodpecker. After a brief walk through scattered car bumpers, stacks of old tires, and briars that lay across her path like booby traps, she pulled out pen and paper and catalogued what she had seen.

MY NEW HOME:

1. Isolated.

2. Woodsy.

3. Dirty.

4. Smelly.

5. Horrible.

6. Mine!!!!

She huddled back in the van, allowing herself a few ounces of water each day and a scant amount of food. For four days she had eaten berries growing on vines and peaches on a gnarled tree near the back of the property. Even with wormholes in them, they were delicious, and she hoarded them like the finest groceries.

Finally, she could stand it no longer. On the seventh day, she gave in to the urge to go into town.

Assignment: fact-finding mission, she wrote. *Explorer: Wreath Willis.*

Assess threats.

Find a shower.

Gather usable objects.

Map the area.

Before she settled into sleep the previous night, she had made plans for the day, going through them again and again. She stepped out of the van and observed her new hideaway with a tiny degree of pleasure and a medium helping of pride.

The sun blasted the hot van by the time she woke up, and she wolfed down the last of her peanut butter crackers and drank a few sips of water, nauseated with excitement and fear of the day ahead.

She pushed her hair back with a black headband and pulled on a pair of track shorts and a T-shirt she had found in the backseat of one of the cars. The shirt looked almost in style—*vintage*, it would be called by fashionistas—and only had one small hole under the arm.

Walking past nearby vehicles, Wreath found a large utility truck with big side mirrors and surveyed her appearance, satisfied that she looked pretty good for someone who hadn't had a bath in days. Her hair wasn't shiny but her dark eyes had a hint of sparkle, and her skin was smooth and clear.

Her pack slung over her shoulder, she headed for the state park, mentioned by the lady who'd given her the ride and the subject of a brochure from the Not-So-Welcome Center. The park claimed to be "spacious" with a swimming area, cabins, trails, and, most importantly, showers. Sticking to the edge of the woods, a thrill ran through her when she found the entrance road, tree-lined and peaceful. A runner sprinted down into the park, waving at Wreath as she zipped through the gate.

The spirit of the moment encouraged Wreath, although she had not expected to encounter others so quickly.

Trying to look as though she, too, was out for a little exercise, Wreath was put off by the large sign at the entrance, demanding all visitors register at the office. The jogger had not stopped, so maybe she could slip by.

But Wreath didn't like to disobey rules.

Three or four rental bikes and a soft drink machine sat out in front of the office, which looked like an old-fashioned log cabin. A bulletin board held announcements and business cards for everything from babysitting to dirt work. She wasn't sure she knew what dirt work was, but maybe she could get a job babysitting.

She looked down at herself and wondered if anyone would trust her with a child.

Probably not.

With a deep breath, she stepped inside the building that looked like an old-fashioned log cabin from the outside. A TV mounted in the corner was the first thing to catch her eye, a weather report on its screen.

A cute boy about her age, dark hair covering his eyes, sat behind the counter, reading. He looked startled when she walked in, and Wreath hoped she did not stink. He wore clean khaki shorts and a dark green state park polo shirt and looked like one of those rich kids who get the plum jobs. When he laid his book down, Wreath noticed it was one of her favorites, a novel she had reread a few months back.

"Day pass, please." Wreath tried to sound as though she did this all the time. She laid a precious dollar bill on the wood surface.

"Great day for a hike," the boy said, writing the date in black marker on a yellow cardboard pass.

Wreath ignored him and studied a trail map tacked to the wall.

"Visiting someone in the area?" he asked.

"No," she said and turned her back on him to inspect a glass case of souvenirs and camping supplies, items that might come in handy over the next few months.

"Not much for talking, are you?" The boy drummed his fingers on the counter.

"Not much," Wreath said. She turned and took the pass that he held out, unzipped her pack, and tried to stuff the piece of paper around the items she had brought with her.

"Enjoy your walk," he said, still friendly despite her rudeness.

Wreath had only gone a few yards when she heard someone yell at her. Panicked, she stopped and thought about running.

"You dropped this." The boy held out a tiny bar of soap that Big Fun had brought back from a cheap motel on an oil field cleanup trip. Wreath felt her face flush and took the soap with mumbled thanks.

She had to get over her skittishness if she was going to make it for the next year.

She walked a step or two and turned to give him a small wave.

He waved back and smiled.

The encounter made her feel rotten. After snakes and lizards, she hungered for conversation, but she didn't know how she was supposed to act around people in Landry.

Heading down a trail, she pretended to inspect a disc golf course and strolled through a picnic area. She sat at one of the tables and pulled out her notebook and a ballpoint pen from the glove compartment of one of the abandoned cars.

In large letters, she dug the pen into the page and wrote.

BAD.

SAD.

MAD.

The words surprised her.

Although she had never lived anywhere long enough to get close to people, she missed her long talks with Frankie, who in many ways had acted more like a girlfriend than a mother. She didn't think she could go a whole year without talking to anyone other than herself.

She remembered Clarice, who had given her the ride, and how good chatting had felt, like a cool cloth on her sweaty forehead.

REASONS TO TALK TO OTHERS, she wrote at the top of a page.

Learn about area.

Get to know cool people.

Prepare for job.

Keep from going crazy.
Lonely.

REASONS NOT TO TALK.

Give away where I live.
Make people nosier.
Remind me of things I don't have. . .family, home, best friend.
Big Fun might find me.
Don't want to get too close to people. (Plan to leave when I graduate.)

She tapped the notebook on the table. Ever since third grade, putting thoughts on paper helped Wreath sort things out. She was always surprised at how the plusses and minuses of life clashed and connected. She was lonely because she didn't have anyone to talk to, but talking to that boy made her think about all she was missing.

She stowed her journal in the pack, checked the zippered pouch, and jogged past a swimming pool, closed for cleaning; past camping sites, where big new motor homes were set up with party lights and welcome mats; and past a screened picnic pavilion. Stopping with an effort at nonchalance, she did a few stretches she had learned in PE class, acting as though she exercised every day. As she bent to touch her toes, she swiveled her head to see if anyone was in sight.

Satisfied that she was alone, she turned down a sidewalk and into a brick restroom. Its windows were high, letting in pale light that only slightly improved the dim bulbs on the ceiling. The smell of mold was strong, but the floor was clean. As advertised in the pamphlet, the facility included two showers, although they did not have curtains or doors, which brought a moan from Wreath. She looked around for a way to lock the main door and stepped outside to see if she could find a rock to jam against it while she took a quick shower. Only a few pebbles and a lot of pinecones lay on the ground, and, other than a squirrel scampering up a nearby tree, the area was still. Feeling the sticky grime on her arms and legs, she decided to take her chances.

With another quick look, she hurried back into the bathroom. She stripped out of her clothes and jumped into a shower.

The cool water streamed down her hair and shoulders, washing away the filth. Frankie was big on cleanliness, and Wreath had gotten so gross she was ashamed. She liberally used the little bar of soap to wash her body and hair, and she scrubbed her skin with a ragged washcloth she had found in one of the trailers at the junkyard.

Watching the dirt disappear down the drain, she hoped the water might wash away the awful sorrow that clung to her. What-ifs had captured her emotions like a steel trap these past few days, and she longed to feel clean and fresh.

Wreath pulled her towel out of her pack, hurriedly dried off, and put back on her shorts and T-shirt. Clean. Dressed. Even the small accomplishments brought a big sense of relief. Combing her hair, she managed a smile as she surveyed her looks in the piece of metal that served as a mirror.

While she was deciding she looked pretty good, considering all she'd been through, the restroom door flew open. Wreath jumped, dropped her comb, and knocked her pack off the sink onto the tile floor.

"Didn't mean to startle you," a woman in running shorts and a tank top said. Red-faced and sweating profusely, she walked to the sink and splashed water on her face.

Wreath picked up her comb and straightened her pack, realizing this was the jogger who had headed into the park in front of her. Casually messing with her hair, she sized up the distance to the door.

"Great hair," the woman said. "If I tried to do that with this frizzy mess, I'd look like a mop on steroids."

"Thanks," Wreath said. Trying to appear disinterested, she studied the woman who had stuck her mouth under the faucet, giving her the look of a contortionist at the circus.

She looked younger than Frankie, in her early twenties, maybe, her body thin. With hair stuck under a ball cap and big blue eyes, she seemed in ways like a fresher version of Wreath's mama. The way Frankie could have looked without the tiredness.

Frankie had been pretty, but this woman looked almost like a model, her legs shapely and tanned. People told Wreath she was pretty, but she thought her own looks were ordinary. She figured she must have gotten them from her dad's family. She wished she could be as beautiful as this lady, like Frankie was before she got sick.

"You camping with your family?" the woman asked. Wreath barely moved her head, neither agreeing nor disagreeing.

"I hope the mosquitoes aren't eating you up," the runner said. "They're worse than usual this year, and there's a junkyard across that road that's a swampy mess."

Wreath watched the woman enter a stall.

"I think I overdid it this morning," she continued, talking behind the closed door. "Central Louisiana has it all today—heat, humidity, and bugs bigger than tennis balls."

Edging toward the door, Wreath froze as the woman emerged.

The time had come to speak. "Are you camping?" Wreath asked.

"Never! I live in the lovely town of Landry. Right now I'm an artist." She washed her hands and took off her cap to straighten her damp hair.

"An artist?" Wreath chalked this tidbit up to "getting to know cool people." She organized her clothes in her pack as she spoke, trying to look nonchalant. "What kind of art?"

"You name it, I do it. Most of my commissioned pieces are for a fleur-de-lis or some sort of pink rose framed in gold." She wrinkled her nose at the description and this time gulped water from the sink with a cup made from her hands.

"If you want to know the truth, I'm an art snob," the woman said, stretching against the wall, pulling her calves and bouncing down to touch her toes.

"I do commercial projects because I need the cash, and people around here don't have a very adventuresome spirit. For fun I paint huge canvases. Someday people will gush over my work and fight to hang my pictures in their homes. Their big, expensive homes." She laughed.

"Oh," Wreath said.

"I'd better get going. I have a workshop today, and they'll have my head if I'm late again. I'm Julia, by the way. Enjoy your visit."

"I'm Wreath."

"Wreath." The woman spoke the name like it was special. "Good to meet you." She jogged toward the park exit, her cap flopping up and down, as Wreath exited the bathroom.

Strolling out of the facility, Wreath was surprised at how much she'd enjoyed Julia's conversation. But Wreath couldn't imagine telling a stranger about *her* dreams, about her own love of art and design, of her plans to go to graduate school and do something that mattered.

And, although she had enjoyed the visit, she would vary her shower times. She couldn't afford to be seen too often by Julia the jogger or the good-looking clerk. The last thing Wreath needed was to get easy to follow. She remembered all too well how easy it had been for Big Fun to find her at the tourism center.

Rounding the far corner of the log building, Wreath couldn't resist looking back. The boy from the office leaned against a split-log fence. He offhandedly waved and turned back toward the office as she walked through the gate.

"Have a good one," he yelled.

She gave a small wave and felt a moment of happiness.

Attract no attention, Wreath had written in her notebook that horrible first day. She was about to put that to the test.

When she wrote out her strategies before Frankie died, they seemed wise and organized. In real life, they felt awkward and stupid. She longed to go right back to the Tiger Van. But she had to have food and learn how to move around Landry without standing out. School would start soon, and she needed to look as though she had lived here for years.

Staying as far from the highway as she could without getting in the woods, she walked and walked, the efforts of her precious shower washing away in a pool of sweat. A few cars whizzed by but no one seemed to pay her any attention, and she tried to get a look at drivers without them noticing. Her feet ached the way they had after the long walk from Lucky to the junkyard, and her shoes rubbed through her worn socks. Her shoulders throbbed from the weight of the pack, and she shifted it to one side, moving her arms, which felt tight and tense.

The distance to town was a lot farther than she remembered from the ride with Frankie and Big Fun, definitely longer than it looked on the map. Seven or eight houses sat back from the road. The occasional dog ran down a driveway, barking fiercely but stopping about halfway. She thought of the sweet dog that lived near her old house, how he wagged his tail and licked her hand.

An auto repair shop and used tire store were the first businesses she passed, and she considered asking for a drink of water but decided it was too risky. She walked on. Her spirits dipped almost in tandem with the backpack sliding off her shoulder.

In the distance she saw a flashing red light, and the highway made a T, veering into town. Her relief was so strong she wanted to lift her arms in triumph. "Yes," she said under her breath. "I made it." A bench with a cover over it, maybe a school bus stop, sat on the other side of the road, and she crossed, hot and thirsty. With a little rest in the shade, she would decide what to do next.

"Hey, Wreath," a voice called.

She skidded to a stop, her heart pounding so hard she thought she might have a heart attack.

"Over here," the voice said, and Wreath turned, feeling like a mechanical toy, jerky and unsteady.

"It's me. Clarice. From the other day. Do you need a ride?"

At the sight of the fancy car and the woman's big smile, Wreath steadied herself. "No thanks," she said. "I'm doing a little hiking." She pointed to the pack.

"Looks like you're about hiked out," Clarice said.

Wreath knew her face was flushed, and she had sweat rings on her clothes. "It's a little hotter in Landry than I remembered." She wiped her brow and forced a laugh. "But I need the exercise. Thanks for the offer."

Walking fast across the road, she turned at the first street, hoping to get out of Clarice's sight in a hurry.

The woman was all Wreath could think about as she tried to figure out what to do. She could scarcely bear the thought of the long walk back to the junkyard, but she didn't want to hang out in town where she might run into Clarice again.

Still, she had to get food and a few other supplies. She had been foolish to think this might actually be simple.

A handful of cars and pickups drove past, and Wreath looked down, expecting to hear the woman's voice at any moment, half hoping she would. Maybe Clarice would butt into her business and put an end to this mistake once and for all.

Almost talking herself into looking for the woman's car, Wreath bumped into a signpost and slapped it with anger. She was hot and hungry, and she missed Frankie so much it hurt.

She rubbed her hand across her face and tried to keep from crying. *Lo, I am with you always.* The words popped into her mind.

Her mind raced. Her guts churned.

She turned around again, to see if Clarice might be near. Her eyes went to the sign she had stumbled against. The Landry Library.

The library! That was on her list of places to investigate.

She would see about public Internet access, maybe check out a book or two. Wreath wasn't sure how she was going to get a new library card, but she'd figure something out. Where there's a Willis, there's a way, as Frankie said.

The cool air of the library hit her so pleasantly it felt like a gift.

Wreath explored every aisle, the familiar sight of rows of books perking her up. Near the teen area, she saw a summer reading display, with a stack of bookmarks and a plate of cookies. A woman shelving books turned to look at her, and Wreath reluctantly walked away.

"Take a cookie or two," the woman said in a library voice. "They're free." The librarian gestured toward a group of kids about her age on the other side of the room. "Maybe you'd like to sign up for our teen reading club."

"Thank you," Wreath said, taking only one of the cookies, despite the desire to grab a handful. She chewed it slowly and sauntered near the shelves where the teens gathered.

She picked up a sheet about "Teen Tales," a book club for grades seven through twelve, and pulled from a display a new novel she had read about in one of her mama's magazines. Curling into a chair, she inhaled the smell of the book, fresh and distinct. Out of the corner of her eye, she watched kids at computers or reading on beanbag chairs in a corner.

She needn't have worried that she would stand out. She seemed invisible.

Suddenly loneliness threatened to crush her, and she put the book back on its table and headed to the bathroom. Alone inside, she examined the space for future use as a place to clean up. It was tidy, with the strong fruity smell of air freshener, and would come in handy, despite its lack of a shower.

Stepping out, she went back to the table and took one more cookie, smiling at the woman who now sat behind a nearby counter. "Thanks," Wreath said, doubting the woman could imagine how much she needed the snack.

She walked out the door into an entryway, licking sugar off the top of the cookie, and sat on a bench, reluctant to go out into the heat again. Her notebook in hand, she made notes.

DISCOVERIES, she wrote.

    1. Good shower, swimming pool at park. Costs a dollar.

    2. Free Internet access at library. (Air-conditioning!!!!!)

    3. Nice people—artist lady Julia, park boy, Clarice.

    4. Need to think more about paperwork and "official" stuff.

    5. LONG walk from Wreath's Rusted Estates into town.

With one last breath of cool air, she headed out to the street, gearing up to spend money she could not afford to spend.

❀ Chapter 6 ❀

The streets of Landry reminded Wreath of most of the places she and Frankie had lived, with a few run-down stores, a mix of black and white people, some workmen speaking Spanish, several churches, and lots of trees. Overall the effect was that of her favorite pair of jeans—frayed but comfortable.

In a small downtown park, Wreath recognized crape myrtles, their blooms the color of watermelon. Frankie said those were Wreath's grandma's favorite "because they bloom boldly in the heat of summer." She decided she'd start a list of flowers she liked when she got back to the Tiger Van.

Living in the junkyard, she liked nature more than she had expected—except for the bugs. She had figured out quickly which birds came around at certain times and what sounds they made. The crows were the noisiest. . .and the nosiest. The woodpeckers were persistent. The blue jays were loud, and mockingbirds dive-bombed her if she went too close to a certain bush. As she walked, she considered checking out a book on birds.

Wandering through downtown, Wreath chose the Dollar Barn for her shopping debut, a store she recognized from Coushatta and Oil City. These stores were cluttered and inexpensive. She figured she would blend in, just as she and Frankie had in the other ones.

As soon as she pushed the smudged glass door open, she could tell the air-conditioning wasn't working. The store smelled like the locker room at her old school, and the girl clerk had a small fan plugged in next to the cash register. An angry woman in an oversized housedress and terry cloth slippers jerked a screaming child by the arm, away from the candy aisle, loudly fussing without any visible results. A man in overalls paid for a gallon of milk with food stamps, and a middle-aged woman browsed through the cheap greeting cards.

No one paid any attention to Wreath as she chose food that met the requirements on her notebook list:

1. *Cheap.*
2. *Will last without a refrigerator.*
3. *Can be eaten without cooking. (Need can opener.)*
4. *Can be lugged back to the junkyard.*

As a treat, she chose a small sack of sale candy, passing over the chocolate for cheaper hard pieces that wouldn't melt. Frustrated, however, she couldn't find the item she most wanted—a big flashlight. She went up and down every aisle three times before asking for help.

"Excuse me," Wreath said to the clerk, who wore a store smock over a cute shirt. The girl stopped scrolling through her cell phone to look up. "Can you tell me where the flashlights are?"

"Those are seasonal," the clerk said, going back to her texting.

"Seasonal?" Confusion and anger blasted through Wreath. "What does that mean?"

"It means," the girl said in an exaggerated tone, "that we ran out, and we aren't getting any more. Seasonal means seasonal." A pretty teenager with a name-brand watch and a small diamond necklace, she looked out of place in the store.

Wreath shuffled back down the aisles, picking up necessities, her head low and her mood lower.

She could adjust to the junkyard. She really could. However, she didn't think she could stand one more night of the pitch-black darkness, the unseen sources of weird noises in the woods, and no way to read or find her way outside. The night was too scary without a light, and her eyes filled with tears at the thought.

Her arms full, she plopped her items on the counter, sensing her money dwindle every time the scanner beeped. She counted a few crumpled bills from her pack and wondered how she was going to keep from starving. Frankie had taught her to be thrifty at a young age, but even that wasn't going to make her little bit of money last.

"You might try the hardware store," the clerk said in a friendlier voice as Wreath placed her purchases in the thin plastic bags next to the register. "They might have flashlights, and sometimes Mr. J. D.—the owner—runs sales."

"Thanks a lot," Wreath said. Her relief must have shown, because the girl gave a small smile before going back to her cell phone. Carrying the sacks and fretting about the lack of a light, Wreath figured she had messed up. Landry didn't look nearly as appealing under this load.

Discouraged, she crossed the street and shifted the packages. Her shoulders throbbed, and she tripped on the curb, a sack tearing and precious cans of potted meat rolling down a slight hill. Frantic, she chased them, dodging a pickup whose driver gave her an annoyed look.

The meat was vital. But at the moment, the cans looked like animated pieces in a crazy video game, rolling along the street, evading obstacles. She watched in despair as one careened right in front of an approaching delivery van, crumpling in front of her eyes. She stood so close she could smell the odor of the smashed heap, but the driver seemed not to notice and sped on down the street.

Snagging the second can, she watched a third roll to the curb and bounce, landing next to the tire of a beat-up red bicycle propped in front of a store. Breathless, Wreath lunged for the potted meat, knocking the bike onto the sidewalk.

Looking around to see if anyone was about to scold her, she righted the bike. Then she noticed the FOR SALE sign taped to the handlebars. Wreath touched the seat and looked at the tires, imagining how good it would feel to put her packages inside the wire basket and ride away. She knew she could not afford it, but after only one foray into town, she was tired of the long walk and dreaded the time it would take to get to school.

The price on the bike, written in blue ink, was smudged and unreadable.

She made a list in her mind. Perhaps having the bike could help her find a job and give her a head start if she needed to leave Landry fast. She could get to school more easily and go to the library to check out books on a regular basis. She'd have more time and energy for fixing up her camp.

She and Frankie had almost always been broke, and she had gotten used to wanting things she couldn't have. But she wanted this old bicycle more than she had wanted anything in a long time.

"Use that good sense God gave you," her mama would have said. But Wreath didn't have money for the bike, and she needed to get back to the Rusted Estates before dark.

With shoulders slumped, she walked five minutes before jutting her chin out, straightening her back, and exhaling the deep breath she had held. She whipped around, arms aching, the supplies heavy. She could at least look at the bike and buy a flashlight at the hardware store, maybe more expensive than one from a discount store, but even a small one would be better than nothing.

Wreath had never been a quitter, and she was not going to start now.

The store with the bike out front was dim and dingy when Wreath stepped in, and it took her a minute to get her bearings.

"A bike and a flashlight, a bike and a flashlight," she said to herself.

Her eyes adjusting, she made immediate eye contact with a woman who looked like she was dressed for church or a funeral. Sitting in a chair, the lady did not bother to get up as Wreath stood uneasily before her.

Neither spoke for what seemed like forever, and Wreath looked around, wondering where the hardware was.

"Excuse me," she finally said, disliking the woman and the quivering sound in her own voice. "Could you tell me where the flashlights are?"

"Flashlights?" the woman snapped. "We don't sell flashlights."

Her heart sank. "Oh, someone told me the hardware store had flashlights."

"This is a fine furniture store, or did you not notice? Durham's Fine Furnishings."

Wreath looked around and saw a few pieces of what her mother and the old lady next door in Lucky might have thought of as fine furniture. Mostly she saw empty spots with dust on the floor, and a pile of junk in a back corner.

"I thought this was a hardware store?" The sentence sounded like a question.

"Of course not." Disdain dripped from the woman's voice. "That's next door. Can't you read?"

"You don't have to be rude about it," Wreath whispered. She knew

Frankie didn't like back talking, but the woman's attitude was uncalled for.

As she turned to walk out, the bike caught her eye, and she remembered what had drawn her into the store. "Are you the one selling that bike?" she asked.

"That's why it's sitting out front with a sign on it," the woman said. She slowly got up from the chair, laid down the magazine she was reading, and walked to a desk piled with paperwork.

"That's what confused me," Wreath said, as much to herself as the lady. "I thought this was the hardware store because it had a bike out front."

"As I told you, this is a fine furniture store. I need to get rid of that bike. Do you want to buy it?"

"How much is it?"

"Twenty dollars. Includes the basket and an air pump."

"That's a little expensive," Wreath said, mentally counting her small stash of money. "Thanks." She headed for the door. Stopped. Turned.

The big desk dwarfed the woman. She looked as out of place as Wreath and Frankie had the time they had gone to a ladies' tea at a big church in Vivian.

"Did you forget something?" The voice had a peculiar sound to it, a coldness.

"Would you be willing to come down on the price of the bike? I might be able to take it off your hands, get it off the front porch of your store."

"This isn't a flea market," the lady said. "I don't haggle over prices."

Wreath walked to the door, not saying a word. She was reaching for the handle when the woman spoke again. "I won't sell it for less, but I'll throw in an old flashlight if you buy the bike for my price."

Wreath felt a smile come to her face, despite her attempt to remain expressionless. "Sold," she said, and put her supplies and the dirty pack on the woman's desk, digging out a twenty-dollar bill.

"That all the money you got, girl?"

Wreath considered lying, but she had grown tired of untruths in a hurry. The lies went against everything Frankie had taught her. "Just about," she said.

"Who are your people?"

"My people?"

"Landry's a little place. Who are your kinfolk?"

Wreath swallowed hard and decided to lie after all. "The Williams family. They live out north of town a ways."

"You visiting for the summer?"

Wreath looked down at the floor. "Yes, ma'am. I'll be here for a few weeks at least."

"You willing to work?" The lady pushed her chair back from the desk.

"Work?"

"Yes, work. As in a job. Are you lazy?"

"Oh no." Wreath's protests were earnest. "I just got to town, and I'm looking for a job."

"I need help around here. I can't pay much, but I'll trade you odds-and-ends and give you a few dollars. Take it or leave it."

Wreath considered her choices. This woman would be a pain to work for, but a bike and a light would be worth a lot of griping. The cash could pay for food, and this woman didn't act like someone who would try to get in her business.

"I'll take the job," Wreath said. The musty smell of the store nearly overpowered her as she uttered the words, but this would be a start.

"You'll have to work. I don't have any use for laziness."

"I'm a hard worker. My mother said—says—I'm the strongest girl she's ever seen."

The woman surveyed Wreath from head to toe. "Come back tomorrow at one." She held the twenty out. "Keep your cash. I'll take the money for the bike out of your paycheck."

Wreath stepped back. "I don't take charity."

"You won't think it's charity when I put you to work," the woman said, waving the twenty in front of Wreath. "If you want the bike and the job, take the money."

The generosity and the words contradicted each other, but after giving it a moment's thought, Wreath pocketed the twenty, relief surging through her.

"Dig around in that pile and find you a flashlight," the woman said, pointing to the rear of the store. "There might even be an old lantern back there. You can take the bike after work tomorrow."

Wreath found a big used flashlight and a lantern in excellent shape and wanted to dance to the front of the store.

"I'm Wreath, by the way," she said as she pulled open the heavy old door to leave. "Wreath. . .Williams."

"Faye Durham," the woman said. "Don't be late for work."

❦ Chapter 7 ❦

As Wreath walked out of town, her packages didn't seem so heavy. She used her renewed energy to look for a new route, a path on which she might go undetected. She walked down three streets, turned around, and finally wound back to the road, still quite a ways from the junkyard.

Taking the bike home today would have been nice, but she knew her new boss didn't trust her to return. Plenty of Frankie's friends and relatives made promises they didn't keep, so Wreath understood.

Faye Durham was the boss's name. Durham, it dawned on Wreath. As in Durham's Fine Furnishings.

Mrs. Durham must be the owner's wife, because she sure didn't seem like someone who ran a store every day.

Wreath thought of the money she could make and the purchases she needed to set up housekeeping. She would have lots of lists to put into her journal tonight.

The slight tap of a horn interrupted her thoughts.

"Hop in, and I'll take you where you need to go. Looks like we're in for a storm."

Wreath looked over to see Clarice's now familiar car. This woman sure showed up a lot of places.

Clarice rolled to a stop, and Wreath's eyes darted from side to side, looking for an escape. "Are you following me?" she asked, walking on, shifting her pack and the plastic sacks from arm to arm.

"I was about to ask you the same thing," Clarice said with a smile. "Every time I turn around, there you are."

Wreath rubbed her right shoulder and glanced at the car.

"I'll pop the trunk, and you can put all that stuff in there," Clarice said. "I'm sure your mother wouldn't forgive me if I let you get rained on."

"My mother?"

"You said you and your mom are visiting relatives. Looks like we might be in for rain. I don't think she'd like you coming in looking like a drowned rat."

Studying the clouds, Wreath inhaled a big breath, and her shoulders sagged. "If you're sure you don't mind," she said. "I hate for you to go to any trouble."

"My pleasure. I told you I live north of here. It's not out of my way at all."

Wreath put her purchases, including the lantern and flashlight, in the trunk and climbed into the comfortable car. She had not noticed the ominous clouds, and she certainly didn't want to get drenched now that she was loaded down with supplies.

"I saw you headed to the library earlier. Did you check out any books?" Clarice asked as they started north on the two-lane road.

"Not today," Wreath said. "But it's a nice library."

"Do you like to read?"

"For sure." Wreath turned in the seat to look at the older woman, a hint of excitement in her throat. "Do you?"

"Always have. I keep a big stack of books I want to read. I like novels about the South and biographies. How about you? Any favorites?"

Wreath paused to think about the question, one Frankie had never asked her. "I like all sorts of books, except not science fiction. I mostly like stories with happy endings."

"My all-time favorite book is *To Kill a Mockingbird*," Clarice said. "What's your number one favorite?"

"When I was a kid, I liked those books about the Boxcar Children, how their grandfather found them and helped them out," Wreath said. "And I like that book about Anne Frank's diary. It got me started keeping a journal."

"I like that book, too." Clarice pointed at a crossroads ahead. "Which way?" she asked.

Wreath was puzzled, caught up in thinking about favorite books.

"Which way to where you're staying?" Clarice asked.

She squirmed, not a clue where to have Clarice drop her. "My family lives out past the state park."

"So who are your people in Landry?" Clarice asked. "Was it a cousin or aunt, you said?"

Wreath flinched at having leaked information. "They're relatives on my mother's side. I'm staying a few more weeks before heading home. They're the Williams family." She realized immediately the lie was a mistake. If she had run into Clarice three times already, there was a good chance it would happen again. And she didn't know any Williamses.

"Or my mama may decide to move down here for good," Wreath said. "Then I'd live in Landry till I finish high school." It was as though the spigot had opened on the garden hose, and untruths gushed out. Having her mother join them would surely be a trick, although Frankie would fit right into the junkyard. Even her ghost would be better company than the frogs and mice and what seemed to be a coyote that made Wreath's skin crawl in the middle of the night.

"This is good," Wreath said as a row of ramshackle mobile homes came into sight. "My cousins live near there where that door is open. They smoke a lot, and they don't have air-conditioning. It's stifling. Not that I'm complaining, because they have been great to let us visit."

She couldn't stop babbling, making up one false detail after another.

The woman pulled into the drive and got out of the car, causing Wreath to panic. She fully expected Clarice to ask to meet her mother and stay for a chat with the Williams family, whoever they were.

However, Clarice merely walked to the trunk and helped Wreath unload her belongings, touched the girl lightly on the arm, and said good-bye, handing her a bottle of water through the window.

"I'll keep an eye out for you," Clarice said, "and here's my card, if you ever want to call. I'd be glad to pick you up, help you out."

Wreath's eyes drifted down as the woman drove off.

Clarice Johnson, Attorney-at-Law, Johnson, Estes, and Johnson in Alexandria.

Clarice was a lawyer!

The dust from the car hung in the air as Wreath set her belongings on the ground and regained her wits.

Moving to the side of the trailer, she walked into a small overgrown area, sat on the ground, and began to kill time, wanting Clarice to be long gone before she walked to the junkyard. With no one else in sight, Wreath pulled her journal out, her brain eager to spill onto the page. She started scribbling, words pouring onto the lined paper.

MORE LESSONS, she wrote.

1. New last name is "Williams." Forget "Willis."
2. Make up an address.
3. Get a library card. (Okay, that isn't a lesson, but I want a library card.)
4. Take a trash sack at all times for possible summer storms. (Use as poncho as needed.)

Maybe one day she could afford one of those snazzy raincoats with the bright boots that went with them. Maybe when she finished college or law school or got her PhD or became a doctor. She might buy Miss Clarice a pair, too, just for being so nice. Wreath flinched when she heard footsteps. Someone had walked out of the ratty trailer with the door propped open. Trying to figure out how not to look like a loiterer, she picked up her awkward accumulation of items, brushed the dirt off her shorts, and took two steps.

She was stunned.

Sitting on the steps of the trailer was the boy from the state park. He was drinking a canned Coke and reading. He set the soft drink down, ran his fingers through his black hair, and acted like he was playing a short song on an invisible guitar.

A moment passed before he looked up and saw Wreath. He quickly quit pretending to play an unseen musical instrument, picked the Coke back up, and stood. His expression was a combination of embarrassment, delight, and confusion. They stared at each other for a moment, the way strangers do when sizing each other up.

He broke the silence. "Hiking girl, right?"

Wreath nodded and tried to figure out what to do.

"You moved into one of these palaces?" The boy pointed to the short row of pitiful metal rectangles, grassless yards, a car up on blocks.

Wreath didn't reply. She adjusted her pack and sacks of supplies and decided she had been wrong about the boy being rich. His home didn't look all that different from the Rusted Estates, although it appeared to have electricity.

"You're *really* not much of a talker, are you?" he said.

Wreath shook her head. Her instincts told her to walk away, but loneliness, dread of the walk to the junkyard, and this guy made her want to stay.

"I'm not real sure why you're standing in my front yard," he said after a minute. "Since you don't seem all that happy to see me, I guess you didn't come to visit."

Wreath shook her head again. The random spot where Clarice dropped her would turn out to be the home of the cutest boy she'd ever seen. And she was acting like a dweeb.

"Ranger boy?" she blurted out, thunder sounding in the distance.

He nodded, a small smile coming to his face, and took a swallow of the soft drink. She noticed he'd been reading a book of guitar music.

"My name's Law," he said.

"Law?" She laughed. "I've never heard that name before."

"It's short for Lawson," he mumbled. "A great-uncle's name or some-thing. You going to tell me your name or just stand there making fun of mine?"

"I didn't mean to make fun. I like unusual names." She glanced at the book of music. "Sounds like someone in a band or something. You play the guitar?"

He groaned. "You saw me playing air guitar, didn't you? I was so hoping you didn't see that."

She nodded.

Law shook his bangs out of his eyes. "I'm saving up to buy one. I've taken a few lessons and am trying to teach myself the rest."

"I've always wanted to learn to play the drums," Wreath said. She had never admitted that to anyone, not even Frankie.

"So you don't like talking, but you like to make noise, huh?" When Law smiled, he made Wreath's heart flutter. He was good-looking enough, for sure, to be in a band.

"I've got to go," Wreath said, suddenly uncomfortable. "My friend dropped me off here by mistake."

"That's strange," Law said.

"I'm new around here. I got the addresses mixed up."

He tilted his head. "So you live around here?"

By now Wreath was backing up, her pace picking up. "Down the road," she said and turned almost at a run.

"Wait!"

Wreath was elated and scared when she heard his footsteps drawing near.

"You never told me your name," he said, falling into step beside her.

"Wreath."

"Wreath." He made her name sound like the title of a poem or a song. "No wonder you like unusual names. You want me to carry that stuff home for you?"

"Oh no!" Wreath said and then tried to give her voice a calmer sound. "It's not far. I've got it. I'd better get going."

"I hope to see you around," he said.

She walked away, wishing she could stay and visit or ask him to walk her home. She was eager to talk with Law and almost as sure she needed nothing to do with him.

"Wreath!" he yelled.

She paused and looked over her shoulder.

"I like your name!"

A few raindrops began to fall, but she didn't care. She smiled all the way to the junkyard.

❀ Chapter 8 ❀

Unlocking the furniture store door from the inside, Faye Durham stepped outside and jumped. Wreath stood silently next to the building.

"Why are you leaning on that wall?" Faye snapped.

The girl looked equally surprised, not expecting her boss to come from inside. "You told me to come back at 1:00 p.m. today. To start my job. Remember?"

"Of course I remember," Faye said. "I didn't think you'd actually be back. Now I have to figure out what I'm going to do with you. Stand up straight. You look slouchy."

Wreath straightened her T-shirt and wiped the palms of her hands on her shorts. She glanced over at the bicycle, still propped out front.

She had to have a job, and she needed that bike, even if it meant putting up with Mrs. Faye Durham.

"Thank you for the flashlight and the lantern," she said. "They work great."

The woman, who wore grouchy like a second skin, did not respond. That was tolerable. Wreath could handle hateful. She'd done it before. Mrs. Durham stared her in the eye. Wreath stared back.

"You're Holly, right?" the woman growled, still holding the door open.

"Wreath," she said, softly but firmly. "Wreath Williams."

"Might as well come in." Faye pulled the OUT FOR LUNCH sign off the outside of the door, ignoring the piece of tape left on the window.

Wreath looked around. Faye's eyes followed hers as they scanned the big old space, more like a warehouse than a retail establishment. Water had seeped through the pressed tin ceiling; a lightbulb was burned out in back, making the rear of the store dreary; and a jumble of furniture and cardboard boxes were piled in a back corner.

An unpleasant odor hit Wreath's nostrils and seemed to settle under her skin, and she wondered about the skimpy furniture and high price tags on out-of-style pieces. The old wood floors were covered with dust, in every visible corner and on each surface of woods that looked like oak and pecan and mahogany.

"Follow me," Mrs. Durham said in a commanding voice.

Wreath didn't speak as they went to a small room in the back of the store, with a refrigerator, a sink, and a small table, plus more piles of old merchandise and a few cleaning supplies on a counter.

"Sweep," Faye said, turning to look at Wreath. "Then sweep again. Once won't cut it. Dust, too. Everything. You will be responsible for keeping the store clean. Don't break anything."

Wreath nodded.

"Here." Faye grabbed a broom and dustpan from the corner. "Make yourself useful."

Wreath took the broom, thankful. Sweeping was an assignment she could handle. "Where would you like me to start?" she asked.

"If you can't figure that out, you're not going to work out," Faye said. "Start wherever you like, and don't nick the furniture."

Wreath slowly swept her way through the store, getting down on her hands and knees to reach under the paltry furniture and taking in the haphazard way things were displayed. The woman returned to her desk, turned the radio up a notch, and shuffled a stack of papers on the desk.

Methodically covering the store, front to back, left to right, Wreath finished back in the workroom. She was surprised at how quickly she had made the store look better.

She wondered what she was supposed to do next. Her new boss had not spoken since handing her the broom. She wiped off the countertop, caught a whiff of something spoiled, and pulled the trash bag out of its can, noticing a handful of empty tuna cans.

Wreath walked out with the sack. "Do you have a cat?" she asked.

"A cat? Of course not. I'm not a pet person," Faye said, walking toward the girl. "Put that trash in the alley." She motioned to a door with a large bolt in place and walked back to her desk, watching.

Wreath pushed and pulled on the bolt until her face was red.

"Darn," she muttered and disappeared back into the workroom. She rummaged around in the cabinets, opening and closing doors and wondering if she was being tested. Wouldn't any normal person have helped her?

She danced a little jig when she came across a small hammer and a can of WD-40 that looked like it had been sitting there for years. Within minutes she had the door open and stepped out into the alley.

Wreath wiped her hands on her shorts, wrinkling her nose. "You sure someone hasn't been feeding a cat around here? There must have been a half dozen tuna cans in that sack. I'll empty that more often from now on."

"That'll be fine," Faye said in a waspish tone.

Twisting the cap off a bottle of lemon oil, Wreath inhaled the smell. She dug out a soft cloth from under a counter and wiped the top of a table. A glow replaced a layer of dust.

"What would you like me to do now?" Wreath asked, stepping back in with a smile.

"Now?" Faye looked at the neon clock hanging on the back wall, an advertisement for a line of furniture. "That's it for today."

Wreath followed her gaze. "But I've only been here an hour. I thought you were going to let me earn the bike."

"Take the bike," Faye said.

"I want to work," Wreath said. "I need a job."

"I don't have any more work for you." Faye spoke in the tired voice Frankie had sometimes used.

Wreath looked around, feeling wild and desperate. She might be poor, but she was not pitiful. She dug in her pocket, pulled out a five-dollar bill, and laid it on Faye's desk. "If you'll hold the bike for me, I'll come back when I have more money."

"I said take the bike," Faye said. She picked up a merchandise catalog from her desk.

"It wouldn't be right," Wreath said. She paused on her way to the door, straightened an area rug, and adjusted the angle of a chair and end table. "Thanks again for the flashlight."

The woman glanced at the rug and back at Wreath. "Be back tomorrow at one, but I don't intend to hold your hand. Take the bike."

❋ Chapter 9 ❋

A feeling of freedom washed over Wreath, a sense of joy she had not felt since Frankie had gotten sick. She hummed one of the country songs that had been on the radio in the furniture store, music her mama loved so much.

She had earned the bike.

Wreath's legs trembled, and the bike wobbled as she headed down the street, thankful to put space between her and her second day at Durham's Fine Furnishings. She pedaled harder, riding through the town, which still looked like Wreath felt—worn out but in decent shape. The ride home was definitely an improvement over the walk, although she was more tired than she'd anticipated. Her workday had been short, and she didn't want to think about Mrs. Faye Durham and how oddly the woman acted, nor the possibility that the job wouldn't last.

Hiding the bike behind a thorny bush in the junkyard, she tiptoed through an examination of her camp, half holding her breath as usual until she was certain no one was near. Listening nervously to various chirps, croaks, and a squealing noise that sounded like a broken radio, she fixed peanut butter and crackers for supper and settled into the Tiger Van.

Restlessness swept over her. She tried to blame it on her boss, a woman who reminded her of shrews she had studied in junior-year English class. But she knew Law and Clarice were the ones who had stirred her up. Law was what her mother would have called a "looker." Wreath appreciated the fact that he worked and was thankful in a warped way that he wasn't rich. She had hoped to run into him again today, but knew it was for the best that she hadn't.

Clarice had made Wreath think about reading, and she wished for a new series to start or one of her old favorites to reread. Some of the best stories she had read three or four times, but she had left all the books she

owned in Lucky. Books were too heavy to carry when your load needed
to be light.

Instead, she had listed them in her notebook, the little library she'd
left behind, mostly books from garage sales or thrown out from the
school library because the covers were beat up or someone had scribbled
in them or torn a page or scratched their initials into the cover. Wreath
couldn't understand people who spoiled books for other people. She
handled books carefully, the way she might a puppy or Frankie's fragile
glass vase.

The night now totally black, she took her flashlight out of its hiding
place under a sack of clothes in the back and fished the journal from
the pack. She picked the old pen up from the seat of the Tiger Van
and tried to remember titles she'd seen at the library the day before.
Maybe she should take a chance and try to get a library card. She jotted
a few novels to read. Clarice was a fan of *To Kill a Mockingbird*, and
her English teacher in Lucky had liked it a lot, too. Wreath definitely
needed to read that one.

Swatting mosquitoes and sweating, she read through her book list,
remembering what she liked most about various stories and reminiscing
about what was going on in her life when she had read each of the
books. A good story took away the loneliness when her grandma died
and Frankie started moving around. Books kept her from having to talk
to kids she didn't know when she went to a new school.

Someday she was going to have a nice house full of books. When she
finished college and had a good job, making lots of money, she would
have one of those rooms lined with shelves and a ladder on wheels.

She had shown a picture of one of those rooms to Frankie, who
smiled and said, "You'll fill that up in no time." Her mama always said
Wreath got her love of books from her daddy's daddy. "That man could
sit for hours with his nose in a book."

Wreath didn't know her father, so she certainly didn't know his
father. She thought instead Grandma Willis had instilled the love of
reading in her, and Frankie agreed that was possible. "She started every
day reading the Bible and after that read everything she could get her
hands on whenever she could grab a minute," Frankie had said.

Until Wreath checked books out, she could read books she had found around the junkyard, many of them mildewed with a slightly distasteful smell but still intact. As the long summer evening grew darker, Wreath started a horror novel she had found in one of the junked cars, a scary, dark drawing on the cover. Its pages were brittle with age and began to fall apart before she finished the first chapter.

She was kind of glad to put it down, the story adding to her anxiety as the night noises got louder, the van stuffier, and her imagination jumpier with fear.

She fell asleep with thoughts of snarling dogs and mean men and a dark jumbled place where evil skulked. She dreamed of a kind woman who helped poor children, and the sight of the woman made her feel safe. She reached out, thinking it was Frankie. When she got closer, she saw it was a beautiful angel, dressed in white, but it wasn't her mama.

Wreath awoke, stiff, as usual, from the hard floor of the van. Except this morning she felt better.

Happier.

The thoughts about being found weren't as close as usual. Nor was she worried about school. . .or the need to turn herself in to some faceless official. Those thoughts, as stuck to her as the hot, humid weather, had shrunk.

On this morning, an odd feeling of peace and tension mixed up inside of her. She knew she had to do a few more things to make her campsite livable.

Wandering through the old cars, she remembered her first glimpse of the place, back in the winter, when the trees were bare and the area deserted, coming out of Landry with her mother and Big Fun. Although she never had much use for Big Fun, she owed him for helping her stumble upon the junkyard, the only good thing to come out of the trip.

Her mother had insisted they drive through the little town "for old times' sake." Even though Big Fun had grumbled, he did so, her mother occasionally pointing to this building or that, not saying much at first. "That's the house we lived in before I quit school," she said, pointing to a small frame home on a street lined with trees.

"I thought you lived up near Texarkana," Wreath said. "Where Grandma lived."

"We moved there right before you were born," she said so softly Wreath could barely hear over Big Fun's radio. "Your grandmother wanted to be closer to her brother and sister. It's hard to believe they're all gone now."

Frankie twisted in the seat to look back where Wreath sat. "Enjoy life, sweetheart, because it goes fast. Faster than you can imagine." She stretched her arm to pat Wreath's knee, the movement seeming to tire her mama. Wreath drank in every word her mother spoke.

Big Fun had interrupted the moment, laying down on the horn when a scrawny dog ambled out. "I was happy to see the last of this place," he said. "Nothing here but white trash and junk."

As Big Fun said the word *junk*, Wreath saw the overgrown sign for the junkyard, a handful of vehicles in sight and not a house around.

The seed was planted, and Wreath filed away details of the towns they passed through, knowing in her gut it would not be long till she needed a place of her own.

"Stop!" her mother yelled suddenly, and Big Fun slammed on the brakes.

"What in the world is the matter with you, woman?" he shouted.

Frankie seemed to shrink into the seat. "This train crossing is dangerous. I don't want anything to happen to Wreath."

"There's not a train in sight, Mama." Wreath rubbed her mother's hair. "Everything's going to be fine." She couldn't quite believe how fast her mother had declined after that day. Frankie went so fast, almost as though the illness *were* a speeding train about to mow her down.

Trying to stay a step ahead of the sadness that wanted to overtake her, Wreath peered every day into smashed cars, sat in the driver's seat of the ancient school bus, pretended to scold the kids behind her, and poked around in overgrown travel trailers, wondering if their owners had ever gone somewhere exciting.

She thought of the van as home, the one place in the whole world that was hers. Each morning Wreath climbed out of the van, nervous about what she might find. The homestead was different, but the feeling was not unlike that at the run-down house where she and Frankie had lived for the past year.

She made herself walk throughout the junkyard both morning and evening, checking for clues that others might have been there, but all seemed well.

Using tricks she had read in a detective novel in seventh grade, she set up traps to let her know if anyone came around when she was gone or sleeping. As she went, she noted the tricks in her journal one morning before work.

SECURITY SYSTEM AT RUSTED ESTATES
1. String tied to Tiger Van doors on left and right sides.
2. Coke can on floor just inside door of travel trailer.
3. Piece of rope across path to pond/mud hole.
4. Leave one item daily on steps of trailer next to van. Monitor item's placement.

Even compiling the list made her nervous, and she quickly dressed.

She collected a few items from trailers, amazed at what people left behind, and silently thanked the previous owners for their generosity, from mismatched dishes to a heavy iron pot that would come in handy if she ever decided to build a fire and cook.

She picked up three tattered books and a handful of T-shirts that had not decayed, but walked away from rotted things that fell apart when she touched them.

The scattered stuff reminded her of the things she had abandoned at the shabby house in Lucky. She could almost see low-life neighbors pawing through them, a lot more concerned about her hand-me-down clothes than they were about her.

Her favorite find on this morning was an assortment of photographs that she lined up on the van's dashboard, next to one of the pictures of her mom she had carefully saved. The children in the found photos would be older than she was by now, she thought, and some of the hippies were probably dead, just like Frankie. Wreath made up stories about their lives, wondering if life had dumped something unexpected on them, too.

Every day she made herself examine at least one different vehicle, and today she added five to her list. They were old and smelly and full of a history that Wreath couldn't understand. She found faded photo after faded photo, greeting cards, cracked dishes, and odd pieces of clothing, some still in good shape even after years in the Louisiana heat and humidity.

The cars and trailers and RVs *were* alive—not with people but with bugs and mice and lizards and something that looked like an oversized gummy worm.

Life here felt much the way it did in the weeks before Frankie died. Wreath felt as though something hung over her head, waiting to drop on her.

❀ Chapter 10 ❀

The pavement was hot, but Julia loved the way it felt to hit the road. She headed out to the state park, her favorite route in any season. Thick green trees came up close to the road, providing enough shade to make her feel cooler. Scraggly wildflowers bloomed along the ditch, and she saw a box turtle trying to make it across the road.

During the sweaty run, she usually sketched pictures in her mind. Today the thought of her art turned her brain back to a subject that was never far from her mind—whether it was time to get out of Landry.

She had come to the high school intent on shaping young protégés and paying off college loans. Instead she was teaching antsy students how to read the newspaper and why the Constitution mattered. Most of her students were good kids, but a few of them made her want to pull her hair out. The subjects bored her, too, so she understood why she couldn't make hyper teenagers care.

She had slid into a paycheck and health benefits and wasn't sure she had enough cash to make a move, even at the age of twenty-four.

Julia wondered if she might turn into someone like her landlady, Faye Durham, whose daily routine seemed closed off and dull. The very idea made her want to pack her car and drive up the road to anywhere but here. She was scared, though, that wherever she went she would find more of the same.

Turning into the park, she sprinted down the entrance lane and headed toward the restroom for a splash of lukewarm water out of the faucet. As she entered the building, she thought for a second about the teenager she'd encountered earlier in the summer. *Wreath. What an unusual name.*

She hadn't seen the girl since, but Julia couldn't quite forget her. She wondered if the family had been camping for fun or if they moved around, living at parks like this. She had heard some families had to do that. Something about the girl Wreath niggled at the edge of Julia's mind.

Lawson Rogers stood outside the park office as she ran past, and she doubled back to speak, hitting PAUSE on the timer on her watch. Law was one of her favorite students, a conscientious boy who didn't sleep in class and made good grades. She'd heard her colleagues in the teachers' lounge say his father was in jail, but he'd never mentioned it to her. He was so polite that it was hard to believe his father was a scoundrel.

"Too hot to run today, Miss Watson." The boy walked from the shade to where she stood. "Where's your water bottle?"

Just like in class, he noticed details. "I forgot it," she said.

"If you have a minute, I'll get you some from the office."

"That'd be great," Julia said. "It probably is too hot to run at this time of day, but I have a meeting later and want to get my run in." While the boy went inside, she sat on a wooden bench, catching her breath.

"How's the job?" she asked when he returned with the water.

He grinned. "It's good, but don't tell my friends. They think it's lame to work here. I like the park. Makes the days go faster."

"Go faster?" Julia gulped a swallow of water. "I thought high school students wanted summer to last forever."

"Not this high school student. I'm ready to graduate and head on to college."

"You have the grades for it," Julia said. "Wish that would rub off on your fellow students." Julia had noticed many of her students didn't even think about college. The principal seemed happy if he could keep them interested enough to finish high school.

Law shook his head, a rueful look on his face. "Most of my friends aren't that interested in school. They want to get a job and buy a new truck." He looked sheepish. "Not that I'm criticizing them. College costs a lot of money, and most of them haven't been out of Landry. They don't think about what's out there."

"So you've traveled?" Julia asked.

"I've read about places and seen them in movies. I want to see them in person, and I want to make money." He stopped. "Sorry. You didn't ask for my life plan."

"If you don't mind my asking, how will you pay for college?" From what she'd seen, the boy didn't have a lot of money.

"Loans. Scholarships, I hope. I'll work, too. My grandparents. Whatever it takes."

"Sounds good," she said. "Let me know if I can help. I'll write a recommendation for you."

Julia glanced at her watch and stood. "By the way, have you seen a girl around here lately? About your age, long brownish-reddish hair, backpack?"

Law didn't pause to think about that one. "Is her name Wreath?"

"That's her," Julia said. "Do you know her?"

"Not really. I've run into her a couple of times, and she seems real nice." He blushed. "Is she in some kind of trouble?"

"Not that I know, but I met her out here and wondered if she might need help."

"She doesn't talk much, but she acted like everything was okay when I saw her," Law said.

"Will you let me know if you bump into her? I want to give her a hand if she needs one."

"Sure," he said. "I hope I do see her again."

❋ Chapter 11 ❋

Wreath had found happiness in being needed by her mother, and she was surprised to find a similar pleasure at Durham's Fine Furnishings.

She still tiptoed around the furniture store owner, always afraid of losing her job, most of the time ignored. But Wreath had begun to feel a level of accomplishment at the store. Some days she looked forward to propping her bike against the post out front and scooting inside, wondering what she could do today to make the place look better.

At the junkyard, she walked to the trunk of a rusty old Chevrolet and pretended to unlock the trunk, though the hinges had sprung long before. She reached inside and counted her small stash of cash, putting most of it back under the spare tire. She also hid cans of food, bottles of water, and a picture of her mother.

Taking her bike out of its hiding place, this time in the bed of a pickup covered with a blue plastic tarp, she pedaled down the road, enjoying the wind in her hair and anticipating a visit to the library before work.

She kept careful track of every day she worked, using little ink marks in her journal along with a comment or two about Mrs. Durham. *Dear Brownie*, she wrote one day. *My boss almost paid me a compliment today. When I finished dusting, she said the spiders must wonder what's happening to the place. Wow! She actually made a joke. She's not the joking kind, but she pays me in cash and lets me have a few old items from the back.*

Mrs. Durham had told her she could take whatever she wanted "out of that pile of junk," and Wreath chose an item or two every day, trying not to look obvious. Today her pack held an outfit she had picked from a cardboard box in the storeroom, and she looked forward to cleaning up at the library and putting it on.

The hot air felt like a blow-dryer on her skin as she rode, and she wondered what cooler weather would be like in her new home. Every time she stepped through the library door, she savored the cool air, tired of being hot and sweaty. She breathed in the familiar smell as she walked in, the scent of paper and ink, a clean scent that felt like visiting the home of a friend.

Walking into the bathroom, Wreath glanced under the stalls to make sure the room was empty, then washed her arms, hands, and face. This was not as good as a shower at the state park, but it was a lot easier and didn't cost a dollar, so she had done it several times in the past weeks. She stepped into one of the stalls and slipped into the cotton skirt she'd paired with a faded blouse. Surveying herself in the mirror nearby, she felt presentable. Almost pretty.

The library had become one of the few public places she allowed herself to linger, stopping in most days before work. The employees were friendly and sometimes offered her a snack from the story hour for little kids or a book club meeting. She read magazines and scanned regional newspapers, curious if she might see her name. Stories about missing children from California to Connecticut always caught her eye, but no one seemed to be looking for Wreath Willis.

Today was the day for another of her big steps.

She went directly to the main desk. "I'd like a library card, please."

The gray-haired man who worked weekdays looked over his glasses and picked up a pen. "It's about time you decided to check out a book," he said with a kind wink, not the creepy kind that Big Fun had sometimes thrown her way. "My grandson's about your age and likes to read. I can recommend his favorites, if you're interested."

"That'll be great," Wreath said, although she already had a long list of books she wanted to check out.

The man handed her a pen and a form on a beat-up clipboard. "Fill this out, and we'll get you taken care of."

Wreath settled into one of her favorite chairs, where the sun came through the window like a pretty lamp, but also near an air-conditioning vent where cool air blew on her face. Her eyes scanned the form, and she relaxed. She hated lying, but the form was brief. She filled in the blocks one by one, listing her real age. She gave the address of the furniture store as her home address.

When Wreath wrote the new last name, she felt a piece of herself slip away. *Williams.* One of the worst things about hiding was giving up her name. "We are Willis women through and through," Frankie always said.

Perhaps getting a library card wasn't such a great idea. The information could be pieced together to track her down. She would take a book in her pack without checking it out. She'd bring it back in good shape. Wreath started to rip the form in half, but longing clung to her as she looked around. She didn't want to be accused of stealing books from the library, and she couldn't depend on the few books at Wreath's Rusted Estates. They were mostly horror stories or technical manuals for various pieces of equipment that had been thrown out, and were falling apart, no matter how careful she was.

Only the old, mildewed Bible had interested her, and she had searched for stories she remembered Grandma Willis telling and looked for the words she'd found in the notebook. *Lo, I am with you always.* They sounded like something you might find in the Bible, but she couldn't locate them. She wondered again who had made the entry in her diary.

But here, at her fingertips in the library, were free books. She didn't have money to go to a movie and had no electricity, even if she could afford a television. She needed a library card. So she kept at it and felt good when she came to the spot for the date under her signature. At least that wouldn't be a lie.

She looked across the room at the big calendar behind the copy machine and sucked in her breath.

Eight weeks ago today Frankie had died. Clenching her teeth, Wreath let her chin droop to her chest. She missed her mother so much that for a second she felt as though she'd suffocate.

By now they should have moved on together, not Wreath all by herself. They would have found a place to rent, and Frankie would have gotten a job as a waitress or a clerk. They could have come to Landry together, and her mama could even have worked at the Dollar Barn. They could have turned the evidence over to the cops and gotten Big Fun sent away for good. Or would he have gotten out again?

Wreath tried to pull herself together when she saw the man from the counter walking over to her chair. "Everything all right?" he asked, his look of concern so intense that she wanted to burst into tears. "Need help with that form?"

"I've got it." Wreath was glad her voice didn't shake. "I'm almost finished."

Nodding, he moved on to a group of toddlers and the women who must be their mothers, and Wreath's eyes lingered on the gathering. The children were adorable, and the women sat cross-legged on the floor next to them, pointing to pictures in colorful books and rubbing their backs or embracing them.

Frankie took her to the library once, when Wreath was about seven. They had chosen a stack of books and practiced reading together. After that, her mama was always working or cooking or "trying to find a nice man," as she put it. Wreath went to the library at school or, when she got older, with a friend or sometimes the old neighbor in Lucky.

Wreath squeezed her eyes shut to block out the sight of the happy children, and gritted her teeth as she finished the short, official-looking form. She walked back to the front counter before she could change her mind, and tried to smile as she handed the man the form, but all she could think about was how Frankie should be here with her, how Frankie had looked that last day, the cover pulled up under her chin, her body so still.

The library employee glanced over the form, his now familiar smile on his wrinkled face, his teeth big and somewhat yellowed. Wreath drew in her breath when his brow furrowed. "You're only sixteen, Miss Williams?"

"Yes, sir."

"I'm afraid one of your parents will have to come in and sign this. You have to be seventeen to get a card on your own."

Wreath felt tears come to her eyes and started to walk away but feared that might look suspicious. "My parents are out of town, and I wanted to check out a book today," she said. "I'll be seventeen in December."

"It's library policy." The regret in his voice was evident. "You're

71

welcome to read while you're here. At least it's nice and cool. Hot as blue blazes outside." He chuckled. "However hot that is."

Wreath frowned, despite herself. "Thanks anyway."

The man went back to his computer, and Wreath walked over to the new releases and pulled out several. Looking around, she started to slip one into her pack but couldn't bring herself to do so.

Dejected, she headed out, knowing it was too early to go to work, but afraid she'd burst into tears if she stayed any longer. Everything was so hard.

As she reached the door, the man at the desk called to her in a loud whisper. "Miss Williams?"

For a moment she didn't realize he was talking to her.

"Miss Williams?" he repeated, louder.

She stopped, nervous. "Sir?"

"Step over to the counter, please."

Once again, she wanted to run. But she was already tired of running, of hiding. Maybe the librarian had figured out her secret, but how would that be possible?

She walked to the counter.

"We have used paperbacks over there for our upcoming annual book sale. Feel free to pick one or two of them up. You can drop them off when you finish them. We have plenty."

Looking at the shelf by the door, she saw dozens of interesting-looking books and was touched by the man's thoughtfulness. She thanked him and left the library with a worn copy of a novel she had read in sixth grade and a like-new biography of a woman named Harriet Tubman, who helped free slaves in something called the Underground Railroad. Both were in much better shape than the books she had in the Tiger Van, in as good of shape as the ones she'd left behind in Lucky.

After carefully placing the books in her bike basket, she sought a patch of shade, pulled out her notebook, and added the new titles to her "books to read" list. Frankie would have liked both of these, and Wreath could have read them to her mama while she rested.

Another tear slid down her cheek, and she got on the bike and pushed off with a wobbly start.

❦ Chapter 12 ❦

The front door of the furniture store was locked, the OUT TO LUNCH sign hanging at its weird angle again today.

Still reeling from the realization that two whole months had passed and wondering why it felt like a lifetime, Wreath settled on the step of the store. She pulled an apple out of her pack, wished for a hamburger and a large order of fries, and watched the man at the hardware store next door, sitting on his front bench, reading.

She craned her neck to seek what the book was, searching for anything to keep her mind off Frankie.

"Did you come here to daydream, or did you come here to work?" The snippy voice had become annoyingly familiar, but Wreath had not heard her boss approach.

She jumped to her feet, the half-eaten apple flying out of her hands and landing right at Faye's feet. The owner had opened the door from the inside, and Wreath was distressed every time it happened that someone could sneak up on her like that.

You'd think she'd be used to it by now. Mrs. Durham's routine was as predictable as Wreath's was odd. "I didn't think you were here," Wreath said. "I knocked on the door." She retrieved the piece of fruit and dropped it, unwrapped, into her pack. She could wash it off and eat it later.

"If I must, I'll tell you again. I'm here every day except Sunday and Monday. I eat lunch inside from twelve thirty to one. As my employee, you should make it your business to know such things." She stood in the partially opened door. "Knock louder next time."

"Yes, ma'am," Wreath said, although she wanted to say something fierce and ugly. She had gotten a similar speech about a half-dozen times, even though she was never late, knocked loud, and worked hard.

"Move that bike away from the door and come on in and get to work." Faye turned and went back in, removing her lunch sign.

"Witch," Wreath mumbled as she pushed the bike past a pile of litter that had blown up against the front of the store. As she thought of ten things she would like to say before riding off in a blaze of glory, she could almost hear Frankie's voice.

"You be nice to them, they'll be nice to you." The words had been her mother's guide-to-life every time they moved and when Wreath fretted about a new teacher or a bully at school. She wasn't sure Frankie's wisdom would work on Faye.

Looking up, the hardware store owner laid the book on the bench, gave her a smile, cleaned his glasses on his flannel shirt, and peered at her closely when he replaced them. Waving, he picked up the book and went inside.

Wreath took a deep breath, adjusted her pack on her shoulder, and walked into the furniture store, the smell not nearly as much like the junkyard as it had been a few weeks earlier. Her boss sat at the old desk, with a pen in her hand and the back of an envelope in front of her. She frowned at the paper, as though not quite sure what to do with it.

Wreath walked over to her and stood quietly. The ticking of a big old clock, advertising some kind of dinette set, sounded like a bomb getting ready to explode, and Wreath's stomach felt the same way it had the night before, when the frogs were too loud and the van too empty.

"Thank you again for the bike," Wreath said when she could stand it no longer. "It helps on hot days like today."

"If it helps you get here on time every day," the woman said finally, "it was money well spent."

"But I paid for it." Wreath frowned.

"At a discount price," Faye said. "But enough of that. I made a list of things for you to do today."

Wreath felt her gloom lift.

For weeks she had come in to silence, swept, dusted, and looked for furniture to rearrange or other chores that might be important. She had scrubbed the storeroom, rearranged the cabinet under the sink, and stacked the boxes of junk like a child's building blocks, in neat order. Her goal was to make herself indispensable, so she could keep the job when school started. Even if Mrs. Durham was rude and the merchandise ridiculous, not too many people came in. Wreath didn't worry that Big Fun or anyone else would find her here.

Best of all, at quitting time each day, Mrs. Durham gave Wreath a ten-dollar bill for her three hours of work. It wasn't much, but it helped keep her fed, and it required no paperwork, no cashing of checks at a bank.

Wreath had been surprised the first time she was handed the money. "I thought employees got paid by the week," she said, stuffing the money into a side pocket in her pack.

"Maybe they do," Mrs. Durham said. "I've never had an employee before. It's easier for me to keep up with my money like this."

What she hadn't said, Wreath figured, was that she didn't expect the girl to show up for work on any given day. She didn't know that coming to work gave Wreath a sense of purpose she needed almost as much as she needed money.

"Here are some duties for you," Mrs. Durham said, holding out a piece of paper.

Wreath eagerly grasped the list, surprised at how excited she was for new responsibility. Some days her life seemed more stagnant than the pool of water behind the junkyard. "I love lists," she said, setting her pack on the cushion of a nearby chair and pulling out her journal. "They help me remember what I want to do. I can write down instructions in here, if you need me to."

"This isn't a management class," Faye said. "The list is self-explanatory."

Only three activities were on the paper: *Sweep. Dust. Rearrange furniture.*

Wreath wondered if this was a joke, or if she was about to get fired. "But Mrs. Durham, this is what I already do."

"Call me Faye," the woman snapped, turned her back on Wreath, and walked toward the rear entrance of the store. "I'm not your mother. Or your grandmother, for that matter."

"You're sure not," Wreath muttered.

"What did you say?" Faye turned around abruptly; her eyes squinted like a villain in a cartoon.

"I said, you're sure not my mother or my grandmother. They were nice." Wreath regretted the words before they made it out of her mouth, but she couldn't stop them. Everyday struggles had worn her down.

For six weeks she had been tied up in knots, and she couldn't stand it one minute longer.

"I quit," she said.

❋ Chapter 13 ❋

Faye didn't know why she pushed the girl so hard.

She didn't remember being harsh when Billy was alive, but running the store was running her into the ground.

That girl Wreath—what kind of name was that?—made all her shortcomings more obvious.

Maybe it was the quiet way the teen had about her, always down on her hands and knees trying to get the last speck of dust out from under a couch. Or the dignity with which she carried herself, whatever the task. Whether told to scrub the toilet or get bird mess off the front of the store, Wreath did it with solemn persistence.

Faye preferred sitting, determined to do things her way. Every day at lunch, she locked the front door and ate a can of tuna with four crackers, washed down with a bottle of fruit-flavored water, and topped off with one small piece of chocolate. Afterward, she wiped her desk with a paper towel, washed her hands in the tiny, outdated bathroom, and returned to the showroom.

Lunch was followed by the small peace of sinking into one of the two recliners still in stock, slipping off her shoes, and pushing back. She did not read, watch television, or nap, but closed her eyes and thought about her husband, mad at Billy for dying and saddling her with this store. Sad.

This was her life. She could find very little she wanted to do these days. But Wreath. . . The girl acted like every task was something she wanted to do, which confounded Faye. She was unsettled by the girl. Wreath made her uneasy, scrutinizing her like she understood far too much.

But she didn't want her to leave. Watching her first and only employee pick up that ratty pack, her back straight, Faye had an irrational urge to tackle the girl, the first surge of energy she'd felt in months. She suddenly felt like she'd perish if Wreath walked out the door. She couldn't bear the thought of the store the way it had been. Stifling. Dusty. Empty.

"Your shift's not over," Faye said.

"I don't work here anymore," Wreath said. Her voice quivered the slightest bit.

Faye tried to imagine what might make Wreath admit she'd been wrong to quit. "If you had an ounce of pride, you'd give me enough notice to find someone to replace you."

The doubt on her helper's face intensified. "I. . .I've never had a paying job before," the girl said. "I think it'd be better for both of us if I left today."

"I didn't peg you for a quitter." Faye looked her straight in the eyes.

"I'm not a quitter." Wreath practically spat the word *quitter*, her shoulders bowed back and a stubborn set to her chin.

Sensing victory, Faye went on. "You've hardly worked here a month. From where I stand, that looks like quitting."

Tension hung in the air.

"Nothing I do pleases you," Wreath said, but she set her pack on a nearby table.

Tapping into Wreath's pride meant Faye would have to swallow her own pride, too.

It was worth it.

Faye took a deep breath and plunged ahead, as though stepping out into oncoming traffic. "I'm not used to running a business. Truth is, up till about seven months ago, I rarely came in here."

Wreath kept her distance. "What happened?" she asked. "Is your husband sick or something?"

"Or something," Faye said, and Wreath shifted her head, the way she did when she was confused, like a blue jay considering a piece of bread on the sidewalk.

"Dead," Faye continued. "Billy is dead. It's been seven months today." She had almost forgotten the girl was there. "He was well respected around town and honored with all the Chamber of Commerce awards possible."

"That's nice," Wreath said, clearly unsure what she was supposed to do.

"No, it's not," Faye said. "Billy was no real businessman. Look at the prices on this not-so-fine furniture. Who in their right mind would pay for this stuff?"

The girl's eyes got larger with every word, but Faye couldn't stop. "I lied to you. I don't have any inventory coming. I can't even figure out what the new styles are, even if I did have money to pay for furniture."

"I don't want to quit," Wreath said in such a hushed voice Faye could barely hear her. "I need a job. I hope you'll take me back. I'm sorry for saying what I did."

"The problem is, I can't seem to think of enough to keep you busy," Faye said. "The sweeping and all is good, but I need a handyman. This place is a wreck."

"I'm strong. And I'm not afraid of heights. If you've got a ladder, I can change that lightbulb. I helped. . .help. . .my mother a lot around the house."

"I don't want you getting hurt. We'll figure something out. Get back to your sweeping."

"I'm sorry your husband died," Wreath whispered before walking to the back. "That must really hurt."

Faye sank down at the antique rolltop desk that Billy had despised, its top cluttered with overdue bills and an old-fashioned adding machine. Less than a year ago, she had trusted the business and all the details of her life to her husband of thirty-six years. While she had lived her life, he had lived his, comfortable and complacent. Their marriage had not prepared her for his heart attack, quick decline, and death—or the problems that suddenly had to be solved.

She looked to the back of the store where Wreath fished new spiderwebs out of a corner with the broom. Each of the teenager's movements seemed intense and focused, and Faye thought for a second that the girl could do a better job running the store than she could. Something would have to be done, but she wasn't sure what. At least Wreath could stay for now and keep it clean.

The familiar car slowed.

"Need a ride?" Clarice called.

"I'm good," Wreath said and kept walking.

"I'd be glad to give you a lift," she said. "Where you headed?"

"Nowhere," Wreath said.

Faye turned up the radio. Now that she was a widow, she could listen to the country-and-western station, enjoying twangy tales of love and loss and cheating and hurt, music that Billy'd had no use for.

"My mama liked that song," Wreath said, broom in hand, on her hands and knees, bringing out dirt and litter that had been there who knows how long.

"She doesn't like it anymore?"

Two red splotches appeared on the girl's cheeks. "I mean she *likes* it," she said. "She loves country songs. She says they tell great stories, and she likes stories. Reading, too."

Looking as though she'd just told a family secret, Wreath turned away and made a great show of dumping a dustpan into a trash sack she carried with her.

Faye liked her occasional chats with the girl. She preferred their calm conversation to the inane chatter of someone who had no intention of purchasing a dining room suite with a huge china cabinet and accompanying sideboard. However, she didn't have to worry about silly customers, since not one person had come in during the two weeks since Wreath had almost quit.

Truth was, she wouldn't go so far as to call the handful of lookers in the store *customers*. Some were bargain-hunters, certain she was desperate to unload her inventory; others thought she had a flea market; and a few were friends and neighbors stopping by to check on her.

She got up from the desk, sat down in a recliner with the weekly newspaper, and gazed at the monstrosity of a store. She looked at the big round clock on the wall, two feet in diameter, its old cord plugged in. She stared as the second hand slowly made its way around, a grinding sound marking the passage of one minute, then two. Faye did not know which she feared most—that no one would wander in or that someone might, that Wreath would leave or that she would stay.

The teen, looking clean and cute in a pair of out-of-style slacks and a knit blouse, put the broom back in the storeroom and opened the door onto the alley as though she had been doing it for years. As the girl brushed out the dust, a wasp zoomed down from its nest under the back eaves. Wreath swatted wildly at the insect before knocking it to the floor and smushing it with her shoe.

"You picked the wrong person to deal with today, mister," the girl muttered. Faye knew the feeling all too well.

Faye wrestled with the heavy back door, wishing she could afford Wreath all day.

Annoyed at the thought, she jiggled the handle again. If that little squirt of a teenager could open it, she could. When it gave way, Faye practically flew out into the alley.

Caught between mortification and triumph, she looked around, wondering where the weeds came from and how so much trash had piled up. The only bright spot was a patch of black-eyed Susans that refused to give up, despite the heat. Something about them reminded her of Wreath.

The screen door of the garage apartment across the alley, part of the store property, creaked. Her tenant walked onto the landing, looked around, and went back in. Billy had mentioned that the woman was a good tenant. Other than that Faye knew little about her.

The young woman stepped back onto the porch, and Faye moved into the shadows near the store, watching.

Julia pretended not to notice her landlady, an aloof woman who seldom spoke and refused to do any repairs, in return for cheap rent, paid on time. Looking around the little porch for her running shoes, she felt like she was spying and went back in, glancing out the window. Mrs. Durham looked around the alley as though she'd never been there before.

Distracted from her search for the shoes, Julia walked over to the calendar she had drawn for summer, reluctant to mark the big *X* on the previous day. The days passed too fast, and she had canvases to paint, pottery to fire, training to do.

She scoured the tiny apartment, rewinding her memory to think where the shoes might be. Stopping to study her latest painting, still on the easel, she touched the canvas with a hesitant finger. An oil of a barn on the outskirts of town, it was framed in weathered wood from the falling-down building. The piece bored her.

She wondered what the customer would say if she offered an impressionistic pastel of the falling-down building instead. She had painted that one for fun, for herself, and she liked the way it looked hanging on her whitewashed plank wall.

Finding her shoes under the bed, next to a stack of other pieces of art, some finished, some abandoned midway, she got ready for her run. She was late and in a bad mood and felt an unreasonable resentment against her landlady. Must be nice to inherit a store like that and not have to work.

Julia dreaded the ongoing continuing education course that would occupy most of her day and hoped the run might wear her out enough to make the class bearable. If it hadn't been required to keep her job as a teacher at Landry High, she would have skipped it.

In-service, they called it on the official paperwork. *In-servant* was more like it. Why should she have to take a course, for no pay, during vacation?

Julia longed to spend her months off creating. She wanted to teach students how to create, wished she weren't stuck in a social studies class. She finished lacing her shoes and jammed her hair under a cap, all the while wondering what was worse—a social studies class or the artistic taste of the people who hired her to do paintings. She stepped onto the landing and waved at Faye, who was still poking around the alley. Irritated at life in general and determined to make the woman acknowledge her, Julia spoke. "Morning, ma'am. How's business?"

"Fine." Faye made a show of inspecting the hinges on the old back door.

"Is it my imagination, or is it unusually hot?" As she spoke, Julia paused to water the hanging basket at the top of the stairs, a pot of wilting impatiens in pinks, oranges, and reds. Her landlady kept her back turned, and Julia tried to think of something else to say. She was in no mood for this woman to ignore her.

"Have a problem with the door?" she asked.

"The door?" Faye looked startled, all dressed up and standing in the alley, as though she'd been dropped off at the wrong place.

"The door there. Is it acting up again? Mr. Billy used to have problems with it." She hadn't known her landlord very well, but he was easier to deal with than his widow.

"He did?"

"All the time," Julia said. "Sometimes he'd walk around the building to get out back. Said it wasn't worth his trouble to get the darned thing open."

"That's good to know," Faye replied. "I thought it was just me."

"These old buildings remind me of my students. They're a challenge, and you never know from day to day what the challenge will be."

"You teach school?"

Julia was surprised her landlady didn't know that. She had lived in the apartment for the whole two years she'd been in Landry.

"High school. Civics and American history."

"Sounds interesting," Faye said, although Julia couldn't tell if she really thought so or not. "Although I confess I never was a fan of those subjects. I liked art and English and gym." The woman stopped. "I'm sorry. I don't know what came over me. That was rude."

Maybe Faye was human after all. "Not to worry. I don't like those subjects either," Julia said. "I'm waiting for an art class to open up. Are you an artist, too?"

"An artist? Me? Heavens, no. I prefer sewing. I haven't picked up a paintbrush in twenty years, other than to paint the trim in the bathroom." Mrs. Durham was definitely flustered. "Are you going to the gym?"

Julia was confused. "Does Landry have a gym?"

"I'm sure I wouldn't know," Faye said. "It's been longer since I've exercised than since I painted. I think there's a dance aerobics class at my church." She said the word *dance* with the slightest hint of a frown.

By now Julia had walked to the bottom of the steep wooden steps, and she and Faye looked at each other as though they were speaking foreign languages the other didn't understand.

"You have on your exercise clothes," Faye said. "I thought you were going to a gym."

"Oh. . . I'm off for my morning run, but I'm getting a late start. Had to prepare for a computer course I'm required to take. I like to use computers for graphics and art projects, but this is about research and timelines."

A completely lost look passed over the other woman's face. "I thought teachers got summers off."

"I need a special certification, so I have to take this course. School starts at the end of the month, so I need to do it now."

"I hope you get paid for it."

Julia raised a brow. "No pay. Just six hours a day in a classroom. Fun, huh?"

"Sounds delightful," Faye said. "I think I'd rather work on the hinges on this back door."

The two laughed awkwardly.

"Nice visiting with you," Julia said. "Better run." She waved, and the woman turned without a farewell and headed back into the furniture store.

While Julia jogged, her feet slapping against the steaming street, she thought about the unusual encounter with her landlady, who rarely stepped foot out of the store. The few times Julia had caught a glimpse of Mrs. Durham, she was alone, lips pursed and mannerisms jerky, as though she wasn't comfortable in her own skin. Today she had seemed different. She said she liked art.

Maybe Julia had misjudged her, the way people in Landry misjudged her art.

❋ Chapter 14 ❋

When Frankie got stressed out, she always said she was about ready to climb the walls.

Wreath wished she lived in a house so she could do that right now. The carpeted sides of the stifling Tiger Van closed in on her and increased the anxious feeling she had. She held her watch up to her ear and shook it, wondering if the battery had died.

She had eaten stale crackers for breakfast and mixed fake citrus flavor into a small amount of water, aware, as always, of how heavy bottled water was to lug back from town and how yucky the pond water was.

While she ate, she looked over her recent notes.

> *Dear Brownie: Mrs. Durham is strange. No, not strange.*
> *Frankie would have called her peculiar. And she wants*
> *me to call her Faye. That seems plain weird. She's old.*
> *But at least she gave me my job back when I quit. I miss*
> *Mama. I wonder if it will always hurt this bad.*

Underneath, she had listed her work duties:

> *Sweep.*
> *Dust.*
> *Keep showroom clean.*

That list was so paltry that Wreath added a few more duties this morning.

> *Other Possibilities:*
> *Rearrange furniture.*
> *Clear out back corner.*
> *Flowers (Fresh flowers always help, according to*
> *magazine at the library.)*

WHAT ELSE CAN I DO?!?! She scrawled the letters in huge print across the page, sideways. She was creative, according to her former teachers, and smart. Surely she could do something else for Mrs. Durham.

She'd have to come up with better ideas if she was going to keep her job and maybe get more hours. Faye wasn't the type to put up with fit throwing, for sure, and somehow Wreath didn't think she'd hire her back again if things went badly.

Worrying about money always made her feel like she needed to throw up, yet counting her money had become a daily ritual. After she counted it, she entered the amount in her journal. Part of the money was now hidden in a small plastic sack near the back of the land, ready to run at a moment's notice. The rest she carried with her.

Using a wet towelette to wash off, she pretended she had a luxurious shower. She'd slipped back into the state park a few more times to take a real shower, avoiding that guy named Law. Wreath dressed, put on a red plastic headband she'd found in a travel trailer, and hoped the furniture lady wouldn't frown at her appearance. The clothes were not only out of style, but worn and faded.

Looking at her watch again, she tried to figure out what to do for the next couple of hours before she went to work.

To work.

Fine furnishings? Not a chance. But the job provided a reason to hang out in town, helped her meet a person or two as "the girl who just moved here," and paid for food and water.

She wished she could tell Frankie about the job, get advice about how to deal with a grouchy boss. Frankie had told her about plenty of those kinds of bosses through the years, but she'd always made the stories fun. Wreath couldn't summon up a fun image of Mrs. Durham, although the woman could be decent when she wanted to. Sometimes she reminded Wreath of herself, as if the death of Mr. Durham had permanently smashed her heart.

Finding a spot of shade, Wreath sat down in a lawn chair she'd rescued from a rusted-out RV, careful to shift her weight away from the broken webbing. She pulled out her journal and started a fresh page.

Wreath Wisteria Willis/Williams, employee.

1. Dress appropriately.

2. Don't be late.

3. Work hard.

4. Be nice to Mrs. Durham no matter how mean she is.

5. Earn money!!!!

6. SAVE money for college.

She groaned at the last entry.

Life had seemed hard with her mama sick and Big Fun hanging around, cussing and drinking, but she'd take it back in a minute. Frankie hadn't believed in feeling sorry for yourself, though, and Wreath could almost hear her mama fussing.

Something stung her ankle, and she looked down to see that her chair rested next to a fire ant bed, a collection of the insects stinging her ankle. She jumped up, knocked the chair over, dropped her journal in the mud, and hopped around trying to brush them off her legs, yelling all the while.

Her loud voice surprised her. She so rarely talked anymore that it almost sounded like a stranger's.

She grabbed her pack and pulled her bike out of an old van where she had hidden it, feeling as though ants still crawled over her.

Jumping onto the seat, she rode hard into town, giving the pedals everything she had, tired of wobbling. Her lungs hurt and sweat ran down her body, causing the seat of her shorts to feel damp, but she pedaled harder and harder.

Hurtling past dense trees, Wreath bumped her way toward town. The route was rough, the pavement full of potholes and rutted-out areas. The shoulders were narrow or nonexistent.

An occasional house, trailer, or run-down wood building was set back from the road, usually with a junky front yard. A station wagon was pulled near the front door of a weird brick building that looked like an apartment. In the back of the car there was a mattress, and the seats were filled with clothes, dotted with garbage bags.

All in all, Wreath thought, it didn't look like those residents lived much better than she did.

She slowed at the entrance to the state park, considering whether to turn in and look around. She needed a shower but was afraid of seeing the boy again. Wreath hated to admit how much she longed to see Ranger Boy, in his green shirt and khaki shorts. She would have thought he only worked a day or two a week if she hadn't seen that lousy trailer where he lived. She certainly had misjudged him. With that mink-brown hair and muscular build, he looked rich. But he couldn't afford a guitar.

With thoughts of Law in her mind, Wreath glanced at the entrance of the park longingly.

Instead of the boy, the artist, Julia was her name, jogged slowly out of the park, sweat flying off her body. Hoping the woman didn't see her, Wreath kept pedaling, but Julia raised her hand in a friendly wave. Wreath took one hand off the handlebars and gave a half wave back, as her pack slipped and the bike headed toward the ditch.

A car sped by as Wreath swerved onto the shoulder and spun in gravel, straining to maintain her balance. Giving up, she pulled over and planted her feet on the gravel.

Julia jogged steadily toward her. "You okay?" she huffed, running in place and gasping for breath.

"I hit a rock." Wreath shifted, hoping the woman would move on. "I'm fine."

"I've been thinking about you. Everything all right?" Julia said. "Anything I can do for you?"

"Everything's good," Wreath said, feeling an extra trickle of sweat pour out from under her arms. She tried to make eye contact instead of shifting her eyes away.

"Your family still camping?"

"Camping?" Wreath thought for a moment. That's what happened when you started lying. You couldn't remember what you'd said, what was real. "We're staying with relatives. My mama liked it so much she's moving us here."

"I'll see you at Landry High, then." She gave a wave and headed off.

Landry High? What was that all about? Julia didn't look old enough to have a kid in high school. Wreath rolled the shoulder she had wrenched when she'd nearly wrecked her bike. Could Julia be a teacher? She looked younger and in better shape than any of the teachers Wreath'd had in Lucky or any of the other towns where they had lived.

Wreath constantly weighed whether something was good or bad when it happened. This encounter could have raised suspicions, one more connection with a Landry resident. What if she had a class under Miss. . .she didn't know her last name. She hoped she didn't get her, because Julia raised too many questions. She might even look at Wreath's files.

She had said she had just been thinking about Wreath. That sounded dangerous.

Maybe it was time to move.

"No," Wreath said out loud. She couldn't. She had to make this work if she was going to finish high school.

She watched Julia move out of sight, thankful to see distance between them. When the woman was nearly around the corner, Wreath climbed on the bike, her feet on the gravel, feeling as though ants were crawling up her legs, and decided to go to the library to clean up.

As soon as she entered the cool building, she perched on a small bench in the entryway and pulled her journal out of the pack, sad to see that its cover looked worn. She fished around for her pen and made a small entry.

Dear Brownie, don't take this too hard, but I have something to share with you. Life stinks.

❋ Chapter 15 ❋

In the evenings, Wreath thought nights were the worst. Weird noises surrounded her, and she fretted that a bum would stumble into her corner of the world. But usually sleep overcame her, and although she woke up with a few bug bites, the darkness was gone.

Mornings hit hard because there was a big hole where Frankie should have been. From the time she was six or seven, her mama had brought her coffee to bed to wake her up. "Rise and shine, baby girl," her mama would say, giving her the tiny white cup that had more milk and sugar than actual coffee. Every day Frankie sat down on the side of the bed and stroked Wreath's hair, which stuck out in every direction when she woke up.

"I'm not a baby," Wreath had grumbled when she turned nine.

"You'll always be my baby girl," Frankie said. "Now get up and face the world."

At sixteen, Wreath figured she was definitely facing the world. She thought her mama must be watching over her, or she'd never have made it this long. When you were doing fun stuff, time flew. But when you were trying to escape, it seemed to crawl by.

Wreath developed a routine. Not a normal one, she had to admit, but a routine anyway. Some mornings she pretended she was at extreme summer camp. "Wreath Willis, from Lucky, Louisiana, will be forced to live by her wits for one week. Can she find food and water? Will she be stronger than the other campers, winning the ten-thousand-dollar prize?" She announced the words into an old metal cup she used as a microphone.

"While other campers are out for activities, Miss Willis diligently takes care of the campsite," she said into the make-believe microphone. "Chosen as camp leader, she must make sure accommodations are up to standard. Now she must begin her daily inventory of the site, making certain that other campers take care of the property and abide by camp rules." Rich people paid good money for experiences like this. She had known a rich boy in Lucky who had gotten sent away to a military school for drinking and generally doing dumb things. When he came back, he described it in much the same way as Wreath felt about her life now.

She went directly to one of her favorite junkmobiles, a travel trailer that looked like one of those cans that ham came in. Maybe she should splurge on a ham at the Dollar Barn. That sounded good. The trailer, even with its share of rust and mildew, had a jaunty air about it, with turquoise trim and bright plastic furniture. She had read about Yellowstone National Park in one of her history books and decided to call it Old Faithful. She could see a family using it to camp in the park, the mom frying bacon while the dad watched for bears.

This morning, she was on a mission. She gingerly opened the door, never plunging in for fear of who or what might greet her. "Not a creature is stirring," she said in her announcer voice, trying to shake the nerves she had when she entered any of the vehicles.

Turning to the kitchen, somewhat of a jumbled mess, she found what she was looking for—a coffeepot, a Dripolator, like Frankie had bought for a dime in a garage sale. She had watched her mama make a hundred pots of coffee and was going to give it a try, once she figured out how to heat the water. She also picked up a cracked flowerpot with a smiley face painted on it.

The floor creaked, and Wreath jumped, then headed back to the Tiger Van. Cute as Old Faithful was, her van felt safer. It was small and secure, not cozy, but contained. Even though she mostly only slept there, it felt like a home. With the coffeepot in the "kitchen" of her van and the flowerpot by the "porch," she sat down in a half-broken lawn chair and pulled out the journal. At this rate, she'd need another notebook before long. She carefully documented her schedule in her journal.

Schedule:
Wake up. Eat breakfast. Clean up Tiger Van.
Write in journal.
Get dressed. Every three days take shower. Yech.
Explore Rusted Estates. Work on home.

> *Go to work.*
> *Eat supper. Read.*
> *Bedtime.*

Writing made her feel in control. She was not a hopeless girl living in a dump. She was Wreath Willis, and if she took life a week at a time, she'd make it, even if she was ignoring the looming weight of school. She hated to admit it, but she looked forward to school starting, even though the idea made her nervous. She missed talking to Frankie and her teachers at school and sitting on the front porch and listening to neighbors argue, TVs turned up loud. She had never watched much television because she didn't like to be in the same room with Big Fun or Frankie's other boyfriends, but now she missed the sound.

Dear Brownie: I wonder if I could get cable out here, she wrote and then got up to explore some more. Sitting still in the van during the day was almost as bad as lying on the floor in the dark, smelly and claustrophobic. Combing the junkyard, she sketched vehicles and listed their contents. It not only gave her something to do, but it made her feel as though she were the landlord, in charge of all these people.

She shrieked when she looked up and saw a face staring at her through a window and then gave a relieved laugh when she realized it was herself.

She had finally found a decent mirror.

Wreath told herself she was making the trip to the state park to shower.

But she didn't fool herself.

She wanted to see Law.

Desperate for someone to talk to, she was crushed when he was not in the little log cabin, replaced by a man in a tan uniform. The man looked more like a prison guard than a park worker, but he paid her scarcely any attention, watching the Weather Channel on a TV mounted in the corner of the office. She stood at the counter for a full minute before he acknowledged her. She supposed that was a good thing.

"Day pass, please," she said, laying one of her precious, crumpled dollar bills on the surface.

The man picked the damp bill up with a slight grimace and wrote the date in marker on the pass. "Enjoy your walk," he said as she turned away. "Watch out for poison ivy. It's bad right now."

The shower always made her feel better, less like a homeless person. The water, lukewarm coming out of the faucet, streamed over her. It washed away not only the grit but also many of her fears. Usually she walked out feeling like a new person, ready for a fresh start.

This morning she felt settled and homesick at the same time.

She wondered where Frankie was buried.

Clarice noticed her as soon as Wreath pulled out of the park, her legs strong as she propelled the bike toward town.

She had been worried about the girl and was happy to see she wasn't on foot.

"Wreath," she called, and the front tire of the bike wobbled a bit but the rider didn't turn. "Wreath," she yelled louder. The teenager kept pedaling.

Hesitant, Clarice put on her blinker and pulled onto the opposite shoulder, in front of the bike. Wreath would have to stop—or run into her car.

The bike swerved a bit, and Wreath's face looked grim.

"I haven't seen you around," Clarice said. "I thought you'd gone back home." She could almost see the thoughts run across the thin face, the beautiful brown eyes hooded.

"We're staying," Wreath said. "I may start school here."

"I see you've got wheels." Clarice pointed to the battered bike, with a silver fender and a large basket, filled with a backpack that was stuffed so full it looked like it would burst.

The teen actually smiled. "I bought it downtown," she said. "It's a lot easier than walking. Thanks again for giving me those rides when I first got here."

"The offer stands," Clarice said. "Do you still have my number?"

Wreath moved her head in what was the slightest nod and looked down at the plastic watch. "I've got to get to work," she said. "See you around."

And off she rode, swerving around Clarice's car and pedaling like a pack of wild dogs was on her heels.

Coming to the edge of town, Wreath slowed down.

She figured she looked crazed flying along the road, but she liked to scoot away from the junkyard quickly on ordinary days. She didn't want a passing driver to notice her near there, raising questions. She supposed it was inevitable that she'd run into that lawyer again, and it had shaken her.

She slowed down. Crashing into a ditch in front of an oncoming car would be a good way to get noticed, and that would have been stupid. *Avoid notice. Avoid notice. Avoid notice. Be more careful.*

Frankie had never fussed at her as much as Wreath fussed at herself. "Don't be so hard on yourself," her mama used to say. "Just do your best." She couldn't let herself get upset by the encounter. Clarice was a good woman. The teen wanted to talk about her job and the books she'd been reading with the lawyer, but she knew that wasn't smart.

Just hearing the voice, though, had helped. No doubt Clarice was smart, being a lawyer and all. She might be able to help Wreath if Big Fun showed up. But that would mean trusting her.

Wreath shook her head and started riding again.

She turned toward Main Street, trying to think of something to do until work. Unless she convinced Faye to let her do more, she didn't think she'd be welcome showing up early. The woman didn't seem too used to having people around and wasn't much for small talk.

Being around her for work could be bad enough, but hanging out with her would be ridiculous.

Wreath couldn't help herself. She groaned out loud at the thought of being chummy with her boss, pulling up a chair and propping her feet on the big old rolltop desk that looked like something out of a history book. She could almost see the woman shrinking back, turning up that rich nose of hers and shooing Wreath out with a broom.

Going to the furniture store was out.

She didn't want to be too obvious at the library, and she'd been there four times this week. If she went to the Dollar Barn, she'd want to spend money she didn't have, and the A/C didn't work so great in there anyway. The cashier's name was Destiny, and she went to Landry High,

Wreath had learned during one of her regular visits for Vienna sausages and peanut butter.

Destiny kept a box fan sitting on the unused counter behind her, blowing hot, damp wind onto the customers as they paid—cash only. Sometimes she was out front on break when Wreath rode up and always seemed ready to talk. No. The Dollar Barn was out.

Wreath's list of options wasn't that long, and she finally took a deep breath and decided to do what she'd been putting off. Today was the day she would scope out Landry High School, where she planned to be an invisible A student, whom colleges begged for and teachers ignored. She wasn't quite sure how she was going to do that, but where there was a Willis, there was a way.

Veering off to the right, she rambled through neighborhoods, up and down side streets until she saw the school in the distance, almost on the other edge of town. She pedaled with a sense of purpose now, excited to get a feel for the place and to work on her plan to get registered.

She ignored the bike rack and rode up the front sidewalk, realizing she was at Apollo Elementary School, not the high school. Disgusted, she turned her bike and rode around the side, jumping a curb into the parking lot and nearly colliding with a trio of sweaty guys, bouncing a basketball between them, shoving and laughing. She slammed on her brakes, skidded, nearly flew over the handlebars, and threw her left leg down to drag her to a stop.

One of the boys had just let go of the basketball, and she was squarely between it and the intended receiver. The ball flew toward her, and she froze, with a split second to decide whether to drop the bike, duck her head, or hope that the overheated parking lot might split and swallow her whole.

"Look out," one of the boys yelled and launched himself at the ball, grabbing it and smashing into Wreath. Wreath, the bike, the ball, and the boy all hit the ground.

"Freak," one of the other boys muttered, grabbing the basketball as it rolled across the playground.

"Are you okay?" the boy sprawled next to her on the parking lot asked, gasping for breath.

"I think so." Wreath winced and tried to get up off the ground with an ounce of pride, gravel stinging her knees. When her scraped hands touched the hot pavement, she gasped and sat with legs stretched out, her best pair of shorts torn and blood trickling from her elbow.

"You didn't mention you're a motocross rider," the boy said, and Wreath shielded her eyes from the sun and looked into Law's flushed face. The boy from the park.

"You didn't mention you hang out with maniacs," she said. She never knew someone who had just gotten smashed could feel so good about it.

"Hey, we weren't the ones riding a bike seventy miles an hour in the parking lot," one of the group, a teen wearing expensive athletic shoes, shorts, and no shirt, said.

"Give her a break, man," Law said. "She wasn't doing a mile over sixty."

"Whatever. Come on. Let's get out of here."

"Wreath, you sure you're all right? Mr. Charm here has a car. He can take you to the doctor if you need to go."

"Doctor? No way. I'm fine." Wreath scrambled to her feet, ignoring aches that seemed isolated to her head, arms, and legs. . .and her neck and feet.

"You know this chick?" She turned her stiff neck and saw that the question came from the guy who had called her a freak. He was good-looking in a preppie sort of way.

"Wreath, this is Mitchell Durham. Mitch, this is Wreath, that girl from the park I told you about." The name woke Wreath's stunned brain with the clarity of an alarm clock set for an early school day.

"Durham?" The word came out practically in a gasp. She glanced at her watch, the face scratched. "I'm late for work." She got on the bike, amazed at how much her body hurt, her knees aching when she tried to pedal.

"She's cute," Mitch said, walking away. "But she acts like a dork."

Law looked at Wreath and rolled his eyes. "You're the one who nearly hit her in the head with the basketball," Law said.

"You're the one who knocked her off her bike," Mitch said.

Wreath decided this was as good a time as any to flee and rolled forward until she built momentum.

"I hope she's not hurt," she heard Law say.

❀ Chapter 16 ❀

Faye stepped outside for the third time in ten minutes, looked at her watch, and frowned, mad at Wreath for not showing up and at herself for caring.

In the first days of Wreath's employment, she'd half expected the girl not to make it to work. But in the more than two months the teenager had been working for her, the girl had always been early.

Rubbing her arm down the sleeve of her linen jacket, Faye could feel the sweat pouring off of her. Most of her outfits were those she had once worn to fund-raising teas or down to Lafayette to shop. Putting them on for work made her feel like she was wearing a costume, but casual clothes would reveal a weakness, a reminder that they didn't even make Oldsmobiles anymore, that her country club membership had been one of the first budget cuts, and her expensive clothes were looking dated.

She pretended not to notice J. D., the hardware store owner and a leader at her church, waving. In his blue jeans and work shirt, he looked more like a field hand than a merchant. She had to admit he was nice-looking in a blue-collar sort of way, but everything about him was too casual, even his name. What kind of name was J. D. for a grown man?

She leaned over and picked up a piece of litter, refusing to admit she still hoped the girl would show up.

"Anything I can do for you, Faye?"

She jumped at the sound and whirled around to see J. D. standing at the edge of the street. "I've got time on my hands. There's only so many times I can sweep my store and straighten my shelves, if you know what I mean." He laughed, as though sharing an inside joke.

"I can manage." Faye turned to walk back into the store. "I was looking for my helper. She's late today."

"Your business must be a lot better than mine if you can afford to pay that girl."

She thought at first he was mocking her. He saw how few customers came into her store, and he had to know she sold scarcely anything in a given week. But he smiled, and she realized he was making small talk, something she'd never been very good at.

"Business is passable, and I thought I'd give a teenager a summer job," Faye said. "But she hasn't shown up today. You know how kids today are. Unreliable."

"I've seen her waiting for you a handful of times," J. D. said. "I hope she didn't run into trouble."

"She quit once," Faye said. "She's probably decided she doesn't want to work after all." The words pricked at her conscience in a way that nothing had since Billy died. Wreath never slacked off, and truth was, Faye was worried about the girl. But she knew so little about her that she wasn't sure where to start looking.

"You'd be doing me a big favor if you came up with an odd job for me every now and then," J. D. said. "It gets pretty boring after lunch. Most people come by in the morning. I've read nearly every one of the new releases at the library."

Faye shoved on the front door, eager to escape his kindness, and had to throw her shoulder into it to get it to open. "Door's stuck, swollen up with this humidity," she muttered.

"Let me work on it. I can fix just about anything, and you're all dressed up. You look too nice to be messing with that old door."

She wasn't sure if her face flushed from pushing on the stubborn door or from the compliment. "I like to look professional," she said. Faye glanced down at the name-brand suit, hose, and pumps. "The customers expect it."

"You look a lot classier than I do, that's for sure," he said. "I'll wear jeans to my funeral if I get the chance."

At the word *funeral*, he paused. "Sorry. I didn't mean to be disrespectful to Billy. I'll grab my toolbox and be right back."

"What about your store?" Faye asked.

"I can watch it from here," he said. "This little project won't take ten minutes."

As he walked off, Faye thought that while he might not look classy, he was a handsome man in his own rugged way. Just as the thought registered, she looked up to see a blur approaching the curb, and a red-faced Wreath slammed on the brakes and hopped off the old bike, flinching as she did so.

"I'm sorry I'm late, Mrs. Durham. It won't happen again. Please don't fire me."

Faye looked at the agitated face in front of her and then at the blood oozing from both elbows. "What in the world happened to you?"

"I won't be late again, I promise." The girl straightened her hair and grabbed her pack. She was clearly trying not to cry, her bottom lip trembling as she stepped onto the store's porch.

"Stop fretting, Wreath," Faye said. "This is the first time you've been late. There's an old first-aid kit in the workroom. I'll find it while you get a drink of water. You look like you're about to keel over."

When Faye came into the showroom with a blue and white plastic box, Wreath was straightening furniture. J. D. had the door propped open, planing the bottom of it so it wouldn't stick. One of Faye's favorite singers was on the radio, belting out words of love.

For a moment, she felt like she'd walked into the wrong place.

Every bone in Wreath's body hurt as she walked over to one of her favorite tables, running her hand across the smooth wood, trying to get rid of a speck of dust. The bike wreck had hurt badly, but she didn't want to let Faye know.

She would show no weakness. Not to Mrs. Durham. Not to anyone.

"Come over here," her boss called, and Wreath nearly cried again when she realized the woman had walked up nearby without being heard.

Wreath tried hard not to let a tear squeeze out, but she was sore and scared. She needed this job.

"Sit down." The woman motioned to one of the nice, soft chairs on the edge of the showroom. A first-aid kit sat open on the desk, a hodgepodge of bandages and tape inside it. A tube of cream that looked like something from Wreath's grandma's medicine cabinet lay on the desk, a tiny bit of brownish gel oozing out the top.

Wreath sat as directed and then jumped up, moaning a bit with the pain of the movement. "I shouldn't sit on the good chair. I'll get it dirty."

"Good point." The woman looked almost surprised. "Move over here."

"Over here" was a kitchen chair covered in yellow vinyl, and Wreath sat down. She felt like she needed to say something, but she didn't know what, so she kept quiet.

"Wipe off with this rag. It's clean." With a jerky motion, almost like she didn't know how to hand someone something, Mrs. Durham gave her an old washcloth, in much better shape than the ones she and Frankie had had back at home.

"I'm sorry I was late."

"So you said."

"I guess I'm a little out of practice riding a bike after all. I used to have a pink bike with training wheels. . . ." The words stuck in Wreath's throat. She had a vague memory of Frankie clapping as she wobbled off when they took those wheels from the bike.

"They say once you learn to ride one, you never forget, but I guess that's not true after all," Faye said.

Wreath was surprised at the creaky chuckle that escaped from Mrs. Durham's mouth. "I've had a couple of wrecks lately," she said.

"I haven't been on a bike in years," Faye said. "Must not be as easy as I recall."

"It's not so hard, but you need to watch where you're going."

"I do remember that." Faye took the cloth from her and gently wiped the scrapes and cuts again. "Let's put ointment on these. You won't be able to work if those cuts get infected."

Wreath felt like a little girl again. She wanted to take the supplies from the woman and take care of herself, but it felt good to have someone mother her. At the thought, she jerked back. "I can do that. I don't want to keep you from doing something important."

If the woman wasn't cranky most of the time, Wreath would have thought the words hurt her feelings. A puzzled look crossed Faye's face, and she pushed the kit toward Wreath. "Hurry up, then, and get to work."

"Thank you for helping me," Wreath said. "Do you have anything extra you want me to do today?"

"Extra?"

"Besides sweeping, dusting, and handling the trash." Wreath pointed to her pack. "I can do more."

"J. D.'s fixing the front door." Faye nodded her head in the direction where the older guy was down on his hands and knees, inspecting the bottom of the heavy door. "The glass will probably need cleaning after that."

"Will do." Wreath smiled. More work. Maybe she could gradually convince Mrs. Durham to give her even more, adding Saturdays after school started.

Hurriedly she applied the ointment, squinting to notice that the expiration date on the tube was five years earlier. She hoped the medicine wasn't worse than her injuries. As she packed up the kit and returned it to the storeroom, she watched Faye pacing around the store, as though she didn't quite know what to do, which struck Wreath as odd since she owned the place.

The woman straightened a cushion on a couch, adjusted the shade on a lamp, turned the lamp on and then off again. She studied the switch as though she'd never seen one before, tightened the bulb, and moved the shade again, tilting it and then putting it back in place.

Wreath took the small trash can out from under the desk and carried it to the back of the store, gathering her dusting supplies, which she had put together in a small cardboard box she had found in the trash. When she walked to the front of the store, the man was standing up, wiping his hands on a cloth.

"Good as new," he said. "At least until our next big rain." He put his tools in a small red metal box, wiping each one carefully before he put it inside. Wreath watched him intently from across the room. Most of the men she'd known were messy.

As she moved to straighten a chair, he saw her and met her eyes with a look of recognition. "You must be Faye's helper." He smiled. "I'm J. D., from the hardware store next door."

"I'm Wreath." The girl looked down at the bottom of the door. "What'd you do to fix that? We have a door that sticks at our house."

She hated to lie, but thought perhaps this man could teach her to handle a couple of problems at the Rusted Estates.

"It was swollen because of the wet weather we had back in the spring," he said. "I trimmed it off just about this much." He held up his thumb and index finger to indicate a tiny amount. "Works smooth as can be."

"Does that work on any stuck door?" When Wreath asked the question, J. D. tilted his head slightly, as though listening for something a long distance away.

"Depends," he said after a moment. "Sometimes an old building will shift, or a shoddy carpenter will put in the wrong size door. Then you have to do something more drastic."

Wreath suspected her home-repair projects fell into the more drastic mode.

"I could come by and take a look if your family's having a problem," the man said. "A group from my church down the street does projects for free."

"That's nice, but we're fine." Wreath turned back to her dusting as though it were the most vital job in the world. "I was just wondering. My mama can probably get it fixed, or my uncle can. We're staying with relatives."

"I thought you must be new in town. I hadn't seen you around until you started working at Durham's. Who are your people? Maybe I know them."

"Probably not," Wreath said. "They live sort of out of town a ways. Near. . .Wooddale. That's it. They live near Wooddale."

"I've been in these parts a long time, sold lawn mower blades and tomato plants and fire ant killer to just about everyone in the parish." The man didn't seem nosy, just interested.

Wreath squirmed. "My uncle works offshore. He's not around much. We're visiting for a while. I may stay for the school year, keep my aunt company. My mama hasn't decided yet if she wants us to move here."

"What's your mama's name?" J. D. asked.

"You don't know her," Wreath said in a rush and scampered to the back of the store, dusting with purpose, eager to get out of the conversation.

"Like I was telling Faye earlier, I've got time on my hands," J. D. called out. "If your parents need me to come out, I'd be happy to. No charge, of course."

"Thanks. I'll tell Mama you said that," Wreath said. "Nice to meet you. Thank you for fixing that door. It sure was getting hard to open."

As she turned away, Mrs. Durham walked up.

"Got her all fixed, Faye," J. D. said. "Anything else I can do for you?"

"Thank you very much, but that'll be all." Mrs. Durham spoke in a formal voice, like a character dismissing a servant in one of the old movies Frankie liked so much.

"Call on me anytime. You ladies have a good afternoon."

The store seemed gloomier when the smiling man left.

❀ Chapter 17 ❀

After the bicycle accident, Wreath missed Frankie so much her stomach felt queasy. . .or was it that old cream Mrs. Durham had put on her?

She went by the Dollar Barn with her precious new ten and was shocked at how much bandages and ointment cost, so she decided on a package of coffee instead. The price was exorbitant, though, and she knew she couldn't afford that either. Without a way to heat water, it was just silly, she decided, and walked out to her bike, her bones hurting.

Destiny waved from the cash register and tried to strike up a conversation, but Wreath pretended like she didn't see her and stepped out into the parking lot. Then she sat down on the curb near the corner of the store and cried.

She absolutely had to talk to someone, and the only person she could think of was the clerk. With the resolution of a general going into battle, she walked back into the store, no customers in sight. "Hey, Destiny," she said.

"Hey," the girl said, looking down at her phone.

"Sorry about not speaking a minute ago." Wreath forced the words out.

"I didn't notice," the girl said, still not looking up.

"I did something dumb today." Wreath pointed to her elbows. "I had a bike wreck." She held up her knee, looking like she was marching in a parade. "Banged myself up pretty bad."

"Did you put anything on it?' Destiny asked. "My mom always uses weird-smelling spray stuff."

Pain tugged at Wreath, not from the injuries but from the casual mention of Destiny's mother. "I got some old ointment at the store where I work."

"Durham's Furniture, right?"

Wreath nodded.

"Is it hard working for Miss Faye?" Destiny asked.

"You know her?"

"Everyone knows her. She and Mr. Billy were big leaders in Landry till he died all of a sudden." The cashier's voice lowered. "Miss Faye used to be a lot nicer. People around town say she's got money problems but is too proud to ask for help."

Wreath didn't say anything.

"Is she hard to work for?" Destiny repeated.

"Not really," Wreath said, uneasy. "Maybe a little. Sometimes she seems a little. . .sort of lost."

The other girl surprised Wreath with a nod, as though she knew what "sort of lost" meant. "That's what people are saying about you, too," Destiny said.

"About me?" Wreath was certain the dismay shone on her face. "Why would anyone be talking about me?"

"Because it's boring around here, and you're new. Some of the kids saw you at the library, and a teacher was asking about you."

"A teacher?"

"Julia Watson. She lives behind the furniture store. Law said she ran into you out at the state park."

"My life is my business," Wreath said, something she'd heard Frankie say on the phone one time.

"You don't have to get snotty about it," Destiny said. "Like I said, it's dullsville around here. People have to talk about something."

A customer with a full basket cleared his throat, and Wreath realized he was waiting to check out. "Well, I'd better go," she said.

"Here." Destiny reached under the counter and pulled out a package of chocolate cookies. "These are out of date. You can have them."

Wreath started to refuse but was drawn by the look of friendship on Destiny's face. "Thanks," she said. "They'll help me forget about my bike wreck."

By now the ride out of town was as familiar to her as her old neighborhood had been in Lucky. Today she varied her route, in case anyone was watching, and she thought about what Destiny had said.

People were talking about her, including that artist. She *was* a teacher.

Behind her she heard a car slowing down. She eased over to what passed for a shoulder, careful to avoid a pothole, but the car didn't pass. An uneasy feeling washed over her, and she tried to speed up, but the bike was hard to ride in the dirt and gravel. She wanted to turn around to see who it was, but she kept riding. Maybe it was the lawyer, Clarice.

"Hey, Wreath, wait up," a voice yelled, definitely not Clarice's, and her head whirled around.

Law, the ranger boy, had his head sticking out of the window of a sporty little car driven by the guy Mitch from the basketball court at the school.

"We've been looking for you," Law said.

Wreath's eyes got wide. They were following her? Did they know she lived in the junkyard? She kept pedaling, slowly.

"We wanted to make sure you were all right. I'm sorry about what happened at the school. We were horsing around and didn't see you. We didn't mean to hurt you."

"I'm okay," she mumbled and rode on.

Mitch honked the horn and yelled out his window. "Would you stop so we can talk to you?"

"Leave me alone," she said, trying to look dignified while teetering along the dirt and gravel, her arms and legs stinging.

"You headed to the park?" Law asked.

"The park?"

"You know. . .the state park. Where you hike. Where I work."

Wreath thought quickly. "Not that it's any of your business, but I am."

"You must really like hiking if you'll do it on a hot day like today, after that fall you took."

"I do, as a matter of fact," she said.

"Maybe I'll see you there," Law said. "I'm working nights for a while. Mitch is dropping me off."

"Maybe so," Wreath said and headed off while Mitch whipped onto the highway and the boys sped away.

Now, in a day filled with problems, she had a new one. If she didn't go to the park, Law might wonder where she was headed or Mitch might see her and figure out where she lived. If she did go to the park, she'd have to talk to Law.

The bike wheeled into the park, as though she weren't even steering it.

She was a goner. Just the thought of visiting with Law made her heart pound, her palms sweat, and her aches and pains seem less. . .well, achy and painful.

As soon as she entered the park, she saw Law, sitting on the bench in front of the office, eating a bag of chips. He smiled when the bike rolled up, and her heart rolled over.

"I thought you had to work," she said.

"Since I caught a ride with Mitch, I got here a little early. I usually catch a ride with someone who lives around us. It's not the most exact transportation."

"Neither is this, as you can see." She held up her skinned elbows.

"Have a seat." Law patted the bench. "I'll share the chips. Want a Coke or something?"

"I'd kill for one," Wreath said, climbing clumsily off the bike, favoring her sore legs.

"Since I nearly killed you earlier today, I guess we'd be even. Hold on a sec."

While Law dug around in his pocket for change, Wreath wiped the sweat from her brow and sneaked a look at how cute he was. He had on his park uniform, his hair shiny and his arms tanned.

"Diet or regular?" he asked. "I'm guessing regular. You don't look like a girl who needs to diet."

"You guessed right. I burn off a lot of calories going and coming to town." As soon as the words were out of her mouth, she knew she'd opened an area for questions she would rather avoid.

"I forgot where you said you lived—where are you going and coming from?" Law handed her the soft drink as he spoke, condensation dripping off the can onto her shirt.

"I live out past your trailer." She waved vaguely. "I stay with relatives. My mother will be coming about the time school starts."

"I heard you work at Durham's."

So much for keeping a low profile. Apparently everyone in town knew about her, but at least they hadn't figured out where she lived.

"I manage the furniture store."

"Really?" Law looked shocked.

"Of course not." She laughed. "I sweep the floors and empty the trash."

"You work for Miss Faye?"

"I do," Wreath said.

"Mitch is her nephew. He tried to help out a little after his uncle died, but she told him she didn't need any help. I'm surprised you got her to hire you. I've heard she's sort of. . .well. . .stingy with her money. And a little hard to get along with."

"She's fine." Wreath suddenly wanted to defend her boss. "It's not the most challenging job, as you probably can guess, but it's not so bad."

"Sort of like mine," he said.

"This looks like fun. I'd love to work at a park. It's peaceful out here."

"You haven't been here when the hillbilly sorts come in or the family reunions descend. It's a cross between a party you weren't invited to and a big family squabble. The office gets two dozen calls on those weekends."

"I've never been to a family reunion," Wreath said.

"You haven't missed much," Law said. "My aunt decided we should have a Jolly Rogers reunion a couple of years ago. Get it? Law Rogers." He grinned big. "Her boyfriend got drunk and fell into the bathtub, the potato salad made three kids and my great-aunt throw up, and my uncle and his buddy got in a fight over a game of dominoes and someone called the police."

"You're making that up."

"I wish I was. That was also the day my mother destroyed our car. She ran into a guardrail on the highway and got her license suspended."

Wreath knew well the look on Law's face. He thought he'd said too much, and she decided to bail him out. "Must be nice to have a fancy car like Mitch has."

"Yeah, he's got it pretty good," Law said. "Are you saving for a car?"

"I don't know how to drive." Wreath laughed, not even self-conscious.

"For real?"

"For real. It'll be two wheels for me for a while. I don't want a car." Truth was, Frankie had seldom owned a car, and Wreath had never thought much about it. She decided she'd add that to her dream list when she got back to her campsite.

"I want a car bad," Law said. "Or a pickup. Something fast."

"I thought you were saving for a guitar."

"I can't believe you remembered that." Law grinned. "I should have enough money at the end of the summer to get a used guitar, but my granddad says he'll buy me a car if I get into college next fall."

"Sweet," Wreath said.

"Well, half sweet. I don't know if my mother will let him."

"Why wouldn't your mother let someone buy you a car?" Wreath couldn't imagine Frankie turning down a car under any circumstances.

"My mother and my grandparents have what people around here call 'bad blood' between them. Most people don't approve of my mother's choices. At least that's how Grandpa puts it." Law smashed a chip between his fingers and watched it fall to the ground. "I probably shouldn't be talking to you about this."

"Why not?" Wreath asked.

He shrugged. "My family's kind of weird."

Wreath could only imagine what Law would say if he knew how weird her life was. "Oh," she said, feeling a real smile on her lips. "Tell me about them."

"My mother says my grandpa's a meddling old jerk."

"Is he?"

"They're probably both right in their own way. My mother acts pretty strange sometimes. What about your mom? What's she like?"

"She's great," Wreath said, thinking of how funny and affectionate Frankie had been. "But she's real private. Kind of shy."

"Like mother, like daughter," Law said. "I thought you were kind of stuck up at first, but I think you're kind of shy, too."

"I guess I am," Wreath said, scuffing her feet against the pavement.

"I never thought about it one way or the other."

Law looked at his watch. "It's time for my shift. Do you want a day pass?"

Wreath shook her head. "I'll head home and make sure my legs don't fall off." She gingerly touched the bandage.

Law grimaced. "Sorry," he said.

"That's all right," she said. "Your story about your family get-together was worth the pain of the wreck. I think I'll suggest we have one in my family."

Law laughed as she rode off, and she hoped he'd forgive her for the lies if he ever found out the truth.

❁ Chapter 18 ❁

Wreath knew she was telling too many lies to too many people. She lived with a made-up family called Williams. Her mama would move in soon.

When she'd made her plan, she knew she'd have to be sneaky. But she hadn't planned on lying every day. The untruths to Law had hurt doubly bad. They'd made her miss her mother, and she'd felt like she was betraying a friend.

She hated it.

Dear Brownie, she wrote, *I messed up. I didn't think about all the people I would have to talk to in my ordinary life. I didn't plan on making friends this year, and now I like a boy named Law. Yes! Me! In less than a summer, I have a crush on a boy. I am Wreath Willis. You know I don't get crushes on boys. You know how boyfriends made Frankie's life harder— and, therefore, my own. But Law seems different. He listens when I talk, and he's good-looking.*

She scratched the last few sentences out and started over, writing, *What am I going to do when school starts?*

SCHOOL YEAR PLANS:

1. Study.

2. Try to keep job at furniture store.

3. Steer clear of organizations and events.

4. Survive.

She had to do well at school, earn enough money to live on, and make the junkyard into a place she could live even when it got cold.

For what seemed like the millionth time, she poked around the vehicles, searching for anything she might use, looking for fire ant hills and watching for snakes and trespassers. In today's search, Wreath found an old Landry High School yearbook and thumbed through it, wondering what had happened to the students who looked so cheerful and. . .well, active.

She sat down on a set of falling-down steps, avoiding a huge splinter, and flipped through the heavy book again, its purple cover padded with an insignia that had *LHS* in gold. Chuckling at the photos of club activities, she realized the clothes in the pictures resembled the ones she was wearing, apparently quite stylish at the time.

Flipping to the back, she drew in her breath. A full-page advertisement congratulated Clarice Janice Estes. Clarice wore a Landry High cheerleader outfit, including a short skirt, and was holding pom-poms. "Future Supreme Court judge?" the headline read. "We are proud of you, Clarice! Love, Mother and Father." Wreath could hardly believe how young and cute the woman was. Nor could she believe how big and alive the school seemed in the yearbook.

Putting the book on the shelf she had made on the dashboard of the Tiger Van, she loaded up her pack and got dressed, hoping she didn't smell after using another of her precious wet-paper wipes to take a bath. She wondered if Mrs. Durham would approve of shorts yet again today.

She scanned the area and went to the clump of bushes where she had hidden the bike the evening before. She was torn over whether to put things in the same spot or to move them around, still not sure if people were snooping around when she was gone.

She hiked around the edges of the field, reassuring herself that no one lived nearby and looking nervously over her shoulder. Thankfully, there was no sign of activity near where she stayed, and she vowed to use her flashlight only inside the van, when she could hide it under her blanket. *Don't lose focus*, she'd written in her small notebook. *Watch for people*.

After arranging her belongings, hiding her money in different places, and setting a trap or two, she hopped on her bike, not sure if her shakiness was from nerves or her accident.

The yearbook prompted her to do what she could put off no longer.

With a sense of determination and a tinge of excitement, Wreath rode right up to Landry High and circled it twice, sizing up the place where she would get her diploma. The old brick building was two stories tall with a sprawling campus. At first glance it seemed almost stately, but a closer look showed peeling paint around the windows, blinds hanging crooked and bent, the flower beds a withered mess. To the side were four tennis courts and a large building that must be the gym. Parking lots had sprouted around the building, probably added through the years. In the very back were six or eight metal structures, the kind called T buildings at her other schools. The parking lot was mostly empty, and the door to the gym was propped open.

Wreath leaned her bike against a back wall, hidden from sight, and tried a side door, which squeaked loudly as she pulled it open. She breathed in the smell of books and paper and the musty odor left behind from students. A janitor waxed a green linoleum hall in the distance, and Wreath turned the other way, dismayed to see that most classrooms were closed up, visible only through a small window on each door. The air was hot and stale.

She tugged at one door after another, eager to see what the school looked like, which classrooms might be hers, but hesitant to cross the threshold into the official world of the office.

"Young lady, what do you think you're doing?" a deep voice bellowed. Wreath turned guiltily from where she had been staring into a science lab. A middle-aged man and a woman walked toward her.

A glimmer of surprise raced across the young woman's face at the same time that Wreath recognized her, looking totally different than she did in her running clothes.

Julia, in jeans and a sleeveless black shirt, turned to the man. "This is one of our new students, Mr. Bordelon. I told her to meet me here later, and I'd show her around." She looked at Wreath and winked. "You must not have been paying attention when I told you I was busy until late afternoon. Mr. Bordelon's our principal at Landry High."

"Nice to meet you, sir," Wreath said, her bewilderment not totally feigned. "I'm sorry I got the time mixed up."

She stood back as the two adults wrapped up a conversation about a training session. "Be on time tomorrow, Miss Watson," the man said, and Wreath turned away, shocked to hear a teacher reprimanded in her presence.

"I'll be here," Julia said and turned to Wreath. "Now I'll give our new student the deluxe tour."

❀

"Thanks for rescuing me," Wreath said as the principal walked away.

"Most interesting thing that's happened to me all day, and that says a lot about the state of my life," Julia muttered. "I've had enough teacher training courses to last a lifetime. But enough about me."

No matter how dissatisfied she was, she knew she should not discuss teacher business with a student. "I do have to wonder why an out-of-town girl is roaming the halls of dear old Landry High in the middle of summer." Her voice turned up at the end, turning the statement into a question.

"Out-of-town girl?" Wreath said. "Oh, you mean when we ran into each other at the park when I was hiking. My mama decided I should finish school here. I'm going to live in Landry, go to high school. I came in to register."

"I see," Julia murmured. "I can help you with that. I'm Julia Watson, by the way. You're Wreath." She looked at the girl from top to bottom, memorizing every detail. She was thin but not unhealthy looking and wore a white eyelet blouse and torn shorts.

The girl nodded. "Wreath Williams. Thanks again for bailing me out."

Julia studied the girl, wondering what trouble she was up to. When she had seen her at the state park, she had been fairly certain she was a camper, taking a shower. Seeing her pedaling toward town had given her a new persona, like a determined woman trying to save herself. Now she was peering in classroom windows as though in search of something dear. "So what grade will you be in?"

"I'm starting my senior year. My mother will be coming later, but she told me to pick up the paperwork."

"Most kids don't move their senior year," Julia said. She doubted Wreath would open up, but it wouldn't hurt to try.

"Bummer, isn't it? We lived in Arkansas for years, but my mother wants to be near family. She knows she'll be lonely when I go away to college."

"College? Good for you," Julia said. "Lots of students here don't get the chance to go to college. I'm happy to hear students talk about their future."

"It's the most important thing to me," Wreath said. "I want to get a scholarship." She couldn't believe she had just said that. "I need to get signed up first. But I *will* go to college."

Julia raised her eyebrows. She hoped the girl was not setting herself up for a disappointment. Landry High did not have the best reputation for sending students off to college.

"You'll need a parent's signature to sign up," she said. "Let me show you around. You interested in art?"

The teacher led Wreath down two halls, filled with closed-up classrooms and lined with lockers. They walked briskly down a flight of steps and moved around a corner, past the room where Julia taught what had to be the most boring social studies class ever. Her feet never slowed.

"Shortcut," she said, her energy increasing as she headed toward the airy lab, which she thought of as her personal studio during the summer months. "This is the art wing."

Wreath stepped with her through the wide door, and Julia glided across the room. She stopped to eye a painting propped by the wall and moved to the back of the room to inspect a kiln.

"So you teach art?" Wreath asked.

Julia was so relieved to be out of the continuing ed class and back in the art room that she inhaled the smell of the room before she answered. "Art? No. I'm social studies. Mostly ninth and tenth graders, one group of seniors, so you may or may not be in my class."

"This is a social studies classroom?" Wreath frowned.

Julia wandered through the room, spreading out large paper canvases and straightening a painting or two hanging next to a large whiteboard. She knew she should not have told Wreath how much she hated the continuing education class and should give her a quick tour of the school and direct her to the office. Then Julia should get herself right back to the training session.

But she couldn't bring herself to. She didn't know if it was the loneliness she saw in the girl's eyes or the boredom she felt in her own heart.

"This is the art studio," Julia said. "It's my favorite spot in the school. My class is in the front wing, near where you were earlier. Not much to it."

"So you *are* an artist," Wreath said, moving over to the easel.

"An artist wannabe, I guess you might say," Julia said, picking up the brush, dipping it in the water again and rubbing it against the thick paint. "I'm experimenting here with a technique I read about. You put the bright paint on heavy and then brush it with water. It gives it a modern look, don't you think?"

"Sort of," Wreath said. "Is this called abstract art?"

"Abstract. Modern. Wild. Goes by lots of names," Julia said with a small laugh. "With this medium you can try so many different things. I'm impressed that you recognized it. Where did you learn that?"

The girl froze. "In middle school, I guess."

"Did you go to middle school and the first years of high school in Arkansas?" Julia asked, trying for a casual tone.

"We moved around a lot," Wreath said, looking like a wild colt about to bolt.

"I see," Julia said, wishing she did.

"I'd better get going," Wreath said but stretched her neck to see a rack of pottery mugs.

"Look over here first," Julia said. "I also use the kiln. I'm firing several pieces right now." A motley collection of pottery pieces lined a shelf at the back of the room; there was a plastic tarp draped over a piece of equipment and the smell of mud in the air. Julia uncovered a block of clay and pinched a small piece from it, rolling it in her fingers and holding it up to Wreath's nose.

"I love the way clay smells," Wreath said. "Like you could make just about anything from it." She took a whiff and pinched a small piece off the block to roll in her fingers. "Which works are yours?" she asked, wandering around the room.

Julia pointed here and there, showing off a huge canvas that depicted a scene in the country, but was painted with an abstract twist, and two small pencil sketches. Lined up on one side of the room was a display of nearly a dozen bold paintings, the hint of a story in each one of them.

Wreath studied the works, and Julia tried to see them through her eyes, the bright colors, the definite strokes, the quirky perspective.

"Why do you do all this if you're not an art teacher?" Wreath asked. "Do you sell your work somewhere?"

"I wish," Julia said with a snort. "I do this because I love art, everything about art. I come in and play here during the summer, when the regular teacher isn't around."

"I bet you'd make a great art teacher," Wreath said.

"I planned to be one, but there wasn't an opening. Maybe one of these days." She looked at the clock in the back of the classroom. "I guess we'd better get out of here."

"I need to head home," Wreath said. "Mama will be looking for me."

"Pick up your registration papers, and get her to fill them out and bring them in right away," Julia said. "The counselor can get your course schedule lined up, but you're cutting it a little close. You'll want to make sure the transcript from your last school gets moved over."

"I have a copy," Wreath said. "My mother requested it before we moved."

"I can guarantee you the office will want an official copy," Julia said. "You might want to have your mom follow up on that."

Wreath's shoulders slumped for a moment, and then she rushed toward the door. Julia walked outside the room and pointed her toward the office.

As she sat in the final training session of the day, she watched Wreath climb on a dilapidated bike and head off, backpack slung over her shoulder.

Julia wondered how the girl had gotten her to do much of the talking. Wreath now knew more about her than lots of people did. . .and Julia realized she knew very little about the girl.

She did know Wreath needed help. Most students did.

Wreath twisted the stack of registration papers in her hands and then tried to smooth them out. Seeing the forms in black and white freaked her out. She was about to commit fraud, forging her permanent record at school. Frankie wasn't coming back, and Wreath couldn't postpone making the lies official.

She used the copy machine at the library to change her transcript, panicking when she thought the nice man at the counter saw her. Using used correction fluid from the Dollar Barn, she whited out the name *Willis* and a couple of the dates and made copies, then filled in the blanks with the name *Williams* and recent dates.

She got on her bike, adjusted her pack in the basket, and headed back to the school.

Perspiring more than usual, she brushed her hair before she went back into the office. Then she straightened her blouse and practiced a smile.

"Do you need something?" a woman asked, coming out of the office.

Wreath forced herself to look her in the eye and held up the paperwork. "I'm registering. My mother asked me to drop these papers off."

"I'll pass those along to the guidance counselor," the woman said, glancing over the materials. "It looks like everything's in order. Report to the office on the first day of school for your schedule."

❀ Chapter 19 ❀

Faye put her feet into her Dearfoam slippers and headed for the kitchen.

With pleasure, she made a cup of hot tea, rescued from the years of bitter coffee Billy had preferred and, thus, expected. Real sugar and half-and-half cream helped start her daily what-if thinking, the closest Faye came to dreaming.

The thoughts used to come almost every day, Tuesday through Saturday: How could she get out of opening the store today? On Sundays that transferred to how to get out of going to church without her absence being noted. And on Mondays she fretted over chores and bills and the dullness of her life.

But now she found herself almost looking forward to going into the store. The girl who was helping her had brought about a change, not only in the shop but in how Faye felt about it. Wreath had come up with quick ways to get the store in order, and she didn't chatter like most teens but kept to herself.

Each day in the tacky store, she watched the somber girl straighten furniture, scrub long-neglected floors, and sort through stacks of junk, and somehow seeing things through Wreath's eyes made the house seem even sillier.

Steadily Faye made her way through her morning ritual in the outdated ranch house, once so fancy with its white carpet and French provincial furniture. She could scarcely stand it anymore, a symbol of the good life she had taken for granted. To pretend otherwise, she pampered the house, tidied it, and acted as though it was still grand, leaving only her sewing room untouched. She wanted others to think her world was as good as it was supposed to be, to overlook the middle-aged woman with the worn-out life. Faye still made a show of driving her aging Oldsmobile through the old subdivision with the big, well-manicured yards. Up until recently, she parked the car directly out front of Durham's Fine Furnishings—her signal that Mrs. Faye Durham was open for business and not going to let the customer have the best parking place. Since Wreath had worked to make the entrance look better, Faye moved her parking place down to the end of the row, grumbling about the bicycle chained to the post but secretly pleased at the tidier appearance of her store. She had smiled when Wreath lettered signs that said PARKING FOR OUR VALUABLE CUSTOMERS and gotten J. D. to help her tack them along the posts on the front of the store.

Today, Faye turned the old key in the stubborn lock in the big glass front door of the store, but the door opened easily, thanks to the hardware store owner's help. She walked in, greeted not by the musty smell she had grown to hate, but by the scent of furniture polish. Wreath bought the product by the dozens at the Dollar Barn, it seemed to Faye, and this morning the fragrance was worth every cent.

Flipping on the store's charming, outdated lights, she refused to turn the OPEN sign around, clinging to a few moments of privacy.

The bell jangled as someone tugged at the front door.

"You forgot to turn your sign around again," Nadine Nelson said, flipping the piece of cardboard over, a chore that made Faye's stomach dip each morning but had gotten easier in the afternoons.

"I must have been distracted by the phone," Faye said.

"J. D. told us you'd hired a helper," Nadine said. "That's great news."

Faye fidgeted with two faded throw pillows on an upholstered chair, not sure anymore what to say to the woman who had been her best friend before Billy died.

"Whose girl is she?" Nadine continued.

"You wouldn't know her. She's new to town."

"Well, Jim and I are so glad to hear you have someone." Nadine sat down on the nicest new sofa in the room. "This store is a lot of work for one person."

"Billy had things organized," Faye said, not willing to confess how hard times were. "The girl, Wreath's her name, does cleanup work, that sort of thing."

"Since you have help now, are you sewing again?"

Faye shook her head.

Nadine sighed. "I need a shower gift for my great-niece, and I was hoping you'd make her one of those sweet jumpers."

"I'm sorry. . . ." Faye let her voice trail off, not sure what she was sorry for.

"Any chance you can join us for bridge one day? We never filled your spot, and we need another player. You haven't been in ages."

"Oh, I don't know if she's ready to keep the store by herself," Faye said. "She's only a teenager."

Nadine stood and headed to the door. "We missed you at Bible study Sunday."

"Business keeps me tied up, but I'll make it when I can."

"Nobody else in the class makes coffee as good as you do," Nadine said. "It's not the same without you." She wiped away a tear. "I miss you, Faye."

"And I don't even drink coffee." Faye tried to sound jolly. "I only learned how to make it for Billy."

"We miss Billy, too. I wish you'd let us help. Anything. We'd do anything."

"You can't bring Billy back." Faye hated the tone of her voice. "Things aren't the way they were."

Nadine gave a sigh. "We have such sweet memories, though, and the promise of a peace we can't even understand." She acted as though she would try to hug her old friend and pulled up short. "That's all Jim and I know to count on when we have troubles. I pray that will help you, too."

"I'll do my best to make it to church Sunday," Faye said. "Wreath is a big help, so maybe that'll free up my time." She forced herself to give Nadine a half hug, waving as her friend walked out and chatted with J. D., who, as usual, was standing out front, book in hand.

Faye didn't turn the OPEN sign around until Nadine drove off in her fancy new SUV.

Peace? She sat down at the rolltop desk. Nadine still had Jim, even if her daughter had made a mess of her life and her son-in-law was in jail. She had money and someone to fix the faucet when it leaked and wasn't saddled with a business that was going deeper in debt by the day.

The stack of bills to be paid grew with each visit from the mailman. Only a couple of customers had been in for the entire week, and they hadn't bought anything. She paid the girl a paltry fifty dollars a week, which she knew wasn't a fair wage, and stuck a little cash back for Wreath because she didn't trust her to manage the money. She ought to be doing the chores herself, but even Billy had had a handyman off and on through the years.

Billy's banker had called to set up a meeting, which could not be good news. Something had to change. First thing she needed to do was let Wreath go. She would miss the girl, who made the place bearable. After getting rid of her, she needed to see about selling the store, although she had no idea who would want to buy a retail dinosaur, nor how to go about it. Maybe the banker would know.

She put her head down on the desk. She hadn't cried once since Billy dropped dead, but today might be the day. She had tried to dwell on the bad parts of life and shut out the happy memories Nadine mentioned because they hurt too much to think about. What right did her friend have reminding her of the life she used to lead?

That part of her died with Billy.

The bell jangled on the door, and she jerked her head up and rolled the chair back so fast that she nearly hit a cherry sofa table that already had two nicks in it and a cracked leg.

"Are you okay?" Wreath asked.

Faye looked at the clock, which had started making a humming sound to accompany its loud ticking. For a moment she wondered if she had passed out. The clock said ten. She was confused about everything.

Wreath followed her gaze and gave a rare laugh. "Oh, it's not time for my shift yet," she said. "I needed to talk to you about something."

The teen held her head down slightly, not quite making eye contact, shuffling her shoe back and forth on the wood floor. "I wondered if you might have more work for me."

"More work?" Faye asked.

"I hoped you could add duties to my list and give me a few more hours. I know I haven't been here long, but I think I've shown I'm a hard worker."

"You are a hard worker, Wreath," Faye said. "But I'm going to have to let you go."

Wreath gasped, and she clutched her ever-present pack to her chest. "No!" she exclaimed. "You can't!"

"I can, and I will. I don't need your help here anymore."

"But I thought I was doing a good job," Wreath said. "I know you don't like me that much, but I have made the store look better."

"Not like you?" It was the store owner's turn to be shocked. "If I had been able to have a child, I'd have wanted a daughter just like you. . . ."

As the words hung in the air, she laid her hand upon her chest, stricken. Faye had never, ever talked to anyone, not even Nadine, about not being able to have children. What was it about this girl that opened her heart?

She cleared her throat and tried to sound stern, mean even. "I'm used to being here by myself, and it works out like that."

"Please give me another chance, Mrs. Durham. I'll do anything. I need this job real bad." Tears rolled down Wreath's cheeks.

"Child, you're sixteen years old. You can't possibly need this pitiful job that bad. Ask your parents for what you need."

Wreath started toward the door. "Thank you for giving me a chance and for helping me buy the bike," she said. "I liked working for you."

The bells on the door jangled on Faye's nerves, and then the store was quiet, except for the clock. Only five minutes had passed, but she felt like she had been through the past year all over again. She walked into the workroom, propped her forehead against the cabinet door, and sobbed.

Then she opened the cabinet and took out the collection of advertising mugs from one vendor after another, for chairs and tables, fabric and office supplies. One by one she threw them against the wall.

"For Billy," she said, crying, as the first one smashed.

"And this stupid store."

"And my friends who don't understand."

"And that stack of bills."

The loud noise of the mugs satisfied her after a year of tiptoeing around, but a whimper crept into the crescendo, and she whirled around. Wreath stood at the door, the traces of tears still on her cheeks.

"What do you want?" Faye asked.

The girl nodded, keeping her distance. "I want my job back," Wreath said. "No matter what it takes. I'll do better. I like working here."

Faye reached into the cabinet, pulled out another mug, and Wreath ducked, but the woman walked over and handed the cup to her. "I can't afford to hire you back. Break something. You'll be amazed at how much better you'll feel."

Wreath threw the mug, which busted into three or four pieces, scarring the already tacky wall. "May I have another one?" she asked, and Faye started laughing.

"Have all you want. There's nearly a hundred years of useless history in that cabinet."

Faye heard a hint of hysteria in her own laugh, and Wreath stepped toward the cabinet.

"A hundred years? You've owned this store that long?"

"Of course not," she said. "How old do you think I am? But my husband's grandfather started it, and his daddy built it up. Seems like me and Billy are the ones who managed to ruin it."

Faye sat down at the table, and Wreath dug through the back of the cabinet, pulling out old cups, mugs, toothpick holders, ashtrays, and commemorative plates. She lined the items up on the counter, eyeing Faye.

"I shouldn't have acted like this in front of you," Faye said. "You'd better go."

"Don't make me go. Please don't make me go. I'll do anything you want me to do—break cups, glue cups back together, even try to sell cups. Please don't make me go."

The path where the tears had fallen was wet again, and Wreath was clearly distraught as she wiped them away.

"Sit down, Wreath." The woman pulled out a chair at the small worktable. She wet a cloth with cool water and wiped the girl's face.

Wreath gave a laugh. "You seem to be doing this a lot."

Faye looked surprised. "I do, don't I? It's kind of nice for a change. It's been too long since I've had someone to take care of."

"So you won't make me go?"

"I'm afraid I have to. As you've probably figured out, this store is in deep trouble. I don't have enough money to pay the light bill, much less to pay a girl to help dust."

"I'll work for less."

"I can't do that," Faye said. "It wouldn't be right. And your parents wouldn't go for it."

Wreath looked at her straight in the eye. "I don't have any parents. My dad ran off when I was born. My mama lives up near Lucky. I don't think she'll be coming down here. That's just a story I made up."

"But you stay in touch with her. You're always talking about her, and she loves you."

"I have to support myself." The girl swallowed as she spoke.

"That isn't right either," Faye said. "I can help you get aid. There are agencies—"

"No, no, no. . . ." Wreath nearly turned the table over as she jumped up. "No agencies. I'll look for work somewhere else."

"Wait, honey. Calm down. We'll figure something out."

"I have ideas on how to bring customers in," Wreath said. "I read magazines. You have a lot of good retro stuff."

"That junk? I'll be lucky to find someone willing to haul it off for free."

"Can't we at least try? If it doesn't work, you don't have to pay me."

The older woman walked over and got the broom and began to sweep up the mess she had made. Wreath immediately stood and tried to take the broom. For a moment, they played tug-of-war, and then Faye gave in.

"We'll give it a try. I'll give you a month to see what we can do."

"Thank you, Mrs. Durham. You won't be sorry."

"I know I won't be. And I don't intend to ask you this again. Will you please call me Faye?"

❧ Chapter 20 ❧

Starting school had always been hard.

Moving around a lot didn't allow her to get too close to people, and she never had many friends. The idea of her first day at Landry High terrified her more than the dark nights in the Tiger Van or the snake she had seen more than once around the campsite.

Now it was the night before the first day of school.

Trying to calm her nerves, she pulled out the old Bible and flipped over to the words in red. The letters were barely legible with her weak flashlight, but she read a few verses and thought of the old neighbor in Lucky who had taken her to church and always told her she was praying for her.

Wreath didn't quite know how to pray and had been meaning to ask Faye whether she prayed or not. If ever there was a time to try praying, tonight seemed like the night.

She pulled out her notebook and wrote. *Dear God, I don't know if You know me. Maybe You know that my name is Wreath Willis, except some people think it's Wreath Williams. I start my last year of high school tomorrow. I'm not sure how this prayer stuff works, but I need help real bad. Lots of people have offered to help me, but I don't know whom to trust. Will You help me? Sincerely, Wreath Wisteria Willis.* She wrote her name in cursive, with a flourish, figuring God might appreciate the extra effort.

Setting the alarm on the windup clock she had found, she squirmed and brushed off bugs she thought were crawling on her in the thick carpet.

She woke up well before the puny bell rang on the old clock, awake every hour during the night, holding the clock close to her face, using her flashlight to see what time it was. Finally at 5:30 a.m., while it was still dark outside, she allowed herself to get up, eat a cereal bar, and grab the supplies she had assembled the evening before.

Propping the flashlight, which flickered a few times, on the seat next to her, she pulled out her journal and started a new list, writing so hard that the lead in the pencil broke.

FIRST DAY OF SCHOOL:
State park for a shower.
Arrive early on campus. Stop by office.
Buy school supplies after work.

The list looked so efficient and easy, but Wreath knew there were big hurdles ahead, including the forged registration papers. They were full of holes, but she'd move ahead.

Not knowing what the kids wore to class in Landry or the school dress code, Wreath chose a skirt and a peasant blouse she had found in one of the campers.

She wrestled her bike out of its hiding place and set out for the park, determined she wouldn't be a weird-looking homeless kid on her first day of school. Riding in the early-morning darkness was different from her usual treks, and she swerved into a pothole a time or two.

When she made her usual turn into the state park, she nearly ran into a gate, closed across the drive, a padlock on it. The park entrance was locked! *How did I overlook this?*

Getting off the bike, she propped it against the gate and walked from side to side, trying to see if she could scoot around the fence. In the two or three places where there were gaps in the fence, chicken wire had been tacked, preventing entry. An armadillo scooted out of the ditch right behind her and, looking like a little dinosaur, nearly ran right into her leg. She yelped and jumped and the confused creature headed back down into the ditch.

"That's it," Wreath said out loud. "That is just it." She yanked her bike upright and started home, riding as hard as she could. She'd been insane to think she could go to school and live in a junkyard.

She packed and unpacked her belongings at least four times, laid down on her mangy blanket and cried, and ran a path around the worn-out vehicles until she had a stitch in her side. Then she lay back down on the blanket and cried again.

So much for prayer.

So much for graduating from high school.

So much for Frankie, for that matter. She still didn't understand why her mother had to leave her.

"I didn't realize it was so late," Faye said when Wreath entered the store. "School out already?"

The girl shrugged.

"Everything all right?" Faye rolled her chair back from the desk, looking at the clock over Wreath's head.

"Fine." Wreath headed for the back room. "I need to sweep."

Faye made a small clucking noise, the kind she used to make when Billy tracked mud onto her clean carpet, and couldn't resist following Wreath to the rear of the store.

"You told me you'd be getting to work about three o'clock once school started," Faye said.

The teen concentrated on the broom and dustpan as though she were hypnotized. "Well?" Faye said.

"Well, what?" Wreath's voice was much louder than usual.

"It's not three o'clock."

The girl slammed the broom against the wall so hard it bounced back and hit her in the face, and she stormed out of the room. As she brushed past Faye, the woman was startled at her urge to grab Wreath and pull the girl to her in a hug. Instead, she spoke in her most matter-of-fact furniture-store owner voice. "Where do you think you're going, young lady?"

"I'll be back at three o'clock, since that's *apparently* when my shift starts." Wreath spoke without looking back, striding toward the front door.

"Since you're here, you might as well stay. You can work on that new display you've been all fired up about."

Wreath stopped but still did not turn. "Really?"

"Really." Faye's emotions were a strange mix, like the sweet-and-sour soup Billy used to get at the Chinese buffet in Alexandria. She wanted to smile at Wreath's interest in the displays, but she couldn't get rid of the worry about whatever problem had brought Wreath in early. When the teen turned, Faye felt a moment of triumph and a happiness long missing from her life.

"You're willing to let me do that sixties room?" Wreath asked. "The one in the catalog?"

This time it was Faye who shrugged. "What's to lose? I'm going further in the hole every day, so something's got to give."

"We've got all the pieces we need to put it together." The girl's voice held a rare note of excitement. "I can use that chair there, and the shag rug over here, and that lamp." She stopped. "But first I need to sweep and dust." She seemed to be thinking out loud. "And the trash needs emptying."

"Get started on the display," Faye said. "I'll sweep for a change. I need the exercise." She patted her stomach. "I don't want to get fat sitting behind this desk."

"You always look nice." Wreath studied the woman as though she'd never seen her before.

"So do you," Faye said. "You've got that look I see in all the magazines." She paused. "What do you call it? Antique? No, that's not it. Vintage! That's it. You have that vintage look."

Wreath looked down at herself and seemed surprised by Faye's description. "Really?"

"That outfit is exactly like one I saw in an article about how retro looks are coming back." She shook her head. "Hard to believe that look is in style."

Wreath wore the oddest assortment of clothing Faye had ever seen, usually clean, often worn, and occasionally ill-fitting. Somehow the teenager gave it panache. "You have great style," Faye said, walking up and straightening Wreath's skirt. "This geometric pattern looks nice."

Then she patted the girl's shoulder. "It looks cute on you, a nice outfit for the first day of school."

Wreath met Faye's questioning gaze and then dropped her eyes. "I didn't go," she said. "I, uh, overslept and, uh, didn't think it'd be that big a deal to miss the first day."

Faye feared she was getting too attached and wanted to walk away, but the defeat in Wreath's eyes kept her standing there. For a fleeting moment she wished she were home in the den, watching her soap opera, trying to decide what to fix Billy for supper.

"I'm surprised you skipped school. That doesn't sound like you," she said. "You're usually so prompt."

Wreath nodded.

"Tomorrow's a new day," Faye said.

"You think so?" Wreath asked, as though the cliché were a piece of deep philosophy.

The woman thought about it for a moment, looked around the store, and nodded. "I really do."

Wreath heaved a heavy red vinyl chair into the front corner and surveyed the showroom for suitable lighting. She remembered a floor lamp she'd seen at the Rusted Estates and wondered if it would be stealing if she brought it to Durham's. The look would be perfect.

She figured that wouldn't be right, though, taking things away from the junkyard. All that stuff must belong to someone, and she hoped they didn't decide they wanted it back during the next year.

Getting down on her hands and knees, she straightened the pale shag rug that had been rolled up in a corner and adjusted a white-and-gold end table that had been grouped with an ugly gold couch. The bell on the front door jangled as she sat back to consider what was missing in her arrangement.

"May I help you?" Mrs. Durham asked in the frosty voice she used for most people who were brave enough to walk through the doors of Durham's Fine Furnishings. Wreath didn't understand how someone who disliked customers could be running a store.

"Yes, ma'am," a confident male voice said. "I'm looking for a girl named Wreath Williams."

Wreath shrank lower and tried to look around the edge of the chair. All she could see was a pair of tennis shoes and jeans.

"Wreath," Faye called out. "Someone's here to see you." She said the last words as though a car had crashed through the front window.

While trying to decide whether to stand up or not, Wreath heard the voice again. "Wreath, is that you?"

She looked up to see Law Rogers headed her way. Her heart flipped, and she slid an inch or so closer to the floor.

"Wreath?"

Wiping her sweaty palms against her skirt, she gave up and stood.

"I'm over here," she said, knowing that sounded stupid, since he was already walking toward her.

"Wow, this looks great." Law surveyed the display Wreath had just put together. "I didn't know this store had cool stuff like this." Then his face flushed, and he turned to Faye, who had scurried over to where the pair stood, clearly curious. "Sorry, Mrs. Durham. I didn't mean that like it sounded."

"No offense taken," she said. "I didn't know you two were friends. Seems like your grandmother would have mentioned it, Law."

"Oh, we're not friends," Wreath said hastily, trying to straighten her skirt and look unconcerned at the same time, noticing Law's slight frown at her declaration. "He works at the state park where I hike some days."

"We were trading summer job stories, and she told me she worked here," Law said. "I thought we were sort of friends, though." He looked puzzled.

"How are your grandparents?" Faye asked.

"Good," the boy said. "My grandmother's playing bridge and teaching that class at church, and grandpa's still at the library. He's always got a new book he thinks I should read."

"I haven't had time to read any books lately," Faye said. "Wreath's got me studying up on design magazines."

The woman almost looked as flustered as Wreath felt. Law, on the other hand, looked downright dignified, chatting with Mrs. Durham as though he were a politician, not a teenage boy.

"The place looks better." He stumbled over the last word. "I like the improvements you've made."

"Wreath gets all the credit for the changes." Faye twisted her mouth. "It's about time, don't you think? Between your grandparents and J. D. at the hardware store, I had to do something or leave town."

Wreath thought Faye's smile made her look years younger as she continued. "This girl has quite an eye for decorating." The compliment hardly registered with Wreath, who watched the casual exchange between the two, feeling both possessive and protective of Mrs. Durham. The place had been a mess all right, but Faye had lost her husband only a few months before.

She never saw the woman anywhere except the store and couldn't imagine her visiting with people in town, but she must have had an outside life at one time. Wreath coughed, and Law and Faye looked over at her.

"Did you want something?" Wreath asked the boy.

"Oh," Law said. "I need to talk to you."

He cast a charming look at Faye and then back at Wreath, and the woman walked away slowly. "Do you get a break or anything?" he asked.

Wreath pondered the question, trying not to let on how shaken she was by his presence. "Not usually," she said. "But Mrs. Durham is pretty nice, so she might let me have a few minutes. Is something wrong?"

Law looked over his shoulder and lowered his voice. "You weren't at school today."

"I couldn't make it."

"Couldn't make it? Who can't make it on the first day of her senior year?"

"I overslept, okay? My alarm clock didn't go off." She wondered if that was considered another lie, since she had turned the clock off.

"Maybe you should get a new clock," he said and punched her playfully on the arm. "They called your name on the roll in at least half my classes."

"They did?" Wreath's heart raced. That must mean her enrollment had been approved. But by being absent, she had violated one of her rules. She had drawn attention to herself.

"Miss Watson asked the whole class if anyone knew you."

"Miss Watson?"

"The jogger you met at the park, remember?"

Wreath felt a jolt of excitement. "I got into her class? I was afraid it would be full. She said she only teaches one senior social studies."

"Are you friends with Miss Watson or something?" He looked

curious. "When she called your name, she seemed disappointed you weren't there. Afterward she asked me about you. She's done that before. Like she's worried about you."

"Nothing to worry about," Wreath said, moving knickknacks around on a table. "I saw her when I registered. She seems nice enough."

He nodded. "She's pushing me to get my college applications finished."

"So you and I have a lot of classes together?" Wreath asked, and realized she seemed even dumber than she had when she tried to hide behind the chair.

She should be concerned about a teacher looking for her and about college applications. But she was very interested in whether this boy was in her classes.

"A few," he said. "If you ever show up."

"I should have gone," Wreath mumbled. "It's a long story."

"Destiny said you probably didn't know which bus to take."

"Bus?" Wreath repeated, thinking she sounded like a parrot she'd seen in a barbershop near her grandma's house when she was in kindergarten.

"The school bus." Law spoke slowly, as though she were dense. "Destiny rides the bus when her dad can't take her to school. She wanted to make sure you know there's a bus stop out near where you live."

"Where I live?"

Law looked almost like he regretted coming into the store. "Out toward my place," he said. "The bus stops at the trailer park where I live and at a few other places down the road. Destiny lives down there. She told the driver you might be getting on out there."

Wreath's hopes rose and then were dashed again. Riding the bus to school would be much easier than taking her bike, especially when the weather got cold. But then she wouldn't have a way home from work.

She glanced up to see Mrs. Durham, who was clearly eavesdropping on the conversation. "If you take the bus to school, I can drive you home from work," her boss said.

Wreath froze and then acted like she hadn't heard the offer. "Thanks for stopping by, Law, but I'd better get back to work."

The boy reached into his back pocket and pulled out a sheet of paper. "Here's your class schedule—and the bus times."

"You told Miss Watson you'd bring this to me?" Wreath whispered, a catch in her voice.

"What's the big deal?" Law asked. "I told her I'd bumped into you a couple of times, and I'd give you the information if I happened to see you."

Wreath's eyes met Faye's and then went back to Law's.

"Thanks a lot," she said. "I'll see you at school tomorrow."

As the door eased shut behind the boy, Wreath stared off into space.

"He's a nice young man," Faye said. "He can be a big help as you adjust to a new school."

"Why would anyone want to help me?" She was genuinely perplexed.

Mrs. Durham looked away, and Wreath caught sight of J. D. sweeping the walk in front of the furniture store.

"Most people are happy to lend a hand," Faye said quietly. "You just have to let them."

❀ Chapter 21 ❀

The school bus pulled over to the shoulder, its lights flashed, and the little stop signs flew out from the sides.

Wreath ran to get on.

She wasn't sure this was the right bus for her, but she was determined to make it to school today. She stumbled on the steps, adjusting her big pack to make it through the doors, which wheezed as the driver opened them.

Wreath didn't move, but glanced back at the empty rows of brown seats. "Is this bus going to Landry High?"

"We're sure not going to Disney World," the driver said, but her tone was joking, not unkind. "Step lively. I don't want to get off schedule the second day." She pulled out a clipboard, wedged beside her seat, and glanced down. "I heard I might be adding a student out this way. Are you Wreath Williams, by any chance?"

"That's me," Wreath said, her face wrinkling with a question.

"One of the kids told me you'd moved out here somewhere. Right?"

"Yes, ma'am," Wreath said, spinning quickly to take a seat.

The woman, who seemed older than the bus driver in Lucky, had long red hair in a knot that was unlike any hairstyle Wreath had ever seen. She stopped talking only long enough to pull the bus out onto the road.

"My list says I'm to pick you up at the trailer park down here," the woman said, meeting Wreath's eyes in the rearview mirror. "Did someone get their wires crossed?"

Wreath drew a breath. "I stay with my relatives over that way." She pointed behind the bus. "The school said I was supposed to catch the bus down by that trailer park."

The woman nodded, her eyes flicking from the road to the mirror and back to the road. "The bus sits overnight at Tire World, past the state park, so I head out of town first and double back," she said. "If you're an early bird like today, I can pick you up first and save you a walk, as long as it's okay with your folks. Or there's another stop right down here, a little closer to where you live."

Wreath squirmed on the brown vinyl seat. What a luxury to be picked up only a few yards from the junkyard, but what if the driver figured out there weren't any houses around? "Thanks for the offer," she said. "I'm not sure if I'll ride the bus every day or not. I have a job downtown after school, and my mom and I haven't worked out all the details."

"The powers-that-be don't like me to make unofficial stops, but if I see you, I'll pick you up," the driver said. "I won't wait for you, though. I'd never get my route run if I waited for all my riders to primp and get their lunch money and kiss the dog or whatever other excuse they have. Let me tell you, you high schoolers can come up with pretty wild stories."

If she only knew, Wreath thought, looking out the window and beginning to relax. No one could make up a story as weird as Wreath's life.

"You're new in town, right?" the driver asked, the bus slowing, its loud blinker clicking. "You didn't go to Landry High last year, did you?"

Wreath met her eyes in the big mirror again but sensed nothing more than an adult's general interest. "We moved here this summer," she said. "My mom's not sure how long we'll stay."

The sound of rocks on the shoulder rattled underneath the tires, and Wreath was relieved and nervous to see a cluster of students waiting. The driver was all business as five kids filed onto the bus, a couple speaking but most silent and sleepy-looking, slumping into their seats.

The un-air-conditioned bus was already stuffy, and it was barely daylight. Students sprawled on entire rows, letting the windows down from the top, hot air from outside blowing through Wreath's hair.

At the next stop, the row of mobile homes where Law lived, another clump of kids tromped onto the bus, including two teenagers who came running up as the others boarded. Law was one of those two and looked out of sorts, but smiled when he saw Wreath. "Glad to see you made it," he said, sliding into the row behind her.

"Looks like you were the one running late today," Wreath said, noticing that his hair was wet and his face had that just-woke-up look.

He rolled his eyes. "My mom was supposed to wake me up, but I guess she forgot. She was still asleep when I left."

"Maybe you should get a new alarm clock," Wreath said with a grin.

"Maybe so," he said and began to gather his things. Wreath's heart jumped, expecting him to move up into the row with her, but instead he scooted over to the window as several more students got on the bus, including Destiny from the Dollar Barn.

Wreath was surprised to see the girl wearing a cheerleading outfit, with her name embroidered in purple letters on the front pocket of the crisp white shirt. She smiled and said hello as she passed Wreath and slid into the seat next to Law.

"Hey, Law, how's it going?"

"Overslept," Law said. "How about you?"

She giggled. "You know my dad. He tried to make me eat bacon and eggs this morning. He said I'd think better if I had breakfast."

"Must be nice," he said. "I didn't even have time to grab a Coke." His stomach growled loudly, punctuating his words. While Wreath would have been mortified, Law and Destiny laughed together, as though they'd been through this drill a dozen times before.

"You really shouldn't stay up so late," Destiny said.

An unfamiliar emotion ran through Wreath, and she tried to identify it. It wasn't exactly anger. The girl Destiny had been nice enough to her at the Dollar Barn, and Law was friendly.

She stared mulishly out the window but listened keenly to every word in the seat behind her.

"Do you have second lunch shift?" Destiny asked the boy. "I didn't see you yesterday."

"Yep, second shift, like last year," he said. "Everything was so crazy yesterday that I didn't make it to the lunchroom."

Wreath's heart fluttered. Maybe he had been trying to help her out with Miss Watson and missed his lunch. That would be sweet.

"Want to sit together today?" Destiny asked.

Wreath's feeling of appreciation for Law's imagined sacrifice screeched to a halt in her brain, and she suddenly identified what she was feeling. Jealousy.

She, Wreath Willis, who had never in her life been jealous of anyone but a girl in first grade who had a toy Jeep you could ride in, was jealous of Destiny's relationship with Law. That girl not only had a father who cooked breakfast for her but was a cheerleader and ate lunch with Law Rogers.

Wreath thought of her own breakfast, a cereal bar and a cup of lukewarm water from a plastic jug, swatting mosquitoes. She imagined Destiny, showering in a beautiful tiled bathroom and using all sorts of hair products, while Wreath was bathing with an antiseptic-smelling towelette that dried her skin out and trying to figure out how to make her hair look like it had been washed.

She didn't like this new feeling at all, and swallowed hard, as though she could push it down into a hidden spot, never to be heard from again.

"Earth to Wreath, Earth to Wreath," she heard Destiny saying and felt a tap on her shoulder.

She wiped the emotion from her face and twisted to look at the row behind her. "Hey, Destiny," she said.

"Hey," the girl said.

"Wreath, do you have anything to eat in that bag you carry everywhere?" Law asked. "I'm starving."

Wreath thought of the precious granola bar she had squirreled away for lunch, but it only took her a split second to offer it to Law.

❃ Chapter 22 ❃

Adjusting her battery-powered lantern, Wreath squinted to read the type in the literature textbook. Maybe she needed glasses.

The light flickered, and she winced. This thing ate batteries like kids at school ate chocolate candy. Between it and the flashlight, she was spending way too much of her money on the *LIGHT* category in her budget.

She pulled out her journal and flipped to the section where she kept track of her money. *$$$*, the heading said, followed by neat columns of the little bit of pay she received and the steady expenditures on everything from expensive batteries to a supply fee for art class to money for the required school notebooks.

Chewing on one of her last peanut butter crackers, her supper for the night, she looked at her food purchases, each listed separately. The amount she spent didn't buy enough to keep her stomach from growling, but it still took a bite out of her budget. With the light she looked around the Tiger Van at the stacks of clothes she had scavenged from nearby cars and wished again she had enough money to purchase something new. A month into school, she wondered what the other kids thought of her wearing identical things again and again, and she knelt down by the tidy rows of clothes, rearranging them into different outfits.

She could already feel a shift in the weather and knew that her next project needed to be finding heavier clothes. While the junkyard had been nearly unbearably warm many times, she dreaded trying to stay warm in the months ahead.

Without a dollar in her budget for fashion, she was going to have to come up with something better than this.

Working at Durham's Fine Furnishings after school and on Saturdays was what Frankie would have called a mixed blessing.

In her journal she had several pages filled with details under the label *MY JOB*.

Under that she had divided the pages into four categories: *DO, DON'T DO, DETAILS*, and *IDEAS!!!!*

The *DO* column was filled with things Mrs. Durham used to emphasize, such as getting to work on time (although she was never late), sweeping first thing, and emptying the trash. The smell of leftover tuna was never pleasant, and Wreath didn't need to be told twice to set the garbage out.

The *DON'T DO* section was still evolving as she got to know her boss better. It included not leaving the back door unlocked, even when they were inside, and not breaking anything. So far she had broken one lamp, when the broom fell from where she'd propped it.

The *DETAILS* list included names of people who sometimes came into the store, like J. D. and the rare repeat customer. One of the regulars in the store was Law's grandmother, Nadine Nelson, who acted like she and Faye were old friends but mostly caused Mrs. Durham to go into the kind of shell that Wreath put around herself in the lunchroom at school.

Details also included what to do when a shipment came in, although that hadn't actually occurred in the more than four months Wreath had worked at the store.

"I'll place an order closer to the Christmas season," Mrs. Durham had said back when school started. "People don't shop until the end of the year."

"But doesn't it take awhile to get merchandise delivered?" Wreath asked, looking through one of the dozens of glossy catalogs that landed on Faye's always-messy desk.

"We don't live in the horse-and-buggy days," her boss said. "Don't you need to dust that grouping in the front window?"

That conversation had led Wreath to her fourth and favorite *JOB* category in her diary—*IDEAS!!!!* Here she let her imagination run wild in the good sort of way, not in the way she did when she thought she'd seen Big Fun on a side street in Landry or when she got a bad grade on an assignment in art class.

Everything, from the way the light shone on her campsite to the clothes other girls wore to school, inspired Wreath's ideas for the furniture store. She wanted to do seasonal window displays, make a display of small home accessories all in one color, and find old books to put on a shelf in a "reading area." Her retro arrangement drew comments from the few people who came into Durham's. *Collect more retro pieces* was on her list.

Stepping into the furniture store after school had become one of her favorite moments of the day. She had recently admitted to herself that she looked forward to seeing Faye and was surprised at the interest her employer showed in the details of life at Landry High. But Mrs. Durham wouldn't be part of Wreath's life long-term, and the girl tried to keep from becoming too friendly with her, although as the days went by it was harder.

Faye seldom preached at her anymore, often asking her opinion instead. Sometimes—like when a stack of bills came in or Nadine invited her out to lunch—she was moody, but Wreath figured she deserved her down moments.

"So you decided to come back," Mrs. Durham said each time the girl came to work, and it had become sort of a joke. Enough people had come and gone in Wreath's life that she knew what it was like to wonder if someone would show up, and she thought Faye always half expected her to quit.

"Couldn't stay away," Wreath replied every day.

Faye's second question on school afternoons was also standard: "Did you learn anything today?"

She'd toss the question out as Wreath walked to the back room to store her pack. Since Wreath expected the query, she considered her answer during the day. At first she had given studious replies, such as, "William Shakespeare had trouble making money as a writer," or "The Vikings first landed in Newfoundland."

During the past couple of months, though, she had gotten more creative with answers. "Landry High's colors were purple and gold before LSU's," or "High school teachers like to wear jumpers to work." She considered it a personal triumph when she made Faye chuckle with an observation. While her boss was considerably nicer than she had been back in the summer, she was not prone to laughter or affection.

Scarcely was the question out of Faye's mouth this particular late September afternoon when Wreath jumped in with an answer. "Customers are more likely to enter a retail business with an enticing storefront or merchandise display," she said, talking as she walked to the workroom.

Faye made a sound that could have been a snort or a choked laugh. "And where did you pick up this piece of information?" she asked, her voice almost echoing in the cavernous showroom.

"From this book on merchandising." Wreath held a heavy volume in one hand and an apple in the other. "I checked it out of the school library. You can borrow it if you want. Thanks for the fruit."

In the past few weeks, the back room was always stocked with fruit. While it seemed to be no big deal to Faye, it helped Wreath enormously. "It's one of the perks of the job," Faye had said when Wreath offered to pay for a banana. "Take all you want."

"What do you think about the seasonal idea?" Wreath asked before biting into the apple, a dribble of juice running down her chin. "Are you ready to let me try a fall window display?"

"I don't suppose it could hurt anything," Faye said. "It's not like customers are arriving in droves."

Wreath did a quick tap dance with her feet and rushed over to give her boss a hug.

Faye stiffened but didn't pull away.

"Sorry," Wreath said. "I got a little carried away."

"It's nice to see enthusiasm around the place," the woman said and walked to her desk, where she commanded the store like a general in a tank. "What do you propose doing first?"

"One moment," she said, flipping through the pages of the book until she came to an eye-catching autumn arrangement. "What do you think of this?"

"Lovely," Faye said, "but I don't see one item in that picture that we actually have in this store."

"We can improvise." Wreath opened the back cover of the book and pulled out a stack of colored paper. "I finished my art test early today and cut out a few fall leaves, in case you said yes."

She fanned the leaves. "These might look good taped to the window, and. . ." She scanned the room as she did a dozen times a day. "We can use that little brown table and that rust-colored velvet chair."

"That ugly thing?" Faye said.

"Just wait till you see what I have in mind. If you don't like it, I'll put it back exactly the way it was."

She tugged on the heavy old piece of furniture, tried to put a rug under it and drag it, and then inched it across the wooden floor.

"You're strong as an ox," Faye said, "but that thing weighs more than a grand piano." She sighed. "We need a man around here."

Wreath tried to hide the gleam in her eye. "Would you mind asking J. D. to help? He said to ask anytime."

"Is that necessary? Can't the two of us handle this?" Faye asked.

The hardware store owner was such a nice man, and Wreath had seen the way Faye watched him when he wasn't looking. Without a doubt, the woman was lonely since her husband had died, and maybe she and J. D. could become friends.

Wreath made a big deal out of being unable to budge the chair. "Even if we get it over there, we can't lift it onto that platform."

"I'll see if I can find him," Mrs. Durham said, acting as though he was a hundred miles away instead of probably reading on a bench next door, a denim jacket having been added to his regular ensemble.

Faye smoothed her hair, the way Frankie always did right before she left the house on a date, and threw her shoulders back as though heading into battle. Wreath climbed up in the window and cleared out the faded furniture that had sat there for no telling how long. She saw Faye approach their neighbor and didn't miss his delighted smile as he stood and listened to whatever she was saying.

He pointed to a pile of pumpkins in the front of his store and handed a medium-sized one to Faye and lifted the largest of the group as though it weighed no more than the apple Wreath had eaten earlier.

"J. D. thought you might be able to use a couple of pumpkins," Faye said, her voice one note lighter than usual. "In keeping with the fall theme."

Wreath clapped her hands together and resisted the urge to do another dance. With money always tight and addresses always changing, years had passed since she and Frankie had bought any seasonal decorations, and the girl could already see the display in her mind.

J. D. put the chair in the window and carried the old pieces to the back corner before a hardware customer pulled up and he had to leave.

"Nice job, Wreath," he said, looking at her intently as he pulled open the door. Walking past the window, he turned back to look again, his head tilted to the side. Then his stance relaxed, and he waved and went into his own store.

Wreath smiled as she attached the leaves to the glass. "I promise I'll get this tape off when I take them down," she said. "I'll even clean these windows."

Faye walked out on the sidewalk to inspect their progress and gestured for the items to be shifted slightly before heading back into the store.

"Doesn't it look better?" Wreath asked, hopping down to grab two orange pillows with brown fringe balls on them.

"It changes the entire look of the store." Faye climbed up on the platform as she spoke, sat in the velvet chair, and patted the padded arms. "This thing was ugly as sin on the floor, but the window showcases it perfectly."

"You look like a queen sitting up there," Wreath said and then put one of the pillows over her face and giggled. "I mean like royalty, in a good way, you know."

"You're not the first to notice," the woman said. "My brother calls me a royal pain. He wants me to sell the store."

Wreath laid the pillows on the platform and tried to make her question sound casual. "Are you thinking about it?"

"I don't think about anything else." Faye picked up the cushions. "Where did you find these?"

"In the storeroom," Wreath said. "There's an amazing amount of stuff in there."

"These things must be thirty years old," she said. "Who'd ever buy a store with inventory like this?"

"Business has picked up a teeny bit," Wreath said, an ugly feeling in the pit of her stomach. A recent compliment from a customer or two had probably gotten her hopes higher than they should be, but she hated to think about the store changing hands.

"Thanks to your displays." Faye lowered herself regally back into the chair. "We've sold three or four pieces of furniture since you rearranged things and made new signs."

Wreath liked the way she said *we* instead of *I*, and the knot in her stomach loosened slightly.

"You're a good shopkeeper," she said and patted Faye on the shoulder.

❀

Taking another quick look at the storefront, Wreath felt an intense feeling of satisfaction.

Mrs. Durham was right. The display made it look like a trendy store at a mall—the kind where someone might actually want to shop.

She tried to keep her thoughts focused on that as she tackled one of her least favorite parts of the day—walking home.

Occasionally she considered asking Faye for a ride. She had offered, after all. But Wreath figured it would open unwanted topics of conversation, such as where exactly she lived and why her relatives didn't pick her up. As it was, the owner asked about her mother from time to time, and Wreath heaped untruth upon untruth.

Wreath vacillated between riding the red bicycle to school and, thus, having it to ride home, or taking the school bus, depending on what was going on at school and what kind of mood she was in.

When she rode the bus, she didn't have to get up so early, and she got to visit with Law, something she looked forward to more than she cared to admit. The bus driver was nice, too, and Wreath liked being the first one picked up, having a moment when it was just her in the squeaky seats. The woman, whose long red hair got wilder by the day, always had a weather report and a comment on how Landry High was doing in football.

When Wreath took the bus, though, she dreaded the long trek home in the evening, especially now that it got dark earlier. She spent so much time looking over her shoulder that she had a near permanent crick in her neck.

145

Even after four months, she zigzagged on her way home, careful of becoming predictable. On rare days she would not think about Frankie, but her fear of Big Fun clung to her like the musty smell of her van.

Once, right before Frankie had gotten sick, her mother had cautioned her to take care around Big Fun until they could run away. "He's not that good at keeping a steady job," her mother had said, "but that man can sure hold a grudge. I never should have let on that I knew. I want you to be careful."

Remembering the look on his face when the security guard sprayed him in the eyes, Wreath had no doubt about the staying power of Big Fun's hatred for her.

The light tap of a car horn made her jump, and she was relieved when she saw it was Clarice, who appeared regularly on the days Wreath walked.

Wreath always acted like she could take or leave the offer of a ride, but inwardly she had started to breathe easier when she saw the lawyer.

She'd never realized how much time survival took, and by the time she walked home, she barely had time to check the junkyard for intruders, eat a bite of supper, do her homework, and get her clothes laid out for school.

Every other day or so, she went to the state park for a shower or to the library for a secret bath in the sink, which added considerably to her day.

"Going my way?" Clarice called out, a smile accompanying the words.

"Yes, ma'am." Wreath didn't waver. She put her pack in the backseat as usual and settled in up front. "Another meeting with a client in Landry?"

Clarice pulled slowly onto the residential street and hesitated at the question. "Not today," she said. "I needed to run a few errands."

Wreath stared out the window. She had been fretting over how to bring the issue up with the lawyer, and today she jumped in. "You're following me."

"What makes you say that?"

"You show up no matter what route I take," the girl said. "Do you just happen to be where I am, or are you looking for me?"

"Have you ever thought of becoming an attorney?" The woman laughed. "You'd be good at cross-examination."

"I take that as a yes," Wreath said. "Stop the car. I want out."

"I'm not going to hurt you."

"Let. Me. Out." Wreath was furious, not at Clarice, but at herself. If the woman could find her this easily, anyone could. She was not as smart as she thought she was.

The car slowed but did not stop. "I'll let you out, but first you have to let me explain."

"I don't have to do anything," Wreath said, leaning as far from the driver as she could but not opening the door.

"Well, unless you're eighteen, Wreath, you *do* have to do certain things," Clarice said in a voice so deliberate that the teen knew instantly how formidable she must be in court. "Are you eighteen?"

"My age and my life are not any of your business."

"I'd like for them to be. My father, my husband, and I have one of the most successful legal practices in central Louisiana. Maybe we can help you."

"Your husband?"

"He's the other Johnson on that business card I keep giving you. My father is the Estes, which was my maiden name. We make a great team, the three of us." She paused and winked. "When business is slow, I drive around and look for clients."

Wreath deliberated over what to do.

"Why would you think I need help?" the teen asked finally. "Because I look poor? Because I don't have a car? Because my clothes are old?"

The lawyer seemed surprised and turned to look at her. "This isn't about how you look or how much money you have," she said. "You're always dressed stylishly. You're a beautiful young woman."

"You don't know me, so what makes you think I need a lawyer?"

"I only *suspect* you need a lawyer," Clarice said. "I *know* you need a friend."

"Do I look like a loser?" Wreath felt tears welling in her eyes and dashed them away with her hand.

"Everybody needs friends, Wreath, and a hand now and then."

"Do you give rides to other kids?"

"Not very often," she admitted.

"Then why me?" Wreath needed to know what made her stand out when all she wanted to do was blend in.

Clarice weighed her words. "Because you're the least-helpless helpless person I've ever seen. You go to school and hold down a job, which is more than a lot of grown-ups I know."

"And?"

The woman looked as though she didn't understand.

"What aren't you saying?" Wreath asked.

The woman nodded, a small smile coming to her face. "Not to belabor the point, but you're going to make a heck of a lawyer if God calls you in that direction."

"You're avoiding my question." Her heart felt easier, but she still was not satisfied.

"In my job, I piece together evidence, and I'm good at it." Clarice didn't seem to be bragging, just stating a fact. "But the evidence about you doesn't add up."

"Evidence about me?" Wreath panicked. "What evidence?"

"The first time I laid eyes on you, you were carrying what looked like your earthly belongings along an isolated highway. You've never let me take you to your house, and I've never seen your mother."

"I told you the other day when you gave me a ride. Frankie's shy, and my cousins don't like company."

"Maybe so. Maybe not. I need to make sure you're safe, and I want you to trust me." Her mouth twisted. "To be perfectly blunt, those two things are somewhat at odds."

"At odds?"

"The law has always been my top priority. Since I was a little girl and visited my daddy's office, I wanted to become a judge, to wear one of those black robes and bang the desk with a gavel and have people stand up when I came into the courtroom."

"And this affects me how?" Wreath tried to sound smart-alecky but felt genuine interest.

"My instincts tell me that you're hiding from somebody, and yet I can't bring myself to turn you in. I've done some very low-key checking. . . ." She stopped when Wreath's eyes widened.

"You have no right to dig around in my business," Wreath said.

"I not only have a right, but I have a responsibility. Children are supposed to be taken care of."

"I'm not a child!"

"You're a senior in high school, eighteen at best, and that's if I'm lucky. Something has caused you to grow up before your time," Clarice said. "You don't appear to be a runaway or to have been kidnapped, and right now that—and touching base with you from time to time—is enough for me."

The car stopped, and Wreath was surprised to see that they were at the dirt road where Clarice usually dropped her off. "I could lose my law license—and certainly any chance of being a judge—by helping a minor stay hidden." She turned to face Wreath. "For the first time in my life, I feel like the law might be wrong, that I wouldn't be doing you a favor by turning you in."

She handed Wreath yet another business card. "I added my father's cell phone to the back, too."

"I know, I know," Wreath said, pulling her pack out of the car. "Call anytime, about anything."

"I trust you with my career," Clarice said. "When you're ready, I pray you'll trust me with your life."

❁ Chapter 23 ❁

Faye struck a match and approached the large candle in the midst of a harvest arrangement on a dining table and smiled in the morning quietness of the store.

"With fall here, it'll set a nice tone," Wreath had said when she asked permission to buy it at the Dollar Barn. The girl must have reminded her half a dozen times before leaving last night to light it.

Even if it didn't add to the warmth of the old store, Faye would have done it to keep from disappointing her young helper. The girl was turning into quite a retailer.

The trickle of daily customers was an improvement over the rare buyer of a few months ago, and Faye almost anticipated coming to work. Her spurt of energy when she opened the door in the mornings still caught her off guard, and she'd even come in on a Monday or two to plan for the upcoming holiday season.

Wreath had printed an article from a retail website about the importance of strong sales during the last two months of the year, and with November fast approaching, Faye knew it was right.

Her helper's youthful optimism and her own small spark of accomplishment wouldn't pay the end-of-year property taxes or buy additional merchandise. With dwindling inventory and scant profits, Faye looked back over the outdated ledger, then added the figures again with the hopes she had made a mistake.

She was rereading the how-to-sell story when the front bell jangled, and J. D. walked in, a small white sack in his hand.

"May I interest you in a doughnut?" he asked, looking cheerful and vibrant in his work shirt and blue jeans, a canvas jacket rounding out the style.

"I had toast for breakfast." Faye deliberately didn't reel in the haughty tone from her voice.

In addition to enjoying the furniture business more these past few months, she had also begun to look forward to her small encounters with the hardware store owner. That worried her.

"Think of this as a midmorning snack," he said, opening the sack and peering in. "Strawberry-filled or glazed?"

Faye looked back at the ledger and opened her mouth to send him on his way. The flicker of the candle in the middle of the lovely arrangement caught her eye, and she caught a whiff of the pastry.

"Strawberry, I suppose. Would you like me to make you a cup of coffee?"

Another of Wreath's suggestions had been that they keep fresh coffee in the workroom and offer it to customers, "at least on Saturdays," and Faye had gotten in the habit of brewing a pot each morning, although some days it hardly got tasted.

J. D. shook his head. "Don't give away my secret," he said, "but I don't drink coffee."

"Really?" Faye thought her voice sounded like Wreath when a surprise occurred.

"I don't tell this to most people, but I'm an Earl Grey man." He winked, and Faye felt herself smile. "I realize hot tea doesn't fit the hardware store image, so I try not to mention it."

Faye giggled. She honest-to-goodness giggled, and she didn't even care. "I've got the kettle ready to go. Have a seat."

By the time Wreath got to work, Faye had a list of questions for the girl, most about trends and how they might best use items left in the storage closet.

"It's now or never," the store owner said, skipping her regular greetings. Wreath looked alarmed.

"Grab your snack and roll up your sleeves," Faye said. "We've got a lot of work to do if we're going to be ready for the shopping season."

A grin creased Wreath's lovely face.

"I've got a few more suggestions," she said.

"I'm sure you do." Faye's tone was dry, and she felt like grinning back.

For the next two weeks, they dug through the storeroom and ventured into the attic on a Saturday in early November.

A bare bulb with a string on its switch threw off little light, and they had to stoop to get to a spot where they could stand up without bumping their heads. The flooring ran almost the width of the entire store, and nearly every inch was full of boxes and furniture.

"Why didn't you tell me this was here?" Wreath looked astonished.

"I haven't been up here since Billy first took over the store, and, frankly, I never planned to come up here again." Faye was recovering from climbing the rickety pull-down stairs and didn't see much cause for enthusiasm. "When my mother died, we stored a lot of stuff up here. I probably should have gotten ridden of it at the time."

"Your mama died?" the girl asked.

"Years ago," Faye said, "nearly twenty years now."

"Do you still miss her?"

The woman nodded, walking over to touch an old brass floor lamp. "You never quite get over the death of your mother. It's a different kind of pain from any other."

She shuddered when a mouse skittered around a collection of boxes, but was glad for the interruption. "There's nothing but junk up here. I don't know what I was thinking."

Wreath walked right over to where the varmint had disappeared and got down on her hands and knees. "We probably need to get rat traps for up here," she said over her shoulder. "That little fellow probably hasn't been living up here by himself."

"Get up from there before you get bitten," Faye said, discouraged by the dust and clutter. "Rodents weren't exactly what I hoped we'd find. I'm going back downstairs."

"Your eyes must not have adjusted to the dark yet," Wreath said, inspecting an array of furniture stacked precariously on top of a table. "There's a ton of great stuff up here."

"If you say so."

"Here." Her employee, designer, and handyman pulled out a ladder-back chair with a cowhide seat. "Have a seat, and I'll show you what I find. You can tell me whether it goes downstairs or gets tossed."

Faye sighed and sat. "Scoot that box over here, and I'll see what's in it while you go through that pile of furniture."

"How about starting with this one?" Wreath asked.

Faye's hands trembled as she looked at Billy's familiar writing on the side of the box, longing churning inside her. *Why did you leave me with this mess?*

"Do you want any of this for your house?" the girl asked, holding up a crystal vase.

Faye shook her head. "I kept the pieces with sentimental value. I'm not even sure why I put all this up here in the first place."

"Some things are just hard to part with," Wreath said.

"By now everything from my mother's house is jumbled up with Billy's leftovers, fixtures and that sort of thing. I'll give you half the money we make on any of this junk, and I wouldn't count on getting rich if I were you."

Wreath's delight and certainty of the worth of the attic's contents gradually drove away Faye's blues. The girl pulled out one piece after another, from collectible pottery to pristine linens in a trunk.

Faye tackled one of the biggest boxes. "My goodness," she said, recognizing the old silver Christmas tree that had come out for years before being relegated to the attic.

"Here's a huge box of ornaments and other decorations, too," Wreath said, her voice more animated than usual. "Perfect timing. I can clean all this up and put it out next week."

"Not before Thanksgiving," Faye said. "I never put up Christmas decorations that early."

"But this is a store. People expect that, and we need to increase our sales."

"You're a persuasive child, but I'm not going to be swayed on this."

She could tell Wreath recognized defeat on this issue. "Okay," the girl said, "but will you at least let me put them out for Thanksgiving weekend?"

"Certainly. You can start the day after Turkey Day."

"How about letting me work on Thanksgiving?" Wreath asked. "That way we'll be ready to go the next day."

"Absolutely not," Faye said. "I will not take you away from your family on the holiday."

Wreath's face crumpled, and the woman could almost see the wheels turning. "We eat our Thanksgiving dinner in the evening," the girl said after a moment. "I can come in and decorate and still be home in time for the turkey."

Seeing her earnest face, Faye gave in. "How in the world are we going to get all of this stuff down those steps?" She realized she had spoken her thoughts when the girl responded.

"Would you mind asking J. D. to help Saturday?"

"He stays pretty busy on Saturdays," Faye said, "and I don't want to ask him to help with every little thing."

Wreath scooted a table a few feet, then put her hand on her hip.

"You look like you're planning to invade a small country," Faye said.

Wreath nodded. "It'll take awhile, but I can get most of it down."

"I suppose I could ask my nephew Mitch to bring a friend and help one afternoon. Maybe that Law fellow you're friends with."

"We don't need their help."

For a split second, Faye heard uncertainty underneath the defiance in Wreath's voice. "You don't spend much time with Mitch and the other kids from school, do you?" she asked.

"I don't have time," Wreath said, closing up a box and moving it to the side. "Besides, most of them have been friends for a long time. I can get this stuff down alone. That's what you pay me for."

Looking into another box of fragile ornaments wrapped in yellowed newspaper, Faye pulled out an old-fashioned glass wreath, its painted green holly leaves and red berries still intact.

"Why don't you take this?" She extended her arm.

Tears came to the girl's eyes, but Faye pretended not to see. "I've had enough grime for one day," she said. "Let's get out of here."

❀ Chapter 24 ❀

Wreath let herself in the store with the key Mrs. Durham had loaned her and looked over at the dining table, a sprinkling of dust apparent in the early morning light.

"Grrrr," she said out loud. No matter how often she dusted, the furniture needed it again.

Come to think of it, everything in her life was like that. Do it once, and then do it again and again.

Not one car had passed her as she pedaled into downtown, the stores locked up for the holiday. Downtown Landry was one lonely spot today.

Putting her pack in the workroom, she pulled out a can of chopped turkey and two smashed slices of bread and laid them on the cabinet. After she got everything out of the attic, she'd have her own Thanksgiving dinner.

Figuring it was worth her batteries, Wreath took her flashlight with her as she climbed up into the attic, the overhead light dim and spooky. Alone at work on Thanksgiving Day was one thing. Alone in the gloom was too awful to imagine.

Slowly choosing what she would carry first, she recalled last Thanksgiving, when the nice next-door neighbor had brought them lunch. Frankie had been too sick to keep anything down, and Big Fun had drunk too much and left the house. Her mama had insisted Wreath eat both slices of pumpkin pie, and they had watched an old movie on television.

All in all, it was quite a good day, and Wreath wished she could go back to it, to Frankie and the pie and that life in general.

But if she could go back, what would happen to Mrs. Durham?

The morning had passed and she was headfirst in a box of antique glassware when she heard the bell on the front door, barely audible. Her mind leapt to the direst circumstance—someone, maybe even Big Fun, sneaking in.

Chiding herself for not locking the door behind her, she lay down on her stomach and looked out the hole where the stairs went.

All she could see was a pair of men's boots.

She leaned out farther, feeling like a frightened acrobat in a circus, and the boots moved toward her.

"Wreath?" a voice called.

Extended too far, she flailed, grabbed for the attic floor, then for the ladder. It reminded her of the time she fell off the high diving board in the public swimming pool in Lucky, having gone too far to pull back.

And then Wreath tumbled right on top of Law.

The boy looked up just as she fell, not giving him time to brace himself. Wreath, thrashing around to catch herself, elbowed him in the eye, and both of them fell to the floor.

"Happy Thanksgiving," Law said.

The girl groaned.

"Are you hurt?" he asked.

"That was the sound of complete humiliation, not pain," Wreath said, although she was shaken. She wasn't quite sure if it was from the fall or from seeing Law. "What are you doing here, and why are you wearing those boots?"

"Mrs. Durham asked Mitch and me to come over and help get something out of the attic." He looked at his feet. "What's wrong with my boots?"

"Nothing. They just scared me for a minute." She tried to stand up but nearly lost her balance.

Law took her arm to steady her, and when she turned, she gasped.

"Is this worse than the boots?" he asked.

She groaned, her head still spinning. "I gave you a doozy of a black eye."

He touched his face, wincing.

"We'd better get ice." Without thinking about it, Wreath took his hand and pulled him to the kitchen. His palm felt warm and solid next to hers.

"Do you tackle everyone who tries to help you?" he asked as she took ice out of the freezer and wrapped it in a nearby rag.

"Only the ones who sneak up on me."

"I called out when I came in. Don't leave that door unlocked when you're here by yourself."

"Yes, sir," she said with a salute. "Quit lecturing me, and put this on your eye."

Mitch arrived ten minutes later, holding a plate of food and breaking the spell Law had woven on her as he sprawled in one of the recliners while she sat at Faye's desk. Mitch held out a large platter, covered in foil. "We ate early, and Aunt Faye sent this to you. She said it would tide you over until you get home for your family dinner."

Wreath's stomach growled automatically as Mitch lifted the cover and pointed out each item on the plate as though he had cooked it himself. "Turkey, cornbread dressing, cranberry sauce, green bean casserole, rolls, candied sweet potatoes, and. . .honestly can't say what that green stuff is."

"This looks great. I'll put it in the kitchen, and we can get to work." Her stomach made another noise that sounded like a lion in a cage.

Mitch grinned. "You sure you don't want to eat now?"

"Oh, no," Wreath said over her shoulder. "I like to work first, eat later."

"Whoa, man, who gave you that shiner?" Mitch said to Law as she walked away.

"Wreath," Law muttered.

"You got a black eye from a girl?" The other boy hooted.

"'Fraid so," Law said. "Don't ever surprise her."

Wreath set the platter on the countertop and hurried back into the showroom. "I know you have better things to do today, so we can try to make this quick."

"We're getting paid by the hour," Mitch said. "No hurry."

One of the first things Law brought down from the attic was an old eight-track tape player, complete with a stack of tapes. "Would you look at this?" he said. "I wonder if it still works."

"Knowing my Aunt Faye and Uncle Billy, it's probably in good shape," Mitch said. "Billy was good with electronics and machines. Let's give it a try."

"Are you sure?" Wreath asked. "We're supposed to be working."

"It'll give us music to work by," Mitch said.

"The store's not open today, so what could it matter?" Law said.

Wreath fidgeted from foot to foot. "Nothing, I guess, but it doesn't seem to go with the, you know, tone of the place."

"Isn't that what you're trying to change?" Law asked. "Mitch and I will put you in charge of choosing the music."

From a stack of tapes by people she'd never heard of, like Jim Croce, the Guess Who, and Iron Butterfly, she chose a Christmas collection by Andy Williams. "I think my grandmother had this on a cassette tape," she said.

"Andy Williams?" Mitch groaned. "I'm working on Thanksgiving Day, and you're making me listen to an old guy sing Christmas songs?"

"My grandparents love that guy," Law said, "but I'll try not to hold that against you, Wreath."

Between clowning around and throwing things back and forth to make Wreath screech, the guys worked out a relay system. They lowered boxes out of the attic, and Wreath unpacked glassware, a stack of leather-bound books, and a collection of salt and pepper shakers in shapes from palm trees to the Empire State Building.

With a quick look she could decide where they would go, pointing here, shaking her head when an item was placed wrong, and smiling big when an arrangement came together.

"How do you do that?" Law asked.

"Do what?" Wreath was peering into a box of weathered gardening tools, seeing them in a garden display, with old clay pots she had discovered in the closet off the workroom.

"Figure out where this stuff goes. You make it look easy."

She pulled out a weathered pair of pruning shears and looked at Law, his words soaking in. "It's easy."

He shook his head, his dark hair falling down onto his face, drawing attention to his black eye. "You figure out where it goes before I've even figured out what I'm looking at. When you talk about all this junk, it's interesting."

Mitch sauntered up in the middle of the conversation and nodded in agreement with Law. "Aunt Faye has been telling my parents that you're a talented designer. This store looks better than it has in years."

"You guys are standing around flattering me to get out of work," Wreath said with mock indignation. "Drape those Christmas lights inside the display window, and we'll be finished for the day."

Mitch picked up the bulging box of old-fashioned bulbs in deep green, red, orange, and blue and started to the window, but Law paused and moved toward Wreath. "You are amazing," he said and kissed her on the cheek.

Feeling as though her heart might explode with joy, Wreath smiled and turned back to the box.

By late afternoon, with Law and Mitch putting leftover boxes back in the attic, the store looked the way the girl had sketched in her notebook, a cozy mix of classic and corny items, clustered so that each grouping could have been a movie set. She pulled out her pack and jotted the scenes the boys had helped her create, thinking of each of them as a story of its own, with sentimental items that had stood the test of time. The red-and-white kitchen area was bright and inviting, the garden "room" restful and calm, and "Santa's library" invited you to sit on a love seat covered with a faded quilt and read a book.

"What's next?" Law asked, brushing his hands against his dusty pants and helping Mitch push the attic ladder back into place.

"All I have to do is put prices on everything, and I'm going to letter a few signs to draw people in," Wreath said.

"You have to eat first," Law said, and the trio meandered into the workroom, where Wreath put her feet up and started eating the best meal she had had in weeks.

"Aren't you going to heat that up?" Mitch asked.

She cringed that she hadn't even thought of warming the food. "It's still good," she said, her face hotter than the food.

Julia clomped down the steps of the garage apartment and put the packages of brown-and-serve rolls and tray of carrots and broccoli in the backseat.

She didn't quite fit in with other faculty members and dreaded the Thanksgiving get-together at the home of another young teacher, married with two small children. But Julia didn't have time or money to go home to Alabama, and she hated to think about eating alone. Four or five other Landry High colleagues were coming, a motley collection of people Julia thought of as strays, mostly singles like herself who didn't have any other place to spend the holiday.

Putting off her solitary entry into the group, she drove down the alley and wove around downtown, sketching in her mind. After a few minutes, the emptiness of Main Street caught at her heart, making her want to create a picture that showed how the empty street mirrored her heart.

Considering going back to her apartment and pretending she was under the weather, she turned around. Instead of eating too much and listening to people she didn't know tell exaggerated stories, she could go for a long run out to the park. She had another project she wanted to finish, too, a portrait of a faceless student, drawn in pastels.

As she circled back down Main Street, she saw Wreath's bicycle propped up in front of Durham's Fine Furnishings and wondered what kind of boss would make a student work on the holiday. Or maybe the girl needed the money. Julia recalled that she had mentioned saving for college.

Feeling guilty for whining about her job and the lack of time for art, she gave an audible groan. Lots of people had it worse than she did, the girl Wreath being one of them. Julia's students, even though not all college material, were smart and energetic and friendly to each other more often than not. The rent on her little apartment was nothing compared to big cities, and she was only minutes from work. Her running times were improving by the week, and even though the weather in Landry was hot in the summer, winter runs were brisk and refreshing, not snow-covered and bitter.

Her mother, who had died when she was a freshman in college, had told her always to expect good things and to appreciate what she had.

"Too many people focus on what's wrong instead of enjoying what's right," her mother liked to say. "You be different."

"You're going to do great things," her father always said with his easy smile. She would call him that afternoon and tell him how thankful she was for her family and how she wished she could be home.

Julia smiled, remembering her mother's hospitality when people gathered around the table, the gentle smile and the faded cotton apron she always wore when she cooked. She looked like something out of an old painting, and Julia often wondered why she had turned out so different—a fan of abstract art and modern trends. She shook her head, then took a deep breath and turned the car toward her coworker's house.

A boisterous crowd greeted Julia at the cute frame house near the school, colleagues throwing out names and introductions, the smell of food drawing her into the kitchen, where she was greeted with warmth and immediately put to work.

"I made rolls. . .sort of," she said, holding up the plastic grocery bag.

"Thank goodness," said a handsome man, snatching the sack from her. He looked to be about her age. "I'll preheat the oven." He leaned over to pull a cookie sheet out of the cabinet and looked back up. "I'm Shane, by the way."

"Julia," she said and was dragged out of the kitchen by a curly-haired preschooler who wanted to show off the new goldfish her Uncle Shane had brought her.

The child's mother shooed them both out of the room. "We're so happy you could come today, Julia. We missed you at the cookout."

"Thanks for having me," Julia said as the little girl tugged on her arm again. "I was feeling homesick this morning."

The day was unseasonably warm, and after lunch most people wandered out into the yard, the men and older children tossing a football, the women groaning about how much they'd eaten and wondering which dessert they'd have next. Julia sprawled on an old blanket on the grass, enveloped by the friendliness of the crowd.

"Julia, it sure is good having you with us for a change," an English lit teacher said.

"You should join us more often," another young teacher said. "We know you don't plan to stay in Landry, but as long as you're here, we're not bad company."

Two or three other women laughed and murmured their agreement. "We eat well, too," another woman said, patting her stomach. "As you can tell."

"Look out," the good-looking man from the kitchen yelled and made a diving catch right in front of Julia, putting his arms up in the air as though he had scored a touchdown.

"I believe my brother's flirting with you," the hostess said as the man rejoined the game.

"Looked to me like he was trying to catch a bad pass," Julia said. The banter made her feel relaxed and connected.

"Shane's a great guy, even if I am a little prejudiced. He works for the sheriff's department out near Wooddale."

"Just stay away from that one," another teacher whispered, pointing to a man with a ponytail and heavy boots. "He's trouble with a capital *T*."

Julia looked over to see a man pulling his shirt off a little too obviously. He'd brushed up next to her when they were filling their plates for lunch, but she'd turned the other way, pretending not to notice. "Who is he?" she asked.

The hostess rolled her eyes. "My husband's sorry cousin. He moved near here a few months ago, and I got the family guilt trip to ask him over. Thank goodness he's only here for the day."

"He's mighty proud of those muscles." Julia tried for a joking tone that didn't quite work.

"He thinks he's God's gift to women. Big Fun's never been married, but every time we turn around, he's got a new girlfriend."

"Big Fun?" Julia blurted out the name louder than she intended, and she saw the man throw her an interested look. "You have got to be kidding me."

"He's been called Big Fun since middle school. If he weren't a relative, I wouldn't have anything to do with him, but he plays on everyone's sympathy."

The teacher reached for a stray napkin that had blown nearby. "My husband says I'm too rough," she said. "One of his girlfriends died a few months ago, and he's been acting different ever since."

"Good different or bad different?" Julia asked, not all that interested but trying to be polite.

"Like he's got something on his mind."

When the football game broke up, Julia hurried into the house. She would have enjoyed getting to know Shane better, but she was afraid she might have to talk to Big Fun instead. That guy definitely gave her the creeps.

With half an uneaten pie pushed into her hands, she prepared to drive off in her little red import, bought used after college. A flashy refurbished Chevrolet pulled out of the driveway as she fastened her seat belt, and the man called Big Fun caught her eye and gave her a casual wave.

She saw Shane standing in the door, watching the other man with narrowed eyes.

Sluggish from too much food, Julia traded her run for a brisk walk through neighborhoods, enjoying the occasional cluster of cars in driveways where families gathered, some waving as she walked past.

"Want a ride, teacher lady?" a male voice called, and the overdone car from the Thanksgiving party pulled into sight. Big Fun. A cloud of smoke came out of the window.

"No, thanks," she said. "I need to walk off that turkey."

For a moment, the man looked like he might argue, but he gave another careless wave and drove away, turning off the main thoroughfare as though heading out of town.

Shaken more than she wanted to acknowledge, Julia turned toward the garage apartment, scanning the area as she cut through the alley. Booming music and laughter came from the furniture store, both sounds she'd never heard there before.

Curious, she ran upstairs to retrieve the leftover pie and pounded on the back door of the store. She had to beat on it repeatedly, the volume on the music lessening and the sound of voices conferring.

"It's me, Julia Watson," she yelled.

Her student Law Rogers opened the door, a piece of gold Christmas garland draped around his neck. He had a fresh black eye, the bruise still red and just beginning to purple.

"Is Mrs. Durham here?" Julia asked, holding up the pie and looking past the boy to where Mitch stood on a ladder with a staple gun, while Wreath smiled and nodded.

"She's not working today," Law said, "but we can take that pie off your hands."

Wreath, wearing a strip of garland around her braided hair, waved and gave an order to Mitch, who appeared cheerfully to comply.

"I hope we weren't making too much noise, Miss Watson," Wreath said. "The guys are helping decorate."

The look of pleasure on the girl's face gave Julia a feeling of gratitude that mirrored the spirit of the day. The store had a fresh look. "Did you do this?" She stepped inside and looked around.

"She designed all of it, Miss Watson," Law said, pride in his voice. "Doesn't it look great?"

"It's nothing really," Wreath said. "We scrounged around and used what we had. Lots of good stuff was going to waste."

Law spoke up again. "Wreath says most people don't realize what you can do with what you've got."

As Julia walked back to her apartment, she thought Wreath had the right idea. Julia needed to do more with what she had.

❀ Chapter 25 ❀

The busy workday was over, and Faye's feet hurt as she walked into her house. She was eager to slip on her house shoes, eat a frozen dinner, and crawl into bed.

Maybe she'd finally finish the paperback she'd started weeks ago, but more than likely she'd fall right to sleep.

Wreath's research had been correct. This was the busiest time of year for the store, and the number of daily shoppers had increased dramatically. The week since Thanksgiving had flown by, busy with customers who oohed and aahed over the old Christmas ornaments and snapped up every one that was for sale. They also bought outdated vases filled with fresh pine and holly branches covered with red berries that Wreath picked somewhere near her house.

Faye was astounded at how much people were willing to pay for the arrangements, and she had even stopped at a garage sale or two to pick up extra containers. She had watched over her shoulders as she paid a dollar for vases they would clean up and sell for twenty times that.

She felt a little guilty and even downright embarrassed, but buying the discarded items was. . .fun. Each time she found a bargain, she wanted to rush to the store and tell Wreath, as though she'd done something special. As though Wreath were her boss and not the other way around.

She leaned against the kitchen counter and wondered what was happening to her. She used to breeze through stores in Lafayette or Alexandria, buying whatever caught her eye, no matter the price. Now she was getting a thrill when she found a piece of glassware without a chip and figured out how to sell it. She knew she owed most of her new happiness to a part-time teenage employee.

Wreath got such a kick out of whatever Faye brought in that she'd taken to going through her closets, relieved to get rid of an expensive accumulation of nonsense and make money in the process.

Sitting on the fancy tufted stool in her pink-tiled bathroom, Faye looked at herself in the mirror. She was not an old woman, although she lived like one. She fingered the costume-jewelry angel Wreath had pinned on her jacket and made a decision. Wearing her pajamas and robe, she held her breath and shoved open the door to her sewing room. A blast of warm air hit her in the face, and a sweet, stale smell tickled her nose. The sewing room looked as familiar as if she'd walked in yesterday.

Pieces of material lay sorted on the daybed, and the iron was still plugged in, the spray starch can sitting next to it. The wall hanging she'd been stitching when Billy had his heart attack almost a year ago was still in the machine.

She walked over and touched the sewing chair, where she had been sitting when Billy had stumbled in, clutching his chest. His face, always pale, had been a chalky white, and his eyes had bulged with fear. "Call 911," he had said and plunged to the floor.

For six days she had sat in the Intensive Care Unit waiting room, surrounded by dozens of people who cared for them both. On the seventh day, the doctor had walked out, shaken his head, and her thirty-five-year marriage was over. The afternoon of Billy's funeral she pulled the door to her sewing room shut and had not gone in since.

The hobby that had gained her a reputation as "quite a seamstress" seemed pointless. The gifts she'd made for women at church or her bridge club were frivolous.

But Wreath had told her today they needed to order more throw pillows, and Faye couldn't bear to pay good money for cheap designs that felt like cardboard covered with low-quality cloth.

Faye had yards of unused material sorted in plastic bins, bought when she had money. She and Nadine spent hours at their favorite fabric stores in Lafayette and Baton Rouge, sometimes making an overnight trip of it. Just walking into the stores made her want to start sewing, and she always had a project under way.

While she could barely remember where she and Nadine ate lunch or what they talked about, she remembered the way the outings felt.

She wanted that feeling again.

She could get Wreath to watch the store one Saturday—or when the Christmas rush slowed down, she'd close and invite her to go with them.

Within ten minutes she found the green- and wine-colored velveteen and bags of polyester batting she had bought on sale last year. She rubbed the fabric against her cheek and tried to summon the feelings she'd had the day it was chosen, a day when she had not known her life was about to change forever, that Billy was about to die.

Memories haunted her, and she stood and headed for the door. "Coward," she said aloud, stopping. She had to make a choice. She could give up and live in the past, or she could buck up and move forward.

She thought of the fierce teenager pedaling to work, scrimping, coming up with one idea after another to try to save the store, friends who kept reaching out.

She would go forward.

Suddenly Faye could hardly wait to sit down at the high-dollar sewing machine Billy had bought her for Christmas two years ago.

Hurrying back to the table, she drew patterns on freezer paper and made a rectangular pillow. She scavenged through her supplies to find buttons to add in the shape of a geometric Christmas tree. She liked the design so much that she made a pillow in the shape of the tree. On a round cushion, she added fringe that had been garish a few years ago but now was all the rage. She made a big square pillow lined with bright green rickrack that she knew Wreath would love.

Threading her machine over and over, she unknotted the bobbin and started on another sample. When her upper back began to throb, she went to the kitchen for a cup of tea and was astonished to see that it was nearly 3:00 a.m. She hadn't stayed up that late since she and Billy were newlyweds and went to a New Year's Eve party at a fancy hotel in New Orleans.

Stashing the dozen pillows in a large plastic bag, she couldn't wait to show Wreath.

"No way!" Wreath squealed, sounding like an ordinary high school student instead of her usual serious self. "You did not! These are gorgeous."

Faye took a step back as the girl touched each cushion and reverently lined them on a sofa, as though she'd never seen a throw pillow before. "You made these yourself?"

"I did," Faye said, ridiculously pleased. "I can sew as many as we need."

Perhaps she had overestimated her abilities, she thought two weeks later, suddenly a pillow-machine. Certain designs flew out the door headed for homes all over the country, and custom orders began to arrive. Wreath suggested free gift-wrapping and shipping for a modest fee, and customers practically played tug-of-war over the most popular designs.

The teenager tracked which sold best and made suggestions on color and trim, and ordered labels that said "Faye's Fine Pillows." On slower afternoons, she shooed Faye out the door to sew more.

When the demand exceeded Faye's ability to keep up, Wreath volunteered to stuff cushions after the store closed. On those days, Faye drove Wreath to the cutoff road out north of town and dropped her off. She always refused to let Faye go farther but clearly appreciated the ride.

On the way to work one morning, Faye stopped at the library, bringing a look of delight to the face of her old friend Jim Nelson.

"Well, Faye Durham, does this mean you've started reading again?" he teased. "Nadine said you'd be back one of these days."

"I don't have time to read," she said. "I'm too busy sewing. I need to see any new crafts books you have, plus I want to peruse the home décor section."

"That helper of yours dashed in two days ago asking for the same things," he said.

"I should have known. Wreath keeps me on my toes."

"Apparently she has that effect on everyone," he said. "My grandson won't admit it, but he's crazy about her. Even if she did give him a black eye."

Faye smiled. "I think Wreath's a little sweet on Law, too, but she'd never confess. He stops by the store once in a while, and she lights up like a Christmas tree."

Durham's Fine Furnishings became a gathering spot for Faye's former bridge partners and church members, who came by to drink coffee and acted like the cushions were art objects from a fancy designer.

"We've never had anything like this in Landry," Nadine said, lingering late one morning. "I always knew my best friend was talented, but now the rest of the world will know, too."

That afternoon as she and Wreath scurried around, filling empty spots in displays, doubt washed over Faye. "You don't think they're just buying things to be nice, do you?"

"People don't spend money to be nice," Wreath said. "They buy your designs because they're original and beautiful."

Faye realized it was Wreath who was original and beautiful. "You might be a little biased," she said to Wreath, who danced around the store with one of the pillows.

"Could be." Wreath grinned. "But this town ain't seen nothing yet. We're going to put this store on the map."

❋ Chapter 26 ❋

Julia stuck her head in the art room and breathed in the smell of papier-mâché.

"May I help you, Miss Watson?" a stern voice asked, and the younger teacher tried not to groan. She had figured the veteran art teacher, Cathy Colvin, would have gone home by now.

"I need to retrieve a few supplies I left here in the summer," Julia said.

"It's December, for heavens' sake," Cathy said. "I had to put those in a box to get them out of my way." She sighed, as though packaging them had been a severe inconvenience. "They're in that corner over there."

Julia looked with dismay at the jumbled mess of paint and brushes in the box and knew it was her own fault. She should never have left them in the art room in the first place. Holding the box like a shield, she headed for the door, unable to resist studying a row of paintings clipped to a clothesline on the side of the room.

Most were traditional in tone, with muted colors and out-of-proportion buildings. But one was a stunning impressionistic piece of an old car, in bright colors that made the soft edges bold and compelling.

"Goodness," Julia said softly, moving closer.

"I know," Cathy said. "It's hideous, isn't it? That student doesn't listen to a word I say. I told the class what the proper colors are for that type of work."

"Who painted it?" Julia asked.

"That new girl. The one with the Christmas name."

"Wreath Williams?" Julia asked.

Cathy clucked and nodded. "She's done well on tests, but she's one of the most untalented artists I've ever taught."

The words echoed what teachers had told Julia in her own early schooling, and she scowled.

"Wreath's doing well in my class," she said, feeling a fierce desire to snatch the piece of art down and lecture the other teacher on how original and excellent it was. "She doesn't talk much, but she's got a high A average. She's very interested in current events and business."

"Maybe that's where her talents lie." The art teacher made the words sound like an indictment. "That girl never asks questions, which automatically brings her grade down. She's so quiet I scarcely remember to call on her."

Cathy had moved to a closet and pulled a piece of peppermint out of her purse.

"Maybe it's because she's new to Landry," Julia said. "She seems shy." The girl had opened up slightly since Julia had seen her on Thanksgiving, but she was still intensely private and accepted praise as though it were a gift someone was going to snatch back.

"Well, she'd better snap out of it. Most of her grade will come from class participation and her art projects, so if she doesn't get better, she's going to be lucky to get a C."

"Just a C?" Julia said. "But she's one of our top seniors. She's a scholarship contender."

"Not from what I've seen." Cathy moved to the door. "I need to lock up now."

Julia's heart felt heavier than the box as she walked out of the room and watched the older woman rush down the hall, as though she couldn't get out of the school fast enough.

"Mrs. Colvin," she called out, surprised at how loud her voice sounded in the empty hall lined with metal lockers. The woman turned, and Julia rushed to catch up with her. "Would it be all right with you if I worked with Wreath a little? Maybe tutored her?"

"It's fine by me. But I wouldn't get my hopes up, if I were you. Her average will be tough to pull up."

Julia's steps were lighter as she walked back to her history classroom, thinking of techniques she might suggest to Wreath. The girl dressed in the most fascinating collection of clothes and obviously had an eye for color.

If teaching art classes was not a possibility, at least she could keep her skills tuned by helping this student.

The next day, as Julia stood in the doorway of her classroom, she watched clusters of rowdy teenagers joke and shove each other in the hall. Her third-hour social studies class would start in five minutes, and she scanned the faces, hoping to catch Wreath before class. She spotted the girl, walking slowly behind a crowd, staying a few steps back. As usual, she wore a funky outfit that could have looked ridiculous but was pulled together with the right touches.

In the wake of the noisy students, Wreath looked small and alone before she noticed Julia watching her. Then she straightened her shoulders and moved forward more quickly, breezing into the classroom with the others.

Julia hesitated, wondering about using her spare time to tutor the girl. . .and if Wreath would even be interested. She had seen Wreath emptying the trash at the furniture store a few times after school and figured there couldn't be much time for art studies, between her job and homework. Most of the kids in Landry High had it rough, and Wreath was probably no different.

Before she could talk herself out of it, Julia called Wreath's name.

The girl, almost to her desk, turned, her brow furrowed as she looked down at her backpack. "Yes, ma'am?"

"See me after class, please."

"Is something wrong?" The girl had stiffened like a character in a stop-action movie.

"I need to talk with you," Julia said. "It shouldn't take long."

Wreath scarcely heard a word of the history video as she tried to figure out what the teacher wanted to discuss. They'd had a good visit on Thanksgiving Day, and Wreath had chatted with her after class a time or two since. Her grades were good in every class but art, and she hadn't missed any school except that first day.

Glad for the lowered lights in the room, she looked down at her faded clothes and wondered if something about her appearance had given her away. Miss Watson was her favorite teacher, and she hoped she wasn't getting moved to another class. She had heard kids talking about a shift in teachers to adjust class sizes.

She glanced over to the next row of desks and saw Law, who watched the documentary intently. She liked sharing classes with him and hated to think about any of her classes with him changing.

When class was over, Wreath collected her textbook and pack and looked up to see a line of students waiting to see Miss Watson. She looked at her watch and thought about her art class, where the teacher already seemed to dislike her. She couldn't be tardy.

As she tried to decide what to do, the teacher caught her eye and waved her on. "Wreath, I'll catch up with you later. I don't want you to be late for class."

Throughout the art lesson, Wreath fretted. Usually she interacted very little with her teachers, and Miss Watson's request worried her.

To make matters worse, the art class had turned out to be her biggest disappointment of the school year. She wanted to ask Mrs. Colvin questions about the color wheel and other store design questions, but found the woman unapproachable and abrupt.

To hear the teacher tell it, art was one big set of rules, which went against everything Wreath had always believed. Her third-grade teacher in Oil City had praised Wreath's artistic ability and told her to go with the flow. That teacher had liked Wreath's yellow skies and blue suns and purple trees, but Mrs. Colvin was a stickler for realism.

In most ways, Wreath was a rule follower, but she thought art was about being creative and expressing yourself. Today's lecture was tedious.

"Miss Williams, would you agree?"

The teacher's voice interrupted her thoughts, and it took her a minute to realize that she was the Miss Williams being called upon. She didn't have a clue what the woman had been discussing. "I'm. . ." She hesitated. "I'm not sure."

"You're not sure about much, are you?" the teacher asked. "You weren't sure when we talked about impressionism last week either."

A handful of students snickered, and the art teacher threw them a look that would have stopped a marching army. Fearing she might throw up on her desk, between this woman's attack and Miss Watson's request for a meeting, Wreath tried to gulp in air.

"The lines of realism are more definite," a voice said from the back

of the room, and Wreath was so relieved she thought she might slide
right to the floor.

"Thank you, Destiny," Mrs. Colvin said. "You are correct." The
teacher favored certain students with praise, including the cheerleader,
but Wreath didn't care. She could have hugged Destiny at that moment.

As Wreath made her way to the cafeteria, dreading the daily
decision of where to sit, the other girl walked up next to her. "Aren't you
going to thank me?" Destiny asked.

Every time Wreath looked at Destiny, who usually sat by Law on
the bus and at lunch, she was reminded of everything she was not,
everything she did not have. Destiny hadn't worked at the Dollar Barn
since school started, and Wreath had learned that her mother was a
popular science teacher and her father a dentist.

Destiny sometimes paid her compliments and once had even
invited Wreath to a youth group at her church.

"I guess not," Destiny said.

"What?" Wreath came back to the present.

"I asked if you were going to thank me for saving you in art class.
That's the last time I'll stick my neck out for you."

"Oh no. I mean, thanks," Wreath said. "I had no idea what Mrs.
Colvin asked me. I owe you big-time. If there's ever anything I can do
for you, just let me know."

The cheerleader offered a small smile. "Will you help me out?"

Wreath frowned. "What's up?" *What could I possibly offer a girl like
Destiny?*

"You can tell me where you get your clothes." The girl's word came
out in a rush.

Wreath looked down at her hand-me-downs. "Just because you did
me a favor, you don't have to be mean about my clothes."

"Mean?" Destiny looked at her as though Wreath were a bona fide
nutcase. "I thought you might let me in on where you're getting those
cool vintage clothes."

"Cool vintage clothes?"

"Some girls say you must get them through suppliers for the
furniture store," Destiny said.

"I suppose you could say that." Wreath recalled the boxes of rags and junk she had dug through to come up with today's skirt and sweater. She had borrowed black embroidery thread from Faye to turn a small hole into a bumblebee.

"All the girls want to know where you buy your outfits, but they think you're stuck up and are afraid to ask," Destiny said.

"They think I'm stuck up?"

"You never talk, and you don't hang out after school or go to any of the basketball games or anything."

"I have to work after school and on Saturdays," Wreath said.

"Is that why you don't take the school bus much?"

"Yeah, I ride my bike. That way I have it after school."

"Can't you bum a ride?"

"I like riding my bike." Wreath hated the defensive note that crept into her voice. In truth, the early morning ride in the dark was wearing her out, and she could hardly drag herself home after work. With the days short and the weather cold, she knew she needed to come up with a better plan. That'd be another good list, but she'd been so busy lately she hadn't taken time to make many new lists.

"Well, if you're ever ready to fess up, I hope I'll be the one you tell."

"'Fess up? I don't have any secrets."

The other girl gave her a playful shove. "About the clothes, silly. That's a great look."

As Destiny walked into the cafeteria, Wreath sagged against the wall. A few weeks had passed since her thoughts had been this jumbled. Her apprehension at being in trouble with Miss Watson mingled with disbelief that Destiny, one of the most popular girls in school, liked her clothes and had bailed her out in art class. That almost felt like having a friend.

"You going in, or you eating outside today?" Law asked, walking up with a group of guys.

"Come sit with us," Mitch said. "What'd you bring for lunch today?"

Mitch and Law were about the only kids Wreath talked to most days, and at lunch they sometimes brought their trays and sat down next to her. Like Destiny, Mitch was popular and seemed to have plenty of money, but he joked around with her and never let Law live down the black eye.

Wreath usually ate an apple and a half a peanut butter sandwich and refilled her water bottle in the fountain near the gym. The boys, who ate from the lunch line, gulped immense amounts of food, sometimes sweet-talking the student cafeteria workers into extra everything from hot dogs to fried pies.

Wreath's worry seemed to have increased her appetite, rather than diminished it, and she debated whether it was worth hard-earned money to go through the cafeteria line. She had adapted to living alone in a dark place without running water, learning how to stay clean and be vigilant, but she never got used to being hungry.

Today her stomach seemed emptier than ever.

She hoped Law would share a school roll with her, as he did some days, because the oversized balls of yeast helped fill her up and were the tastiest things she ever ate these days.

Mitch, however, was the one who caught her staring at the tray of food and held out a roll. "My aunt's not paying you enough to buy lunch?" he joked.

"Here, have part of my mystery meat," Law said. "I had a bag of chips after English, and I'm not all that hungry."

Wreath sat on her hands to keep from reaching for the plate. "No, thanks. I brought my lunch."

Destiny and a trio of other cheerleaders made their way to the table, and the boys shifted, bringing Law much too close for Wreath's comfort. He smelled fresh and clean like soap, and his tray smelled like meat and gravy.

Wreath stood up, accidentally pushing the table in her haste. "I forgot that I'm supposed to talk to Miss Watson," she said. "See you later."

She grabbed her miserable lunch and her overstuffed pack, stained and ragged, and rushed out of the room.

"What's her problem?" she heard Mitch ask.

In the courtyard, Law walked up to Wreath, who was wolfing down the scant sandwich and thinking that finger foods were grossly overrated. Thunder rumbled in the distance, and the temperature was dropping.

She knew from an online weather report that there was a good chance she'd get drenched on her way home this evening, an ordeal that had become too frequent as the wet days of a Louisiana December settled in. A cold rain was miserable.

"I thought you had a teacher conference," Law said, sitting on the concrete bench next to her.

Wreath bit into her apple and chewed deliberately. She couldn't bear for him to think she might want something different to eat. "Miss Watson wants to see me about something," she said after a moment or two. "I figured I might as well finish lunch before I got in trouble."

"Why would you be in trouble?" Law asked. "You're the best student in every class. The other seniors are taking bets that you'll be in the top three and get to speak at graduation."

Wreath took another bite of apple to buy time to adjust to Law's words.

"What've you got now? A four-point-oh?" He reached up to brush a small piece of apple off the corner of her mouth.

Wreath's heart galloped, and she took another bite, stalling.

"I'm going to be super mad if you beat me out for valedictorian," Law said. His broad smile was so appealing that Wreath wanted to lean over and hug him, until she reminded herself she didn't hug anyone but Frankie. And Frankie was gone.

"That must be one fascinating apple," Law said.

Wreath chewed on.

"You are the strangest girl I've ever met."

"Thanks a lot," she said, still chewing.

"I mean strange in a good way," he said. "You're smart and artistic and not like the rest of the girls at Landry High. What's up with you anyway?"

"Nothing's up with me. Just because I wanted a little peace and quiet to eat my lunch out here doesn't mean anything." Law Rogers thought she was smart and artistic! Her mind did cartwheels.

"What's up with you?" she asked, needing to turn the conversation.

"Nothing's up with me," Law said, "other than work and school and practicing guitar and trying to get to know the most interesting girl in Landry."

Wreath took one last bite into the core to make sure she hadn't left any fruit and tossed the apple into a trash can ten feet away.

"Three points," Law said as it thudded into the container. "You are in such great shape that I'm surprised you don't play sports."

"I don't have time," she said and offered him a teasing smile. "I have to study extra hard to beat you out in the class rankings."

"Where do you go when you leave work anyway?" he said. "It's like you vanish into thin air and appear on the school bus the next morning. Some of the kids are joking that you're the opposite of a vampire. You come out during the day and disappear at night."

Wreath stood up so quickly that her unzipped pack fell to the floor and her diary, granola bar, and container of deodorant fell out. She scrambled to pick them up, trying to make sure the inside pocket was still closed, but Law beat her to each item and held them out in outstretched hands. As she reached for them, he laid them on the pack and took her dry, cracked hands.

"Are you in trouble, Wreath? Miss Watson or one of the other teachers might be able to help you, or my grandparents. They're old, but they're super nice."

"I'm not in trouble." She tried to pull the pack and herself back together. "Not that it's any of your business."

He stayed seated but reached out to take her hand when she started to walk off. "I don't want to offend you or anything, but you can sign up for the free lunch program without much of a hassle," he said. "That's what I did."

Wreath's eyes widened, not only at the thought of free food but at the realization that such a cute, popular boy had to eat for free.

Law twisted his shoulders in the way Wreath had noticed he did when he was uncomfortable. "My mother's not all that reliable," he said. "And you've probably heard that my dad's in jail."

"Your dad?" She was stunned.

"He's a major loser," Law said. "That's why I work harder at school, so I won't turn out like him."

Wreath knew she should pull her hand away from Law's but loved the feel of his fingers against hers.

"So what I'm trying to tell you is that help's available if you need it," Law said. "I'm living proof."

Wreath weighed her words carefully. "You've lived here your whole life. My family moves around. It's harder to get help when you don't know people."

Instead of blowing off her comments, Law seemed to consider Wreath, his head cocked, his expression intense. "That's a valid point, but no one's completely alone."

"I am," Wreath said.

"At least you have your mother," he said, the words sounding more like a question than a statement. "She sounds a lot more dependable than my mom." He let go of Wreath's hand and patted the bench next to him. "Sit down and tell me about her."

"I've got to go," Wreath said.

"You always do that, you know. You run off when I try to talk to you."

She gave him what she hoped was a sassy look, ran her hand through her hair, and tried to think of a comeback. But her spunk fizzled. "I do better with books than people. I've never been very talkative."

"My grandfather says he sees you in the library all the time."

"How does he know me?"

"He's the librarian," Law said. "He's worked there for decades."

"Mr. Nelson's your granddad?"

"One and the same," Law said. "He's my mother's father."

"But why. . ." Wreath stopped the question, knowing it sounded rude.

"Why do I eat free lunches and live in a crummy trailer with a mother who's addicted to prescription pills?" Law asked. "Is that what you want to know?"

"It's not my business," she said. "I don't like it when people pry into my life, and I shouldn't ask you personal questions."

Law stood up and studied her face, then looked right into her eyes. "My grandparents don't like the decisions my mother's made, but I can't bring myself to go off and leave her." He hesitated. "It would make life a lot easier in certain ways, but it doesn't seem right."

"Do you see them a lot? Your grandparents, I mean."

"A few times a week," he said. "I usually go by the library one afternoon and to their house for supper. Gran's an outstanding cook. And they take me to church." He winked. "Believe it or not, I like going, and I eat lunch with them every Sunday. You should come sometime."

"I work on weekends," she said.

"On Sundays?" he asked. "I thought the store was closed."

"Oh, it is," she said, the hot feeling of a flush creeping up her face. "But I have homework and housework and that sort of thing. I haven't gone to church much since my grandmother died when I was five."

"Think about it," Law said. "I'm practicing with the new youth band, and we're playing a concert in a few weeks. You could come hear us and eat lunch afterward."

She glowed at the possibility of going anywhere with Law, and her mouth watered at the thought of a home-cooked meal.

But she knew she couldn't let it happen. Things like that never worked out in her life.

❀ Chapter 27 ❀

Wreath took the school bus the next day, determined to get to Landry High early enough to confront Miss Watson. The dread had hung over her throughout the night, bringing the night noises closer in her mind.

The talk with Law about free lunches had made her potted meat and crackers more distasteful than usual. She wanted to sign up for the food program but was afraid of the paperwork. Lying to a girl like Destiny was one thing, but lying to the federal government was something altogether different.

Miss Watson was writing on the old-fashioned chalkboard, outlining the day's question and topics of discussion when Wreath entered. The teacher referred to the textbook several times before she saw the girl.

"You needed to see me?" Wreath asked, holding out her social studies notebook. "I've been paying close attention in class and keeping up with the homework assignments."

The young teacher waved the notebook away. "You're an excellent student, Wreath. Surely you know that. I wanted to talk with you about your approach to art."

Looking at the clock on the wall, Julia motioned for Wreath to sit on a nearby stool and rolled her chair over until they were almost knee-to-knee. "I saw your painting in the art room," Miss Watson said.

"I'm not very good at drawing, am I?"

"You're an excellent artist," Julia said.

"Mrs. Colvin doesn't think I'm paying attention to her directions," Wreath said.

Once more, Julia spoke over her. "You've got an unconventional eye."

The two laughed at the clumsiness of their conversation, and Julia held up her hand to silence the girl. "Different art teachers have different opinions about what makes a work good or bad."

"It's pretty clear that Mrs. Colvin's opinion of my work is not very high." Wreath waited, wondering where this history teacher who preferred art was going with the conversation.

"There are basics skills students need to learn, however, and your art teacher has more traditional views on those than other teachers might have."

"Like you?" Wreath asked.

"Let's just say that Mrs. Colvin and I were trained in different schools of thought. That doesn't make either of us right or wrong."

Wreath looked at her watch, knowing her homeroom class started in less than ten minutes. "I'm not sure I know what this has to do with me. I plan to pull my grade up with my next project."

"I'd like to help you with your art studies," Julia said, the words coming out fast. They almost made a whooshing sound.

"You mean like a tutor?" Wreath frowned. "I can't afford a tutor."

"There'd be no charge, of course," Julia said. "We'd just need to find a time when you're available."

"But I still don't get why you're suggesting this. I've got plenty of time to pull my grade up."

Julia shrugged. "You're trying to get a scholarship, and your grade point average is important. I might be able to help you understand what Mrs. Colvin is looking for, and teach you techniques for use at other times."

Slowly it dawned on Wreath what Miss Watson was not saying. If she kept using her own instincts, no matter how much she liked them, she would not please the old-fashioned teacher. "You mean you can teach me what Mrs. Colvin wants?" Wreath asked.

Julia nodded. "That's one way of looking at it."

"I work after school and on Saturdays," Wreath said.

"Since I live in the apartment across the alley, I can meet you at the store, if it wouldn't get you in trouble. Is there a slow time when I can stop by?"

Wreath gave a laugh. "Some days are slow, but not like they used to be."

The bell rang.

"How about Saturday afternoon?" Julia asked, standing.

"That might work."

"Nice outfit," Julia said as the girl headed to the door.

Wreath looked down at the teal stretch pants and floral cotton blouse she had found in a chest of drawers in a rusty mobile home. The art teacher was right. Everyone certainly had different tastes.

The temperature turned cold overnight, pleasant days replaced by a chilly drizzle, Wreath's constant companion. Hardships were commonplace in her daily life, but getting caught in a cold rain ranked right up there in her least favorite things.

KEEP UP WITH WEATHER, she wrote in her journal and tracked the temperature online at school or the library or on the television in the state park office.

A cheap umbrella from the Dollar Barn turned inside out during a gust of wind, and Wreath became obsessed with finding a jacket with a hood. She scoured dozens of vehicles at the junkyard and dug through box upon box of old stuff at the store, but came up with only a couple of sweatshirts, a snazzy but impractical nylon Windbreaker, and a double-breasted wool jacket with several large burn spots in it.

While reading a newspaper in Miss Watson's class, a picture of an all-weather coat in a thrift shop advertisement caught Wreath's eye. "Winter clothes, home accessories, and more!" the advertisement said. Wreath pulled out her journal and copied the store's name and address before heading to art class, which had gotten much more bearable since Miss Watson had started helping her earlier in the month.

"Art is a matter of perspective and individual taste in some regards," Julia told her. "But if you learn the principles from Mrs. Colvin, you'll be able to adapt them to all sorts of artistic endeavors."

The lessons were also paying off at Durham's Fine Furnishings, where Wreath looked for ways to incorporate what she was learning about color, and she seemed to be getting along better with the cranky art teacher, too. Destiny slipped Wreath a note as the chattering students settled into their desks, and Wreath unfolded it with care. She had never, in twelve years of school, gotten a note from a student.

The lined notebook paper was decorated with flowers and smiley faces. *Haven't seen U on the bus 4 a while. Want to come to PZA party at church Fri. nite? W8 for me after class.*

Wreath smiled, thinking the note looked like something she would write in her journal, and was astonished that Destiny had invited her to a party.

"Do I have your attention, Miss Williams?"

Closing her eyes for a second, Wreath held in the groan that tried to slip out. Just when things were getting better with the teacher, she had been caught with a note. The woman was standing two steps from Wreath's desk, holding up a fashion drawing Wreath had done, using props from the junkyard.

"I, I . . ." Wreath stammered. "I'm sorry, ma'am. . . ." Her voice trailed off as she eyed the drawing, which looked different hanging there from her teacher's hand.

"I thought my announcement would surprise you," Mrs. Colvin said. "I'll admit it caught me off guard, but your work is improving now that you understand the rules better."

When Wreath was a little girl, Frankie would lie next to her at bedtime and talk, and sometimes Wreath would be so sleepy that she had no idea what her mother was saying, although she could make out the words. She had that feeling at this moment and wondered what had managed to surprise Mrs. Colvin.

Wreath slid Destiny's note off the desk into her lap and waited.

"Thanks to the efforts of me and Miss Watson, your fashion design has been chosen to be printed in a regional magazine, and you'll receive a laptop computer," the teacher said. "What do you have to say about that?"

Stunned, Wreath wondered how those around her would respond if she admitted she didn't have electricity or running water. The laptop sounded like a dream, though.

A handful of students around her cheered, and a smattering of applause rang out.

"Way to go, Wreath," Destiny yelled, and Mrs. Colvin didn't even frown.

❀ Chapter 28 ❀

On Wreath's seventeenth birthday, four days before Christmas, the sun shone, and the air was crisp and clear.

Stepping out of the Tiger Van, Wreath blinked at the glare, grabbed a sweatshirt from one of her tidy stacks of winter clothes, and moved her single folding chair so she could sit in the sun to eat her cereal bar. Two bright red cardinals flitted in and out of the small cedar tree she had draped with a string of store-bought popcorn. In the van, she had a three-inch tree that had come with tiny ornaments glued to it, and hanging on the rearview mirror was her prized glass wreath from Mrs. Durham.

Wreath could not remember the last time she had been this excited about her birthday—not because she was turning seventeen or expected presents or attention. She hadn't told anyone it was her birthday, but today they were having the long-awaited Christmas open house at the furniture store.

Faye had kept her word and paid her extra for all the merchandise they sold out of the attic, which meant she had been able to buy a raincoat at the thrift store and add another hiding place to her cash stashes. Her savings accounts, as she thought of them, were now scattered in five places around the Rusted Estates.

Wreath couldn't have been any happier about the store's success if it had been her own business. Nor any more exhausted.

Between her semester finals, which she had aced, and work, which was full time while school was out for the holidays, she barely had a minute to think about life in the junkyard, worry about Big Fun, or write in her journal.

Today she absolutely had to make a list, a birthday tradition she'd started when she was ten. Each year she came up with five things she intended to do in the next year, pushed in the past by her mama to "make them bigger and better than ever."

"You have to dream and set goals," Frankie had said, always talking to Wreath as though she were older. "Otherwise you'll drift along and turn out like me."

"That'd be good, Mama. I want to turn out like you."

"No, you don't, honey. No, you don't."

Every year since, Wreath had made a Give Me Five list for Frankie. "I want you to be proud of me, Mama," she whispered as she started writing.

> *GIVE ME FIVE: AGE 17!!! J*
> *1. Graduate from high school in the top ten in my class.*
> *2. Get a scholarship to college.*
> *3. Find someone to work for Mrs. Durham when I leave.*

That entry made her melancholy, but the months were flying by, and Faye depended on her. Wreath intended to find a responsible girl—or guy—to pick up the slack when she moved on.

She debated long and hard over her fourth goal, but wrote it down anyway.

> *4. Go to prom with Law.*

She'd never even been out on a date, but she wanted to get dressed up and go to the prom and have her picture made. When Wreath was little, Frankie had told her about her prom at Landry High, making it sound like a fairy tale. Wreath had dreamed of going to prom since. And to go with Law? That seemed like too much to hope for.

> *Dear Brownie, Law and I are only friends, but friends sometimes go to the prom together, don't they?*
> *5. Visit Frankie's grave.*

She'd considered postponing this goal until she turned eighteen but didn't think she could wait that long. When she started college, she needed to know Frankie was resting in peace.

With the list made, Wreath set her morning traps around the campsite and got dressed for the day. Apparently the former residents of the vehicles had not been festive people, and Wreath's holiday wardrobe was severely lacking. The best she had come up with was an old pair of black stretch pants and an oversized forest-green sweater. She'd cut a

Christmas tree out of felt and stitched it over a moth hole on the sweater and even bought a tube of pale pink lipstick from the Dollar Barn.

One detail remained before she could start to town. For the past few days, she'd been working on a Christmas gift for Faye, a wreath made out of vines she'd foraged from the woods and trimmed with bright red berries and cedar sprigs. Using red-plaid ribbon, she'd topped it off with a bow.

With the wreath in hand, she decided to walk into town, knowing the store would stay open late and willing to ask Faye for a ride home. Letting her drop her at the road down the way was a risk but worth it on cold winter nights when her feet ached from moving around the store so much.

Not five minutes into Wreath's walk, Clarice's car appeared, coming from town. The lawyer did a quick U-turn and rolled down her window.

"Going my way?"

Wreath just smiled, put her pack in the back, and laid the wreath on her lap as she climbed in.

"What a beautiful wreath," Clarice said. "Is that for the store?"

"It's a Christmas gift for Mrs. Durham," Wreath said, straightening the bow. "Do you think she'll like it?"

"She'll love it, not only because it's pretty but because you made it."

Wreath grinned, picturing the way Faye looked when they came up with a new design.

"You look awfully happy today," Clarice said.

"It's my birthday." She hadn't intended to tell anyone, but she couldn't hold it in.

"So you *were* a Christmas baby," Clarice said.

Wreath blushed as she remembered her first encounter with the lawyer. "Instead of naming me Holly or Noel, my mother chose Wreath."

Clarice laughed. "Well, at least she didn't name you Jingle Bell."

Wreath was relieved to have cleared up one small deception. She looked forward to the day she could wipe all of them from her life, and vowed that once she turned eighteen, she would never tell so much as a fib.

"Happy birthday!" Clarice said. "Dare I ask how old you are?"

"Old enough to know not to tell you how old I am." Wreath cut her eyes at the attorney. "And old enough to know you're going out of your way today to give me a ride. You were heading out of town."

"I'm killing time until the big holiday open house at Durham's Fine Furnishings," she said with a wink.

"You're coming to the open house?"

"Daddy and my husband and me," Clarice said. "I've only been in the store a few times over the years, but my father has been a *preferred* customer for years." Wreath liked the way Clarice put air quotes around words every now and then, steering the car for a second with her knee.

"Billy Durham was the first person in Landry to give my daddy a charge account, as a matter of fact. Back when African Americans were not allowed in the front door at some businesses, the Durhams were always welcoming."

Wreath wouldn't have believed that of Faye when she had first started work, but she could easily see it now. "Hmmm," she said.

Clarice stopped the car near the front of the store and reached into the backseat, handing Wreath a small present. "I didn't know it was your birthday, but I bought you this for Christmas."

"But I don't have anything for you," Wreath said.

"This isn't much," Clarice said. "I just wanted you to know I was thinking about you."

"Feels like a book," Wreath said, ripping into it like a child and smiling broadly when she saw what it was. "My own copy of *To Kill a Mockingbird*," she breathed. "Your favorite book."

Clarice was smiling as she pulled off, promising to be back later for the party, and waving at J. D., in his usual spot on the bench in front of the hardware store.

"Good luck with your shindig today," J. D. called to Wreath as she practically skipped up the walk.

"You're coming, aren't you?" Wreath asked, smiling so big that she felt like she was beaming.

He studied her face for a long moment before answering. "Wouldn't miss it for the world," he said.

Faye looked like one of the stars of a soap opera, wearing a tailored red silk suit and pearls. But instead of looking happy to see Wreath with gift in hand, she was clearly dismayed, giving a quick frown and blowing air out of her nose with a little huff.

"You didn't tell me you got a new outfit," Faye said and pulled a wrapped package from underneath her desk. "I made you one."

It took a couple of seconds for Wreath to comprehend. "You think *this* is a new outfit?"

Faye sighed. "You look darling as usual, but I wanted to surprise you. That felt tree on that sweater is the perfect touch. I should have known you'd come up with something good."

Wreath, still holding the decoration she'd made, looked down at the old sweater with her hurried design covering a hole and looked back at the present Faye held. "You made me an outfit?"

Faye held out the package, and Wreath started to reach for it as though she'd ever seen one before, brushing the package with the wreath. "Oh! I almost forgot," Wreath said. She held up the wreath, framing her face. "I made this for you."

"For me?" Faye asked, laying her package down and taking the wreath as though it were a priceless antique. "This is beautiful."

"I thought you could hang it at your house, since you didn't decorate much there."

Faye cleared her throat and cleared it again, as though something had lodged there. Then she nodded at the package, wrapped in the store's trademark green paper with a twine bow, Wreath's idea. "Open yours."

Wreath tore into the package, shredding the paper, the string flying.

"I copied that old-fashioned style you seem to prefer," Faye said as Wreath pulled the short skirt, blouse, vest, and a tie out. "Part of the fabric is from old linens, a little is new, and I cut that tie down from one of Billy's."

"A Faye Durham original design." Wreath fingered the silk tie and leapt at Faye, hugging her fiercely. "This is the best birthday present I've ever gotten!"

"Today's your birthday?" The woman looked flustered. "I whipped that outfit up as a thank-you present. You should have let me know it was your birthday."

Wreath blushed. "That's even better. No one's ever given me a thank-you gift before. I'm changing into it right now!"

When she stepped out, she noticed that the tear in her eye was mirrored in that of her boss.

The open house felt like Wreath's own birthday party and Christmas celebration rolled into one, and she was overwhelmed at the affection she was shown.

For someone who had intended to avoid attention, she received enough notice to warm her heart for weeks. She decided she was glad she had failed at her goal. She could go back underground when school started again. Today, she would soak up the good wishes.

"That is the most precious outfit I've ever seen," Clarice said, reaching up to touch the vest. "Are those vintage linens?"

Wreath grinned. "Faye made it for me."

Clarice turned away, seeming to wipe her eye, and then rushed to introduce Wreath to her father and husband, who greeted Wreath like a long-lost relative or dear old friend. Each handed her a business card and told her to call them anytime she needed anything, day or night.

In addition, Mr. Estes, Clarice's dad, slipped her a hundred-dollar bill on his way out.

"I can't take your father's money," she whispered to Clarice, but the lawyer smiled and said, "Help someone else along the way, Wreath."

J. D., looking downright snazzy in a pair of khakis and a red plaid shirt with a sweater vest, gave her a bird feeder and seed from his store and an envelope with fifty dollars in it. "Thank you for being such a help to Faye," he said. "God sent you along right when she needed you most."

The look on his face was so nice that she didn't even try to turn the gift down, and she was too embarrassed to ask what he meant about God sending her. She was unsure how you knew if God was sending you anyplace.

The party was in full swing when the deputy sheriff stepped through the front door, and Wreath ducked into the workroom, heart thudding. More than six months had passed since she'd run away to Landry, and she still expected to be discovered, dragged back to Lucky, and put into the care of someone she didn't care for.

"Has anyone seen Wreath?" she heard Miss Watson ask.

Her heart beat harder, and she gauged the distance to the back door, hating to leave but not wanting to spoil Mrs. Durham's event by being hauled off by the law.

"Wreath?" Faye called. "Are you in the back? Someone's here to see you."

Her shoes, bought at the thrift store, felt like they were made of lead as she stepped back into the crowded showroom. For a moment, before anyone saw her, she soaked it in, thinking how different it looked from that first day in June. The smell of fresh pine that she had cut in the junkyard permeated the air, and tall fat green candles lined an old mantel she and Faye had rescued from the trash after work one day.

"That looks like something we can put to good use," her boss had said, swerving to the side of the road as she drove Wreath home. Since then, the two of them had made it a point to see what people left by the curb on trash day, in addition to their garage sale runs.

A heavy crystal bowl from one of the boxes from the attic was filled with punch made with strawberry sherbet and ginger ale, a recipe Faye said her mother had always made at Christmas. The lights hung by Mitch and Law twinkled, and even though it was only late afternoon, Wreath could see the sun beginning to set through the plate glass windows.

The bells on the door, so often silent when Wreath first came to the store, jangled again, and Law, Mitch, and Destiny walked in, all grinning and scanning the room. Wreath knew they were there to visit her, and she started to wave, then remembered the deputy again.

"Oh, there you are!" A woman's voice rang out.

Turning her face away from Miss Watson, Wreath intended to run but didn't. This moment felt so right that she couldn't walk out.

"Wreath, I want you to meet Shane." Her teacher's voice sounded excited, and the teenager turned to see the handsome deputy smiling at her.

"Julia has told me how talented you are," he said, reaching out his hand to shake hers. "She says you're responsible for all this." He gestured at the crowd and the store. "Congratulations."

"I'm only a helper," she said, casting her eyes down.

"You're a catalyst," Miss Watson said. "Oh! And this is for you."

The teacher handed her a book about fashion design with a red bow tied around it. "I'm enjoying working with you on your drawings."

Wreath held the heavy book up to her face and inhaled the smell of new paper. Flipping through the smooth pages, she saw sketches and tips on how to design everything from bedspreads to evening gowns. Not one page had a smudge or a hint of mildew, and the corners of the cover were sharp and straight.

For a moment she was dismayed when she saw that someone had written in the front, but a tear came to her eye as she saw what it said: "To Wreath—Remember you were designed for something special. Best wishes in the years ahead. Julia Watson, Landry High School."

"It's the most beautiful book I've ever had," she said. "Thank you so much."

The deputy gave both Wreath and Julia another big smile, his eyes piercing as they looked at Wreath, and for a split second, the girl's joy faltered.

"I'm sorry we can't stay longer," Shane said. "I'm taking your teacher out for an early Christmas dinner since she's going to visit her family tomorrow."

"Enjoy your school break!" Julia called out as they walked off, holding hands. "Your outfit is adorable, by the way."

Wreath exhaled the breath she had been holding.

Faye insisted that Wreath go out to eat with the other kids. "Mitch can drop you off afterward."

"But we have all this mess to clean up," Wreath protested, wanting to go out for a change but reluctant to spend money or to ask the boy for a ride.

"J. D. offered to help," Mrs. Durham said, her voice higher pitched than usual. "And Law's grandparents want to stay, too."

"We've got lots of catching up to do," Nadine Nelson said, looping her arm around Faye's waist. "We can talk while we pick up."

Faye motioned Wreath over to the big desk, which had been cleared off and polished. Opening a drawer, Faye pulled out an envelope. "This is a small bonus for all the hard work you've done this Christmas season. You can put it in your college fund."

The girl, hands trembling, opened the envelope and saw ten crisp one-hundred-dollar bills. "Are these real?" she asked.

"Just for you," Faye said.

Wreath jumped a foot off the floor and tackled her with a hug, topping it off with a kiss on the cheek. "You are the best boss ever!" She hesitated and looked Faye straight in the eye. "And this may sound weird, but you're my best friend, too."

They hugged again. "You're not so bad yourself," she said.

"Come on, Wreath," Destiny called. "Law's grandfather gave him money to buy our supper! And you've got to tell me where you found that new outfit."

On Christmas morning, Wreath built a small campfire, glad she had gathered sticks the week before, and hung her new birdfeeder within sight of the van. She ate an entire package of doughnuts and an orange for breakfast, the citrus smell and sticky juice reminding her of Christmases past when Frankie put fruit in her stocking.

She read the Christmas story in the old Bible she had found, remembering the passage from the one time a year Frankie took her to church, Christmas Eve. "Fear not," part of the story said, and she felt protected and loved as the words jumped from the page.

She had wrapped a new sketchbook to give herself for Christmas, and drew in it for a while after reading the art book from Miss Watson. She gave herself permission not to do any chores for the day and to eat as much as she wanted, including most of a small canned ham, packaged rolls, and a large chocolate candy bar.

Finally, she wrote Frankie a letter in her diary, telling her about the past few months. *I miss you, Mama*, she wrote, *but I want you to know I'm doing okay*.

Restless in the middle of the afternoon, she gathered up a small package she had wrapped for Law and pedaled over to the row of mobile homes. They looked even shabbier in the bare winter light.

A pickup was pulled up on the grass, and Wreath had to work up all her nerve to tap on the door. A pretty, somewhat droopy-looking woman opened the door. Before Wreath could open her mouth, the woman yelled, "Law, you've got company."

Law's eyes lit up as he walked into sight, wearing jeans and a Landry High jersey. "Wreath. . ." he said and then stopped as he noticed his mother's curious look. "Let me get my jacket."

"I'll wait out here," Wreath said and practically ran down the steps.

"I was kind of bored," she said when Law reappeared. "I probably shouldn't have just dropped in like this."

"Are you kidding? This is the best thing that's happened to me all day," Law said. He ran his hand through his longish brown hair and lowered himself to the steps. "Have a seat."

"Are you sure it's all right with your mom?"

"She doesn't care," Law said. "I'm killing time till we go to my grandparents' house for supper, and she's coming up with her usual excuses not to go." He shook his head. "She makes life harder on herself than it needs to be."

Wreath was surprised as she reflected on his words. "I've never thought about it like that, but my mother was the same way. She was so smart, but she couldn't figure life out like most adults do."

"Was?"

Wreath grimaced, dismayed that she had again used the past tense when talking about her mother. "I meant *is*. She makes things hard."

"Wreath, is your mom in jail or something? You always act kind of weird when we talk about her." Law reached over and put his hand on her knee.

He looked so serious and so sympathetic, Wreath couldn't lie about Frankie. Not today of all days.

"She's not in jail. She's dead."

"Dead!"

"She died right before I moved here."

"Oh Wreath," Law pulled her close against his chest. "No wonder you don't like to talk about her. My mom's messed up most of the time, but I don't know what I'd do without her."

Wreath breathed in the scent of him, the warm, comfortable scent that she would recognize anytime, anywhere.

"So your cousins took you in?" he asked.

"What?" Wreath was momentarily lost in the feel of Law against her cheek.

"Your cousins? You moved here when your mother died?"

Wreath jumped back as though burned. What was she thinking? She had five more months till graduation, and she couldn't be lulled into trusting anyone, not even Law. She had to do damage control and do it in a hurry. "Yes." She avoided his eyes. "They brought me home with them after the funeral."

"I'm sure glad you moved to Landry, instead of someplace else."

"Me, too." Wreath was tempted to lay her head back against his chest. About to give in to his comfort against her better judgment, her eyes fell on the package in her bike basket, and she jumped up, bumping her head under his chin.

"Sorry," she said. "I have something for you."

He rubbed his chin, smiling. "It's not another black eye, is it?"

"This is something you've been wanting," she said, shoving thoughts of her confession about Frankie back inside and pulling out her cheerful smile.

"But I don't have anything for you," he said.

"Yes, you do." Wreath handed him the small gift bag. "You look out for me, and that means a lot. Open your gift."

He laughed as he pulled out a toy guitar.

❀ Chapter 29 ❀

Business at Durham's skidded to a halt in the first week of the New Year.

"Have you ever noticed it's not nearly as much fun taking Christmas decorations down as it is putting them up?" Wreath asked, pulling a string of lights from the window.

"Why don't you wait till I can get the boys over to help?" Faye asked.

"This'll keep me busy," she said, "since we don't have any customers."

The girl had had something on her mind after Christmas, but Faye couldn't get her to open up. In the last days before Christmas, Wreath had become almost a chatterbox, replaying the details of the open house, outlining the gifts she had gotten and thanking Faye repeatedly for the bonus. When the store reopened for business, though, she was quieter than she had been in months.

"Are you worried about the store?" Faye asked, boxing up seasonal fixtures while Wreath swept and dusted.

Down on her hands and knees getting a spiderweb out from under a chair, Wreath twisted her head. "I will be if business doesn't pick up."

"You know January is slow in retail," Faye said. "You're the one who told me our business would be best during the last two months of the year."

With her legs crossed, the girl sat in the middle of the floor and looked around the store. "I had started to believe things were going to stay good."

Once more, Faye had the idea that she was not only talking about the store but something altogether different. "You're not getting pessimistic on me, are you?" Faye asked, smiling and moving over to the big desk where she now felt at home as she did at her sewing machine.

"I was naive. I thought all of that business would continue, even though my research said otherwise."

"Billy always expected January to be slow," Faye said. "We'll just have to put our heads together and figure out a new approach for the entire year, or at least until graduation."

Wreath looked downright glum. "It's so bare in here without the Christmas merchandise, and I wanted to leave everything in good shape when I finished school. Now look at it. . . ."

Following Wreath's eyes, Faye smiled, despite herself. "You think it looks like it did when you first started work here, don't you?"

"Sort of, I guess."

"It wasn't that great, was it?"

"No, ma'am." Wreath was perking up. She stood up straighter, squinted her eyes, and appraised the room.

"You'll just have to come up with a plan," Faye said. "Why don't you take stock of what's left upstairs? I'll work on the numbers."

"There's not nearly as much in the attic," Wreath said, "but we have some stuff left." She sighed and headed toward the back, pulling the folding stairs down and nimbly climbing up them.

Faye punched numbers into the ancient adding machine, its motor whirring each time she pulled the handle to compute profits. Using a ruler and a pencil, she drew a graph of the store's business, watching Wreath haul a half-dozen boxes down the attic stairs.

"Well, I'll be!" Faye said.

"What?" Wreath looked around in alarm, sliding a box down the last few rungs of the ladder.

"We almost made it."

"So we're in the hole?" Wreath's mouth drooped.

"That's one way of looking at it, I suppose. But we're a lot less in the hole than we were a few months ago. Look at this." She pointed to her chart. "We've made more money every month after you arrived. I may not be an economist, but even I can tell we're headed in the right direction."

"You think so?" Wreath asked.

"I know so." Faye felt upbeat, despite the lack of a profit.

"We've got to come up with new ideas," the teenager said, swatting her forehead. "I should have been planning for the slump."

"That's what we're doing now," Faye said. She glanced at the clock. "I'll share my tuna with you, and we'll do some of that brainstorming you're so fond of."

Wreath pulled out her beloved journal as Faye fixed lunch, but the pen remained still, her thoughts adrift about telling Law about Frankie. With life in Landry beginning to be enjoyable and the end of high school almost in sight, she feared everything was going to unravel now that she had confessed that key detail.

Law had been so sweet, though, and reassuring. His soft words and deep voice had eased the burden Wreath had carried for months. He promised he wouldn't tell anyone, and she believed him. She had even wound up going to his grandparents' house for Christmas supper and had felt like part of the family, adding her own amen when they bowed their heads, held hands, and said the blessing.

"My mom was on her best behavior because you were there," he'd told her as she got on her bike at Law's house.

"I had a great time," she had said and was happy when he gave her a gentle kiss before she left. She steered her bike with one hand and touched her fingers to her lips with the other. Big Fun's touch had been rough and mean. Law's was tender. Her first real kiss.

But, her morning voice told her the next day, becoming attached to others had a downside. The more she let people help her, the more she needed them. She felt disloyal to Frankie, like she was using others as a substitute. She left for work undecided about her life.

With the hustle and bustle of the busiest retail season over and the nights so cold in the Tiger Van, she experienced a letdown. School would start back in a couple of days, and Wreath wasn't looking forward to the hassle of getting there each day and then making it to work. She liked the routine of the store, with no homework in the evenings and a later start to each day.

"Well, that's a first," her boss said, placing a plate with a sandwich, chips and a pickle in front of her. "You pulled out that notebook of yours and didn't write a word. Are you feeling ill?"

Wreath gave a slight shake of her head, both a no and a signal she was clearing her thoughts. She took a bite of sandwich, appreciated the taste on her tongue, and started writing.

SEASONS:

1. Winter, bare

2. Valentine's

3. Easter

4. Spring

5. Summer

6. Fourth of July, patriotic

7. Back-to-school

8. Football

9. Autumn/Harvest

10. Christmas

"I've got it!" she said, putting the sandwich down with reluctance. "We take these basic themes and decorate the store around them." She read each to Mrs. Durham, elaborating as she went along. "We take what worked with the holiday rooms and expand on that."

"So we use more vignettes?" Faye, too, had put down her sandwich and looked at the list of seasons. "We can add seasonal books, flowers, and other foliage, different styles of furniture."

"Exactly," Wreath said, pushing her chair back with a burst of energy. "We can do a garden theme for spring, a little study or home office for back-to-school. There are lots of possibilities."

"As much as I hate to say it. . ." Faye took a bite of tuna, chewed, and swallowed. "We're going to have to go back up into the attic."

Wreath laughed for the first time in several days, and then she closed her eyes for a couple of moments. "Before we do that, I need to tell you something."

She opened her mouth, but the words stuck in her throat.

"Wreath," Faye said carefully, "are you in some sort of trouble? Are you sick? Do I need to call a doctor?"

Shaking her head, Wreath looked at the table.

"Do you want me to call Clarice or her father? Do you need a lawyer? What can I do to help?"

Touched by Faye's insistence, she gulped a drink of water and met her friend's eyes. "I hope you won't fire me, but I can't lie to you anymore. My mother is dead, and I don't want anyone else to know."

❋ Chapter 30 ❋

The awkwardness that Wreath had expected did not materialize. Faye scolded her "for bearing such a burden alone" and asked questions about Frankie's death. Her voice was gentle and kind, and Wreath could see affection in her eyes. With Wreath evading inquiries as much as possible, Faye consoled her, still believing she lived with relatives who weren't all that happy to have her.

"Why don't you come live with me till you go to college?" Faye asked. "I'm in that big house with more than enough room for both of us."

Enticing as it sounded and as touched as she was, Wreath tried to rebuild the shell she had kept around her heart. "I've got a comfortable place to live," she said. The Rusted Estates had become her domain, and she cherished her independence. The promise of warmer weather ahead, Wreath intended to prove to herself that she could make it on her own. While she hadn't heard a word from Big Fun or any officials, she felt more secure in the secluded junkyard, as though moving to town would make her vulnerable.

"Well, if you ever want to spend the night, you're more than welcome," Mrs. Durham said. "We need to go through all that junk in my attic at home anyway, so I could even put you to work."

By the middle of January, Wreath had made a list of inventory from the closet in the workroom and store's attic, and sketched potential rooms to draw people in. "I'll put the window display together tomorrow," she said.

Law sat by her in the cafeteria most days now, and Mitch and Destiny treated her like part of their old group of friends. A time or two Mitch even flirted with her, but usually backed off when Law scowled. Since the night they had gone out for burgers after the Christmas party, they had invited her to a myriad of activities, many involving their youth group at church. Wreath continued to resist.

Some of the other students, especially the other cheerleaders, acted like snobs and made fun of her when she pulled up to school on her bike. She thought it best if she had as little to do with her classmates as possible and stuck to her routine of school, work, library, and home.

"If you change your mind," Destiny always said, "let me know, and we'll pick you up."

The new semester started enthusiastically for Julia, who was relieved that her longing to be the art teacher wasn't quite so keen. She had several paintings under way at home, was working a couple of afternoons a week with Wreath on sketches for the store, and had committed to train for a half-marathon with Shane.

Scanning her computer at work, she noted that Wreath Williams was making excellent grades in all of her courses and still in the running to be one of Landry High's top three grads.

"How are your college plans coming?" Julia asked the girl one day after class.

Wreath squirmed. "I'm behind on the application process, but I've heard from a few places."

"You haven't committed to a school yet?"

"Not exactly."

"You need to tie up the loose ends immediately," Julia said. "Frankly, I'm surprised you haven't taken care of that. It's much too late."

Her words came out harsher than she intended, and Wreath bolted when the bell rang for the next class.

"I've got to hurry. I'm late for art class," Wreath said when she reached the door.

Wreath huddled in the Tiger Van that night, her old blanket pulled around her shoulders, unable to get warm.

Miss Watson had speared her in the heart with her questions about college. She had gotten letters of interest and packets from a host of great universities, mailed to the furniture store. She had explained the mail to Mrs. Durham offhandedly, saying her cousins were messy and might lose something important. The storeowner seemed happy to have Wreath use the address and had tried again to get her to move into her house.

With her flashlight, Wreath sorted through the stack of envelopes, the appealing logos of grand universities making her dream of possibilities, the letters from area junior colleges dousing her with reality. She had alphabetized the list of interested and interesting schools in her diary. Passing up the early-admission dates had been a stupid mistake. Trying to console herself, she argued that at the time it had seemed unavoidable. She was doing her best. That was all Frankie could expect. Right?

She picked up her journal and started a new section in her notebook on *COLLEGE QUESTIONS.*

> *1. What will happen if the college finds out I enrolled with a fake last name?*
> *2. How do I best qualify for scholarships and grants?*
> *3. Can I file paperwork to be an adult upon graduation from high school?*
> *4. Research universities with best academic reputations.*

She updated her running list called *POSSIBLE CAREERS* and was enthused and confused by its complexity.

> *Dear Brownie, Some days I want to be a lawyer, like Clarice, and help kids like me. Other days I plan to own a chain of stores and be a trendsetter across the country. Or I could be a fashion designer or an artist, like Miss Watson.*

Between school and work and trying to survive, she'd taken her eyes off her bigger goal. Berating herself, she didn't know if she could even get into a two-year school.

The life she wanted would require scholarships and loans. Listening to other seniors and talking to Miss Watson, Wreath had realized that, good grades or not, a top-notch school was no longer an option.

The kind of college Frankie had insisted she try for was out of reach, and it was her own fault. "I'll do better, Mama," she whispered out loud and then threw her stack of mail across the van.

The next day she asked Mrs. Durham for permission to use the phone, and her boss made a tsking sound. "Of course you can use the phone," she said. "This store is as much yours as it is mine."

Wreath smiled slightly and pulled Clarice's card out of her backpack. "You go to church, right?" she asked Faye.

The woman hesitated. "Most of the time, although I used to be more faithful before Billy died."

"Do you believe in prayer?" Wreath asked.

This time Faye didn't stop to think. "I couldn't have made it through this past year without it. You are an answered prayer, as a matter of fact."

"That's silly," Wreath said. "You didn't even know me. How could you have prayed for me?"

"God knew you, and God knew I needed someone to help me. You saved this store. . .and you probably saved me."

Wreath seemed to be taking in the words, not quite clear what they meant.

"Why were you asking about prayer?" Faye asked. "Do you need help with something?"

"I need you to pray for me. I've got an important call to make."

A questioning look settled on Faye's face, but she nodded, laid her hand on Wreath's shoulder, and bowed her head. She stood there for a moment or two in silence, then nodded again.

"Place your call," she said. "I'll be in the workroom if anyone comes in."

Wreath dialed Clarice's cell phone number and asked the attorney if she had time for a few questions.

"Absolutely," Clarice said. "Would you like me to come to Landry to meet with you?"

Wreath recognized the sound of delight and concern in Clarice's voice. "Not yet," Wreath said. "I need to ask you about getting into a college."

"Wonderful!" Clarice sounded a bit surprised, although her tone was professional.

"Will you bill me for this call?" Wreath asked.

"You're a friend, Wreath. There's no charge for friends."

"I read online that I need to pay to gain attorney-client privilege."

"There's some truth to that, although the law is complicated," Clarice said.

"I want your assurance that what we say stays between us," Wreath replied.

"Unless you're in danger, I can make that promise. Pay me a dollar, and I'll send you a bill for the rest when you get out of college."

❊ Chapter 31 ❊

Law's first guitar solo finally got Wreath to church and resulted in Durham's new fashion line.

"You have to hear the band," he insisted, walking her to work after school. "Besides, I'll feel better if you're there."

"I don't know," Wreath said. "I haven't been to church much, and I might embarrass you."

"That's ridiculous." He burst out laughing, as though he thought she was kidding.

"Seriously, I don't know much about the Bible or some of those things people do at church, like praying and singing hymns and all that."

"So Frankie didn't like church?"

"Not much," Wreath said. "She told me once she was ashamed of choices she had made. After my grandmother died, I only went every now and then."

"My mother doesn't care much for church either, but Grandma and Grandpa keep praying for her," Law said. "It helps me to go to church, and there are no secret handshakes or anything. You already know a bunch of the kids in the youth group."

The next day Mitch and Destiny hounded her until she said yes. Unsure about college after her talk with Clarice, she figured it couldn't hurt to check out the church and learn more about prayer. It might be the only thing that would save her at this point.

"I'll go this once, but I'm not promising to join or anything," she said. "What should I wear?"

"Any of those darling outfits you wear to school," Destiny said, "and I'll ask my mom to pick you up."

"Oh no, that's not necessary." Wreath panicked. "I'm spending the night with Mrs. Durham."

All three of her friends looked amazed. "Really?" Law asked.

"You're staying with Aunt Faye?" Mitch said.

"You'll sleep over at her place but you'll never come to my house?" Destiny's voice had a hint of a whine.

Deciding she had dug a hole too deep to get out of, Wreath plunged ahead. "She needs me to sort through antiques in her attic, that sort of thing. I can ride with her Sunday morning."

"Great!" Law said.

"Whatever," Destiny said.

Faye was clearly as surprised as the students had been when Wreath casually asked if she was still invited to spend the night sometime. "Well, of course. I'd love to have you."

"Can we look through the boxes you mentioned? Our merchandise is getting thinner by the day."

"Certainly. And I want to show you the pillow designs I've come up with for the seasons. I have hearts for Valentine's Day and flowers for that fresh spring look you keep talking about."

❀

Staying in a real house for the first time in nearly eight months was harder than Wreath expected. The bed was soft, the bathroom a luxury, and the refrigerator stocked with snacks that Faye had bought especially for her. But the walls closed in on her, as though she were a wild animal in a cage.

Faye tried to get her to rest while she cooked supper, but Wreath insisted on helping. "You've been working all day," she told her hostess.

"So have you."

Wreath shrugged. "I always cooked for Frankie. I won't eat unless you let me help."

When they settled in the den to watch television, Faye handed her the remote control. "Choose what you want to watch."

At first, Wreath held the remote as though it were a live snake and then thrust it at the older woman. "I'm not familiar with these channels. You decide."

The evening improved, though, when Faye led her into the sewing room, almost a fantasy world to Wreath.

"Where'd you get all this fabric?" she asked, picking up a shiny piece of satin and rubbing it against her cheek and a swatch of red velveteen that she fingered as though it were precious.

"Here and there." Faye opened a closet full of bins. "Want to see the rest of it? There's more upstairs."

More comfortable in the dark attic and the little walk-in closet than the guest bedroom, Wreath exclaimed repeatedly over trunks of linens and Faye's old clothes. "You must have saved everything you've ever worn," she said as she examined outfit after outfit. "Your old clothes are in better shape than most people's new clothes. Don't you ever spill anything or rip something?"

She didn't think Faye heard her because the woman was fingering a pair of white bell-bottom jeans, with an elaborate pattern down each leg. "I bought these to go to the state fair on my first date with Billy," Faye said and then looked up. "Take any of these things you want, and we'll throw the rest away."

"We've got enough here to open a boutique!" Wreath's enthusiastic words came out before the idea had formed fully, but once the thought hit her brain, it was off and running. "That's it!" she continued. "We can add a boutique over on the left side. It'll fill in that empty spot and add another dimension to the store."

"But we're a furniture store. . . ." The doubt was deep in Faye's voice.

"We'll be an all-around furnishings store—home and body. We'll give it a name of its own and segment it off. Fine furniture and fine fashion. . . They go together like pen and ink."

"Bread and butter," Faye said.

"Sales and money." Wreath laughed.

"We can only hope," Faye said. "It'd sure be nice to get things stable again."

"We'll make it happen. I know we will." Feeling like she was jabbering, Wreath pulled one of the trunks out of the attic and shoved it into the sewing room. "We'll have to have help with those others, but this is fantastic."

"It is?" Faye asked.

"Anything you don't want, we can sell." Wreath thumbed through a pile of stamped cotton tablecloths. "These are cool. I've seen them in lots of magazines."

"I have seen those in antique shops with Nadine," Faye said, a calculating look on her face. "I can starch and iron them."

"You have designs for all our seasons." Wreath practically hopped up and down with excitement. "They'll fit our seasonal rooms perfectly. And these. . ." She held up pieces of white linen, some embroidered, some plain. "What are they?"

"Those are dresser scarves and doilies." Faye laughed. "I guess people don't use them much anymore. My mother did that tatting on the end of those."

"Tatting?"

"That's the little stitches there on the end. She tried to teach me, but I never was good at that. I liked the machine better."

Wreath remembered the boxes of older clothes at the store and inexpensive items she'd seen at the thrift shop. "Maybe we can combine this material with out-of-style clothes and come up with more new outfits."

Now Faye was smiling and pulling out items faster and faster. "You can design some like those outfits you wear all the time. My friends asked me if we sold those. I think they'd buy them for their granddaughters."

"Girls at school might buy them, too."

"They'll be unique and handmade," Faye said. "But we'll have to make people want them. For some reason, women like things with designer labels."

"The name needs to be catchy. Something fun-sounding," Wreath said.

"Let's sleep on it. If I don't get you to bed, you'll never be up in time for church tomorrow."

Wreath sang in the hot shower and wrapped her tired body in the thick towel. She might not need a fancy house, but she would never take hot water for granted again.

Mrs. Durham called good night to her as she pulled the soft sheets and down comforter up around her and started to doze off.

Suddenly Wreath sat upright, a name in mind. She knew it carried a slight risk, but it set the tone they needed.

Junkyard Couture.

❀

Law waited in front of the church, right where he said he'd be.

"Right on time," he said. "Hey, Mrs. Durham. Thanks for bringing Wreath."

The older woman smiled, something Wreath had noticed her doing much more often these days. "My pleasure."

J. D., almost unrecognizable out of his hardware store clothes, rounded the corner, and Wreath saw Faye's smile grow.

"Was he watching out the window for her?" Wreath whispered to Law. "I think he likes her."

"J. D. and Faye? I don't see that happening. A train killed his wife and son a long time ago. My grandmother says he'll never marry again."

"Hit by a train?" Wreath grimaced. "That must have been horrible."

"The warning signal failed at that crossing out past where I live," Law said. "They were coming back from Alexandria, and I heard they never even saw it."

Wreath thought of her mother's fright on the drive through Landry, the mention of a scary train crossing. "I wonder if my mother knew J. D.'s son. Maybe she even knew your mother."

"I didn't know she ever lived in Landry." Law guided her toward the youth room as they talked, his hand on the small of her back.

"Up through high school," Wreath said.

Their conversation was interrupted by Mitch, who gave Wreath a hug and introduced her to some kids she didn't know, while Law practiced with the youth band. Remembering Sunday school as a sober, withdrawn kind of place, Wreath absorbed the lesson from the book of Ezekiel in the Old Testament and was intrigued by the forthright ways the youth leaders answered questions from class members.

The discussion went back and forth, and Wreath wanted to take out her journal and jot a few notes. They talked about "dry bones" and whether they would live again, and Wreath felt as though this conversation was aimed straight at her.

She wanted a better future, and these teachers seemed like they might help her figure it out.

She sat with Mitch and Destiny during church, giving a small wave to Mrs. Durham, who was one section over, with Nadine and Jim Nelson, J. D., and a few other people who came by the store to drink coffee.

"Aunt Faye always sits in the middle there," Mitch said with a smile. "Uncle Billy asked her one time if they paid rent on that pew."

The youth band led all of the songs, some traditional hymns Wreath had heard before and one or two unfamiliar songs that sounded like something Frankie would have listened to on the radio. Two girls from the senior class at Landry High sang a duet, and Law played his guitar solo, a moving ballad that made Wreath want to cry for reasons she could not fathom.

"Lo, I am with you always," the pastor said when he stood to speak.

Wreath sat up straighter, straining to hear what he would say next.

"That is the reminder Christ gave us, words for days when we are nervous or tired or uncertain or feeling lonely. God is with us always."

Wreath drifted in and out after that, thinking about the words written in the back of her diary, wondering how they came to be there and why the preacher would speak on that sentence on the first day she attended church in Landry.

She glanced across the church and met Faye's eyes, and the woman smiled at her.

After the service, church members poured out into the sunny day, standing on the front walk and visiting as though soaking up the sunshine, which had been rare the past few weeks.

Wreath stood on the edge and watched the expressions of affection between young and old. Grandmothers gave Law and Mitch hugs and hellos, while men shook their hands, sometimes yanking them forward for a semi-hug. Young children played tag, yelling until their parents admonished them, and families grouped around to discuss lunch and the day ahead.

The warmth of the people was more potent to Wreath than the warmth of the day, and hollowness expanded inside her until she thought she might collapse in on herself. These people were connected to one another, and she had no one.

As she turned to slip away, thinking perhaps she could wait in Faye's car until the impromptu gabfest ended, the preacher walked through the front door and met her eyes, his expression thoughtful. "Lo, I am with you always," she remembered him saying. She would have to ask Faye or Law's grandfather what that meant, because she was not quite sure she understood.

The pastor walked over, shaking hands with the men on his way, and gave Wreath a pat on her hand. "Welcome," he said.

"This is Law's friend Wreath," Nadine Nelson said.

"And my friend, too," Faye said, her smile drawing Wreath into the circle and erasing the sudden melancholy feeling that had enveloped her. "This girl is the brains behind the transformation of Durham's Fine Furnishings, and you're not going to believe what she's got coming next."

The pastor, interrupted by an occasional churchgoer, stood for a few minutes near the group, looking at her. The first couple of times, Wreath thought he was trying to include her in the conversation, but then he stepped closer, making her nervous. "Are you from Landry, Wreath?" he asked.

"No, sir." She looked down at the sidewalk. "I moved here from Lucky."

He shook his head slightly, as though trying to dislodge a thought. "You remind me so much of somebody, but I can't think who." The pastor turned toward Faye and J. D. "Doesn't Wreath remind you of someone?" he asked.

He smiled at Wreath. "Sure hope you'll come again," he said to her.

Wreath looked at the people around her, at the blue sky, anywhere but at the preacher.

"I will," she said, but as much as she regretted it, she didn't think it was a good idea.

When the crowd broke up, Law's grandparents insisted that Wreath, Faye, and J. D. join them for Sunday dinner.

Wreath declined, and Law pulled her aside to talk her into it. "I know it sounds boring," he said, "but Grandma's a great cook, and they're fun to be around. They don't treat you like kids or anything."

"It's not that," she said. "It's just that I don't want to. . ." She stopped.

"You won't be imposing, if that's what you're thinking," Law said.

The older adults had walked closer, too, intent on convincing the girl.

"I'll take you home in plenty of time to do your schoolwork for tomorrow," Faye jumped in.

"It's fried chicken and mashed potatoes day," Nadine said, "plus I made rice for Law. I even cooked a peach cobbler this morning."

Wreath thought of the peanut butter crackers in her pack and gave in.

❋ Chapter 32 ❋

Julia popped into Durham's Fine Furnishings nearly every day after school.

She used the excuse of checking on Wreath and her schoolwork and teaching her graphics shortcuts on her prized laptop, which had finally arrived. In truth, the new liveliness of the place made Julia happy, and she liked to visit with Wreath and Faye.

Apparently the store's zest had a similar effect on a lot of people. In late afternoon, there was usually a crowd gathered. What passed for society women in Landry looked at accessories. Young women discussed redecorating their bedrooms or family rooms. High school girls tried on the new line of clothing Wreath had come up with.

Certain customers consulted with Faye about new colors for a tired room, while others bought gifts and chatted about Landry news. Wreath flitted from the furniture to the new boutique, often suggesting outfits, quickly telling teens when something looked good and when it didn't.

"Those colors wash you out," Julia heard Wreath say on this February afternoon. "Try this instead."

Julia shook her head and wondered if Wreath needed art tutoring anymore. She had pulled her grade up to an A and learned how to communicate with Mrs. Colvin as well as Julia could. The girl's fashion drawing had caused a small stir when it was published, and the art teacher had gotten a lot of attention for coaching Wreath, the irony of which was not lost on Julia.

While a flock of girls tried on clothes, Faye demonstrated the store's new website, using Wreath's laptop computer on a vintage 1950s desk. "You can look at our accessories, fashions, or furnishings from here," Faye said, pointing a finger at the screen. "Wreath made it simple enough that even I can use it. You have to call to order, but this gives you a peek."

Faye wore a pair of rolled-up jeans, red sneakers, and a red-and-white cotton sweater. For a moment Julia had trouble reconciling the image with the woman she had ignored and judged for more than two years. A trio of older women, friends of Faye's, Julia thought, took turns looking at the site, murmuring and nodding as they scrolled through the simple screens.

"We have free shipping for a limited time, and a discount on phone orders, so tell your out-of-town friends and relatives," Faye said, offering them a plate of home-baked cookies in the shape of flowers.

Julia knew the old desk came from a garage sale because she had seen Faye and Wreath unloading it last weekend. When she jogged on Saturdays, she often saw the two going from garage sale to garage sale, lugging an array of items to Faye's Oldsmobile. As she scooted by a yard sale, she'd hear them animatedly discussing this item or that, haggling over prices and carrying various items to Faye's car.

When Julia jogged back each week, sweaty and tired, they would be taking stock of their purchases in the alley, Wreath proclaiming what they could do with a rusted metal chair or a tin pail. Sometimes Julia would help haul the items into the store, amazed at the goods they managed to wedge into the car, from backseat to trunk.

Wreath told her that frequenting garage sales was part of their new inventory strategy, and they hoped to add flea markets and estate sales when they had time.

"You have to learn to see the potential in discarded objects," the girl said. "People overlook things that are in plain sight."

Today Faye offered Julia a bottle of water from a small display Wreath had arranged in an old galvanized tub, and motioned to a used garden glider.

"Let's have a seat," Faye said, scanning the room to see if any customers needed a hand. "I may be able to grab a minute or two."

Wreath had spray-painted the metal piece a tangerine color and strategically placed Faye's big, handmade cushions on it. New ones appeared daily, and Julia had watched women gush over them, asking about the designs.

"This looks like something straight out of one of Wreath's decorating books," Julia said as they swayed slightly back and forth. She held up a small cushion that had been wedged behind her back as she spoke.

"With our orders from the website and in-store shoppers, I can hardly keep up with these pillows," Faye said. "Now Wreath's pushing me to consider comforters and curtains."

"She's a natural entrepreneur, isn't she?" Julia watched the giggling teenagers in the boutique area.

"Junkyard Couture," Faye said, following Julia's gaze. "Do you think my husband is turning over in his grave?"

"Hardly," Julia said. "He's probably wondering why he didn't bring you into the business earlier."

"I doubt it. I was too critical of him, and he didn't pay much attention to me." Faye covered her face with her hands and added a muffled groan to the statement. "I don't think I've ever admitted that to anyone."

"I'm glad you told me," Julia said. "I'm around high school kids all day. I need adult conversation." She sipped the water, wiping condensation off with a bright napkin with tulips on it.

"Are you still seeing that handsome deputy?" Faye asked. She put her clasped hands in her lap and turned to meet Julia's eyes.

Julia felt herself blushing like one of her students. "I am, and I have a crush on Shane bigger than the one Wreath has on Law. Shane's an incredibly nice guy."

"Take care with him," Faye said. "Have fun. Life will pass you by if you don't pay attention."

Impulsively, Julia grabbed Mrs. Durham's hand. "Well, it certainly doesn't look like it's passing you by now. Look what you've done! This store is fantastic."

"I'll say it again. Wreath gets the credit. She thinks up things like the website and special promotions. I just nod and do whatever she tells me."

"I doubt that's true," Julia said. "You strike me as a fighter."

A look of incredulity came to Faye's face, and she sat perfectly still. "Maybe I am," she said finally, "but I'm not nearly the person she is." Faye nodded at Wreath.

"That girl's something, all right," Julia said. She shredded her napkin as she thought about how to ask the question on her mind. "How much do you know about Wreath's background?" she finally asked.

"Not much." Faye shook her head, a measure of grief in her eyes. "She won't open up about that. I know she can't have had it easy. She works harder than most adults I know."

"Have you met the family she lives with?"

Again, Faye shook her head in regret. She started to speak and then stopped. Then she started again. "There's something I ought to tell you, but. . ."

"What is it?" Julia interrupted.

Faye looked across the showroom, jiggled her leg up and down a few times, and sighed. "You promise you won't spread this around?" she asked softly. She stared at Wreath, who was holding up a shirt and smiling at a young customer.

"Of course," Julia said. A knot grew in her stomach. "Please. Tell me."

Faye breathed in, held it for a moment, and exhaled. "Wreath confided in me that her mother passed away last May, but she won't say much more than that."

Julia moved her head up and down slightly. She had wished for more information. "Law told me about her mother—in strictest confidence. He worries about her, too."

"Did he tell you anything else?" Faye asked eagerly.

"No. He's cautious when he talks about Wreath. I hoped she'd opened up with you," Julia said. "She's so much more at ease around you than she is at school. Wreath needs guidance if she's going to get into college."

Faye's stomach churned. "Wreath's behind in the process, isn't she?"

"Not hopelessly, but she needs to stay focused if she's going to make it all work. That's a tough process even for students with very involved parents."

"What can I do?" Faye asked.

"Let me fish around at school and check with the counselor," Julia said. "Maybe you can get her to confide in you. She's hiding something, but I cannot for the life of me figure out what it is."

Faye's voice was so soft that Julie had to lean in to hear. "I wonder at times if I'm fooling myself about Wreath. I tell myself that she's clean and healthy, never misses work, does well in school, has started going to church. Everything seems right, but I'm not sure."

"I know," Julia said.

"I'm ashamed to tell you this, but I'm afraid to dig too deep," Faye said.

Julia didn't reply.

"I'm afraid of what I might find." Faye sat up straighter, giving the glider a quick push. "I'm afraid I might lose her, and I don't know what I'd do without her."

❀ Chapter 33 ❀

Wreath began to feel sick to her stomach after morning worship. The roast beef Mrs. Durham had cooked for lunch wasn't sitting well in her stomach.

She took a rare nap on the guest room bed at Faye's, the room beginning to feel more like her own. She now spent most weekend nights there. She was chilled when she woke up and chided herself for not wearing a sweater, fooled by a warm March morning that had turned cloudy.

"You look pale," Faye said when Wreath woke up. "Would you rather go on home and skip youth group tonight?"

"No." Wreath shook her head adamantly, even though the motion made her feel dizzy. "That's one of my favorite parts of the week."

She picked up on Faye's disappointment instantly. "Other than my work at the store, of course," she added.

Faye smiled. "You don't have to explain to me. I remember youth group when I was in high school as one of the highlights of my week. My mother said I loved the boys more than I loved the lessons, but it felt like home away from home to me."

"That's exactly the way it feels to me," Wreath said. "I thought it was because my mother died or that I hadn't been to church much before. Then Law said he feels the same way."

"Through the years I've found that church means different things to all of us. After Billy died, I could hardly bear the familiarity, the pew where we sat together, the friends we shared. Now I can't believe I stayed away as long as I did."

"You want to hear something corny?" Wreath asked, not sure if the congestion she felt was from a cold or from the eloquent way Faye spoke. "Even though it's all new to me, I feel love when I'm there."

"That's the way it should be," Faye said, clearing her throat.

❀

Wreath passed on the snack supper that evening and had trouble concentrating on the discussion. Watching Law play the guitar with Mitch on the drums cheered her somewhat, but she felt as though someone had taken a box of Kleenex and stuffed each one of them in her head.

Mitch, as usual, drove Wreath and Law to Law's house after church, where Wreath sometimes left her bicycle locked near the end of the trailer on Friday afternoons. At times she smiled when she thought about anyone trying to track her down. Her transportation system was so complicated that she could barely keep up with herself.

"Are you sure you won't let me drive you all the way home?" Mitch asked. "You don't look so hot."

"I'm fine." Wreath said, although getting out of the car took all of her energy. "I have my bike."

With a wave and a good-bye shout, Mitch drove off.

"I'd better get going," Wreath wheezed. Her voice sounded hoarse and weak.

"Are you all right?" Law asked.

"I'm fine." Her head was so full that she could barely sort the words coming out of her mouth, and her knees buckled as she walked toward the bicycle.

"Are you sure you're not sick?" Law said.

An unwanted sob came out of Wreath's throat, and her hand trembled when she brushed tears from her eyes. "I'm just a little tired, I guess."

"Hey, shhh," Law said as though speaking to a cranky infant and pulled her up against him. "It'll be okay."

"There's not a problem!" Wreath insisted, but her slurred words lessened the impact of her proclamation.

"We need to get you home. One of the neighbors can drive us."

"No!" Wreath said, summoning her energy. "I can ride my bike."

"Then I'm going with you."

"You can't!" The vehemence in Wreath's voice surprised even her, and Law took a step back and held up his hand.

"Calm down," he said. "I didn't mean to freak you out. I just want to take you home. I think you have a fever."

"You know my cousins don't like me bringing people over," Wreath said.

"I won't go in or anything, but if you think I'm going to let you ride alone late at night and sick. . ." He shook his head. "Isn't going to happen."

Wreath was touched but panicked at how to keep him away from the junkyard. "Don't you need to study? We have those big social studies reports tomorrow."

"Nice try. I'll look over my notes when I get back."

"Did anyone ever tell you you're stubborn?" she asked.

Law laughed. "You make me look like a lightweight when it comes to stubborn. You're absolutely the most stubborn person I've ever met. Probably the smartest, too, but don't tell anyone I said that."

She bent down to pick up her pack. Law was going with her, whether she liked it or not. She'd have to think of something along the way.

"Let me carry that for you." He reached for the pack. "What do you have in this thing, by the way? Rocks?"

"Rocks and books." Wreath forgot for a split second how lousy she felt. "I look for the heaviest things I can find."

Law grunted. "As usual, you succeeded." He patted the bike seat. "Climb on behind me. I haven't tried this in a while, but I know how to keep us moving."

Not a single car passed them on the dark highway, and Wreath was glad for Law's presence. She didn't feel like herself at all. With Law pedaling, she felt like a queen on a parade float. A sick queen, but a queen nonetheless.

For a few bumpy minutes, Wreath allowed herself to think that things were turning out all right after all.

When they got to the junkyard, she pointed on past it down the road. "Just stop over there."

Instead of riding to the spot she'd intended, Law stopped on the shoulder. Wreath's head whirled, and she steadied herself by gripping his shoulders.

"You ever noticed that place?" Law turned slightly and pointed to the junkyard where she lived. "It's creepy."

Wreath's heart thudded, and she thought she might throw up. Letting go of Law, she shook her head like one of those dolls with a spring for a neck. She managed a casual glance at the property she knew so well. "No," she said, and then "no" again. "I haven't paid much attention to this area. You stopped too soon. My cousin lives farther out."

"I wasn't sure," Law said. "You all right back there?"

"Not so great," she said. "Please go on. I need to get home."

Thankfully Law started pedaling again and talked as he did. "That's an abandoned junkyard," he said and gave a spooky, dramatic laugh. "They say it's haunted."

"Haunted?" Wreath's voice squeaked. "That's ridiculous."

"People say they've seen lights there lately, that ghosts live there." Law kept up the weird voice, like he was announcing a horror movie.

"You're creeping me out," she said, punching him halfheartedly in the shoulder. "Quit talking like that."

"A homeless person is probably camping up there," Law said. "With the leaves off the trees, it's easier to see up in there."

A coughing fit consumed Wreath, and the bike wobbled. "Quit talking about that," she said. "I don't like it."

"I'm sorry," Law said. "I didn't mean to scare you. Nobody could possibly live up in that place. Mitch and I used to explore there when we were kids, and it was a disaster area even then. They don't even let people go up there anymore."

Wreath drew her first full breath since Law had first mentioned the junkyard.

"No one in their right mind would attempt to live there," he said and reached back to pat her leg.

Wreath coughed again. "Turn there," she said at a small dirt road on the other side of the highway from the junkyard. "Turn!"

"Your cough is getting worse," Law said, crossing over to the dirt road.

"I want to go home." She glanced at the bare outline of the old junkyard sign, and Law draped his arm around her shoulders for a sliver of a reassuring moment.

"Let's get you to your cousins,'" he said.

Wreath reluctantly pulled away. "This is far enough," she said. "You've got a long walk home as it is."

"I'm taking you to the front door," he said. "I want to make sure you're okay."

"Wait." Wreath unzipped the pack, still on his back, and pulled out her flashlight. "I've got a light, and I'll be fine. It'll upset my mom's cousin if you bring me home, and that'll just make it harder."

For the first time that evening, Law looked doubtful. "I don't want to make things worse," he said. "But why would your cousin care if a friend brings you home?"

"His wife's not all that happy about me moving in." Sometimes the lies rolled off her tongue so fast it scared her. "I should stay out of their way as much as possible."

She shone the thin beam of the flashlight onto her watch. "It's late, and I'm going to have to sneak in as it is." She turned the light off and pointed down the dirt road, dotted with the occasional homestead. "It's just around the corner. I'll be there in two minutes."

"If you're sure. . ."

"I'm sure. Thanks, Law. See you at school tomorrow. I intend to ace the big project, so you'd better do your best."

He smiled and kissed her on the cheek. "Be safe, Wreath."

With her chapped hand against her face, she could almost feel his warmth as he headed off into the night. Wreath rode down the unfamiliar road, stopping twice to make sure Law wasn't following, relieved when she turned a small curve, and he was out of sight. Turning off the flashlight, she shivered as a cool wind blew down the lane.

She made herself wait in the shadows for a few minutes to be certain she was alone. A few feet away she watched a gray cat stalking something in the brittle weeds, and jumped when he pounced and walked out with a mouse.

Unnerved, she pedaled back toward the highway, staying close to the brush. A car sped past on the open road, and she swerved into the trees, scraping her hand on a branch. The small cut stung worse than the time she'd snagged her leg on a barbed wire fence, and she had to force herself not to cry.

Her eyes moving from side to side, she scanned the highway as she approached, halfway hoping Law would be waiting there for her. Her legs felt like they couldn't push her the rest of the way home.

But the late winter moon shone on a desolate strip of road and nothing more.

✿

Locking herself in the Tiger Van, she tried to work on her homework. But her thoughts were jumbled, and she gave up and lay down under her blanket. She'd rest a few minutes and look for an aspirin.

Within seconds she was sound asleep.

A persistent rustling sound awakened Wreath, and she sat up, reaching for the baseball bat she kept nearby.

Her breathing was loud and raspy, and outside she heard steady movement.

She considered calling out but decided not to reveal her presence. The element of surprise was about the only protection she had. Weakly, she crawled to the back of the van, listening. The noises retreated, and the night grew quiet again.

Unable to get warm, she fumbled for warmer clothes, including a moth-eaten knit cap. She pulled an extra sweatshirt over her head and put on the insulated coveralls she'd found in the big toolbox on the back of a wrecker. A wrecked wrecker. As she struggled into the stale, heavy outfit, she thought her life and that wrecker had a lot in common. For years she had done her best to pull her mother out of one mess or another, and this was what she had come to.

The outside noises drew close again, and she slithered on her stomach to the front of the van, the old carpet tickling her face, dust threatening to make her sneeze. Something bumped against the van, and she could stand it no longer. "I have a gun," she yelled in a hoarse voice. She heard sounds like men arguing, low and indistinguishable. "Big Fun, go away!" Her thoughts were muddled.

A thud sounded near the front fender. "I'll shoot you. I will." Her voice was muffled in the padded vehicle, and it trembled.

Silence.

She sat with her legs crossed, the bat raised, trying to watch both front doors, wondering how much it would take for someone to break the locks. When her feet went numb, she rose to her knees. The waiting was paralyzing, and she knew she had to take action.

She peeked around the old sheet she'd used to cover the windshield and tried to make out shapes in the darkness. She wished for a brighter moon. A low movement near the pristine VW bug next to her van caught her eye. Then another. And another. She heard the grunting noise again, and wondered if Big Fun was in a fight, rolling around on the ground. She'd seen him do that once with a man who came to their house to play poker, and it had looked primitive, beastly almost.

Staring so hard her eyes hurt, she couldn't make out what was going on, but it was clear that whoever was out there was distracted. She eased the van door open, gripping her pack in one hand, the bat in the other.

When Wreath stepped out, she didn't know whether to run or laugh. A half-dozen of the biggest, ugliest hogs she had ever seen were foraging approximately three van-lengths away.

As she took a cautious step toward her bicycle, the largest of the animals charged toward her. She jumped back into the van, slamming the door. She thought at first the animals were making the loud squealing noise, but then realized it was her.

No matter how brave she might think she was, no way could she face those beasts. She slumped to the rough floor.

❀ Chapter 34 ❀

Julia was disturbed.

Wreath had missed two days of class during a week of big presentations, something so out of character that the teacher knew something was wrong.

After class, Law Rogers had asked her if she knew where the girl was, looking troubled and hinting that she might be ill.

"I need to know what you know," she told the boy. "If I'm going to help, I need more to go on."

He had shadows under his eyes, as though he'd not gotten much sleep.

"I don't know much, Miss Watson," he said. "I walked her home after church Sunday night, and she was planning to give her report yesterday."

Julia could tell he was considering how much information to offer, the way students sometimes did when covering for a friend, and she saw the minute he decided to shut down. "Wreath wasn't feeling very good," he said. "She probably has a bug or something. I'm sure she'll be back tomorrow."

"Law," the young teacher said as gently as she could, "you and I both know that Wreath doesn't have much family support. If you know something that can help, you need to tell me."

Two other students crowded near, trying to ask questions about their projects, and the boy pulled back.

"I'll let you know if I hear anything," he said and bolted from the room.

With a weight in her stomach, Julia turned to the other kids and tried to push the thought of an ill Wreath from her mind. During her next class period, she searched her files for Wreath's student profile, something she asked each of her students to fill out.

No such sheet was available, and she wasn't surprised when she looked at her early semester list and saw that Wreath was among a dozen or so students who had never turned their paperwork in.

Julia groaned. If only she'd paid more attention to her students and less to being forced to teach history...

As soon as the afternoon bell rang, she rushed from the school, passing Mrs. Colvin in the hallway.

"Leaving early today, are we?" the old art teacher asked, her tone disapproving.

At first Julia ignored her, but then she turned around. "Mrs. Colvin, was Wreath Williams in your class yesterday and today?"

The teacher shook her head. "She not only skipped two days of class, but she missed a test, and she can't make it up. She's been doing much better since you've tutored her, but she'll have to work to hold on to her A."

Julia tilted her head to the side. "What do you mean she can't make it up?"

"I checked with the attendance clerk. Miss Williams's parents didn't call in either day, and no one checked her out of school."

"Maybe she'll have a written excuse tomorrow," Julia said. "Wreath's a very conscientious student."

"If you say so," Mrs. Colvin grumbled and walked back toward the art room.

The school office after school was like a beehive, with teachers submitting various fees from students, club leaders trying to get their events on the master calendar, and the attendance clerk, the queen bee, ordering volunteers around and tallying the day's absentee rate.

"I hate to interrupt, but did Wreath Williams's guardian call in yesterday or today?" Julia asked.

The clerk gave a put-upon sigh and looked through the list. "I haven't heard from anyone regarding a student by that name."

"Can you give me her home number and her guardian's name? She lives with a cousin north of Landry."

Julia could tell that the office worker was in a hurry to finish, but she turned to the computer and logged into the enrollment files, Julia watching over her shoulder.

"Wreath Williams?"

Julia nodded, anxious. "She's the new student who transferred in from Lucky this year. One of the top students in the senior class."

"I see her name." The clerk frowned. "This is odd, though. We never got the official transcript from her last school, plus she's missing the required medical records."

Julia winced as another piece of the mystery of Wreath fell away. "It's probably an oversight. She's an A student, a very bright girl."

"I'm glad you mentioned her," the clerk said. "If she doesn't get this information turned in, she can't graduate. I need to follow up with her parents."

"Not parents," Julia said. "She lives with a cousin. I'll mention it when I talk to him."

"Make sure you do. She can have the best grades in Rapides Parish, but she won't graduate without straightening this out."

Julia exhaled the breath she'd been holding. "What's that phone number, please?"

The clerk looked closer at the screen, still frowning. "Apparently they didn't have a phone when she registered," she said, "but I have an address." She wrote the street name and number on an index card and handed it to Julia. "Be sure Wreath stops by to see me. I'd hate for her not to get her diploma over a filing error."

"She's not only counting on a diploma, but on a scholarship," Julia said and walked out in the hall, looking down at the address on the card. She knew it was not where Wreath's cousin lived.

It was the address for Durham's Fine Furnishings.

An error had not caused the missing records.

Something very strange was going on with Wreath Williams.

The front door swung open, the bells ringing loudly with the force of a hard shove.

Faye hurried from the workroom, hoping it was Wreath, who had missed work yesterday without letting her know.

A large man was silhouetted near the plate glass window, the glare making it hard to see his features.

"Hello, Mrs. Durham, how are you?" The voice was higher pitched than his size suggested, his hair was pulled back in a ridiculous tiny ponytail, his fingers covered with rings. "It's me, Fred Procell."

"Oh Fred, for heaven's sake," she said. "It's been a long time."

"I was sorry to hear about Mr. Billy," he said. "He was one of the best men I ever worked for."

One of the only men Fred ever worked for, if Faye remembered correctly. Fred had been Billy's deliveryman for about a year but had left work one day and never come back. They'd suspected he'd stolen the day's receipts, but Billy said it wasn't worth fooling with.

"I was wondering if you might need a worker around here," Fred said. "I'm looking for a job."

"Oh, I have help," Faye said. "She's. . ." Suddenly she shut up. Something about this man made her uneasy, and she didn't want to discuss Wreath. "J. D. next door fills in for me from time to time, and the Nelsons from church have been good to me."

The hulking man studied the store, as though memorizing it. Faye wondered if it were her imagination, or if his eyes lingered on the desk drawer where she kept cash, checks, and credit card receipts.

"Do you know of anyone who might be hiring?" he asked.

"No. Business is slow most places these days," she said. "You'd probably do better somewhere besides Landry."

"I've heard you're doing well here." He walked over to the clothing area. "Junkyard Couture. Do people buy this old stuff?"

"Sometimes." Faye inched toward the door. She could see J. D. on the sidewalk near the hardware store and hoped he might wander in as he so often did these days.

"Well, if you don't mind, I'll check back in with you later," Fred said. "Maybe you'll hear of something."

"Probably not." Faye did not want him to come back in the store. He was definitely a shifty-looking sort. "I don't hear much news around town anymore. You might check at the hardware store."

She felt guilty foisting him off but knew J. D. was plenty strong enough to handle him. She'd never thought about it before, but J. D.

looked quite fit for a man his age.

"Could I trouble you for a drink of water before I get going?" Fred asked, moving farther into the store as Faye walked toward the door. She couldn't think of a way to turn him down without showing her nervousness, and she didn't want him to think she was afraid of him. Which she was, although she couldn't pinpoint why.

"Water's in the back." She strode past him, leaving a wide circle between them. He seemed to notice, and something like a smirk came to his lips.

As Faye ushered him to the rear of the store, she looked over her shoulder at the clock. It was almost time for Wreath to come in, and Faye was going to do her best to keep the man from laying eyes on the girl. A sweet, pretty young woman like Wreath didn't need any contact with a man like Fred Procell.

Her eyes were as watchful as his as they moved through the showroom.

Right as they reached the rear, the back door, left unlocked during business hours since Julia had started coming over frequently, flew open. The door opened easily now, thanks to J. D. and what Wreath called his Magic Hardware Juice.

"Faye, have you seen Wreath today?" Julia asked and then stopped so fast she nearly fell over. If the moment hadn't been so tense, it would have been comical. "What's he doing here?"

Faye's eyes widened, while the man's eyes narrowed.

"Do you know this man?" Mrs. Durham asked.

"Did you say Wreath?" Fred said at the same time.

Suddenly Faye gave a hyena-like laugh, so forced it sounded like something out of a horror movie. "No, Julia, I haven't found you one of those old *wreaths* you keep hounding me for."

Turning to Fred Procell, who apparently had some connection with Julia, she gave an exasperated sigh. "You were asking me if people buy this old stuff, and my tenant here is one of those people who won't let up on collecting."

Fred's eyes moved from one woman to the other, and he looked like he was trying to decide whether to believe Faye or not. Julia's expression was a blend of consternation and indignation.

"Faye, whatever in the world. . ." The teacher's voice trailed off as Faye furrowed her brow and tried to gesture with her eyes.

Julia looked over the man's shoulder. "Is that a new lamp?" she gushed, suddenly rushing closer to the front of the store.

Trying to get close enough to whisper instructions, Faye followed. Fred strolled through the showroom, touching this item or that, stopping by the desk.

"Get J. D.," Faye hissed as softly as she could.

"Where's Wreath?" Julia asked under her breath.

The shake of Faye's head was almost imperceptible, and Fred took a step toward Julia.

"I don't believe I've seen you since Thanksgiving," the teacher said. "I didn't know you and Mrs. Durham were friends."

"I used to work here," he said. "I'm hoping she'll take me back on."

Faye looked around with feigned regret. "I told Fred that business isn't very good in Landry these days."

Julia wrinkled her face for a second and then smoothed it to give Fred what appeared to be a sympathetic look. "I'm about the only person who buys Faye's junk," she said. "She told me she might better go back to fine furniture."

The door jangled again, and Faye froze, Fred whirled around, and Julia sucked in her breath.

J. D. walked in, a potted geranium in his hands. "I brought Wreath one of those pink geraniums she was so crazy about."

Faye interrupted before he could continue. "J. D., do you know of anyone in town who's hiring? You may remember Mr. Procell here. He used to work for Billy and is looking for a job."

J. D.'s congenial look fell away, and his eyes hardened. "I remember Fred very well. I'm surprised you'd show your face around here again."

"I don't plan to be here long," Fred said, edging toward the door. "I've got a few loose ends to tie up and then I'll be heading out. Was hoping for a little work, but I'd best be going."

He pushed the door rather than pulled it, cursed, and then pulled it back against his heavy boots. Muttering, he hurried off down the street.

Faye rushed over to J. D. and threw her arms around him, nearly knocking the plant out of his hands. "I can't thank you enough for coming in when you did," she said. "That man is trouble."

"You're probably going to want to call the police," Julia said and pointed to the desk. The middle drawer was standing open, the money bag unzipped. "I think you've been robbed."

The door flew open again, and Faye hoped to see Wreath walking through, safe and sound. Instead, the boy, Law Rogers, stepped in. His gaze was full of hope as he looked around the store, but it turned to dread after a moment.

"Wreath's not here?" he asked without his usual polite greeting.

"I was hoping you had heard from her," Faye said, her heart sinking.

Law shook his head, his dark hair falling into his troubled eyes.

Faye drew a deep breath and offered a silent prayer. For a second, she thought of the quiet days when no one came in. Now she desperately wanted Wreath to walk through the door and greet the trio who had come to help.

"She wasn't in class today," Julia said. "That's why I came over in the first place. She had a big oral report to give yesterday, and she didn't show up then either. That's not like her."

"Law, have you ever met her guardian, this cousin who lives north of town?" Faye asked as the ominous air continued to grow in the room.

"No, ma'am," Law said. "Wreath said he's grouchy and doesn't like visitors. I don't think his family is all that keen on having her live with them."

"I've never laid eyes on him," Julia said.

"Neither have I," Faye said.

"This doesn't add up," Julia said. "Did you know she listed the store as her home address?"

"I know she's been getting mail here," Faye said. "This came today." She held up a large manila packet, addressed to Wreath Williams. The return address included the logo of a nearby community college. "She's gotten two or three others the past several weeks."

Julia put her hand on her forehead. "She wants to go to college so badly," she said. "We have to help her."

"We need to look for her," J. D. said.

Law headed for the door. "I don't have a good feeling about this," he said.

❊ Chapter 35 ❊

Wreath walked to the edge of the woods, as far from her campsite as her weak legs would carry her, and threw up.

With her ragged blanket around her shoulders, she stumbled back to the Tiger Van. She wasn't sure how much school she'd missed and hoped she could make up the class work. She hoped things were good at the store. Her throat burned, her head ached, and even her skin hurt. She wondered if this was the way Frankie had felt right before she died.

Pulling herself up into the van, she barely managed to close the door and lie down on the hard floor, thankful for the carpet as she shivered. She heard the sound of a male voice calling her name from a long way off and thought she must be delirious.

"Wreath! Where are you?"

Sitting up, the gold-and-black-striped carpet spun around her, and she put her palms on the van floor to steady herself.

"Answer me," the voice called. "One way or the other, I'm going to find you."

Wreath groaned and pulled the blanket over her head. He had no way of knowing where she was. Maybe he would go away.

She drifted back off to sleep.

The sound of the van door roused her, and she propped herself on her elbows, blinking. The outside light hid her visitor's face.

"Wreath! Are you okay?" Law crawled through the middle of the bucket seats and into the back where she was. "Can you hear me?"

"Of course I can hear you. Did you bring my assignments?"

The boy gave a hoarse laugh. "Do you know how worried we've been about you? I've got to get you to a doctor."

"No doctors." Wreath feebly pushed on his chest. "I'm not sick enough for a doctor. No money. . ." Her voice trailed off. She looked at him, the picture of health and vigor, squatting there, and felt the first dose of hope she'd had since he'd dropped her off Sunday evening.

"What time is it?" she asked, squinting at her watch. "What day is it, for that matter?"

"It's Tuesday night, and you've got half the town in an uproar. Why didn't you call one of us?"

"No phone," she said. Short sentences seemed to be all her brain could form at the moment.

"When was the last time you had anything to eat?"

"No food."

"You don't have any food." Law looked around. "You've been starving yourself."

"No." She doubted she sounded as indignant as she wanted to. "I have food but can't eat." She remembered the trips to the edge of the woods. "Ugh. No food."

"You must be dehydrated," he said. "Let me get you some water."

Again he looked around, as though trying to figure out where her kitchen was in the darkness.

"There's a jug on the front seat," she said, suddenly realizing her tongue felt like it was covered with one of the fake fur coats in the boutique. "Please."

Holding a cup to her lips, Law brushed her hair off her face, and Wreath tried to pull away. "I must look horrible," she said.

"I can't lie to you." He tried for a smile, which came out lopsided. "You look rotten. How do you feel?"

"About like I look," she said.

"Do you think it's the flu? That's going around at school." He felt her forehead and then took her pulse, which raced with his presence. "You don't seem to have fever."

"I'm better today. For the first time since I saw you Sunday, I feel like I might actually live."

"Did your cousin kick you out when you got sick?"

"My cousin? What?" Her head still felt fuzzy.

"Why are you sleeping in this van? I don't understand. Why didn't you come to us for help? We're your friends. Mrs. Durham and Miss Watson are worried about you. Mr. J. D., too. They have the police looking for you."

Immediately Wreath's head cleared. "The police! They called the police because I have the flu?"

"They didn't know what happened to you. You didn't show up for school or work. A man came to the school looking for you."

"Who?" she whispered, dismayed at how little energy she had.

"Some big guy who used to work at Durham's. He went by there supposedly looking for a job. He emptied the cash drawer at the store and left."

The flu paled at the reality of Law's visit, and the information he piled on her. "He must be one of Frankie's relatives or something. I've got to get out of here," she said, half stumbling, half crawling to the front seat.

She pushed hard on the door and nearly tumbled out into the junkyard. But the campsite looked ordinary, no swarms of people, no strange man.

In recent days, spring had started to come, and the woods smelled fresh and welcoming. The air was cool, but it lacked the brittle feel of winter, and a clump of small flowers bloomed over near an old pickup.

Suddenly her legs felt rubbery again, and she sank down into her one chair. "I'm sorry I don't have a place for you to sit," she said to Law, who was looking around like he'd never seen a wrecked car before. She saw his eyes move from the clothesline to the ashes from her campfire to her bird feeder hanging in a nearby tree. He even looked at the pictures on the dash of the van, visible through the open door.

After what seemed like an hour of surveying the junkyard, he turned to Wreath, who had stretched her legs out and laid her head back on the chair, liking the feel of the fresh air on her face.

"No wonder we couldn't find your house," Law said. "Do you even have a cousin?"

"Maybe somewhere," Wreath said.

"But they don't live anywhere near Landry, do they?"

She thought for an instant about trying to keep the lie going but didn't have the strength. She sighed and shook her head. "I don't actually have any cousins."

Law looked around again. "So you've been living here, in a

junkyard, all this time?"

"'Fraid so. How'd you find me?"

"You didn't make it easy, that's for sure. I retraced our steps, thought of every hint you'd ever dropped, and made one of your famous lists." He pulled a piece of paper out of his pocket. "I spent two hours riding around with Miss Watson. We couldn't find anyone on the road where you supposedly lived who even knew your name."

Wreath groaned.

"Miss Watson's boyfriend, that deputy guy, is looking for you, too, and Mrs. Durham and Mr. J. D. They left their stores the minute they figured out something was wrong and tackled some of the neighborhoods around school."

"Oh no," Wreath said, her head in her lap.

"When Miss Watson and I didn't get anywhere, I got her to drop me off on that road." He pointed toward the highway. "She's gone to meet Shane to get more help."

Law reached out and touched Wreath's dirty hair. "You scared me so badly, Wreath. I kept playing our conversation Sunday night over and over in my head, and I finally gave up and prayed."

"You prayed for me?"

"Yep," he said. "I asked God to watch over you and to help me find you. Then it dawned on me that unless you had been vaporized, you had to be somewhere in the junkyard. It was the only place we hadn't looked."

He held up his arm, brandishing a long scratch. "I came through the woods. This place is huge."

"Tell me about it." She couldn't keep from smiling.

He knelt on the ground in front of her chair and grabbed both of her hands. "You're amazing, did you know that?"

She shook her head.

"Amazing and possibly a little crazy."

"More than a little," she said. "You should hear this place at night."

"You're the bravest girl I ever met, but why? Why, Wreath? Why not let someone help you?"

"I didn't know who to trust, and I want to finish high school." She started to cry softly. "I've got to get my work done, but I don't feel so hot."

She stumbled to her feet and walked around the van, out of sight, to throw up again.

Law rushed around the corner and wiped her face with the corner of his shirt. "Let me take you somewhere. To my grandparents' house? Or to Mrs. Durham's?"

Wreath sagged against him. "On one condition."

"Name it," he said.

"You can't tell anyone where I live."

"That's impossible," he said. "You can't keep staying out here."

"I'm staying here until I finish high school. If you can't keep that secret, I'm not going with you. I'll leave Landry."

"I won't do that, Wreath." He looked around. "This is dangerous. It's a miracle that no one has bothered you out here already. An absolute miracle."

Wreath covered her face with her hands, speaking through her fingers. "I won't go with you then," she said. "This is my home. This is where I live."

"You mean that, don't you?"

She jerked her head in a nod.

Law took her fingers from her face. "Do you promise you'll stay with someone until you're well?"

"I promise."

"Are you sure you won't move into town? Maybe stay with someone till you graduate?"

She shook her head. "It's the way you feel about staying with your mother, instead of taking the easier way with your grandparents. I can't explain it, but I've got to do this on my own."

"I don't like it," Law said. "Please let someone help you."

Wreath's voice quivered. "I only need three more months. Please, Law. I know you understand."

He sighed. "I won't tell people you live here, but I have two conditions of my own."

"I've already given you my word, that I'd stay with Faye."

"That's not my condition," he said. "You have to promise me that you'll come to me if you're ever in trouble again."

Wreath looked at him. "I promise."

Law looked into her eyes, as though trying to see if she was lying, and she squirmed and spoke.

"You'll be the first person I come to if I have a problem." She did not take her gaze from his. "What's your second condition?"

"Agree to go to senior prom," he said with a tiny smile.

She put the back of her hand on her forehead. "I think I'm feverish again."

"Is that a yes?"

"A most definite yes," she said.

"Let's get you out of here," he said, picking up her pack. "We've got to put Mrs. Durham out of her misery. She's more shaken up than she was when her husband died."

❋ Chapter 36 ❋

For the first time in her life, Wreath was waited on hand and foot.
When Wreath and Law emerged from the woods, Mitch's car waited near the school bus stop. He was walking back from investigating another trail and came out of the woods as they did. He galloped back to his vehicle with a loud whoop and a big, questioning smile as he saw them.

Wreath saw Law give Mitch a small shake of the head, and Mitch didn't ask anything. He just gave Wreath a tight hug and tucked her into the front seat and told her about ten times how glad he was that she'd been found.

"You don't look so hot," he said with a smile.

"That's the same thing you said the last time you saw me," she said.

"We need to get you some help," Mitch said, a surprisingly tender note in his voice. Wreath couldn't believe she used to think he was a snotty rich kid. He and Law stood just out of earshot and whispered for a few moments, and Wreath wondered if her secret would come out, no matter what promises had been made.

Mitch used his cell phone to let the others know Wreath was safe, but other than that the three had little conversation during the drive to Faye's, with the boys looking at Wreath and asking her repeatedly if she was sure she was all right.

Faye, Julia, and J. D. were sitting at the kitchen table drinking hot tea when Wreath tapped on the door and slipped in.

Faye leapt to her feet. "Oh, my darling girl," she exclaimed and swept Wreath into a hug. "Oh, thank You, Lord."

"Thank goodness," Julia said, moving next to Wreath. "Are you all right?"

"I think so," Wreath said.

"I need to call Shane and confirm that you're safe and sound," Julia said, pulling her telephone from her pocket and moving into the den.

Wreath clutched the edge of the counter.

"How is she?" J. D. said to Law, as though Wreath weren't in the room.

"She's a little worse for the wear, and she hopes Mrs. Durham will let her stay here for a few days. She didn't have any way to call to let us know she was sick."

"I was so afraid that horrible man had snatched you," Faye said, her hand trembling as she touched Wreath's face. "You're so pale."

"I'm sorry I scared you," Wreath said. "I should have figured out a way to get in touch."

"Do we need to take her to the emergency room?" J. D. seemed to be asking himself the question as much as asking the others.

"I hate hospitals," Wreath said, shaking her head. "I'm getting better."

"Let's get you in bed, and I'll make chicken soup," Faye said. "J. D., do you think you could. . ."

Without another word, the man picked Wreath up as though she were a small child and carried her into the guest room. His gaze was so intense that Wreath closed her eyes until she felt the soft mattress.

Faye pulled a warm blanket up around Wreath's shoulders and wiped her face with a cool cloth.

"We'll get this sorted out," J. D. said, but Wreath was so drowsy and secure that for once she didn't try to figure out what he meant.

Law and Mitch said their good-byes from the hall, immediately banned from the sickroom.

"Don't forget to pick up my assignments," Wreath said, already sounding stronger.

Julia, who stood just inside the guest room, chuckled. "We'll take care of that, Wreath. Don't fret about it."

"I've got to get my grades up," Wreath murmured.

"You mustn't worry about that now," Faye said, tugging on Julia's arm.

The two women followed Law and Mitch to the back door. "Thank you for bringing Wreath here," Faye said, patting both the boys on their backs as though they were small children. "Thank you, Julia, for everything. We can find out more later."

"I hate to leave her, but I suppose I'd better go, too," Julia said. "I'll let the other teachers know."

"You let them know I intend to do battle with anyone who tries to lower Wreath's grades because of her absence," Faye said. "Clearly Wreath is quite ill."

"I'm with you on that," Julia said. "And Shane said to tell you that they're doing everything they can to find Fred Procell."

Faye stepped forward and hugged Julia. "Be safe," she said.

Law and Mitch started to follow Julia out to the car, but Faye took Law by the arm, holding him back as Mitch stepped onto the carport. "What did her cousin say when you picked her up?" Faye asked.

The teenager fidgeted and seemed to be looking everywhere but at her. "He didn't have anything to say. Wreath thought she'd be more comfortable here for a few days."

"I see." Faye didn't think Law was the kind of boy to lie, but his answer sounded vague.

J. D., who had been sitting on the sofa, joined them at the door. "You said a man asked about her at school, correct?"

"Yes, sir," Law said.

"Do you think that the man who was looking for her at school was the same man who came into Faye's store?" J. D. asked.

"No doubt," Law replied.

"Did Wreath give you any idea about who he was?" Faye said.

Law shook his head. "She didn't act like she knew anyone who used to work at Durham's, but she was super freaked out that he'd asked about her."

"What about Fred Procell? Did that ring a bell with her?" J. D. asked.

"She was so sick that I didn't mention that. I mostly helped her gather a few things and got Mitch to bring us here. We didn't talk much."

"Good job, young man," J. D. said, closing the door behind him.

After checking on Wreath, who was in the stage between wakefulness and sleep, Faye started a pot of homemade chicken soup.

"She may not be able to keep this down right away, but I want to have it ready when she wants it."

"That smells great," J. D. said.

"There'll be plenty for us to have for a late supper, if you can stay." She felt her face getting hot, as though she had leaned too far over the pot of boiling chicken. "Or you can take it home with you."

"I'd like to stay," he said. "There's probably a better time to say this, but I've wanted to have dinner with you for months."

Faye dropped the lid off the stockpot, and it clattered on the gold Formica countertop. "We eat meals together all the time. Our Sunday school class had dinner together four nights ago."

"I want to ask you out on a date, but you don't make it easy," J. D. said.

Faye turned to chop two carrots, dicing them with the precision of a samurai warrior. She swept them into the boiling broth with a swift motion, her mind more on Wreath than J. D. She was relieved to have the child back under her roof.

Her life had a purpose that had been missing since Billy died. She looked through the steam from the pan at J. D. And a joy, now that she thought about it.

"Did you say a date?" she asked.

"Yes, a date," J. D. said. "Is it that outlandish? I haven't been on a date in many a moon, but I don't recall women looking quite that incredulous."

"You had your Lynn and I had Billy," she said. "Going out with you seems. . .odd. Do people our age *date*?"

"Beats me," he said. "If it makes you uncomfortable, I'll step away. I don't want to ruin our friendship, nor dishonor the memories of Billy or Lynn. But they're gone. That doesn't mean we forget them, but life goes on."

Faye pivoted to face the handsome man sitting on her kitchen stool. "I'd be delighted to go out to dinner with you sometime."

"How about Saturday night?"

"That quickly? I'll have to see," she said. "I may not be able to leave Wreath."

"There's no rush," he said, looking toward the end of the house where Wreath rested. "We both want to make sure she's well."

"I think Wreath's on the mend," Faye said, stirring the broth. "But there are so many questions."

"Yes," J. D. said quietly. "There are."

Wreath awoke the next morning hungry and weak. She couldn't recall where she was and thought Frankie had checked on her during the night.

Then she remembered Faye slipping in and out and recognized the lace curtains on the window.

"You feeling better, sleepyhead?" Mrs. Durham appeared as though magically summoned.

"I think so." Wreath's tongue felt thick, but her legs didn't feel quite so boneless.

"Let me get you a glass of water, and we can talk about what sounds good to your stomach. You slept right through supper."

Wreath wound up having chicken soup for breakfast, but Faye only let her eat a small amount with three plain crackers. "We don't want to push it," the woman said, fussing over her like she'd been near death.

"I've never had homemade chicken soup before," Wreath said. "This is delicious."

Faye tilted her head. "What did your mother fix for you when you were sick?"

Wreath pondered the question. "I don't think I've ever been sick before. I did get Popsicles once when I had a runny nose."

"I hope you never get sick again," Faye said. "You gave me quite a scare when you didn't show up for work."

"How's the store doing? Any sales?"

"That couple from Lafayette came in and bought that chair you found in the attic and ordered a new duvet cover, curtains, and a shower curtain."

"Wow. Did you price everything for a good profit?"

Faye gave a little laugh. "I'd say we came out all right. I put your share in your bonus pool. It's at the office—hidden. I won't ever leave our cash in an unlocked drawer again."

Wreath bowed her head. "Do we need to talk about what happened?" she asked. "About that man who. . ."

"Not now," Faye interrupted, her voice almost as firm as it had been when Wreath started work. "The police are looking for him. There'll be plenty of time to sort things out."

"Whew," Wreath said, relieved.

"What's wrong? Are you sick? Do you need the trash can?"

"No, I need a shower." Wreath wrinkled her nose. "I'm surprised you let me sleep inside. I smell awful. What I'd really like is a hot shower."

"I've put shampoo and conditioner in your bathroom." Faye beamed. "And pajamas and a robe in that closet."

"Thank you," Wreath whispered.

When she opened the chest of drawers, she found a new hairbrush and toothbrush, an assortment of lotions, T-shirts, and underwear and a brand-new pair of pajamas and monogrammed robe.

When she came out into the den, Faye was dressed for work, and Wreath shyly gave her a hug. "Thank you for all the new things," she said. "I feel like I'm at a fancy hotel."

Faye laughed, a loud, unexpected sound. "You *are* feeling better, aren't you?"

"Who wouldn't be with all those gifts?"

"You deserve them."

"Do you want me to come in to work today?" Wreath asked.

"Definitely not!" Faye said. "You are banned from work until you're one hundred percent well."

"Thanks." Wreath choked up as she spoke. She missed her job but was tired from the effort of showering and dressing and didn't have the strength to go to work . . . or worry about the stranger.

"Call if you need anything, and I mean anything," Faye said. "And don't unlock the door unless it's me or one of your other friends."

Friends. The word had healing power.

Dear Brownie, Wreath wrote in her journal for the first time in days, *I got sick, and so many people took care of me. I am very thankful.*

***

When Faye got to work, she wasn't surprised to see J. D. in front of his store, reading. He was an early riser, and he spent his free time with a book in hand.

"How's the patient?" he asked, standing back a few feet farther than usual.

"On the mend, but still peaked."

He stepped back another foot or two. "Thank goodness."

Faye moved toward him. He moved back. "Is it my imagination, or are you rethinking asking me out on a date?" she teased.

His look was serious. "It's not that at all."

She walked over and stuck the key in the door, trying to act as though her heart wasn't racing. "Then what is it?"

J. D. spoke as the heavy door swung open. "I think Wreath may be my granddaughter."

Faye staggered into the store, J. D. walking in behind her.

"Why would you even say such a thing?" she asked, whirling to look at him.

"Wreath needs help," he said. His usual easygoing expression was markedly absent.

"Of course she needs help," she said, "but that doesn't mean you need to rescue her." *Could it possibly be true?*

"I have to rescue her," he said. "There's a chance I'm the only relative Wreath has left."

"Where did this come from?" Faye asked, trying to piece together hints she might have overlooked.

"I've always suspected John David's girlfriend might have been pregnant when he was killed. The girl and her mother left town right before the funeral, and I never heard from her again. Things were a blur for me for a long time, and I tried not to think about John David. It hurt too much."

"But Wreath?" Faye said, looking at the range of emotions moving across J. D.'s face.

"This is probably all wishful thinking on my part," J. D. said. "But to have a chance to help John David's child. . . What if it's true, and my own granddaughter is here, in my life?"

"It doesn't seem likely," Faye said. "But something drew her to Landry."

"There are a lot of coincidences. . .similarities," he said. "I've tried not to notice them, but looking at Wreath is like catching a glimpse of my son. It's uncanny how her expressions favor his."

Faye's heart turned over. "You know I've been trying to figure out how to get to the bottom of Wreath's secrets. Why haven't you told me this before?"

J. D. hung his head. "I care for you, Faye, and I care for the girl. I didn't want to mention it until I knew more. But with her missing and sick, I couldn't stand it any longer."

"I don't want to go behind her back," Faye said. "She's so independent that if we take the wrong approach, she might up and run."

"John David was like that. From the time he could walk, he wanted to do everything for himself."

Having a hard time pulling her thoughts together, Faye motioned toward two matching recliners, one draped with a furry throw she had made. A vase of greenery sat on a dark Mediterranean-style table, next to a stack of design magazines, fanned out, and a heavy glass dish with a few pieces of candy in it.

J. D. sank into one chair and Faye eased into the other. For a moment, she felt like they were an old married couple and wished Wreath could be her granddaughter, *their* granddaughter.

"Do you remember John David's girlfriend's name?" she asked after a moment. "Was her last name Williams?"

He shook his head. "John David's girl was a Willis."

"The names are close enough. Perhaps Wreath's mother changed her name, or married someone else."

"Wreath could have a whole family out there looking for her," J. D. said. "I'm trying to bring a piece of my son back."

"Do you remember the girlfriend's first name?" Faye asked, afraid to get their hopes up, yet longing for this to be one of the answers for Wreath's future.

"Her name was Frances," J. D. said. "But John David called her Frankie. I tried to track her down a time or two through the years, but she moved around a lot after she left Landry. I decided I was being foolish and quit trying."

Faye could barely take in what J. D. was saying, her ears ringing with the name Frankie. "Oh my" was all she could manage to say at first. Then she was adamant. "We cannot stir things up for Wreath until she's stronger."

Never in Faye's life, not even when Billy had died, had she been so tied up in knots.

On one hand, she was thrilled beyond belief that Wreath could have an honest and good man like J. D. to look after her. On the other, she feared Wreath wouldn't be able to fathom why her father's family had abandoned her for all these years.

When Faye remembered the thin girl who first stepped into the store in need of a bicycle, an almost physical pain shot through her. All that time, a family and someone who cared had been only a few yards away.

Piecing the puzzle together made it all look so obvious. At times she had seen a similar expression on the faces of the man and the girl and not quite been able to place it. The two were both voracious readers, and they kidded each other constantly about what the other was reading. Wreath was never without her journal, and J. D. carried a small notebook in his shirt pocket, jotting down one list after another.

They even had the same nose.

But Faye didn't know whether the teenager would be thrilled by the revelation or brokenhearted, whether it would stir up questions and issues best left undisturbed or bring a new wave of joy. She could not bear to see the girl hurt, even if it meant she never knew her father's family, and insisted they not tell Wreath until they were completely certain.

"We simply cannot bring this up without more to go on," Faye said on their first supper date, a few nights after their conversation at the store. "She's just now beginning to get over the death of her mother."

"I'm concerned, too," J. D. said. "Have you heard anything more about this cousin she's living with?"

"Not a word," Faye said. "It's as though he doesn't exist."

"What if she rejects me?" J. D. said. "Or hates me for leaving her and her mother on their own all this time? Clearly she and her mother did not have much going for them."

"They had each other, and that mattered a lot to Wreath." Faye laid her hand on his. "Frankie told her that her father was a good boy, that they were kids when they met, and he was killed."

"My mind keeps thinking of the ways this might affect her, and about half of those aren't great."

"You won't know unless you tell her," Faye said.

"I'm afraid to tell her."

"We need to wait until the time is right," Faye said. "I couldn't love that child more if she was my own flesh and blood, and I won't have her hurt. To top it off, she's worried about college."

"I want to help her with that. I have more than enough money stuck back," he said.

"Wreath's not much for taking money from others, and she's about as stubborn as anyone I've ever seen. I'm not sure she'll accept your help."

J. D. paused. "John David's mother said he had the personality of a mule, and she blamed that on my side of the family."

"Maybe you should hold off for a while and see what happens."

"As long as you're convinced Wreath's not in harm's way," he said. "No one—and I do mean no one—will hurt that girl if I have anything to say about it."

A week after her bout with the flu, Wreath confirmed her acceptance into a community college up in Alexandria, buying a money order for her deposit.

"It'll be okay," she told Julia while doing makeup work at lunch. "It's not exactly what I dreamed of, but it's a start."

"At least you'll be close to Landry," Julia said.

Wreath grinned and tried to overcome her disappointment at not making an A-level university. "That's what Faye said, too."

"Wreath. . ." The sound in Julia's voice caused a knot in her stomach. "Is all of your paperwork cleared up for graduation?"

"Sure." Wreath closed the textbook and stood. "I think I'm done with this. And my project was satisfactory, right?"

"Your project was outstanding, as always," Julia said, but the look on her face didn't match her words.

Wreath grabbed her pack and hurried to the door, but her teacher spoke again before she could escape. "Sometimes transfer students have loose ends to tie up. Be sure to check in with the counselor."

"Will do," Wreath said and headed toward the cafeteria, checking her watch and wondering how she could clear up the mess she was in.

Law, Mitch, and Destiny were nearly finished with lunch when she slid into a cafeteria chair at their table.

"What's up?" Law asked. "You look worried."

"Nothing," Wreath said, fumbling to get an apple out of her pack. "There's just a lot going on."

"Does it have something to do with Aunt Faye?" Mitch asked.

Wreath threw him an exasperated look. "Of course not," she said and then glanced at Law. "She didn't want me to move back in with my cousin, but she's all right with it."

"My dad thinks Aunt Faye's up to something," Mitch continued. "He says she's as jumpy as a cat in a room full of rocking chairs."

Wreath laughed, but a butterfly flitted through her stomach. "I think she's falling for J. D. They spend a lot more time talking lately."

Wreath had moved back to the Rusted Estates after only a week at Faye's house, much to the woman's dismay, but reassured Faye that she would stay every weekend with her and keep going to church. Law had kept his word and not told anyone that she lived at the junkyard.

"That doesn't mean I have to like it," he'd said when Wreath came back to school. "Are you sure you're safe out there? Miss Watson said they haven't found that Procell guy yet."

"I'm safer out there than I'd be in a metropolitan area," she said with a laugh. "I have a baseball bat that will keep all varmints away."

She set her traps each day and settled easily back into her routine, her legs strengthening again on the bike rides into town. In the evenings in the Tiger Van, she read and reread the junior college catalog and filled out more paperwork.

She was still neck and neck with Law in the senior class standings, and Wreath had begun to believe that maybe God did have a plan for her life after all.

❧ Chapter 37 ❧

Faye and Julia teased Wreath about "The Great Prom Project" when April arrived.

Confident she'd find a used dress, she had decided to scrimp on her outfit but splurge on extras for the evening with Law, digging up one can of her savings. *Dear Brownie*, she wrote in her diary, *I'll never be a senior again, and I want this to be special*.

Her prom list included choosing a dress (*TEAL or AQUA!!!*), finding killer shoes, and deciding whether she wanted to put her hair up or not. She asked Julia and Faye for opinions on where to get her hair done and what color her nails should be. She experimented with an expensive tooth-whitening paste from the drugstore and frequented the thrift shop in search of the perfect dress and matching pair of shoes.

As the days passed and no dress appeared, she repeated her strict instructions to Faye to be on the lookout at garage sales. "It needs good lines and a soft fabric," Wreath said. "I'm hoping for something in green or blue, maybe black, but only if it doesn't look like a funeral dress."

"We'll find you one," Faye said. "If we don't, we'll drive to Lafayette, and I'll buy you a new one."

Wreath shook her head. "I want to look pretty, but I don't want to waste money on a dress. The school applications cost more than I expected, and I'm trying to save more money for moving to college."

Julia had gotten into the prom spirit, too, and signed on as one of the chief faculty sponsors and chaperones. "I haven't gotten involved in school activities before," she said at the store one afternoon. "Now's the time."

Wreath clapped her hands and did one of her happy hops. "I'm so glad," she said. "It'll be more fun having you there."

"How about Shane?" Faye asked. "Will he be wearing a tux that night?"

"Unfortunately, he's on duty the entire evening. He did promise to stop by and check out my dress."

"You've already got a dress?" Wreath whined. "I can't find one."

"Not yet, but I'm thinking about it."

Wreath's excitement about the prom and graduation spilled over into her enthusiasm for the store, and she came up with a long list of possible rooms to put together. "I have a new idea for the window," she told Faye, rushing in from school. "Let's do a prom thing, featuring clothes and furniture from the fifties."

Then another idea hit her. "We can offer to let girls who buy dresses here have their picture taken in the store displays, wearing their dresses." Wreath, generally fairly calm, buzzed around the store, framing imaginary pictures. She even dashed to the sidewalk to see how the idea could work from outside.

Faye followed with a bemused look. "You have a talent for this, Wreath. This could be your best idea yet."

"Maybe the school yearbook will publish some of them. Think of the publicity for Junkyard Couture," Wreath said. She had her journal in hand and stood sketching ideas, Faye looking over her shoulder.

"You ladies casing the place?" J. D. asked, wandering over from the hardware store. His voice had a gentle quality.

"Wreath's coming up with those marketing ideas she's so good at," Faye said. "She's making one of her famous lists."

"I like to write things down," she said to J. D. as he looked down at her notebook. "What do you think about this look?"

The man laid his hand on her shoulder as he peered at her drawing. "That's imaginative," he said. "Where'd you get that artistic talent?"

Wreath shrugged. "From my father, I guess. Frankie—my mama, that is—said I sure didn't get it from her."

"So your parents passed away?" he said.

"Yes, sir," Wreath said, moving back toward the store, not wanting to mar her excitement with thoughts of Frankie. "If you'll excuse me, I need to finish this up before closing time."

"I shouldn't tell her yet, should I?" J. D. said to Faye.

"I don't think so," Faye said, taking both his hands in hers. "Let her have the joy of prom before we blow up her life again."

Julia threw her artistic energy into the Durham's Fine Furnishing prom window design, laughing as she and Wreath sketched and experimented.

One day she arrived at the back door carrying three huge canvases, an old-fashioned ball gown painted in a pastel color on each canvas. "We've been hoping you'd let us display your art sometime," Wreath exclaimed. "We can hang one in the boutique, one in the new prom parlor I'm putting together, and one in the window."

"Just what I hoped," Julia said.

Excited by Wreath's quest for an old dress, Julia had called her father, who dug around in the attic and shipped her senior prom dress to the store. She ripped into a box covered with brown paper and tied with twine and pulled it out in front of Wreath and Faye. A beautiful plum color, it had spaghetti straps and a small ruffle around the neck and hem. "You can wear it if you want," she offered, holding it out.

Wreath fingered the soft fabric even while she shook her head. "It looks just like you," Wreath said. "You have to wear it."

"I want you to wear it, though."

"No," the store owner said to Julia. "Wreath's right. That dress was made for you."

"I hope I can still fit into it."

"All that running has to be good for something," Faye said. "Try it on, and we'll see if I need to do any alterations."

The girl and the older woman drew in their breath when Julia walked out of the workroom, gliding like a glamorous model.

"That is stunning," Faye said.

"I would laugh at the looks on your faces," Julia said, "but I'm afraid I'd tear a seam."

Within minutes Faye was seated on the floor with her old red pincushion shaped like a tomato. She pinned here and basted there, mumbling to herself about nips and tucks.

"Stand still," she said, the words garbled by a host of pins in her mouth.

"Aye, aye, Captain," Julia said with a salute and then winced when a pin poked her. "You did that on purpose," she said.

"I most certainly did not," Faye said, and Wreath laughed.

❀

Wreath felt as though she had gotten on a tall slide at the park and started down before she was quite ready. With homework a priority, college plans gradually settling, and work at the store, she was constantly busy.

Nearly every girl in the senior class had come by to look at the store's Junkyard Couture collection of party dresses. Faye had updated some, with touches suggested by Wreath, and the result was an amazing array, lacking in only one thing. The perfect dress for Wreath.

One afternoon Faye was at her desk assembling a box in the purple and gold colors of Landry High when Wreath came in from school.

"So you decided to come back," Faye called out automatically when the bell sounded.

"Couldn't stay away," Wreath said.

"What'd you learn today?"

"That my boss is holding out on me."

Faye's mouth fell open for a moment. "What?"

"Miss Watson told me about your marketing ideas," Wreath said.

Faye exhaled. "Oh, you're talking about my prom-shopping box."

"What'd you think I meant?" Wreath asked, plopping down next to her.

"Nothing." She held up a brown box with a pink ribbon. "*Voilà!* Open it and see what you think."

Inside were a tube of lip gloss, a small piece of high-end chocolate, and a packet of tissues with fancy high-heel shoes printed on them.

"Let's give the prom shoppers the red-carpet treatment," Faye said, "including punch and cookies and a box of favors. The shopping experience can be like a party."

"I love that idea," Wreath said. "How'd you think of that?"

"I've been doing research myself," Faye said with a smile.

Wreath couldn't resist and threw her arms around Faye's neck. "We need a sign on the highway," she said. "We're about to go big-time!"

❋ Chapter 38 ❋

Between a billboard hastily designed by Julia and Wreath and word of mouth, the store exploded with customers.

Students, best friends, and moms from all over the region oohed and aahed over dresses, sipped punch, and nibbled on cookies while declaring they had to watch their diets. They bought dresses by the shopping sack full, gearing up for proms at every high school in the area.

Grandmothers began to tag along, too, putting their feet up and sipping Faye's new blend of tea, often leaving with a custom-ordered designer pillow or one of the pricey candles that she had ordered wholesale.

Faye paid off a line of credit Billy had carried for years and opened a savings account in which she deposited regular amounts for tuition without telling Wreath.

Through all the busyness, she and Wreath bought leftover belongings from others, needing more and more merchandise to keep up with the demand, visiting house after house in Landry's old neighborhoods. They had started getting phone calls from people with merchandise to sell, and Faye recruited Julia to watch the store in late afternoons so they could check out potential goods.

"These people heard about us from a neighbor," Faye told Wreath one afternoon as they drove to a worn neighborhood to look over the contents of a house. "The owner is moving to an independent living center and wants to get rid of a lot of furniture. "I do believe we're developing a bit of a reputation as junk lovers."

"We're called pickers," Wreath said matter-of-factly. "I looked it up at school."

"I suppose I've been called worse," Faye said and punched the gas on the old car. "Although technically I believe pickers are people you hire to do the dirty work for you."

Wreath cast a sideways glance.

"I keep telling you that I'm doing my research, too," Faye said with a smile and turned the big car onto the street where the house sat. She even drove differently these days, faster, with more confidence. She had begun to imagine herself in a sports car instead of the gigantic model.

When they pulled up next to the curb, Wreath visibly stiffened, and Faye's lighthearted mood shifted. "You're awfully quiet all of a sudden. You're not having a relapse, are you?" Ever since Wreath had gotten sick, Faye hovered over her. She regularly served her fruit juice and lectured her about getting enough rest.

"I'm all right," Wreath said, "but I think I'll wait in the car."

"You're sick again, aren't you?" Faye touched her forehead. "You're clammy. I'm taking you home. I can reschedule this anytime."

Wreath drew a deep breath. "I'm not sick, but I can't decide if I want to go in this house or not." She paused long enough for Faye to look puzzled. "It's where my mother grew up."

"Oh, Wreath, this must be so hard for you," Faye said. "Why don't I take you to my house, and I'll come back."

But Wreath was already climbing out of the car. "Maybe seeing it can help me learn more about Frankie and my grandmother. Besides, I don't trust you to buy the right pieces from the owners." She offered a small smile and reached for Faye's hand. "Let's get this over with."

While Faye dealt with the owner and the owner's daughter, Wreath wandered through the rooms, touching the walls and trying to sense her mother's presence. She had intended to come over here since arriving in Landry, but every time she started by, her heart got that heavy sick feeling. She'd turned back at least five times before deciding she didn't need the grief.

"I miss you, Frankie," she whispered when she walked into the bedroom that she guessed would have been where her mother slept.

From where she stood, she could hear the elderly owner's daughter apologizing to Faye for the clutter. "People say your store has cute things," the daughter said. "I hope this isn't too junky for you. There's even a box or two left from the former owners on the closet shelf in that bedroom."

"You don't mean it," Faye said in what Wreath thought of as her bargaining voice. "We'll take a look at all you've got."

"Those boxes were up in the attic when Mother moved in, and she stuck them in the closet, thinking the people would come back," the daughter said. "Apparently those folks left town in a hurry."

"You never know what you'll find lying around," Faye said. Wreath felt like she was about to crawl out of her skin as she listened to their conversation, and she couldn't keep her eyes from darting to the closet.

"Let me know if you have any questions," the woman said. "I'll be with my mother in the living room."

Faye entered the bedroom at about the same time that Wreath pulled the first of the boxes down. "Don't get your hopes too high," she said quietly. She touched the small of Wreath's back, as Frankie had done sometimes at night. "We don't know if someone else lived here between your mother and the current owner."

But Wreath was already opening the box. It contained one dingy pillowcase, a set of unfamiliar chipped grocery-store dishes, and a set of ragged pillow towels. She sighed, despising the musty smell.

"You're right, Faye. I should have known Grandma wouldn't have left anything here."

Before Faye could reply, the owner of the house walked into the room. Her cane thumped on the hardwood floor.

"Don't like what you see?" the old woman asked, her eyes moving from Faye's face to Wreath's.

"We'll purchase the kitchen items and most of the furniture," Faye said quickly. "I believe I'll come back tomorrow and go through the rest, if that works for you."

The woman nodded but spoke to Wreath. "Would you mind getting that other box down?" she asked. "I've lived in this house for nearly eighteen years, and I've never even looked in there. I reckon it'll have to go out on the street."

Wreath stretched on her tiptoes and finagled the box from the back corner. As she placed it on the floor, she saw it was labeled MY STUFF. She turned to Faye. "Should I look at it?" she whispered.

"I doubt you'll be able to sleep tonight if you don't," Faye said. Her face reflected Wreath's anxiety.

"Do whatever you want with it," the home owner said and headed for the door. "I'm just glad to have that closet empty. All this stuff has to go."

Settling onto the floor, her legs crossed, Wreath peeled brittle masking tape off the top. Faye sat on the edge of the bed. Layer by layer, Wreath pulled artifacts from the box: a Landry High yearbook with an unfamiliar name inside the cover and a few silly handwritten messages in the front and back, a stuffed animal whose fur reminded Wreath of the carpet in the Tiger Van, and a school picture of a boy. "I wonder who he was?" she murmured.

Finally, Wreath pulled out a dried corsage, the flower's odor stale and sweet. She held it briefly against her cheek, squeezing her eyes shut. "I wanted this to be something of Frankie's," she said. "But it's not."

"I suppose it could be," Faye said.

"No," Wreath said firmly and pulled out the small card that had been wedged in the corner of the box. She held it up like an exhibit in a courtroom. "This is not my mother's name. Not my grandma's, either."

"I'm sorry, Wreath." Faye stood as she spoke. She wore a solemn expression.

"How stupid was I to think this could be Frankie's stuff," Wreath said, kicking the box. "This is just anonymous junk, the kinds of things we buy every day for the store. They mean nothing! Nothing!"

"I know it hurts," Faye said, once more putting her hand gently on Wreath's back. There was a long quiet moment, the only sound the television from another room. "I should have insisted you stay outside. I hoped coming inside might. . .well, settle some things in your mind."

Wreath looked at Faye, trying to get her bearings.

"I guess I had to come sooner or later," Wreath said. "This house is one of the main reasons I came to Landry." She threw her hands up. "This! Like I was somehow going to find Mama in this place."

Faye remained silent and continued to rub Wreath's back.

"I loved her so much," Wreath said.

"I know you did," Faye said.

"She'd really have liked you," Wreath said and followed Faye out of the room.

❧ Chapter 39 ❧

"How do I look?" Wreath asked Faye for the tenth time, adjusting the bodice of her dress and fidgeting with the wispy curls that touched her face.

Faye, a smile on her face, rolled her eyes, sighed, and threw up her hands. "Wreath, you look beautiful, just like you looked when you asked me five minutes ago."

"But are you sure this dress is all right?" Wreath glanced at the clock by the bed. "If I hurry, I probably have time to run and swap it."

"That's not such a good idea since Law's on his way," Faye said, patting the bed. "Let's go sit down with J. D. and relax."

"I can't sit down," Wreath said. "You know how bad this chiffon-y stuff wrinkles."

Faye made a small noise, almost like a choking sound, and Wreath's eyes flew to hers. "You're laughing at me, aren't you?" Wreath said, and, despite her jitters, she could feel a laugh work its way up her own, pink-chiffon-covered body. "I'm nervous."

"I'd have never guessed," Faye said, standing up and carefully putting her hands on Wreath's shoulders. "Look at yourself." She turned Wreath toward the full-length mirror on the closet door. "You're so pretty I can hardly stand it."

"Do you like my hair up like this?" Wreath fretted.

"It's my favorite of all the hairstyles you tried," Faye said.

"And the pink's okay? I'd planned on a blue of some sort until I found this."

"The color is lovely. I think it's much better than the dresses you tried on in Lafayette."

"I couldn't buy a new dress," Wreath said. "But I still can't believe you made this one fit so perfectly." She gave a small twirl. "I bet I'll be the only girl at the prom who paid a dollar for her dress."

Faye chuckled and fingered the thin straps. "Your dress is special, just like you."

Moving from foot to foot in her first pair of high heels, Wreath looked at Faye again. "What if I don't know what to do?" she asked, holding up her fingers and counting off her fears. "I've never been to a big party before. Never been to a country club. Never been on a date." She moaned. "I think I'm going to be sick."

"Child, what am I going to do with you?" Faye asked. "You'll have a wonderful evening. Let's go in the living room and show J. D. how you look."

When Wreath stepped from the hallway into the den, J. D. was reading a magazine, and she silently struck a modeling pose, a grin on her face.

"Ahem," Faye said.

J. D. looked up and then leapt to his feet, almost stumbling over the coffee table. "Oh, Wreath," he said. Then he said her name again, softer.

"Well?" she said. "What do you think?"

He opened his mouth, closed it, and then opened it again, almost like no words would come out.

"J. D.," Wreath demanded in a playful voice. "Are you speechless?"

He drew a deep breath. "As a matter of fact, I am," he said.

Faye looked a little flushed when she spoke. "Well, it won't be long now."

Wreath nodded. "Law and Mitch are picking Destiny up first, but it'll only be a few more minutes."

Faye looked over at J. D. with a tentative smile. "Let's go into the living room and wait," she said.

With J. D. on her heels, Wreath followed Faye into the formal room, where they seldom sat. With its white carpet and brocade sofa, it looked like one of the displays at Durham's Fine Furnishings. She stared at herself in a mirror with an ornate gold frame and opened her mouth to speak.

"Yes, Wreath," Faye interrupted. "You look beautiful."

They all three laughed, and Faye jumped when the doorbell rang. "Well, I'll be," she said, walking toward the door. "We have company at the front door. It's been a long time since that happened."

Giving a last look in the mirror, Wreath couldn't resist touching her shiny, soft hair and sliding her fingers along her neck where small feathery strands lay.

Beaming, she turned as Law walked in. His eyes widened, and she blinked.

"Whoa," Law said. "You look fantastic."

"You don't look so bad yourself," she said, drinking in his dark tux, freshly trimmed hair, and the corsage box in his hands.

"No, I mean you look great," he said.

Wreath felt the creep of a blush working its way across her cheeks. "Thanks," she said. "I guess we'd better go. We don't want to keep Destiny and Mitch waiting."

Law reached for the door and then gave his head a brief shake. "I almost forgot." He thrust the box forward. "This is for you. I hope it's the right color."

Wreath looked at the wrist arrangement of pink roses and baby's breath and wanted to cry. "Look, you two," she said, holding it up. "Isn't this the prettiest thing you've ever seen?"

They both looked at her. "It most certainly is," Faye said.

Julia, in her high school dress, and Shane, in his deputy's uniform, sat down with Wreath and Law at a small table in the ballroom.

"So, Wreath, what do you think of the décor?" Julia asked. "Does it meet your standards?"

Looking at the purple and gold balloons and baskets of ferns, Wreath gave a small smile. "It'll do," she said.

"It's not as good as if you'd done it," Law said.

"Thanks," Wreath said, "but Julia gets the credit for our prom displays. She's the one with the super artistic eye."

"You bring out the best in me," Julia said and felt happiness seep through her. Shane reached over and squeezed her hand.

The walkie-talkie he wore on his belt interrupted with a quick squawk and a hard-to-decipher message. Shane held it up to his ear, listened intently, and then gave a brief answer, standing as he spoke.

"Duty calls," he said. "Some guy's hanging out in the parking lot, causing a little trouble. I'd better check it out."

Julia didn't miss the shadow that passed over Wreath's face as Shane headed for the door. "Don't worry, Wreath," she said. "He deals with this kind of stuff all the time."

"Wreath's been a little jumpy since that man was asking about her," Law said.

"Have you heard from him again?" Julia asked, concerned.

"No." Wreath shook her head, almost as though trying to shake off the thought. "Shane said they think he's long gone."

The junkyard burst forth in color in the spring, with beautiful wild azaleas, dogwood trees sprinkled through the woods, and the intoxicating smell of wisteria, showering her with purple petals. It no longer felt like an escape but instead like a refuge, her private garden. With the days staying light longer, Wreath sat outside in the warm air, writing in her diary, trying to figure out her next steps. Graduation was only two weeks away, and she was considering taking Faye up on her offer to stay with her for the summer.

Wreath Wisteria Willis, she wrote in her book, loving her name and life more than she could have imagined. Often her future plans were interrupted by dreamy memories of prom night, and she wrote page upon page about it.

She had labeled one section *FAVORITE PROM MEMORIES*:

> *1. My dress. It looked gorgeous on me, if I do say so myself.*
>
> *2. Going with Law. He was the best-looking (AND SWEETEST) date there!!!!*
>
> *3. Double-dating with Destiny and Mitch. They say they aren't a couple, but I can tell they like each other.*
>
> *4. The midnight breakfast at Faye's. She made all of our favorite foods, and J. D. and Law's grandparents served us like we were in a restaurant.*
>
> *5. Seeing Julia Watson and her deputy, Shane, slow-dancing. He looked so handsome in his uniform, even*

if he did have to leave early to check on a prowler downtown.

I've never been so happy in my life, Wreath wrote. *I wish Frankie were here to be part of it.*

She did not write about the one blemish on the near-perfect evening, a glimpse of a fruit-punch-colored car driving slowly around the meeting hall where the prom was held and the rumor that "Miss Watson's deputy" was on the heels of a stalker.

Big Fun had not surfaced since she'd run away from him nearly eleven months ago, but she expected she'd hear from him again. She had the evidence of his crime.

Wreath was pleased when Clarice pulled up to the store at quitting time with the offer of a ride.

"You might not be so glad to see me when I tell you what I learned today," Clarice said. "Your life is tangled up in red tape."

"It's bad, isn't it?" Wreath asked.

"We can get this taken care of, but you may not get to graduate on time."

"But I have to. All of my friends will be there, and I promised Frankie."

By now everyone knew her mother had died, but only Clarice knew her last name was Willis. Wreath continued to let them believe she lived with a reclusive cousin. Law regularly tried to convince her to come clean and move in with Faye, but Wreath dug in even harder when he pressed her.

"Can't I plead insanity or something?" she said to Clarice.

"Believe me, I've thought about that. Using a false name on college applications is a thorny issue. I need more information."

Wreath had been obstinate with Clarice, even though she knew the woman only wanted to help her. During the fleeting moments when she thought of giving in, she remembered the rage on Big Fun's face at the rest area or her mama's frightened voice when he threatened both of them.

She recalled Frankie dragging her through deserted streets to catch a bus to run away from one abusive boyfriend, and their sneaking through bushes to elude Big Fun when he had been on a drinking binge.

"Everything in my life has always been complicated," Wreath said.

"These aren't the easiest waters to navigate, unless you're willing to use your real surname publicly. Plus you stonewall my efforts to get a statement from your guardian." Clarice's voice held a sterner quality than usual.

Wreath's head drooped. "You're not going to back out on my case, are you? If I can graduate, I'll go back to being who I really am and start fresh."

Clarice squared her shoulders the way Wreath imagined she did when entering a courtroom. "Don't send your cap and gown back. I'll see what my father can do. He has connections in the state department of education. One way or the other we'll work this out."

She pulled the car over. "Are you certain you won't let me take you to your house?"

As Wreath had done so many times before, she declined and gathered her pack from the backseat.

"Child," Clarice said, "you are going to gray my hair. But one way or the other, you are going to get your diploma."

❧ Chapter 40 ❧

Faye wanted a special design in the store window for the week before Wreath's graduation.

"I don't know for sure that I'm graduating," Wreath said.

"Oh, be serious," Faye replied, moving a fern into a spot of sunlight in the store. "You've made excellent grades all year, and you said you did well on your finals."

"But"—Wreath gnawed on her fingernails, something she rarely did—"I haven't gotten the official word."

Faye knew there was a problem. She just wasn't sure what it was. "Wreath, you know that I try not to butt into your business, right?" she asked.

Wreath slid the plant a few inches. "Sure."

"I feel like I have to ask you about this matter with Clarice," Faye said. "I'd like to be involved."

Straightening slowly, Wreath turned, her face calm. "It's all under control, Faye," she said. "Clarice is working out some official issues with my school transfer." She shrugged. "It's not a big deal."

"But you're so concerned about not graduating."

"I know," Wreath said. "I've wanted this for so long. For me and for Frankie."

Faye could not resist stepping over to Wreath. "I'm going to keep praying, and I know this is going to work out before the ceremony."

"Can we change the subject?" Wreath asked.

"Certainly," Faye said. "Let's hear your ideas for a special graduation display."

"I already know what I want," Wreath said. "Let's make a lush garden, a design where you have to study it to see what's there. We can put geraniums and even shrubbery, with the yard sculptures we've been saving." Her head turned this way and that in the look that had become so familiar. Faye knew an idea was about to burst out. "I've got it!" she said. "What if we turn the entire store into a garden, just for the month of May? We'll bring in small trees in pots, bushes, all sorts of plants."

"Would that be a good setting for a party?" Faye asked.

"A garden party, I suppose." Her eyes widened. "Are you planning a spring open house? What a great idea!"

"Actually, I'm planning a graduation party for a very special girl. A garden theme would be perfect because this girl has blossomed in front of my eyes."

Faye could tell it took Wreath, who so seldom had something given to her, a moment to realize she was the honoree.

Wreath's eyes lit up. "We can do it for all of our customers who are graduating," she said. "We can sell exclusive sponsorships."

Faye shook her head. "It will be exclusive, all right, designed just for you. This party's not for sale. I intended for it to be a surprise, but I want you to look forward to it."

Wreath did her funny dance and walked over to give Faye a hug. The woman, so alone a year ago, drank in the strawberry scent of Wreath's hair, the warmth of her affection. "Why don't you go next door and ask if J. D. might have a few plants he'd be willing to loan us? He's the one with the plant sources."

"You sure you don't want to go?" Wreath asked with a cheeky grin, and Faye swatted her lightly on the rear and sent her out, hoping Wreath would understand when the time came.

J. D. grew still when Wreath walked in the store; she thought he looked almost ill.

"Are you all right? You don't have the flu, do you?" she asked.

"Yes. No." He shook his head, but his eyes were glued to her face. "I was wool-gathering. What brings you over today?"

Wreath outlined her design plans in great detail, J. D. hanging on every word as though listening to a foreign language. "Do you understand what I'm going for?"

"Absolutely. I'll round up what you need and bring it right over." He pulled the small notebook out of his pocket and started jotting something down.

"What are you writing?" Wreath asked.

"A list of what you're looking for. I use lists to help me think."

"Oh," Wreath said. "So do I."

"I've noticed," he said.

"Well. . .thanks for the help."

"Wreath," he called as she headed out the door.

She stopped and turned.

"When you have a few minutes, I'd like to talk about your plans for the future."

"Sure." Lots of people had asked her about college. She didn't know why J. D. looked so sober as he mentioned the topic. "Let me get the window done," she said, "and we can visit. Maybe Faye'll join us for a cup of tea."

"That'd be nice," he said.

Wreath pulled the stepladder out of the closet and noticed the messy remnants of a package of cookies. "You must have had a hungry bunch in today," she yelled to Faye, who stood staring out the front window.

"We had a few lookers, and I sold that wicker settee you liked so much," Faye called back.

Wreath dug through the cabinet. "Who ate all the snacks? I'd better put the grocery store on my to-do list." She dug through her pack, stuffed in its usual spot under the workroom table, and made a few notes. "We need extras for that bride and her mother coming tomorrow to look for favors."

Walking back out into the showroom, she sniffed the air with a frown. "Did you have a workman here today?"

Faye didn't look up from Wreath's laptop, where she now compiled her sales records, but shook her head absentmindedly. "We agreed to put that off until summer, remember?"

"Oh right," Wreath said, trying to identify the scent while she arranged a bouquet of bright tissue-paper flowers. She felt antsy and attributed it to the odd exchange with J. D. "These paper flowers'll be perfect in that corner. Will it be all right if I go up in the attic and dig around, see if I can find anything else for our garden theme?"

Faye glanced at the clock. "Are you sure you want to start on it this late? It's getting dark. Let's wait until tomorrow."

"I'll just be up there a sec," Wreath said, waiting for a slight nod before pulling the staircase down and climbing up with the agility of a monkey. Hearing the familiar rustling noise, she added rat poison to her mental shopping list and fumbled for the string to the dim light.

As she wrapped her fingers around the pull, she inhaled and caught a whiff of the odor again, not musty like the attic usually smelled, but musky, like a man's cologne. . .like Big Fun. . .

Taking a shallow breath, Wreath made herself act as though nothing was amiss. She yelled an inane question down to Faye and stood still, trying to see without turning the light on or moving her head.

Out of the corner of her eye, she saw them, the heavy boots that had once kicked Frankie off the front porch when Big Fun thought she was hiding tip money from him. "You didn't think you could run away from me, did you?" he asked from the shadows.

Wreath dove for the opening to the stairs, looked down at the shop floor, and pitched forward. As she hit the floor, she wished for half a second that Law had been there to break her fall, as he had at Thanksgiving, and then she stumbled to her feet, unsteady but propelled by fear for her and Faye.

"What in the world?" Faye asked, rising from the desk. "Wreath?"

At that moment, Big Fun's legs, looking like tree trunks, started down the steps, his torso hanging briefly in the small entry space.

"RUN!" Wreath screamed at the top of her lungs, heading for the back door.

"Fred? What are you doing here?" Faye sounded baffled for a moment before reality hit, and she jumped up. "Wreath!" she yelled.

"I'm okay," Wreath shouted back. "Get J. D.! Call 911! Hurry!"

Faye hesitated and then ran toward the front door, screaming louder than Wreath would have imagined possible.

Desperate to divert Big Fun, she glanced back to see Faye gesturing wildly to J. D. on the sidewalk out front and pushed open the door, thankful it no longer stuck. As she had hoped, Big Fun followed her, and she sprinted down the alley.

"You can't escape," he roared. "You're going to pay for what you've put me through this past year, and you're going to tell me what you did with the bracelet!"

Wreath kept running, using every shortcut and decoy she'd memorized over the past months, wishing she had her bike but knowing she'd be more agile on foot.

"I'm going to wring your scrawny neck and kill that old lady you're so crazy about and that uppity teacher and that boyfriend and your grandfather. I'll kill them all!"

Dashing around a corner, her fright was covered with sorrow. She had brought harm to innocent people who had tried to help her, people she loved. The look of shock on Faye's face was seared in her mind, and she remembered the woman calling out the name "Fred."

Of course! Big Fun was the mysterious Fred Procell who had come around looking for her. Now he was more insane than ever, talking out of his head, threatening to kill a long list of people, including her grandfather. She didn't even have a grandfather. He had lost his mind, and she had to save the people she cared about.

She jumped over a low fence, a downtown neighbor's dog barely acknowledging her. "Good boy," Wreath mouthed to the dog she saw regularly. The animal charged at Big Fun, tripping him.

Wreath dashed through the back gate before Big Fun got back to his feet, and she zipped through another yard and zigzagged out of town, wondering if she should avoid the junkyard altogether. She had enough in her pack to run.

Her pack! She had left her pack at the store.

A car drove by, and she jumped behind a tree. She didn't know what to do. If she went back to the store, Big Fun might hurt Faye and Julia, even J. D. But she needed the pack, which contained half of the money she had saved, her journal, plus a change of clothes. And the bracelet. He would kill for it.

After months of living in the woods and relaxing enough to roam Landry's sidewalks with little fear, Wreath suddenly felt exposed, no cover around to hide her as she tried to decide what to do. She stayed close to houses, figuring that trespassing was better than being caught by Big Fun.

"Wreath!" a familiar voice called out. She spun around so fast she nearly fell.

Clarice pulled to the curb, a calm smile on her face. "Need a ride?"

Wreath looked wildly around but saw no sight of Big Fun. "That'd be great." She practically leapt into the car and slouched down in the seat, gulping in air.

"What in the world is wrong?" Clarice handed her the standard bottle of water with a look of alarm. "Are you running from someone?"

"Being followed," Wreath gasped, sounding like she had when she'd had the flu. She looked back over her shoulder.

"Wreath, this cannot continue," Clarice said. "You must let me help you."

"No. You shouldn't be seen with me." Wreath tried to push the door open, even though the car was moving. "He'll hurt you."

"No one's going to hurt me." The lawyer gave a small laugh. "I'll beat up anyone who tries."

"Joke all you want, but Big Fun is strong and mean."

"So am I," Clarice said. "You have to tell me the truth. I cannot help you unless you do."

"I'm being chased by a very bad man," Wreath said, her eyes moving back and forth so rapidly she got dizzy. "He'll kill you. I know he will."

"Wreath," Clarice said in the tone television lawyers used in court, "does this have to do with Fred Procell?"

"You know him?"

"Every lawyer in Rapides Parish knows him. That man has a rap sheet longer than my arm. I'll call the police." She pulled over and started to reach for her phone.

"Don't stop the car," Wreath said. "Please keep driving." She felt lost, the way she had the day Frankie died. Big Fun would never give up, and he would hurt everyone who loved her, even Clarice, who only thought she was tough.

"I must notify the authorities." Clarice left the engine running but didn't drive on. "It's my responsibility."

"Please, no," Wreath said.

"I won't tell them you're with me for the time being," she said. "But they need to know where Procell is."

Wreath tried to hold back the sob that was perilously close to jumping out of her mouth. "I guess I don't need a ride today after all."

"You've trusted me for months, Wreath. Trust me now."

Wreath sniffed, still not one hundred percent recovered from the gallop through town. Trust? She knew all about trust. People you trusted moved to other cities or took the cash you had hidden in your closet or died and left you alone. They wound up getting hurt because you came into their lives.

"I'm serious. Let me out," she said.

"Wreath," Clarice said. "I'm going to call the police. Collect your thoughts, and let's figure out what you need to do. I'm here for you." Her voice was now so kind that it almost sounded like Frankie's.

Wreath sat for a moment and then looked at the woman as Clarice punched in the numbers. She spoke precisely and made a few comments before ending the call. "The police are on the scene," she said to Wreath. "They are looking for Procell."

"Is Faye all right?"

"I don't know, but we can check on her."

"No," Wreath said and took a deep breath. "I need to get my backpack from the store. But I don't want anyone to see me."

"What if I went in and picked it up for you?"

"Faye's in danger. . . ." Wreath's voice trailed off as she remembered Big Fun barreling away from the store. "Do you have a piece of paper and a pen?"

Without a word, Clarice reached into the backseat, hoisted up a leather satchel, and pulled out a yellow legal tablet and her fancy ink pen. She handed them to Wreath.

Dear Mrs. Durham, Wreath wrote, then crossed out the words and started over. *Dear Faye: I am sorry for running out on you, but I'll be in touch when Big Fun, a/k/a Fred, is gone. Clarice is giving me a ride home. Will you please give her my backpack? Love, Wreath Wisteria Willis.*

She was so upset that she did not notice she had written her real last name.

Rarely was Clarice this unsure about whether she was doing the right thing, but she had felt from her first encounter with Wreath that she had been sent into the girl's life to watch over her.

Faye, the young teacher, and J. D. were pacing when the lawyer walked in, their disappointment obvious that she wasn't Wreath.

"Have you seen Wreath?" they asked in unison.

Clarice nodded slowly.

"Where is she? Is she hurt?"

"She's fine, although a little shaken up. She asked me to give you this, Mrs. Durham."

Faye nearly ripped the folded yellow paper from the attorney's hand.

Scanning it, she again looked past Clarice. "Is she in the car? I want to talk to her." She started for the door. "We need to tell her that Fred Procell is behind bars and will never lay a hand on her again."

"Wait," Clarice said in a voice she sometimes used on hostile witnesses. "Let me take her the pack and ask her if she's ready to talk, if you don't mind."

"I can't wait," Faye said.

"Me, either," Julia said.

"We have to go with you," J. D. said.

"I expected that's what you'd say," Clarice said. "I know we all have Wreath's welfare at heart."

Clarice's car was empty when they rushed up to it.

Wreath was nowhere to be seen.

Another note was in the driver's seat. *I hate to be so much trouble, but please leave my backpack with Law Rogers at the state park. I'll get it from him later. Thanks for all your help. Wreath.*

Clarice called herself every kind of fool for letting the teen out of her sight, and the worried group jumped in her car, speeding toward the park.

"Dear Lord," Faye prayed out loud, "please watch over Wreath, and give me another opportunity to help her."

J. D. patted her leg and then leaned forward. "We've got to do whatever it takes to find Wreath," he said. "I can't live with myself if we don't."

Pulling into the park, they piled out of the car and ran into the office, where a ranger stood behind the counter, his hands flat on top of the smooth wood surface.

"May I help you?" he said.

"We're looking for Law Rogers," J. D. said.

The man shook his head. "You just missed him. His shift ended not fifteen minutes ago. He's not in any trouble, is he?"

"We have a message for him from a friend," Clarice said.

"Must be a pretty important message," the ranger said. He pointed toward Landry. "His grandpa picked him up today for band practice at church."

Wreath crouched in the woods close to Law's trailer, more scared than she had been since Frankie died.

She looked at her watch. Nearly two hours had passed since she'd run from Clarice's car, but she still felt winded. J. D. and Faye had come by earlier, pounding on the door and calling her name in a hoarse voice. "Wreath, please come out," J.D. begged, while she huddled nearby. *I'm so sorry, I'm so sorry*, Wreath thought.

"She must have gone somewhere else," Wreath heard Faye say.

"But where?" And then they left.

Within minutes, a battered pickup pulled off the road and drove right up to the front steps, bypassing the driveway for the little bit of grass in the front yard. Law's mother stumbled out of one side, laughing loudly, and a man walked around the truck.

The door had hardly closed when Law and his grandfather turned into the drive. The two talked for a couple of minutes, but Wreath could not hear what they said.

When Law got out of the car, he leaned over the window and spoke. "If you hear anything, let me know. I'll start calling everyone I know."

Wreath sighed with relief. Her pack was slung over his shoulder.

She stared as the taillights of his grandfather's car disappeared into the night. Law, illuminated by a streetlight, looked at the old truck on the grass of his front lawn and at the still-dark trailer, and stepped away from the mobile home, his head up, as though searching the sky.

She drank in the sight of him and wished her life didn't have to be so weird.

"Law," she called out so softly that she wondered if he would hear, but he turned instantly.

"Wreath?"

"I'm over here. Near the end of your house." After the close encounter with Big Fun today, she intended to stay in the shadows as much as possible.

Law rushed toward her. "What in the world?" he asked, embracing her so fiercely that her feet came off the ground. He ran his hands over her hair and down her arms. "Did that man hurt you?"

Wreath clung to him, barely shaking her head.

"You scared the living daylights out of me. We've got to call Mrs. Durham and the others. They came to the church, and they're out of their minds with worry." He was wild-eyed, speaking rapidly.

"No, I can't go over there," Wreath said loudly, and a light came on in the end room.

A minute later a woman's slurred voice called from the front of the trailer. "Law, is that you?" Then the light went off again, the sound of muffled voices inside.

"We have to get you over to Mrs. Durham's," Law said. "They need to talk to you."

"She was hurt, wasn't she? Faye's hurt." Wreath's heart broke at the thought.

"She's fine. Everyone's fine." He scanned her face. "Except for you. Wreath, we have to get you to them. They can work all this out for you."

"I can't be near them," she said. "He'll find me. He'll hurt me."

"Has he been stalking you all this time?" Law curled his hands into fists. "That guy won't ever hurt you again. Shane arrested him. He chased him all over downtown and tackled him. He's in jail."

"Is Shane okay?"

"Yes. Shane's fine. And you're safe. Listen to me." He put his hands on each side of her face, as though she would break. "That jerk's behind bars."

"He's been arrested before." Wreath sighed and leaned against Law's shoulder. "It never sticks."

"He won't get within a hundred miles of you again. No one is going to let you get hurt again." Law swallowed and put his arm around her. "All of this is going to work out. The whole mess will."

Wreath didn't think it was possible to tense even more, but at his words, she did. "What's wrong?" she said in a rush. "Something else happened, didn't it?"

"I don't know if I should tell you or not." Law's arm lay heavy on her now, the comforting feeling gone.

"Tell me," Wreath hissed, sitting up and jerking back.

He hesitated.

"What is going on?" Wreath's mind skidded around horrible possibilities.

"J. D.'s son, John David, who was killed by that train, was. . ." Law paused.

"Was what?"

"He was apparently your father."

"My *father*?" Wreath could scarcely take in the words.

"J. D.'s your grandfather," Law said.

Matter-of-factly. Just like that. *Your grandfather.*

She sank onto the ground, and Law knelt by her, holding her hands.

"Now do you see why you need to get to Mrs. Durham's?"

Wreath knew she had to get back to the junkyard, retrieve her hidden money, and lose herself again. Growing up with Frankie, she knew when it was time to run—and the time had come, while Big Fun was out of the picture.

She also could tell by the feel of Law's grip and the look in his eyes that he had no intention of letting her get away. "I don't know what to do," Wreath said. "Big Fun—Fred Procell—hurts people." She nudged her pack with her foot. "He *kills* people."

"You're safe," Law said, stroking her hair. "You're safe. All safe."

Wreath didn't believe that.

"Will you walk with me to the junkyard to get my things?" she asked. "You can call and let the others know I'm all right and that we'll be there soon."

"Are you sure?" Law said. "That's a long walk, and they need to see you for themselves. They'll want to come pick you up. This has to end, Wreath."

"I need time to think," Wreath said. "A grandfather. . ."

Law looked at her intently. "That's a good thing, right?"

"I can't take it in." She did not have to pretend to tremble. "I need a few minutes."

"Fair enough," Law said. "Come inside with me, and I'll get you a glass of water."

Wreath gestured toward the trailer. "Your mom's in there," she said. "I'd rather wait here."

Law looked at the light and looked back at her. He kissed her on the forehead and got to his feet. "I'll be right back."

"And, Law, will you tell Faye I love her?"

He smiled. "Will do."

As soon as the boy opened the door to his home, Wreath started running, across the road and up into a stand of trees, weaving back and forth, again calling upon every shortcut she'd ever used, looking over her shoulder until she entered the unofficial boundaries of Wreath's Rusted Estates.

The familiar array of cars and oddball landmarks didn't calm her tonight, nor did the grip of fear around her heart ease. Without using a flashlight, she dug up the cans where she had hidden her earnings from the furniture store, stuffed her old Bible and a couple of shirts in her pack, and headed for the brush.

She could already hear Law calling her name and thought she heard Faye's voice, too, and possibly J. D.'s. He was her grandfather?

She hopped on her bike, crashing down the escape trail she'd cleared months before, with enough money to buy the bus ticket she needed.

❊ Chapter 41 ❊

*D*ear Brownie, Wreath wrote in the diary. *I never thought I'd say this,
but I miss the junkyard.*

She looked around the shabby motel room near Lucky, rented with
a wad of her hard-earned cash.

TO-DO LIST:

1. Find a job.

2. Write Faye, Miss Watson, and Clarice a note.

*3. Figure out why Frankie never told me about my
grandfather.*

4. Get an apartment.

Anguish churned in Wreath over running away; she was missing her
friends more than she'd imagined. She'd seen her mother pick up and
move a dozen times and didn't know how Frankie had done it. Waking
in the middle of the night, Wreath looked at the floral bedspread
dotted with cigarette burns and the crooked drapes. She thought of the
way Durham's Fine Furnishings looked when she first walked in. She
thought of the cozy Tiger Van and her campsite.

She went to the lobby and bought a stale pastry from a vending
machine, studying a big calendar from a bait and tackle shop. Someone—
probably the grumpy clerk behind the counter—had marked a big *X*
through each day of the year, as though wishing the time away.

Today's date swam in front of her eyes. Tonight would have been
her graduation ceremony.

She figured her disappearance had cost her the honor spot she had
held, but maybe she could still get her diploma. Her grades were good,
and she'd only missed school when she had the flu and that first day
when she'd been too nervous to go. And these last three days.

She would love to hear Law give his speech, with his deep voice and
sweet smile as he stood before the crowd. The safe crowd. Wreath out of
their lives.

Staring out the window, the darkness closed around her until a hint of gray tinged the sky. As soon as there was a trace of daylight, she hurried to her former neighborhood, stunned that it could look as though nothing had changed.

With quick steps, she walked up the elderly neighbor's sidewalk and rang the doorbell. "I'm sorry to come so early," she said when the door opened. "I need to see my mother's grave. Can you take me there?"

"I knew you'd come back one of these days," the neighbor said, opening her arms to Wreath. "Frankie left a letter for you. She didn't trust that boyfriend of hers to give it to you."

The daybreak visit to the cemetery choked Wreath up but didn't break her down. Frankie would always be a part of her life, and her mother's letter answered questions that had nipped at her all of her life.

J. D. *was* her grandfather.

A small picture of her father, was in the envelope. Studying it, Wreath didn't know how she'd missed the resemblance between herself and the hardware store owner.

The sight of Frankie's handwriting felt like a visit from her mother.

I know I haven't always been the mother you deserved, she'd written, *but you are a treasure, Wreath. I hope you'll find it in your heart to forgive me for always running away from my troubles. Never forget that God is with you wherever you go. I hope you found my note in Brownie to remind you. All my love forever and ever, Frankie.*

Wreath unzipped the small inside pocket in the pack and pulled out the bracelet. She had to go back.

Wreath called Clarice from the neighbor's house.

"Wreath?" the lawyer said. "Oh, thank You, God, Wreath. Thank You. Oh Wreath... Where are you? Are you all right? Oh Wreath..."

The lawyer's outburst was so unlike her usual self that Wreath gulped back tears, remorse rolling over her like a tidal wave.

"I need a ride," she said.

Using every persuasive word she knew, Wreath tried to talk Clarice into picking her up without telling anyone else.

"I have to let people know you're all right," the attorney said. "They're heartbroken and afraid for you. They love you."

"I love them, too. Just do this one last thing for me. I'll never ask you to hide anything again."

"Let me tell them I've heard from you, that you'll be back soon."

Wreath thought of Faye's worry, of J. D.'s kind face. "I'd rather see them. Please. Hurry."

Clarice sighed. "I got your graduation paperwork cleared up. I guess, as your attorney, I do need you to sign the papers." Then it seemed to dawn on her. "The ceremony's tonight," she said. "We don't have much time."

"I've been so stupid," Wreath said. "I thought Big Fun would hurt more people."

There was a beat of silence, and Wreath thought maybe she'd been disconnected. Then Clarice spoke. "You did what you thought you had to. I'll come get you."

"Thank you," Wreath said. "I promise I'll never keep secrets after this. Please, please hurry."

"I'm on my way," Clarice said. "I'll be there before noon. Do not go anywhere."

❀

They rode mostly in silence, Clarice glancing at Wreath from time to time.

"I went to the cemetery," Wreath said. "I saw my mama's grave."

"How'd that go?" Clarice asked.

"Sad. But good." Wreath reached into her pack and pulled out the bracelet. "I have something I need to give you."

Clarice looked puzzled.

"Big Fun—Fred Procell—killed a woman," Wreath said. "He stole this from her, and Frankie found out. He told Mama he'd kill me if she ever told."

"Oh Wreath." The car slowed as Clarice glanced at her.

"He hid this under Frankie's mattress," Wreath said in a rush. "I took it the day Mama died." Her hands shook as she dropped the bracelet onto the seat. "I don't want to run from him ever again."

279

"You don't have to," Clarice murmured, reaching over to clasp Wreath's hand. "This will help put him away for a nice long time."

"Clarice?" she asked as they approached the site where Wreath had first hitched a ride with her. "Will you take me home first? By the junkyard, I mean."

"Are you sure, Wreath? You know we're cutting it very close."

"I need to pick something up," she said. "It's important."

Clarice turned off the highway and drove a few yards before stopping the car, the rusty vehicles sparkling in the afternoon sun.

"Welcome to my home," Wreath said with a smile.

Clarice, who had laughed and cried and uttered prayers of praise as they had driven from Lucky, looked dumbfounded. "I can't believe you lived here almost a year," she said.

"It's not as bad as it looks," Wreath responded, surprised that she meant it. "This'll just take a sec."

Inside the Tiger Van, Wreath reached into the plastic sack near the back, changed clothes, and strolled out.

"Going my way?" the lawyer asked with a smile.

"Can you drop me downtown?"

"It'd be my pleasure," Clarice said.

Faye looked at the clock and gave thanks that closing time was near. With graduation this evening, the afternoon had been long and empty, her hopeful graduation party decorations ridiculous.

Walking into the workroom, she looked at the overflowing trash can and sighed, just as the bell on the door made a short, light sound. She went back into the showroom and gave a small smile when she saw J. D.

"It's been a hard day, hasn't it?" he said as he hugged her.

"Almost unbearable." She leaned against his cotton shirt. His sturdiness helped steady her.

Over his shoulder, Faye noticed a car pull up. She wished she had turned the CLOSED sign around and locked the door. Then she recognized Clarice, who leaned over to say something to the person getting out on the passenger's side.

Faye moved closer to J. D., afraid to hope. The front post where Wreath often locked her bike partially blocked the view, and she grew still. Her breath caught.

Unable to speak, she watched Wreath run up the steps and burst through the door. The bell jangled loudly.

For a heartbeat, Wreath stood before Faye, wearing her Landry High cap and gown.

Wreath took in a deep breath, and Faye did likewise. The store smelled like fresh gardenias, and the late afternoon sun made the old wood floors glow. As though someone had flipped a switch, the two ran to each other. They cried and hugged, working their way close to J. D. in their exuberance. He seemed glued to where he and Faye had stood. His eyes were wet with tears, his tanned face now pale.

Faye took a step back from Wreath, not letting go of her. "So you decided to come back," she said.

Wreath bit her bottom lip, which trembled. "Couldn't stay away," she replied.

"Did you learn anything?"

"That running away doesn't solve problems."

The two hugged again, no words spoken for a moment.

Wreath stepped back and looked at J. D., who remained a step or two away. When she spoke, her gaze included both Faye and J. D. "I'm so sorry. Please forgive me."

"Forgive *you*?" J. D. said, his voice deeper than usual. He cleared his throat, and Wreath lowered her head. "I'm the one who did wrong, not you."

Faye interrupted by grabbing Wreath again. She held her at arm's length, looking her up and down. "Are you all right, Wreath?"

"Yes." The word sounded almost like a prayer. "Are you?"

"I am now that you're back," Faye said.

"I was scared, and I didn't know what to do."

"You could have come to me," Faye said, still holding on to Wreath. "I was scared, too." They clutched at each other, crying harder.

"I will never keep a secret from you again," Wreath said. "And I'll never run again. Never, ever. I will always come back, wherever I go."

Faye smiled and touched Wreath's hair. Her hand shook. "I should hope so," she said.

"May I live with you?" Wreath asked. "This summer? And when I'm back from college?"

"Oh sweet child, your room is waiting for you. Anytime. Always."

Faye exhaled, looking at the big old furniture-store clock. She looked at J. D. and Wreath and smiled.

"Wreath Wisteria Willis," she said, "we've got to hurry or you're going to miss your graduation."

Wreath nodded, the tassel on her mortarboard flopping, and she gazed shyly at the hardware store owner.

"Do you think my grandfather might drive us?" she asked.

Tears rolled from J. D.'s eyes as he nodded, but the back door crashed open before they moved. Law raced in, dressed in his cap and gown, Julia on his heels.

"Clarice told us Wreath's all right," Law said. His head moved from side to side as he scanned the room, the hat almost sliding off his head. "Where is she?"

Then Law met Wreath's eyes.

He and Julia stopped, as though they had slammed on the brakes. "Wreath!" they said at the same time and ran toward her.

Reaching her first, Law wrapped Wreath in his arms and swung her around once, putting her feet on the floor and hugging her fiercely. "You're home!" he said. "Wreath, you're home!"

Julia, Faye, and J. D. drew closer, smiling, crying, embracing.

A joyful laugh erupted from deep within Wreath, and she threw her graduation cap into the air. "It's true," she said. "I'm home."

Author Judy Christie started keeping a diary when she was nine years old and still has all of them. A former journalist, her first newspaper job was as editor of *The Barret Banner* in elementary school. *Wreath* is her first Young Adult novel She and her husband live in North Louisiana, where she loves to sit in the porch swing and read. For more information about Christie, see www.judychristie.com.

Discussion Questions

1. Why does Wreath decide to live in a junkyard? How would you describe the junkyard? Is it a frightening place or a comforting place? What does Wreath learn during her time in Landry?

2. What are some of the hard decisions Wreath makes throughout the story? What do you think she should have done differently? Have you ever had to make a hard decision? What helps you make good decisions?

3. What words would you use to describe Wreath to a friend? How do those words compare with words you might use to describe yourself? Do you and Wreath share any traits? If so, what are they? What quality of Wreath's do you most respect?

4. Wreath keeps lists in her journal. Why does she do this? What role does her diary play in her life? Do you keep a journal or have you considered keeping one?

5. The idea of God's guidance is new to Wreath. How does she begin to understand it as the story unfolds? What part do faith and prayer play in the lives of the characters in *Wreath*? What does Wreath discover about church?

6. What do you think of Wreath's mother, Frankie? Did Frankie learn from her mistakes? What is Wreath's opinion of her mother? What does she learn from Frankie? What lessons have you learned from your own mother?

7. Who helps take care of Wreath during her senior year in high school? Why do they help Wreath? Who guides you in your life? Have you had an opportunity to help someone else? What did you do?

8. How do Law and Wreath become close friends? How does Law influence Wreath?

9. What do you think of Big Fun? Why is he chasing Wreath? Why is she afraid of him?

10. How does Wreath discover her talents in Landry? How does she use those talents? Have you ever considered what you are good at and how you might use your talents?

11. What does the idea of "home" mean to Wreath? What does it mean in your life?

12. What are Wreath's plans for her life? What does she do to make her dreams come true? Do you think she will achieve her goals? Do you have dreams and goals for your life?

If You Enjoyed
Wreath,
be sure to read

THE WISHING PEARL
by Nicole O'Dell

Sixteen-year-old Olivia Mansfield can't wait to escape the confines of her home, which promises nothing but perpetual torment and abuse from her stepfather. When poor choices lead her to the brink of a complete breakdown. Olivia comes to a crossroads. Will she find the path to ultimate hope and healing that her heart longs for?